PENGUIN BOOKS

HAPPY ENDING

Chloe is a *USA Today* bestselling author who writes romantic fiction reflecting her belief that everyone deserves a love story. When not dreaming up her next novel, you'll find her reading, trying new recipes, savoring nature, and soaking up time with her big, beautiful family.

Praise for Chloe Liese:

'A stunning mix of hilarious tropes, swoony romance and lovable, relatable characters'
Ali Hazelwood

'Witty, smart, thoughtful, and tender in turn'
Hannah Bonam-Young

'Chloe Liese is a force to be reckoned with'
Lyla Sage

'Absolute romantic perfection'
Christina Lauren

'I could curl up in Liese's writing for days. I love it so much!'
Helen Hoang

Also by Chloe Liese

The Bergman Brothers:

Only When It's Us
Always Only You
Ever After Always
With You Forever
Everything For You
If Only You
Only and Forever

The Wilmot Sisters:
Two Wrongs Make a Right
Better Hate Than Never
Once Smitten, Twice Shy

HAPPY ENDING

CHLOE LIESE

PENGUIN BOOKS

PENGUIN BOOKS

UK | USA | Canada | Ireland | Australia
India | New Zealand | South Africa

Penguin Books is part of the Penguin Random House group of companies
whose addresses can be found at global.penguinrandomhouse.com

Penguin Random House UK,
One Embassy Gardens, 8 Viaduct Gardens, London SW11 7BW

penguin.co.uk

First published in the US by Simon & Schuster 2026
Published in Penguin Books 2026
001

Copyright © Chloe Liese, 2026

The moral right of the author has been asserted

Penguin Random House values and supports copyright. Copyright fuels creativity, encourages diverse voices, promotes freedom of expression and supports a vibrant culture. Thank you for purchasing an authorised edition of this book and for respecting intellectual property laws by not reproducing, scanning or distributing any part of it by any means without permission. You are supporting authors and enabling Penguin Random House to continue to publish books for everyone. No part of this book may be used or reproduced in any manner for the purpose of training artificial intelligence technologies or systems. In accordance with Article 4(3) of the DSM Directive 2019/790, Penguin Random House expressly reserves this work from the text and data mining exception.

Interior design by Karla Schweer

Printed and bound in Great Britain by Clays Ltd, Elcograf S.p.A.

The authorised representative in the EEA is Penguin Random House Ireland,
Morrison Chambers, 32 Nassau Street, Dublin D02 YH68

A CIP catalogue record for this book is available from the British Library

ISBN: 978–1–911–74620–1

Penguin Random House is committed to a sustainable future
for our business, our readers and our planet. This book is made from
Forest Stewardship Council® certified paper.

**For my girls,
my heart's greatest happiness**

AUTHOR NOTE

By the time this book is published, I'll have been writing love stories for six years. The storyteller in me can't help but admire the irony that I began writing love stories when my own love story was ending, that at my most heartbroken I began to write the most heartfelt stories I could imagine.

Divorce was devastatingly painful, and for years I tucked away that part of my life into the untouched corners of myself when I sat down to write. When it came time to draft my next book, I opened my laptop and knew I couldn't hide that pain anymore.

This story deals with the raw ache of being newly divorced, and maybe that doesn't sound well suited to a feel-good romantic story. But there's a reason love and loss are intertwined beats of the human story—we experience loss because we loved what we had; we love because we don't take for granted what we one day might lose. And so, yes, this story foregrounds the ravaging sadness of divorce, that is necessary to capture the depth of happiness that can shine out in its wake—unexpected joy glimmering through the bleakest days, love that blooms from the soil of loss, hope that reaches beyond the realm of what we've known and illuminates the vastness of our heart's landscape.

So here it is, untucked from those once-hidden corners of my heart, a story about sad endings and new beginnings, my encouragement to all of us that, while loss is inevitable, love is indefatigable; that when we cling to that truth, we see our life story for what it is—a gift.

Love,
Chloe

CHAPTER 1

NOW

July 14. ? days until I finally take a vacation

When you spend so much of your life in stories, it's hard not to think of your life as a story, too. At least, that's what I tell myself—that I'm not the only book lover who's parsed life's defining moments into chapters, scoured it for themes and foreshadowing; who's been so captivated by a good beginning, so *sure* it would lead to a happy ending, because how else could something that began so well possibly end?

I have a theory that all book lovers grow up doing this, seeing their life-as-story. But by the time we're adults, so few will admit it because, having read enough stories, lived enough life, we've learned the hard lesson that life isn't a polished story but a jumble of messy drafts, and even the best beginnings can't save some stories' ends. We grow up when we learn how uncertain life is. That's when some give up on stories altogether. The rest of us clutch them even tighter.

I'm one of those still-story-lovers—I'd be a pretty terrible bookseller, if I wasn't. And while I could do without uncertainty in life, I love it in books. Because in books, even after you've grown up, a kernel of your childlike trust can prevail. You can still free-fall into the magic of a good beginning, endure each shocking plot twist, even a terrible ending, and still say to yourself, *This was worth the journey.* In books, hope in the face of uncertainty is safe.

In life, it's not that simple, of course. It's not so easy to hope for a happy ending once life has taught you a good beginning is hardly a guarantee. Which is why, though my life still revolves around stories, I try not to think of my life-as-story anymore.

That said, lifelong habits are notoriously hard to kick, so I do relapse on occasion.

Thea Meyer thought back to the day of her interview, when she'd stopped beneath a patch of summer-leaf shaded sidewalk, took one look at The Bookshop, and fell head-over-heels in love at first sight. Little did she know, that first blush of love for bookselling her way through the day would fade as her days ended in the most miserable of tasks—cleaning toilets.

I tap the brush on the toilet bowl's edge with my rubber-gloved hand and return it to its holder.

"Dear God," I say—I'm not generally the praying type anymore, I just find myself reverting to it in desperate moments—"I ask your mercy for whoever came in here and committed such a heinous crime to this toilet. And I ask that you keep them far from The Bookshop for the rest of their life. Or mine," I add, "whichever ends first. Amen."

It takes three seconds of eerie quiet for me to realize the Get Sh★t Done playlist I've had blasting through the bookstore's speakers has come to an end. Deeply annoying, when I'm so close to being finished.

Just as I start to peel off a rubber glove so I can grab the store's laptop and restart the playlist, my phone rings in my overalls pocket. I yelp and fall backward, my elbow knocking over the toilet brush and plunger set. I have unique ringtones for my favorite people, so I know who's calling—Lauren—and then I remember why—I was supposed to call *her*.

An hour ago.

"Shit. Shoot." I pick up the toilet bowl and plunger set, yank off both rubber gloves, chuck them in the bucket of cleaning supplies, then finally manage to unearth my phone from my pocket. "Hey, Lo—"

"You're lucky I love you," Lauren says. "And that I just upped the dosage on my anxiety meds."

"Sorry! I lost track of time. I didn't mean to worry you."

"I think we should reenable location tracking," she tells me. "The anxiety meds are good, but they aren't *that* good."

"Lauren." I put the phone on speaker and set it on the sink's edge so I'm hands-free. I still have to refill the paper towel and hand-soap dispensers. "We agreed that was *not* a good idea."

"Did we?"

"We did, after that time I tracked you because you hadn't shown up for dinner and found out it was because you were tied up at a kink club. Literally."

"Ah." A beat of silence. "So?"

"Lauren, that was how I found out you were *part* of a kink club."

"Exactly," she says, rallying. "It brought us closer."

"At the time," I remind her, "it really pissed you off."

"Well, speaking of being pissed, since we no longer use location tracking, I spent the last hour worrying you were dead and chucked in a dumpster. Abducted at the bus stop. Lost without a trace!"

"You could have texted or called!"

"First of all, I did call. Three times."

"Oh." I wince as I rip off the wrapping on a fresh pack of paper towels. "Well, I had music blasting in the store, so I couldn't hear my phone—"

"And texting?" she says. "What for? So your abductor could answer for you? I don't think so. I needed auditory confirmation that you were okay."

I roll my eyes. "You need to lay off the true crime podcasts."

"Listen here, my true crime podcasts keep me—"

"Paranoid?" I offer.

"Informed," she says.

"Well, you can relax now; I have not been abducted." I catch my reflection in the mirror and grimace. Tired hazel eyes, a wild high pony of brown sweat-frizzed curls, flushed tomato red cheeks. "But, oof, do I look *rough*."

"Is your hair at the porcupine stage? If so, please send a pic."

"You're a turd." I drop the paper towel pack into the dispenser and flip down the lid. "My hair is *slightly* frizzy from the sweaty work of deep cleaning this restroom, which I'm proud to say no longer reeks of the bowels of hell."

Lauren makes a retching sound. "Ew."

"The joys of the job." I dab sweat from my face with my forearm and sigh. "I really need a vacation."

"Yes, take one!" she says. "And come visit me, crash my hotel. I'll work all day, you'll relax all day, then we'll party all night."

I laugh. "When would you sleep in this scenario?"

"I wouldn't," she says. "But it would be worth it. So why are you closing today? You never close on Tuesdays."

I never *used* to because that was one of our nights—Tacos and Tequila Tuesdays, Fried Food and French Wine Fridays—until Lauren moved away almost two years ago for a new job that has her racking up frequent-flyer miles and living out of a suitcase. Since then, we're rarely in the same time zone, let alone the same city.

"Typically," I tell her, "Tuesday is not one of my days to close, but Jordan, who was supposed to close, got a call from her son's day care that he'd puked and needed to be picked up early, so I said I'd cover for her."

I squeeze soap from the giant refill jug into the dispenser, and it makes a loud fart noise that echoes in the bathroom. "That was the soap. Not me."

"Sure it was," she says.

I slap the cap down on the soap jug. "Rude."

Lauren snorts. "So did Jordan offer to swap you a closing shift to make up for covering for her?"

"Not . . . yet," I hedge.

"Thea."

"I *will* follow up with her." I scoop up my phone, taking it off speaker mode, and walk down the hall, then set the cleaning supply bucket back in the closet. Shutting the door, I sigh with relief. My least favorite task at the bookstore, finally done.

"You've said that before," Lauren reminds me. "Because Jordan has done this before."

"I know. But she's juggling new motherhood and a full-time job, and that has to be hard. I don't want to push her."

"You could stand to push a *little*, Thea."

I head into the office and grab my cross-body bag along with the stack of children's books I keep forgetting to take with me, then head for the staff-only exit. "Guess what," I tell her.

"A blatant subject change?"

I smile as I yank the door shut. My friend knows me well. "I'm finally free! Store's closed."

Lauren yells, "Huzzah!"

"Now, tell me what's been going on," I say. "Get me all caught up."

"Eh." I hear the glug of liquid poured into a glass, a margarita in the making—Lauren is the queen of routine, and it's Tequila Tuesday. "The job is finally not perfect anymore."

"I'm sorry, Lo. Have a gulp of that margarita and tell me all about it."

"Oh, I've already had two."

"Gulps?"

"Margaritas," she says.

I laugh. "Go on."

"I am," she says. "Margarita número tres is ready to go."

"I was talking about *work*."

She sighs. "I kicked off a new project with the client from hell at the end of last week. It's already a nightmare. I don't need to get into it beyond that."

Pinning the phone between my ear and shoulder, I jiggle the key in the door's lock until the bolt slides home. "Why not?" I ask.

"Because you just survived the bookstore-restroom-cleaning trenches, hours after you should have clocked out, and I'm pleasantly buzzed. The last thing we should talk about now is our jobs."

"Well, I had my turn to vent about work, but you didn't. *I* think we should talk about it, so you can have your vent session, too. Look at me, pushing! Please clap."

"Sure, we'll call that 'pushing.'"

"We'll call that progress."

"Progress," she concedes.

"Speaking of progress." I cross the small gravel driveway reserved for The Bookshop's staff, then start walking up the side street toward the main drag.

Summer dusk is in its glory, dripping tangerine down the shops that have closed for the day, the restaurants that spill crowded two- and four-tops across the sidewalk. I wend my way around them, walking the curb like a balance beam, and pass tables littered with the dregs of happy hour—nearly empty glasses, half-finished plates of food. Laughter floats on the humid air, everyone's bodies turned like flowers toward the sun.

"Speaking of progress?" Lauren reminds me.

"Right. Progress." Stopped at the intersection, I press the crosswalk button and squint a smile at the sunset warming my face. "I managed to run a whole two miles nonstop yesterday without you barking at me to keep going—"

"I do not bark," she says. "I encourage with vigor. Also, I'm proud of you!"

"Thank you. There's even more." I indulge myself in a dramatic pause. "I, for the first time ever, prepped, cooked, and served an entire meal on my own."

Lauren gasps. "Thea! You buried the lede!"

"I know!" The crosswalk signal tells me I can safely cross, right as a car whizzes through the intersection. I wait another second, look both ways, then step off the curb.

"So," she says, "what's this meal Hot Chef taught you to cook?"

I scowl. "Stop calling him that."

"Why?"

"Because his name is *Alex*."

"Not because you don't want me to remind you that he's a hot chef?"

"I don't need to be reminded of that. I'm aware."

"So jump his *bones*, already!" she yells.

"Lauren, we've been through this."

She sighs, then says flatly, "Because he's your *local* best friend"—a distinction she makes every time Alex comes up, and every time it makes me smile—"and friends don't jump friends' bones."

"Especially *local* friends," I remind her.

"So move away," she says. "You've been talking about it for years. *Then* visit the 'burgh and jump his bones."

To Lauren, this is a simple problem with a simple solution. To me, it is anything but.

She doesn't know I see it differently. I haven't admitted to Lauren how much Alex means to me, because I can barely manage to admit it myself. Lauren doesn't know, because I haven't told her, that I love Alex, that I love him so much that loving him as anything other than my friend will be the last thing I do. Because loving him as anything other than my best friend would mean loving him in a way that could end badly. And I will never risk that.

"It's not that easy," I tell Lauren, a sliver of the truth. "I can't just move away. I'm still working on getting full ownership of Argos."

"Oh my god, Thea, just take the dog from your shitty ex-husband—hell *I'll* come steal him for you—so you can get out of there already."

"I'm not positive I'm going to leave. I'm . . . still weighing my options, here. Professionally, that is."

Lauren's quiet for a beat, then says, "You think you want to go for it, submit the co-ownership proposal for The Bookshop?"

"Yes. And no."

"Those would be conflicting answers."

"That's because I'm feeling conflicted."

"About what?" she asks.

I glance over my shoulder at The Bookshop, the dark charcoal-painted brick façade burnished bronze by the sunset. The thriving glossy green ferns I planted out front, in honor of my boss, Fern, that made her smile in a way I'd never seen before. And then I turn, facing ahead, toward Alex's house. My heart twinges.

I used to be so sure, after the divorce, that I wanted out of Pittsburgh, the city my ex had dragged me to. Two messy, healing years later, I find myself pinned between a rock and a hard place of loving my life here so much that I can't stand the thought of leaving it, and dreading all the ways I could get hurt if I stayed.

"Thea?" Lauren says. "What aren't you saying?"

"Compromise," I tell her.

Lauren groans, then audibly gulps her margarita. "I'm listening."

"You talk about the reason you wanted me to call, everything that's making you miserable at work, and stop acting like a protective older sister who never lets herself have any problems—"

"You sound like my therapist," Lauren mutters.

"I'll take that as a compliment," I tell her.

"And *your* part of this compromise?" she says.

"Tell me what's going on with you, and I'll tell you . . . some of what I'm weighing—"

"Only *some*?" she yells

"And," I add, "my plan to get Argos."

Lauren's silent for a beat, deliberating. "You really, truly, *actually* have a plan to get the dog for good?"

I hike the stack of children's books higher in my arm and tell her, "I do. And I think it's going to work."

"Does it involve Ethan's prolonged physical suffering?"

"Not likely, but definitely acute humiliation."

"Fine," she sighs, "but I want to switch to FaceTime first. I want to *see* the sinister, scheming glint in your eye when you tell me your fiendish plan."

"Fine," I say back, "but if I trip on the sidewalk and eat pavement because I'm looking at my phone instead of what's in front of me, you have to jump on the next plane from . . ." I have no idea where she is right now, just that she isn't where she was the last time we talked. "Not-Chicago?"

"Or, as most call it," she says, "San Francisco."

"San Francisco," I tell her, "and nurse me back to health."

"No deal."

"Wow. Some friend you are."

"Oh, I'm the best kind of friend," she tells me. "Because if I stayed put, your *local* best friend, whose house you're walking to now, would nurse you back to health instead."

"Lauren!" I come to a dead stop on the sidewalk. "No location tracking!"

"I'm not tracking your location," she says. "Just working off a hunch, which you've now confirmed."

I shut my eyes and sigh. "Dammit."

"Answer my FaceTime request, would you?"

I jab at my phone and hit the accept button. Her flawless, infuriating face pops up—bright green eyes, that sleek ink-black bob, a shit-eating grin.

"You," I tell her, "are going to talk about work. Right now. Or I'm hanging up."

She's sprawled across a chaise on a sunny balcony, the blurry background of a bougie hotel behind her shifting as she sips her margarita. "Sure thing," she says. "Just one request, before I start. Please make sure we're still FaceTiming when you get to his place. I haven't seen Hot Chef's hot face in way too long."

*

My walk from the bookstore to Alex's house isn't far, the weather so dreamily perfect, that even if it was a hike, I wouldn't notice. By the time I'm coming up on the alley behind his house, I've told Lauren about the professional side of my stay-or-go dilemma as well as my get-the-dog-for-good plan, she's filled me in on her client from hell misery, and Lauren's wrapping up her second room-service taco. My stomach growls loudly.

"That looks so good," I tell her.

"It is," she says around her mouthful. "Have Hot Chef make you some."

I roll my eyes as I turn into the alley. "He's not my personal chef, Lo. And he's busy right now, working on his next cookbook. If he's testing recipes and whipped up something, I'll eat it. If he hasn't, I brought my leftover SpaghettiOs."

"Thea. SpaghettiOs are barely edible to begin with. *Leftover* SpaghettiOs?" She gags.

"Back off my 'Os," I tell her. "You and Alex are such haters."

"What can I say? Hot Chef and I know good food."

I open Alex's backyard gate on a rusty squeak, then drag it shut behind me. "You're fancy-food snobs, is what you are."

"Uh-huh." She pops the last bite of taco in her mouth and leans in, eyes narrowed. "Well," she says, "I can see you've made it safely to your destination. And that Hot Chef keeps as messy a backyard as ever."

I smile at her FaceTime view of the scene behind me. Lumpy grass and weed-ridden flower beds, chewed-up tennis balls, a kid-size soccer net that's seen better days.

"It's not messy," I tell her. "It's lived in."

Lauren says, "It's messy."

"He's got a high-energy six-year-old! And Argos is here all the time, tearing up his yard."

"*Is* he." She grins. "Meaning *you*'re there all the time, too."

I lift my chin, defiant. Yes, I hang out with Alex most nights of the week. What's the big deal? "So?" I ask.

"That's an awful lot of time to spend with your local best friend whose bones you say you *don't* want to jump—"

"I'm hanging up."

"No, you're not! I get to see Hot Chef's hot face first, that was the deal."

"Actually," I tell her, "that was what you requested. I didn't agree to it."

Her mouth falls open. "You little shit."

"Guess I'm getting better at pushing after all, huh?" I smile and wave. "Love you, bye!"

She flips me the bird, leans in for a smooch to the screen, then ends the call.

I'll send you a pic of Alex, I text her.

Olive branch not accepted, she texts back. Unless it's a pic of Hot Chef's hot ass.

I laugh as I pocket my phone and step over another Argos-chewed tennis ball. The warm breeze picks up and stirs the trees, whips my hair, lifting it from my sweaty neck. I stop, savoring the moment as I glance out across the yard and drink it in—the sunset that's turned hazy nightlight soft as it hovers on the horizon, the comforting glow of Alex's string lights that kick on, zigzagged above the yard.

It feels so right. And two years ago, standing in this exact place felt so wrong.

Two years ago, everything felt wrong. That's when my life story unraveled, when my happily ever after ended in my ex-husband, Ethan, at my suggestion of couple's counseling, suggesting that we get divorced. Then, *very* soon after, falling for another woman. It felt like I was living a nightmare that I couldn't wait to wake up from. And yet, it led me to this—a moment that feels like a daydream that I never want to end.

Smiling to myself, I take the three steps up to the stoop and open the door.

CHAPTER 2

THEN

July 17, two summers ago

I loved this house—what used to be my home—but what I loved most was its door. Original to the home, dark polished wood with ornate carvings, it reminded me of the doors in some of my favorite stories, portals that transported their characters and me to a magical, otherworldly place.

When Ethan and I bought the place, I wanted our home to feel that way—warm and inviting, whimsical yet cozy, each room unique, telling a story, like you'd stepped into a new adventure. But Ethan wanted our home's aesthetic to be "tranquil" and "cohesive," and Ethan got his way. He always got his way. Because I let him. I thought that's what love did—sacrificed, accommodated, did whatever it took to make the person you love happy.

Turns out, all it did was get me a house I never made my own before I had to give it up, and a simmering resentment that I'll be reminded of this every week from now on, when I come either to pick up or part with Argos, my golden retriever.

The weather is miserable, which feels apropos for my first trip back to the house since I moved out. Gloomy skies, disgustingly muggy. Still, I chose to walk from my new apartment to my old house—knowing Ethan, he's barely walked Argos the past week, and the dog will be desperate for exercise.

Brushing my humidity-frizzed hair back from my temples, I take a fortifying breath and start up the stairs. On my fifth step, I catch a noise ahead of me. I glance up and freeze.

There's a man walking up to my house.

He seems oblivious that I'm behind him, which is awkward, though probably not as awkward as it would be if he knew I was staring at him as I trail him a dozen steps behind. I can't help it, though. My curiosity is piqued.

As I hit the first stretch of flat concrete preceding the second long flights of stairs, I study him. Faded black Pirates baseball cap worn backward, black basketball shorts, beat-up white Nike high-tops, a white T-shirt. Tan skin. Dark licks of hair curling up beneath his ball cap's brim. Tall, maybe an inch or two taller than me.

By the time I'm climbing the second set of stairs, I've moved on to theories about why he's here. Repairman, coming to fix something (Ethan is *not* handy)? Landscaper hired to maintain the garden I started? Maybe he's here to ask Ethan if he wants to switch from Verizon to Comcast.

When he stops abruptly, I yelp, startled as I realize that while lost in my curious thoughts I significantly narrowed my following distance. I stumble sideways to avoid plowing into him.

The man spins and faces me, startling me again. There's something familiar about him.

I stare at him, trying to figure out why. Deep-blue eyes, dark circles beneath them. Thick, scruffy stubble on his jaw and neck.

His shoulders are slumped like he's exhausted; his mouth is set in a hard, flat line. He exudes the same bleak aura of misery that I do. Maybe that's why he feels familiar.

"Sorry," we both say at the same time.

The man clears his throat, then says, "Didn't realize someone was behind me."

I start to force a smile because politeness, no matter how awful I'm feeling, was drilled into me growing up. Then I remember my parents are six hundred miles away, I'm a grown-ass thirty-three-year-old woman whose life just fell apart, and I don't have to make small talk and smile if I don't want to.

"I'm just going to, uh"—I point up the stairs—"keep going..." Then I add, because the people pleaser in me is dimmed, but she's not dead, "Feel free to join."

The man hesitates for a second, then falls into step beside me.

I thought it couldn't get more awkward when I was trailing behind him. I realize, now that we're taking the steps side by side, that I was wrong.

Glancing at him, I say, "This is weird."

He peers over at me. "Yep."

I clear my throat. "But we will persist."

"Been doing a lot of that lately," he mutters.

His honest words hit my heart like it's a struck tuning fork. Suddenly my throat is tight, my eyes wet. An embarrassing laugh-sob jumps out of me. "I, on the other hand, am doing *so* great."

"Same," he says quietly.

I dab my nose and the corners of my eyes. "Yeah?"

"Hell, yeah." His mouth lifts at the corner, a commiserating, weary, not-quite smile. "I'm living the dream."

We keep trudging up the steps. There are so many damn steps.

"So," I say, trying for a breezy tone, like I didn't just have a mini breakdown three stairs below. "What, uh, brings you . . . here?"

"I'm here to pick up my daughter."

I freeze. My stomach drops. "Your what?"

The man stops, too. "My daughter," he says slowly.

"Why . . . is your daughter here?"

He glances at the house and sighs. "I had the same question for my ex-wife."

I stare at the house that Ethan took. That I *let* him take. My heartbeat thunders in my ears.

Ethan is already spending time with another woman, after saying he wanted to divorce, or, in his words, "consciously uncouple," in order "to explore an unattached life and reconnect with himself." Ethan is with a woman who has a *daughter*, after telling me for over a decade that he wasn't ready to be a father.

"What about you?" the man asks.

I very rarely get angry. I am *very* angry right now. Between clenched teeth, I tell him, "I'm here to get my dog from my ex-husband."

"Your ex-*husband*?" he says. "This is his place?"

I tear my gaze from the house and meet his eyes. "Yes."

"Jen said . . ." A muscle jumps in his jaw. "She was sleeping over at a *friend's*."

I laugh emptily. "We've been divorced for a week."

"Same for us." He scrubs at his face and mutters, "Jesus Christ."

I turn toward the house and start marching up the stairs.

"You're pissed," he says, catching up to me.

"I am *livid*."

"Why? You're divorced. What do you care who he spends time with?"

"It's not about that. It's about . . ." I reach for words, but they're all too embarrassing, too confessional. "Don't *you* care?" I say instead.

He's silent the length of two steps, then as we reach the last stretch of flat concrete, says, "I care that my daughter spent the night here, instead of in her home, in her own bed, which is where she's *supposed* to be, since I moved out and let her mother keep the place so she could have that 'continuity.'"

"Oh." I bite my lip. "I'm sorry. I shouldn't have pried."

He sighs. "I pried first. I'm sorry."

"That's all right." We've slowed to a stop, standing nearly shoulder to shoulder, our gazes fixed on the house.

A sudden wind picks up and wipes away the heavy, claustrophobic mugginess. As the breeze curls around us, I let out a steadying breath and glance over at him. "Maybe this is selfish," I say, "because I wouldn't wish this on anyone, but . . . it's kind of nice to find someone else who's as not-okay as me."

His eyes meet mine. "Yeah," he says. "It is."

"Selfish?" I ask. "Or nice?"

The breath he huffs out sounds like it wants to be a laugh but can't quite muster the will. "Nice," he tells me.

Our gazes hold for a moment, silence settling between us. Then, he says quietly, "I'm Alex, by the way. Alex Bruscato."

My own not-quite-smile tugs at my mouth. I wish it didn't make it so obvious, how miserable I am. But it still feels better than plastering on a lie. "Thea Meyer."

His eyes narrow a little, scouring my face. "You . . . seem familiar."

"So do you," I tell him.

An almost wariness comes over his expression, like he's bracing himself, waiting for me to say more. I have nothing else to say though, and after a beat of awkward silence, he seems to relax a little. "You from around here?" he asks.

"No, I just moved here three years ago. I grew up in St. Louis," I tell him, then add, "well, a St. Louis suburb. Webster Groves."

"Hmm." He frowns as he lifts his ball cap from his head and scrapes back dark loose curls of hair.

That's when I recognize him. "Mia's dad!"

The frown deepens as he tugs his hat back on, this time with the brim in front. "How do you know that?"

Slowly, I lift my hands, pointers up, then start to sing, "I am here and you are here—"

"Wait." Alex's eyes widen. "StoryTime at The Bookshop?"

I drop my hands. "Yep."

He's staring at me, brow furrowed.

"I know. I don't look like the perky, smiley bookseller you've brought your kid to for StoryTime. But I promise it's me."

He clears his throat, looking guilty. "I didn't say that."

"This," I tell him, drawing a circle with my finger around his face, "very much did."

"Listen," he says, "you didn't recognize me at first, either. It's not like I look too 'perky' myself."

The sound of the front door banging open makes both of us glance over our shoulders.

"Daddy!" Mia yells from the porch, hopping up and down. She's in rainbow-striped pajamas, and her dark, wavy hair is poking out in every direction. "Come hug me, Daddy!" she yells. She waves her arms, still hopping. "Hurry up!"

"Hi, Sunshine," he tells her. "I'm coming."

Argos barrels out onto the porch behind Mia in a frenzy of manic tail wags and loud whines.

"Easy, pup," I tell him. "I'm coming."

Alex and I briskly walk the flat stretch of concrete toward the last five steps leading up to the porch. And then we both come to a stop when our exes make their entrance.

I now recognize the woman standing beside Ethan from the few StoryTime visits she made with Mia—Jen, Alex called her. She's beautiful. Petite, hourglass curves, sky-blue eyes, honey-blond hair swept into an artfully messy bun. She's rocking skin-tight bike shorts better than I ever could and swimming in one of Ethan's WashU T-shirts.

My brain snags on that last detail, but I tear it away with a rip, dragging my focus to Ethan. My ex-husband is in lounge clothes, too. His normally pale cheeks are flushed, his light-brown hair mussed as if hands have tousled it. I used to think he had such handsome soft brown eyes; now I just notice they're avoiding mine.

Alex crouches as Mia rushes down the stairs, right into his waiting arms, at the same time that Argos loses the battle with his obedience training and barrels down the steps into my knees. I bend to hug him, lavished with licks to my chin and cheeks in greeting. I wrap my arms around him and squeeze, burying my face in his neck. I missed him so much.

"You're late," Jen says to Alex.

"Sorry," he tells her, eyes on his daughter as she shows him a painted pebble in her hand. "Construction traffic. I texted to let you know."

Mia glances my way, and her midnight-blue eyes go wide. "Miss Thea!" She waves up at me. "Hi!"

I smile down at her. "Hi, Mia. I like your pajamas."

"Thanks," she says. "I wore them all day."

"Nothing better than a pajama day," I tell her.

"Mommy says I can't wear them to preschool, though."

"Well," I say, trying to be diplomatic, "that . . . makes sense."

Mia huffs like she thinks it really doesn't.

It makes me smile. Alex smiles, too.

"So," Jen says. She tugs at the hem of Ethan's shirt that she's wearing, glancing between Alex and me. "You two . . . know each other?"

For a second, I'm thrown by her question, but then I consider what this must look like to her: Alex and I showed up at the same time. We're standing, albeit unintentionally, quite close, as if banded together. Mia knows me and was happy to see me.

"Sure seems like it," Ethan says. His eyes are fixed on Alex. He has yet to look at me. "Judging by the fact that the Ring camera showed you two being all chummy out here for ten minutes before you made it to the door." Ethan adds, still locked in on Alex, "Just think. If you hadn't been out here wasting time, you wouldn't have been nearly as late to get your daughter."

Alex stands from where he's been crouched with Mia. His eyes are hard.

My gaze ping-pongs between Alex, Ethan, and Jen. Tension thickens the air. I peer down at Mia, glancing between the adults surrounding her, her little face drawn tight with anxiety. My heart twists.

I know, down the road, I'm going to look back on this moment and have to admit that I wasn't solely motivated by my desire to protect Mia. I'm angry at Ethan for his rude, manchild behavior. My pride is wounded that I'm standing in front of my ex and a beautiful woman he's obviously already tumbled into bed with, while I look like a disheveled hedgehog in worn-out Birkenstocks who's been crying for the better part of the last twenty-four hours. And I feel an odd sense of camaraderie with Alex, whose life, much like mine, seems squarely in dumpster-fire territory.

Before I can think better of it, I do the first thing that comes to mind—I tell a story. In other words, a big old lie.

"Yes," I say to everyone, "we do know each other. Alex and I are actually friends." I fumble for a beat then add, "*Old* friends."

Everyone's focus snaps my way.

"What?" Jen says.

Ethan's eyes narrow as they finally land on me. "*Old* friends?"

I glance at Alex, who's staring at me, one eyebrow arched. *What are you up to?* his expression says.

With my wide-eyed look of panic, I tell him, *Hell if I know*.

A sly smile curves at the edge of his mouth. "It's true." He glances toward Jen and Ethan. "I met Thea when we were teens," he fibs smoothly. "In the parking lot outside Busch Stadium. A tailgate for the Cards-Buccos game when we stopped in St. Louis on the Bruscato-family road trip." He glances back at me and grins. "We hit it off *right* away."

I'm a pretty bad liar, even worse at thinking on my feet. If I'd read fewer books, this is when I'd botch this ridiculous, snowballing deception. But I've read a lot of books, so I pull from one of the many stories I've loved and add, "Instant friendship. Pen pals for years. This guy," I tell Ethan and Jen, "can write a letter."

Jen slips a little closer to Ethan. Ethan's got his hands shoved in his sweatpants' pockets. His jaw is clenched, his eyes hard.

"We lost touch over the years," I explain. "You know how life goes." Smiling down at Mia, then up at Alex, I say, "Until these two walked into StoryTime at The Bookshop."

I've conveniently left out *when* that first visit to StoryTime happened because adrenaline's wiped my memory.

"I couldn't believe it who it was!" I tell them. Clasping Alex's hand, I squeeze. My breath catches when he squeezes back, his hand, warm and solid, wrapped around mine. "It was Alex, my long-lost friend."

Alex tugs me close and says, "Aw, Ted."

I bounce into him and blink, surprised by the maneuver, wondering who Ted is. Then I realize that's what he's calling *me*.

"No need to downplay it," Alex murmurs, still loud enough for Jen and Ethan to hear. "Just *old friends*?" He glances their way and grins. "We were each other's first *love*."

CHAPTER 3

THEN

July 17, two summers ago

I'm perched on Alex's back stoop, palms pressed against the cool concrete, eyes shut, as I replay the most surreal evening of my life. It feels like a chapter of a book that caught me so off guard, I need a reread to be sure I know what actually happened.

Thea Meyer stood at the foot of her old home's porch, spiraling as Alex Bruscato took her astronomical lie and blew it up to planetary proportions.

As he did, Thea decided it was a good thing she was looking at Alex rather than their exes, because her eyes widening to saucers was hopefully much less noticeable in profile than it would have been head-on.

A stunned silence followed, before Jen said, "Oh . . . I see." Ethan said nothing.

Somehow, Thea managed not to go even more bug-eyed when Alex smoothly fibbed that she and Mia were heading back to his place for dinner, so they had to get going.

And then, mercifully, Thea and Alex made their exit—Argos by the leash held tight in Thea's hand, Mia in Alex's arms, her small yellow backpack thrown over his shoulder.

I flop onto the stoop, the concrete cool against my sweaty back and arms, as the little narrator in my head continues,

Fifteen minutes later, after a car ride filled with Mia's one-sided chatter with Argos making up for Thea's and Alex's incredibly awkward silence, Thea found herself walking through a fenced-in backyard leading to a quaint redbrick and cream-trim Craftsman bungalow. Mia skipped ahead, clutching Argos's leash as he dashed across the grass.

Thea turned to Alex and said, "I really don't have to stay for dinner."

And Alex said to her, "No, you don't. But you're welcome to."

Inside Alex's tidy kitchen, Thea sat, watching Alex make Mia dinner—the fanciest grilled cheese she'd ever seen, a fruit and veggie smiley face of hummus and carrot-coin eyes, a grape nose, a mouth of green and black olives, and raspberry hair.

Mia's meal finished, a homemade frozen-yogurt popsicle for dessert, chased by a few yawns, Mia told Thea good night as Alex carried her up the stairs. Then, five minutes later, Thea found herself coming up the stairs, too, at the request of a certain overtired four-year-old who wanted her to sing the "I Am Here" StoryTime song so she could fall asleep. Halfway through her third encore, Thea watched Mia's eyelids droop, then peacefully drift shut.

It had been a truly bad day, but singing a sweet little girl to sleep hadn't been a bad way to end it.

I open my eyes slowly, returning to reality, the crickets singing, the intermittent whir of cars passing on the street, Argos's happy snuffle as he pokes around the yard, finally worn out from an hour of zoomies.

"It all really happened," I mutter to the sky.

"It did indeed," Alex says.

I glance his way as he lowers beside me, a baby monitor in one hand, a cigarette in the other.

"I was doing a reread," I tell him.

Understandably, he seems confused.

Sitting up, I brush off the tiny concrete pebbles stuck to my palms, and explain, "I had to double-check that everything I thought happened actually did."

"Ah," he says, placing the cigarette in his mouth and lighting it. "Trying to wake up from the nightmare?"

"I just . . . needed to process, I guess."

He peers my way, exhaling out of the far side of his mouth, so the smoke doesn't come my way. "Fair enough." After a beat of silence, he says, "Sure you're not hungry?"

I shake my head. "Thanks, though."

He nods and taps the ash of his cigarette into the dirt of an otherwise empty planter beside him.

I have a lot of questions rolling around in my head. What did we get ourselves into? What do we do about it? But what comes out first is, "Why'd you call me Ted?"

He shrugs, eyes on his cigarette. "You look like a Ted."

"No one's ever called me that."

"I have," he says.

I smile faintly. "Besides you."

"Theodora is your full name, I'm guessing?"

I nod.

"Theodora," he says. "Thea. Ted. Just seemed right. Like . . . a good reduction."

"A what?"

He peers my way. "Like a sauce." At my blank look, he adds, "In cooking?"

"I don't cook," I explain.

"At all?" he asks.

I shake my head.

He looks concerned. "And you eat . . . how?"

"Poorly."

Alex sighs. "Right."

"So the reduction?" I remind him.

"In a reduction," he explains, "the flavors are . . . richer. It's everything you had to begin with, just intensified. Theodora to Ted . . . felt like that."

"Ted." I tip my head. "I think I like it."

"I think it was a bad cooking metaphor," he mutters, peering out at the lawn, where Argos is sniffing around. "Thanks," he says, "for singing to Mia."

"Happy to." I don't tell him that singing his kid to sleep was the best part of this awful day, that singing my own kid to sleep has been something I've wanted to be the best part of my day for years. But I almost want to.

He glances my way and like a mind reader asks, "You have any kids?"

My stomach knots sharply. "No." I watch Argos roll onto his back, pawing at a firefly. "I wanted them. Ethan didn't. 'Not *yet*,' he said."

Alex taps the cigarette against the planter's edge again. "You'd be a good mom."

My heart lodges right up in my throat. I swallow thickly. "What makes you say that?"

"Mia," he says, "is an excellent judge of character. She doesn't ask just anyone to sing her to sleep. And she sure as shit doesn't go to sleep for just anyone, either."

I smile faintly. "Well, I'm flattered."

For a moment, we sit in silence, watching Argos being weird, as he froggy crawls across the grass, a not-so-stealthily prowl toward who knows what.

"Hey," Alex says, "remember how I told you I didn't care about our exes banging each other?"

I groan. "I was trying not to think about that."

He takes a drag on his cigarette, then blows out. "I *do* care."

"Of course you do. You were married to her. For . . ."

"Eight years," Alex says.

"Thirteen for me," I tell him.

His eyebrows lift. "That's a long time."

I nod. Then, for some reason, maybe because he's the first person I've met whom I can freely talk to about this, I ask, "How'd yours end?"

He peers my way. "Slowly. And painfully. Yours?"

"Quickly. And painfully."

"So . . . it's new," he says. "Things being bad between you. I mean, bad enough to end the marriage."

I stare up at the sky. "I think it had been bad for a while . . . I was just in denial about that for a long time."

"Still," he says gently, "makes sense, you being upset that Jen was there, when it hasn't been that long."

"I'm not jealous that Ethan already wants someone other than me. I'm just . . . mad at him. For a lot of things. And I'm tired of being mad. But I can't seem to stop being mad, either." I peer over at Alex. "What about you? How do feel about all of this?"

Alex's gaze drops to the ground. "Also not jealous. Also mad. Jen being with someone already is going to make things harder for Mia."

My heart twinges. "That makes sense."

"Maybe I am jealous," he adds, his voice quieter. "Of both of them. That they're just . . . fine, apparently. Or, at least, fine enough to be with someone like that again."

A sigh gusts out of me. "Yeah. I'm jealous of that, too."

"I can't imagine wanting that right now," he says, "being in a relationship, no matter how casual."

"Same. I'd be way too in my head." I also haven't ever found casual relationships to be something I enjoy, but admitting that has always left me feeling oddly vulnerable, and also just . . . odd. Anyone I've talked to about this seems to enjoy the thrill and no-strings, unstructured nature of casual relationships. But to me, the desire for a relationships has always been about longing for comfort, connection, that unique sense and sensuality of belonging just to each other. "I couldn't do it."

Alex grunts in agreement. "I can barely keep my head above water, as it is. The last thing I need is the added weight of trying not to fuck up *another* relationship."

I stare at him for a moment as he rakes a hand through his disheveled hair and sighs heavily. He looks so forlorn.

I nudge him with my knee. "It's not like you *couldn't* find someone else right now, if you wanted, though. You've got strong DILF energy."

He slants a look my way, something like surprise flashing in his eyes. A faint smile tugs at the corner of his mouth that he tries to hide behind a draw on his cigarette. "Shut up."

"You're like Prince Eric," I tell him. "With a solid tan. And *dark*-blue eyes . . . And a stronger nose."

"Broke it," he explains through an exhaled plume of smoke. "Twice. And you're full of shit about the Prince Eric thing."

"Am not."

He shakes his head as he drags on his cigarette again, another faint smile peeking out. "My sisters had the biggest crush on him when we were kids."

"So did I. And on Aladdin. The Beast-slash-prince. Robin Hood—"

"Robin Hood, the *fox*?"

"An *anthropomorphized* fox."

"Which of those was your first crush?" he asks.

I make a prim face. I'm not telling him it was Prince Eric. "A bit personal for conversation with a stranger, isn't it?"

That gets me a sidelong glance. "I thought we were *old friends*."

"Not to mention *first loves*," I say pointedly.

Alex grimaces as he flicks ash off the end of his cigarette, staring at its red-orange ember glowing in the darkness. "Guess we should talk about that at some point." He clears his throat. "Obviously, I got a little carried away."

"I got it started," I concede.

"Yeah, but I dialed it up to an eleven. I do that a lot, dial myself up to an eleven." He sucks hard on the cigarette and exhales a stream of smoke up into the night sky. "It's my fatal flaw."

"Mine is dialing myself down to a one."

He glances my way. I expect him to say something, like, *Why would you do that?* the way others have before, like there's a simple answer—like, if I just tried harder, I could change how small I've learned to make myself.

But he doesn't. He simply nods, flicking the cigarette's ash in the planter.

"Well, Ted," he says, "we've backed ourselves into a pretty tight corner."

"That we have." I stare up at the stars and sigh. "If we come clean and say we made it all up, we look—"

"Pathetic," Alex says.

"*Deeply* pathetic," I agree.

"And if we don't . . ." He watches me out of the corner of his eyes.

I glance his way. "Then we get a very satisfying upper hand. A mysterious history of first love that was too precious, too dear to our hearts to ever talk about with our exes. Now, a rekindled friendship that spans decades."

"Sounds great," he says. "Let's do it."

"Before you commit," I tell him, "I need to warn you that keeping up appearances will require something I'm not sure you're prepared for."

He frowns. "And what's that?"

I point to my face. "Being my friend."

His frown dissolves, and in its place a full, wide smile lifts his mouth. A little thrill runs through me. "I think I'll manage," he says. "That is, if you can handle being friends"—he points to his face, too—"with me."

I shrug. "I think I can make that work."

"Friends it is," he says.

"Friends," I agree.

"And for the purposes of appearances, in front of the exes?" His gaze travels my face. Like he's studying me. A swallow works down his throat. "What about then? Would we act like friends or . . ."

Heat creeps up my cheeks, as his meaning dawns on me. "Or more?" I ask.

He nods. "They think we were first loves, after all."

"It would probably be very satisfying at first," I say slowly. "To act romantic in front of them, rub it in their faces."

I let it play out in my head, this scenario in which I get to cozy up to an attractive man like Alex, flaunt a romantic relationship in front of my ex and show him I'm doing fine, too, in that department, thank you very much.

"To really sell it," Alex says, "we'd have to pretend in front of more than just Ethan and Jen, though, and more often than when we saw them."

"Your family?" I ask.

He nods. "And friends. Everyone, honestly. Pittsburgh might be a midsize city, but it is a surprisingly small world. Someone's always connected to someone else, and that someone else has some connection to you."

"I've noticed that," I tell him. "Not so much for me, since I'm newer here, but for people who are established here. I think it's kind of lovely."

"Yeah, well," he grumbles, "trust me, after a while, it starts to feel suffocating." After a beat he says, "Maybe they won't last, though. So we wouldn't have to lie for long."

Alex makes a good point. To really hold the upper hand on our exes, we'd have to keep up the romantic ruse for as long—no, *longer*—than Ethan and Jen. Maybe their relationship is a fling that'll fizzle in a week, like Alex said. But what if it lasted? We'd have to keep pretending we were romantic, too. My stomach sinks at the thought of that possibility, the two of us trapped in a lie told on Ethan and Jen's timeline, caught in playing out a future that isn't ours, not only because it's untrue but because it's still inextricably constrained by our past.

I want my petty vengeance on my ex. But I want to be free of him even more.

"I'll admit," I say to Alex, "that I don't have much figured out about what I want down the road. But I do know I don't want it to be dictated by my ex."

Alex grunts in agreement as he leans back and unearths the lighter from his pocket.

"And," I add, "I don't see any scenario in which acting romantic to get back at Ethan and Jen doesn't do just that. Plus, neither of us wants a *real* relationship right now. Why pretend something we don't want? I think it'll just make us—"

"Miserable?" Alex flicks his lighter, and its flame dances to life. "Exactly."

"Then that's that," he says, watching the flame fade as his thumb lifts, then with another flick of his thumb, reappear. "Whether we're in front of them or not, no pretending, no performing, just being ourselves, two . . . friends." Alex peers my way, his eyes holding.

It feels like that lighter's flame is suddenly right beneath my ribs, sparking, warming. A glimmer of light in a part of me that's felt so utterly dark.

Slowly, I reach for his cigarette that's gone out, take it from him, and bring it to my lips. Alex leans in and lights it for me. I've smoked weed and cigars—I know how to inhale and how not to. I do the latter and blow out. "Thanks, friend."

He stares at me for a beat, then carefully plucks the cigarette from my fingers, smiling softly. I smile, too.

Holding my eyes, Alex brings the cigarette to his mouth. "Ugh." He looks accusingly from the cigarette to me. "You lipped it. Where do you even get this much spit from?"

"I have robust salivary glands. And it's the least that cigarette deserved." I rub my tongue around my mouth, frowning in disgust. "Blech. That tasted like the burned edge of a gas station hot dog wrapped in mildewed mint leaves."

He snorts. "Mildewed mint leaves." Alex wipes the cigarette's filter dry with his thumb, then brings it to his mouth and draws in one last lungful before he shoves it into the planter beside him. "They're foul," he admits, grinding it hard against the dirt. "But *nothing* is as foul as a gas station hot dog."

"Gas station hot dogs," I argue, "have a time and place."

"And it's called rock bottom."

"Exactly."

"Same as cigarettes," he says. I watch him squeeze the dregs of tobacco from the filter, brown crinkled slivers flitting into the wind. "And before you judge me," he adds, "for *my* rock-bottom vice causing cancer, I'll have you know research has proven gas station hot dogs are carcinogenic, too."

I bite my lip guiltily. "I had one earlier today," I tell him, "a gas station hot dog."

He gives me a deeply disappointed look. "Ted."

"No judgment!" I remind him.

Alex is silent for a moment, before he nods. "No judgment but . . . no more." He tips his head toward the planter and his smoked-to-the-filter cigarette. "Of either of them. Sound like a deal?"

I stare at the ghost of his vice as the wind sends it rolling around the planter. My stomach rumbles, the ghost of my own poor choice making known its imminent plans to haunt me.

I meet his eyes and tell him, "Deal."

CHAPTER 4

NOW

*July 14. ? days until
I finally take a vacation*

I walk into Alex's house and, with a nudge of my butt, shut the door, smiling at the familiar sight that greets me. Alex at the stove, his faded black Pirates ball cap turned backward, its brim barely restraining curling licks of dark hair. A white undershirt stretched across his shoulders and back, old threadbare jeans, two black apron strings tied low at his waist.

Slipping off my Birkenstocks, I say, "Smells good!"

Alex's response is a monosyllabic grunt.

Not a good cooking day, then.

Scooting my Birkies toward the wall, out of the way, I breathe in. Fresh-baked bread, butter, lemon, and . . . thyme, maybe? I'm still learning my herbs. Whatever it is, it sure smells like a good cooking day to me. Then again, my culinary wheelhouse is meals that start in the freezer and end in the microwave, so what do I know?

I try to steady the wobbling tower of books in my arms as I set them down, but they end up tumbling domino-style across the kitchen table. I sigh, defeated, as I shrug off my messenger bag and set it beside the pile of books. I'll straighten them out later.

Judging by the grunt, this is not the time to ask Alex if there's anything edible up for grabs, so I pull the container of leftover SpaghettiOs from my bag and unsnap the lid.

Alex lifts his head and goes still. He's caught a whiff. The man has a bloodhound's sniffer.

"Bold move," he says, "bringing that trash into my kitchen."

"Bold move," I tell him, "calling early copies of highly anticipated children's literature 'trash' in the presence of a bookseller."

That earns me a small shake of his head, a wry smile I can't see with his back to me, but I feel it all the same. "Not what I was talking about," he says, "and you know it. Put the trash where it belongs, Ted."

Gambling, I ask, "Got something better to offer?"

"Working on it," he mutters, whisking as he adds a pinch of something to the saucepan.

I grab a spoon from the silverware drawer and scrape it around the container. "I don't know," I tell him, peering down uneasily at the SpaghettiOs. Lauren was right, darn her. Leftover 'Os are gross. "This is some tasty 'trash' I've got. I think it's too tempting to toss."

"Ted." He sounds exasperated.

"C'mon, you know you want to taste it." I lean his way, extending my spoonful, and chant-whisper, "Do it, do it, do it."

Alex turns, facing me, and our eyes lock. My belly does a swoop.

Hot Chef indeed, Lauren's voice says in my head. She drives me up the wall when she calls him that, but she's not wrong.

Blue-flame eyes, hard-work muscles, tan skin tattooed with high-heat burns. Loose curls of coffee-dark hair that he scrapes his fingers through when he's stressed and tucks inside a ball cap when he's cooking. Thick brows and lashes, a five-o'clock shadow that shows up at noon. There's an attractive intensity to Alex's looks, but even more so there's an intensity in his gaze when he looks at me that feels like the first time I flicked on the light switch in my apartment and a jolt of electricity barreled through me.

I found an electrician who fixed the light switch. I have yet to find anything that fixes what happens when Alex looks at me.

"Ted," he says again. I shouldn't, but I love when he says my name like that. Frustration shot through with fondness.

"Alex." I smile impishly as he leans in, commanding my heart not to fly in my chest.

He smells like he always does, woodsy spice and lemon kitchen soap. But then I catch a whiff of another kind of spice, the kind I haven't smelled in nearly two years. My eyes widen. I point with my spoonful of SpaghettiOs, and say, "Nicorette!"

"Yes, Nicorette." Alex plucks the container and spoon from my hand, then unceremoniously chucks them into the sink.

My smile drops. "What's going on?"

"Have you checked your email recently?"

"Of course I have. You know how often I check my email."

He nods, working the Nicorette in his mouth. "Right. Which is why I'm confused."

"Makes two of us."

"When did you check it?" he asks.

I wrinkle my nose, trying to remember the specifics. "An hour ago, maybe two? Why?"

He closes his eyes and presses his palms against them. This is clearly stressing him out. "Would you just... check again? Please?"

"Okay, okay." I unearth my phone from my stretchy overalls pocket and open up my email.

Alex leans in, his chest brushing my shoulder.

"Oof," I tell him. "Nicorette smells awful."

"Tastes awful," he says, then he nods his chin at my phone. "Email, Ted."

"Right."

We both scan my tidy inbox. Its contents are unremarkable, with the exception of an email that came in this morning from my water provider, explaining they're going to charge me three hundred dollars for using water that I didn't use, but that's a problem for Tomorrow Morning Thea, who doesn't go in to work until noon.

"This month's water bill?" I ask.

"It doesn't make sense." Alex yanks off his ball cap and scrapes his fingers through his hair. "You were on the email, too."

"*What* email?"

"The one," he says, tugging his ball cap back on, "from your ex-husband and my ex-wife."

I blink, stunned.

An email from Ethan and Jen means it's Capital N News—something too important to text about, too awkward to say in person. Alex and I have discussed this before, that at any point these past two years, the moment could come when they'd announce their engagement, elopement, pregnancy. It's seemed inevitable. My stomach still knots.

Alex leans a hip against the counter, arms crossed over his chest. "You still have Ethan's email filtered out of your inbox, don't you?"

I point to the hidden garbage cabinet behind him. "Straight to the Trash."

"Not just any 'Trash' folder, though." Alex lifts his eyebrows after a beat of my silence, confusion etched in his expression. "If I remember correctly? Why are you looking at me like that?"

"I'm not looking at you," I tell him. "I'm thinking."

"*At* me?" he asks.

"I frown when I'm thinking, you know that."

Suddenly, the memory of what he's referring to comes rushing back. Peering down at my phone, I tap my way to my email's Trash. It's been so long since I made that vindictively titled subfolder, let alone looked at it, I honestly forgot it existed.

"You remember correctly," I tell him. "The Buttface McGee subfolder remains." My frown returns. "Why has Ethan been forwarding me scammy home warranty offer emails?"

Alex leans in, staring at my phone. A notch forms in his brow. "Ted, when's the last time you checked this folder?"

"Never. That being the point of filtering my ex's email address—oh, God, there it is."

I stare at the screen, my thumb hovering over the newest email.

Subject: Family Vacation!!!

"Three exclamation points," I say to myself. "Which means—"

"Jen wrote it," Alex says. "Yes. But it came from Ethan's email address. Obviously. Since it went straight to—"

"Buttface McGee." I stare at the unopened email, biting my lip. What would possess Jen and Ethan to email us about a family vacation?

I peer up at Alex. "How about you just tell me what it says?"

He gives me his most disappointed look. "Ted."

"How about I guess?" I take a step back, pocketing my phone. "Guess one: your mom accidentally sent the Bruscato family beach vacation itinerary to Jen again and now Jen's forwarding it to us . . . from . . . Ethan's . . . email?"

Alex gives me a flat look. "Mom only did that the first summer, right after we divorced, then she removed Jen from the family email list and hasn't done it since."

I feel immediate, tail-between-my-legs guilt for bringing that up. Alex's mom, Lydia, is one of my favorite people, and she told me herself she felt terrible when she did that, an honest mistake born out of habit.

"That was poor form," I admit. "I rescind my guess. And I apologize."

"Apology accepted." He takes a step toward me. "Now open the email."

I take another step back and give him sad-puppy eyes. "Right now?"

"Yes," he says, unmoved in the face of my puppy pout. "Right. Now."

I freeze. And then Alex hits *me* with his sad-puppy eyes, which is bad news. My resolve against them is pitiful at best (when he's being playful), hopeless at worst (when he's being sincere, which he is now). Holding my gaze, he says, "Please, Ted."

Sighing, I drag my phone from my pocket, tap my way to the Buttface McGee subfolder, and rip off the Band-Aid.

My eyes fully scan the email. My brain barely processes the first line. Breathing out slowly, I pocket my phone again. "I opened the email."

"And?" he asks.

"I read one line."

"Jesus," he mutters.

"I will read the rest, I promise." I let out a wheezing breath. "But first, I'm going to need a gas station hot dog."

"The hell you are," he says.

"You've got Nicorette!" I holler.

"It's not a *cigarette*!" he hollers back.

"Well, I'm sorry there isn't a gas station hot dog Nicorette analogue for those craving a hit of a week's worth of sodium and nitrates!"

"That's what you think," Alex says. Opening his refrigerator, he unearths the last thing I ever expected to darken its pristine door.

"Grass-fed organic-beef hot dogs," I read aloud from the package. I peer up at him. "You got these for me because . . . you knew I'd need them?"

He points to the Nicorette in his mouth by way of confirmation.

"Well," I tell him, "now I'm *really* excited to read the rest of that email."

"It's bad." Alex tosses the hot dogs on the counter and finally pulls me in for a warm, hard hug. "But it's not *that* bad."

"How do you know?" I whine into his shoulder.

"Because I actually read the whole thing," he says. "And even after that, I still managed to bake damn good hot dog brioche buns."

*

There is no delicate way to eat a hot dog, even as gourmet as the one Alex put together. Char-grilled casing that cracks as I bite in.

Light-as-air, subtly sweet brioche bun, finely diced shallots scattered across it. Two slim spears of crunchy homemade dill pickle. Tangy brown mustard. And of course, because this is Pittsburgh, a hearty drizzle of Heinz Ketchup.

My hands have a pleasant stickiness to them from the humidity clinging to my skin, the ketchup and mustard that leaked from the bun. Salty grease lingers on my lips. My stomach is wonderfully full. I breathe in and taste the scent of grill smoke hanging in the air as a chorus of crickets chirps in the backyard, the steady thuds of Alex traipsing through the kitchen like a comforting heartbeat.

My first hot dog from Alex's kitchen. Knees knocking as we sat side by side and ate in comfortable quiet. Eyes meeting over just-right bites. His thumb sweeping ketchup from my mouth. Smiling so hard it hurt when I noticed he had mustard on his nose.

For a moment, I am utterly content.

Then I remember the email I just read.

The back door thuds shut, followed by the pleasant *crack* of a beer being opened. Alex lowers himself to the edge of the stoop beside me and hands me the can of beer he went inside for. He always offers me the first foamy, ice-cold sip.

"Well?" he says.

I take a long gulp of beer. And then I take another.

"Easy, tiger." He plucks the beer gently from my hand.

"I read the email," I tell him.

"I inferred," he says, "from the chugging." His eyes search mine. "Talk to me, Ted. Tell me what you're thinking."

"I'm thinking this is not the kind of vacation I had in mind when I pictured finally taking a vacation." I take the beer from him and this time have a measured, throat-wetting sip. Then I hand it back. "And I'm thinking our chickens have come home to roost."

Alex peers at the beer, brow furrowed, then brings the can to his mouth and takes a drink. I watch it wet his lips, his Adam's apple rolling in his throat as he swallows.

"Sometimes," he says, "I think about how wild it is that they believed the story we cooked up."

I take the beer from him and have another drink. "They didn't just believe it. They took it and *ran*."

A montage of moments since that first night on his stoop flits through my mind. All the things we've done together, been through together, that Ethan and Jen inevitably witnessed. I can admit we've given them plenty of material—in person, on social media—but all of it was in the context of friendship. They just seem incapable of seeing it that way.

"I *did* say we were first loves," he admits.

"And then we told them that was in the *past*," I remind him, "when we were teens." I swig the beer again, then hand it back to Alex and pick up my phone, so I can reread the email.

> Thea and Alex,
>
> We would like to invite you to join us for a two-family beach vacation starting the last week of July into the first week of August.

"'Two-*family* vacation,'" I mutter. "We've been telling them we're just friends for two years. Why don't they believe us?"

"I think . . ." Alex clears his throat. "It's because they don't find us very convincing as 'just friends.'"

"What," I say to him, "about our behavior is so unconvincing? We've never done anything that had a whiff of romance."

Alex stares at me. I squint-grimace as I rethink that statement. The truth is, there have been slipups, moments between Alex and me in the past two years that very much had a whiff of romance. What mattered then—what matters now—is that they were unintentional, incidental moments that were bound to happen between two people going through a hard season of life together, being each other's safe person, comfort person, steady person. Being each other's best friend.

"At least," I amend, "not in front of them."

Alex frowns down at the beer in his hands. "Ted, we've done more with each other—*for* each other—than a lot of romantic couples. No matter what we call it, we're good to each other in a way they'd only expect people to be if . . . they loved each other."

I stare at him, my heart pounding in my chest. "We do love each other." My throat's turned tight and dry, but I push out the words because they're the life raft I cling to, my insurance, my guarantee that we're safe: "As friends."

Alex is silent, still frowning down at the beer. I watch him take a sip, then a longer sip that turns into a chug.

"Now who's the tiger that needs to go easy." I reach for the beer, and Alex lets me take it, dropping his elbows to his knees, his hands clasped together.

I cup the cold can, tracing the condensation with my fingertips. Then I go back to rereading the email.

> Of course, we know things haven't always been easy between the four of us, and we recognize that might make this idea less than appealing, but all of us being there would mean so much to Mia. As we anticipate a significant development in her family life (which we would like to share with

you during this vacation), we think she would benefit from the comfort and consistency of time at her favorite place with her favorite people and dog (Argos is included in this invitation!!!). Ethan's family has offered us the use of their beachfront property in Bethany, DE. We also recognize this is short notice, so even if you can't come the full two weeks (though that would be wonderful, for Mia!!), you're invited to come for however much time you can get off. Please consider and let me know if you're willing to join and how long you are able to stay as soon as possible. I truly hope you can make it. Your presence would make Mia so happy.

Warmly,

Jen and Ethan

I slip my phone into my pocket, tip the beer back, and drain the last swig that's left.

"Reread?" Alex asks.

"Yep." I set the empty can on the step beside my feet. "I'm thinking they're going to tell us they're engaged, maybe pregnant, too."

"Hmm," Alex says.

I glance his way. "Don't you think so? What else would 'a significant development in Mia's family life' mean?"

Alex rubs his thumb over a burn scar on the inside of his wrist. "I don't know what else it would be." He meets my eyes. "If that *is* the case, will you go? Knowing it's likely they're going to say to our faces that they're getting married, having a baby together?"

"Will you?" I ask.

A swallow works down his throat. "I asked first, Ted."

My eyes search his, one of those moments in which the tug between us feels more weighted than it should. "Yes," I tell him finally. "I'll go."

I didn't realize his shoulders were tucked up tight and high, the way they are when he's anxious, until I watch them fall. "I'll go, too," he says. He looks like he wants to say more, ask more. But he doesn't.

"We'll do it for Mia," I tell him.

He sighs heavily. "Yeah."

"But . . ." I lean my shoulder into his and say, "I do have one condition."

Alex glances over at me. With how close I've put myself, leaning into him, our noses nearly brush. His eyes hold mine. "So help me god, if you say it's a gas station hot dog . . ."

"No." I smile. "You've ruined me for every other hot dog now."

He smiles, too, slow and satisfied. "Glad to hear it." As the wind drags a tendril of hair into my face, Alex combs it back, tucking it behind my ear. "What is it?" he asks. "This condition?"

"We *have* to kick their asses at euchre."

His eyebrows lift. "We're playing euchre with them?"

"That's the Bruscato beach vacation tradition, is it not? Kids in bed, cards on the table."

He grimaces. "I was picturing more of a 'play nice while Mia's awake, go our separate ways the moment she's in bed' type of 'two-family' vacation."

"Well," I say, "me, too. But I really don't think I can pass up the chance to crush them at cards." I give him big sad-puppy eyes, a pathetic pleading pout. "At least one night?"

Alex's mouth twists, then twitches at the corner. His *I'm exasperated with Thea* smile. He rolls his eyes. "Fine, Ted. One night.

But *just* one night. This vacation is going to be rough enough as it is. Deal?"

I stare at him, trying to unravel the knot of worry twisting my stomach.

A beach vacation with our exes. The last thing I need is to spend that much time around people who press my tender points and dredge up the aches of the past, who see Alex and me as the very thing I will never risk us becoming.

This vacation will be hard, Alex is right. It'll be Ethan and Jen versus Thea and Alex, and "Thea and Alex" is a concept I already have a hard enough time keeping in its safe, sure place. Friend love. Steady love. Love that can never crash and burn and break our hearts.

Resting my head on Alex's shoulder, I cling to what I always tell myself. That I'm good at being content with this; that what we have is enough; and that we've stayed this way, just friends, for a reason. Because wanting anything more could end in losing everything.

And then I tell him, from the same spot on his stoop, the same thing I did, two years ago, "Deal."

CHAPTER 5

THEN

July 19, two summers ago

This morning, I woke up in my sweltering shoebox of an apartment, got ready for work, and, as I brushed my teeth, made a bargain with myself—if I could make it through the day without crying, I would buy myself gelato. Expensive, delicious, terrible-for-my-stomach gelato.

It's not even noon, and the odds that I'll get that gelato aren't looking good.

Today would have been Ethan's and my fourteenth anniversary. I woke up on the verge of tears, a tangle of grief and relief and loss knotted into a lump in my throat. I don't want to cry today, even if feeling all of that makes sense. I want to focus on my job and feel a sliver of happiness. Because The Bookshop is *my* place. My happy place.

I love working at this bookstore. I love books. I love helping people find books *they'll* love. I love the crisp scent of paper mingled with rich espresso brewed at the coffee bar, the shush of pages being turned, the hum of patrons speaking softly as they browse. I love the bubbly laughter of students who trickle in on their walk home for oversize cookies and a chance at the coveted front-window alcove seats; the hiss of city buses coming to a stop right outside, spilling out people, some of whom walk toward our door and, as they drag it open, usher in the familiar whoosh of North Side traffic, even the wail of a siren barreling toward the hospital where we've donated books, reminding me The Bookshop isn't just located in the heart of this neighborhood—it's part of the heart of this neighborhood.

I still feel like an outsider in this city, most of the time. But when I'm at The Bookshop, I feel a sense of belonging, connection—happiness. I want that to hold true even on a hard day.

I suck in a breath, trying my best to tune out the world's most emo playlist ever filling the speakers; apparently one of my coworkers felt that's the vibe we needed today.

As I scoop up a box of new releases to restock, I mutter on my exhale, "Gelato. Gelato, gelato, gelato."

I've just ripped open the box of new releases when The Bookshop's door swings open, and in walks Lauren, looking like a pissed-off supermodel. She spots me immediately, only a few feet away, and flashes me a smile.

Through the speakers above us, Tori Amos wails about being lost in the rearview. Lauren's smile evaporates.

"Who the fuck," she asks the store at large, "put on Tori Amos?"

Dan shrinks on his barstool perch at the front register. "Well, um. I did—"

"Daniel." Lauren stares him down. "Do. Better."

Patrons have tuned in, a tableau of wide eyes, lowered books, coffee cups suspended midsip. They are captivated by Lauren's profane drill-sergeant entrance.

"Sorry," Dan whispers.

"I don't need a sorry." She hikes her bloodred designer bag higher on her shoulder. "I need a solution. Play something happy. Please," she adds offhandedly as she walks my way, an attempt at politeness for my sake. She knows I'm allergic to offending people.

Dan salutes her as she marches past him. "On it."

For the first time today, I don't feel like I'm about to cry. I wrap my arms around Lauren and hug her hard. She squeezes me back.

"Thanks," I whisper.

"Such a dumbass," she mutters. "What did he pull up on Spotify, the heartbreak special?"

I laugh. "Let's just say Damien Rice opened for Tori today."

"Jesus." She rolls her eyes. Suddenly, Pharrell Williams's "Happy" floods the store's speakers. "Men," she sighs. "So literal."

"I like this song," I tell her, trying to throw Dan a bone. I turn and give him an encouraging thumbs-up.

Dan smiles nervously, his gaze darting from me to Lauren. She does not acknowledge him. Dan wilts. He has a brutal crush on her.

Everyone who meets Lauren has a brutal crush on her.

Because Lauren Vaughn is the whole package—gorgeous, smart, and, beneath that tough exterior, deeply kind. Lauren is the one friend I'm proud to say I've made on my own in my three years since moving to Pittsburgh. Every other friend I had was through Ethan, and, along with the house and the newer car, he walked away with them. If I had to have only one friend, I couldn't have picked a better one than Lauren.

Pharrell croons that contagiously upbeat chorus, the perfect soundtrack for this moment—finally, once again I am in my happy place and actually happy.

Thea stood at the store's threshold, smiling at her friend, brimming with gratitude for her happy place, which gave her not just a job she loved but her best friend. Lauren was a successful architectural designer, health nut, and marathon runner, a fancy-food and fine-wine and designer-everything gal, and Thea was none of that. She truly believed their lives would have never crossed paths if it weren't for The Bookstore.

"Thea?" Lauren says. "Where'd you go?"

I blink, snapped out my bad habit. "Nowhere," I tell her.

Lauren tips her head. "You were clearly *some*where."

Lauren swears under her breath as her phone starts to ring. She rummages around, finds it, then groans. "Dammit, I have to answer this."

I watch her walk to the alcove on the other side of the door, and like the little narrating traitor my mind is, it picks up right where it left off.

Thea was in only her second week of work when she found Lauren perched on a kid-size chair in The Bookshop's children's section, wearing an office-chic outfit and sighing as she opened books, shut them, and tossed them aside. After Thea asked her how she could help, Lauren told her she was browsing for her nephew but had no idea what an eight-year-old would enjoy. Thea nudged her toward the graphic novels and away from the picture books, suggested a few well-loved middle-grade titles, and somehow they ended up talking for so long, they learned they'd both grown up in St. Louis (Thea, quaint Webster Groves; Lauren, affluent Ladue). Then Lauren asked Thea if she'd want to grab a drink and bond over being St. Louis gals stranded in Pittsburgh. Two glasses into their first meetup, Lauren clasped Thea's hand and said, "We're going to be best friends, Thea Meyer. I just know it." And, like always, Lauren was right.

"Okay," Lauren says. "I'm back." She slips her phone into her purse and smiles, the portrait of style, as always—a white sheath dress that makes her sun-kissed skin pop, red kitten heels that match her bag.

"So," I say to her, "what can I help you find today?"

She shrugs. "I'm looking for a best friend who'd want to take a lunch break with me." She glances around. "Think you can help me out?"

I peer at the wall-mounted clock. It's noon, and since I'm scheduled to work more than seven hours today, my lunch break is a full glorious sixty minutes.

Smiling, I tell her, "I'll get my bag from the back. Meet you outside?"

"God, yes." She throws open the door. "This obnoxiously happy song is pissing me off."

*

The sun is shining, my belly is full of wood-fire pizza, and I haven't felt the urge to cry once during lunch. Maybe I'll earn my gelato, after all.

Basking in the sun, I slouch in my café chair across from Lauren and slurp the last of my root beer. Lauren sucks down the dregs of her Aperol spritz.

Our waiter, who's been very attentive since we were seated—unsurprisingly, he has the hots for Lauren—sweeps in, clearing our glasses and asking if we want another round.

I tell our waiter I'll pass on a refill. Lauren orders another Aperol spritz.

My eyebrows lift.

Having two drinks at lunch, when she's headed back to the office, is very un-Lauren.

"You okay, Lo?"

She peers my way, a notch in her brow. Also very un-Lauren. Lauren doesn't believe in frowning: it "leads to premature wrinkles."

"Yep!" she says brightly. She tugs down her sunglasses, hiding her eyes.

Suspicion, then guilt hit me, a swift emotional one-two punch. I've been such a mess the past few months—have I missed the signs that Lauren's struggling, too?

Asking directly will get me nowhere. Lauren's so protective of me, she'll tell me what she thinks I need to hear rather than the truth.

Leaning down to my messenger bag at my feet, I lift the flap and rummage around for the embroidered birthday card I fell in love with and bought at The Bookshop this past winter.

"What are you digging around for?" Lauren asks.

"Mind your beeswax," I tell her. My messenger bag is a black hole. Where the hell is that card?

"Theodora Meyer." She swats my arm. "Do *not* get out your wallet."

"I'm not!" I straighten, triumphant, card in hand.

"What," she says, eyes narrowed, "is that."

I hold off on answering and instead thank our waiter as he sets down Lauren's Aperol spritz. Our waiter misses this. He's otherwise occupied, smiling dreamily at Lauren.

Lauren peers up at our waiter. She does not smile back. I clear my throat, hoping that snaps him out of it.

The waiter blinks, then asks, "Do you ladies need anything else?"

"No," Lauren says.

I knock her knee with mine from beneath table.

"Thank. You," she adds flatly.

Our waiter finally takes the hint and makes himself scarce. Lauren sucks down half of her second spritz.

"Must be tough," I say. "Being that hot *and* possessed of a snort that works like a mating call."

She flips me the bird.

I laugh. Lauren laughs, too—a loud, throaty cackle.

It's been a while since I can remember her laughing. And I've been too distracted with my own pity party to pick up on that. Guilt hits me again, though a bit gentler this time. A shove nudging me forward.

I slide the card across the table. "Happy almost birthday, Lo."

Lauren glances from the card to me. "My birthday is over a month away," she says.

I shrug. "You know me, I hate waiting to give gifts. Honestly, I'm proud I lasted this long. Pretty sure last year I gave you your gifts in—"

"May." She rolls her eyes, but it's softened by a smile. "Which is ridiculous."

"Come on, open it."

"Thea." Her smile falls. She peers warily at the card. "Your cards make me emotional. You know I don't like public displays of emotion."

I nudge the card closer to her. The card teeters on the café table's edge. "Lo," I say dramatically, "don't let my gift fall! My precious gift! Oh no, it's going to—"

She swipes the card from the table.

"You and your damn gifts," she mutters. She slides a finger beneath the envelope's edge, careful as she opens it.

"How," I ask, "can you open it that slowly? Don't you just want to rip it off?"

"Nope." Lauren pulls out the card and traces the embroidery. She smiles softly. I can tell she loves it. When she opens the card and sees what's inside it, her mouth falls open. She swats me with the card. "Theadora—"

"Don't you dare finish that sentence," I tell her. "Bon appétit, friend."

She stares at the gift card in her hand. "It's too much."

"Is not," I say.

"Savoureux," she says quietly.

Savoureux, Lauren's told me, is the first restaurant she visited after moving to Pittsburgh for work. It's the place that made her fall, in her words, "just a *little* in love" with the city. Since then, she's had the worst luck trying to get a reservation. They book months out, and any time she's tried, they haven't had openings that lined up with her demanding work schedule.

She peers up at me, and, shockingly, her eyes are wet. Lauren is *not* a crier. "Thea, thank you."

I squeeze her hand. "You're welcome. And that's not all. I got a reservation on your birthday weekend! The first opening they had was the second Sunday in September, which I figured was pretty safe, since you usually only work through Saturday on the weekend . . ." My voice dies off as Lauren bursts into tears.

"Oh my god." I lean in, clasping her arm. "Lauren, what's wrong?"

"Nothing," she chokes out. She drops her forehead to the table.

"Lauren, clearly something is wrong."

Her chest rises and falls with a deep, yogic breath as she gracefully sits up, then dabs beneath her eyes.

"I'm fine," she says.

Giving me another one of those too-bright smiles, she grabs her Aperol spritz and sucks down the second half.

She is definitely not fine.

Before I can press, Lauren reaches inside her bag and says. "Funnily enough, I have something for you, too."

"Lo," I whine. "Can't I just give you a gift for once?"

"Don't be petulant." She unearths from her purse a rectangular something wrapped in beautiful floral paper.

"I've been a shitty friend the past few months. I haven't been tuned in. I've been a self-absorbed Debbie Downer, and I wanted to do something nice for *you* for the first time in—"

"Excuse me." She drops my gift with a thud on the table.

"Hey." I scoop up whatever she's giving me, cradling it to my chest. "Be nice to my gift."

"You listen here, and you listen good. You haven't been a shitty friend. You've been going through *hell*."

"I mean, those two things aren't mutually exclusive—"

"Thea," she says. "Stop it. You are a good friend. I love you, and I know you love me, and I haven't doubted that one bit the past few months."

"Lo." I clutch the gift tighter to my chest, pressed against the ache in my heart.

"Now, no more mushy feelings." She nods to my gift. "Open it!"

I tear off the paper, ripping at it eagerly.

Lauren sighs. "You open presents like a feral squirrel."

"I get excited! I can't help it . . ." My voice dies off.

I'm looking at a book, on whose cover is none other than Alex Bruscato. Above him, in a striking gold embossed serif, *Come Viene, Viene*.

What is Alex doing on the cover of a book? What is his *name* doing on a book? I open it, flipping through the pages.

A cookbook. A very beautiful cookbook. I shut it, staring at the cover again. At Alex. He's wearing in an indigo chambray button-up, cuffed at his elbows, that matches his eyes. His dark hair is styled so that a rakish curl falls on his forehead; flour covers his hands and the table he's leaning on. I turn the book over. On the back, he's in the same outfit, leaning on the same table. *Licking* a half-melted cone of what is, I presume, because the universe is cruel, and because the front of the book is in Italian, gelato.

"Oof," I mutter.

Lauren says, "It's obscene, right? How fine he is?"

I nod.

"I know cooking isn't your thing," she tells me, "but I figured maybe this book could be your gateway, now that you've got your own place, your own kitchen. Crack this sucker open and you and the hot chef can enjoy some"—she leans in and says meaningfully—"one-on-one time."

"Lo!"

"Seriously, though, this cookbook is hailed as *the* best intro to Italian cooking, which I know you love. And if you don't want to try cooking, you never have to open it and you've still got your money's worth. Just feast your eyes on the cover."

I open the book again, this time turning the pages slowly so I can take it in. Mouthwatering food photos—heaping twirls of homemade pasta scattered with fresh herbs, cracked pepper, and coarse sea salt dusting a pan of colorful roasted veggies, luscious desserts flecked with chocolate shavings, raspberries, a sprig of mint. I peer closer to read what look like hand-scribbled notes around the tidy recipes, the up-close photos of the chef at work in his kitchen, in profile, sweat on his temple, flour at his throat. They feel so intimate, these peeks of Alex woven throughout.

I flip to the back, to the author bio. My stomach drops. I've watched enough cooking shows, since Ethan loved them, to know the prestigious terms. *James Beard. Michelin star.*

My not-really old friend and first love is a culinary prodigy.

"You look upset," Lauren says. "I'm sorry, if it seems like pressure, giving you a cookbook—"

"I'm not upset," I tell her honestly. "I'm just . . . surprised."

"Well," she says, "that's fair. Like your gift to me today, this was meant to be given on a relevant occasion."

"What occasion?" I ask.

"It was going to be an apartment warming gift." She lifts her dark, expertly shaped eyebrows. "But that would require my *being invited* to your apartment."

"Ah." I flip the book shut and plant my hand over Alex's face. I can't keep staring at him. "Well, I was going to invite you. Eventually."

"When?" she asks. "Thanksgiving?"

"Lo." I sigh. "It's just . . . not . . . presentable yet."

"*Presentable?* You really think I'll care what your apartment looks like?"

I stare at her.

Lauren tips her head, receiving my meaning. "Okay, I take your point. Generally, I care very deeply about interior design and architectural aesthetics and can be quite judgmental, but I'm not going to say anything about *your* place."

"True." I lean in and tap her temple. "But you'll think it."

"Will not!"

"Fine. You can see it. Soon. Ish."

She glares at me.

"Just give me a couple days," I tell her, "to zhuzh it up."

"But I want to zhzuh it up with you!"

"Nope. You've done enough for me the past few months."

She rolls her eyes. "Thea, I got sad drunk with you a couple times and dragged you to a pedicure—that's hardly anything."

She's done a lot more than that. But I know better than to argue with her.

"Next Tacos and Tequila Tuesday?" I ask. "How's that sound?"

She smiles. "That sounds lovely. What can I bring?"

I think of my sweltering third-floor apartment, how miserable Lauren will be. "A lot of ice?"

"Sure," she says. "I'll bring a bottle of tequila, too."

"No you won't." I scoop up the cookbook and slide it into my messenger bag. "*I'll* provide the tequila. And the margarita fixings."

"Bringing tequila," she says.

I tell her, "Paying for tacos, then."

"Speaking of paying." Lauren pulls out her wallet and glances around, looking for the waiter. "Of course. Now that I actually want him here, he's nowhere to be seen."

I smile.

She narrows her eyes. "You got the tab, didn't you?"

"Told him it was on me when he walked us to our table."

"Thea!"

"I'm so sorry I treated on your almost-birthday!"

"Almost-birthday that's a *month* away," she mutters. Standing, she hikes her bag onto her shoulder. "Not forgiven."

"Lauren." I stand, too. "All you've done lately is steal tabs when we eat out."

"Well," she says, as we start down the sidewalk, "only one of us is divorced and not collecting alimony from her dirtbag ex."

"I don't want Ethan's money. I don't want anything of Ethan's."

"Why not?" she says. "You should clean that fucker out, Thea."

I peer at her. There's an edge in Lauren's voice, a level of anger toward Ethan that, even for her, seems unprecedented.

"You sound more pissed at him than I am. Which is impressive. And up till now, I thought, impossible."

Lauren's mouth tightens.

"What's going on?" I ask.

She adjusts her sunglasses but doesn't answer me.

"Lauren."

Lauren peers up at the sky and mutters, "Fuck." Then she rips off her sunglasses, meets my eyes, and says auctioneer fast, "I saw Ethan on a date with a woman last night."

My stomach tightens. Ethan. On a date. With Jen.

Or maybe it wasn't Jen. Maybe they just banged and moved on. If that's the case, I'll have no reason to be friends with Alex.

That thought leaves me oddly sad. Alex and I haven't texted since exchanging numbers that night at his house, but I told myself it was fine for there to be a stretch of quiet following the chaos that threw us together. He said he'd have Mia the next few days, so I'm sure he's been busy. And I've been fully booked with work at The Bookshop and tears to cry and also maybe waiting for Alex to text and make the first friend move. It's only now, when faced with possibly having no cause to stay in it, that I realize I was weirdly looking forward to this pickle Alex and I got ourselves into.

Or maybe I was only looking forward to, for the first time in a while, being in *anything* with somebody else. Not feeling so deeply alone.

"So this woman," I say to Lauren. "Was she by any chance petite? Annoyingly pretty? Natural honey blond with sky-blue eyes and killer curves?"

Lauren blinks. "That . . . was a disturbingly accurate guess."

"Not a guess," I admit.

"Wait, you *knew* about her already?" Lauren throws up her hands. "Why haven't I heard about this?"

I bite my lip.

I was going to tell Lauren about Alex, about our lie, about Ethan and Jen, over lunch. But then I realized something was up with Lauren, and the last thing I needed was to spend more time talking about me and my dumpster-fire life.

She steps closer, eyes locked on me. "First, you steal the tab. Then, you don't tell me your ex is out there swinging his dick around mere weeks after your divorce. Happy almost-birthday to me!"

"Oh so *now* you're fine with calling it your 'almost-birthday.'" I lift the flap of my bag and pull out the cookbook. "Her name is Jen. I met her at Ethan's when I picked up Argos on Monday. Their vibe was . . . postcoital."

Lauren shudders. "Ew."

"Very ew. And very awkward. Also." I lift the cookbook and point to Alex's face. "This guy was there."

Lauren blinks. "I'm sorry, did you just say the hot chef was there?"

I nod. "He's her ex-husband."

"Get the fuck out of here," she says. "Wait, that means you've *met* him." Her voice is getting louder. "You didn't tell me you'd met the hot chef! What kind of best friendship is this?"

"A loving but dysfunctional one," I remind her. "In which, say, one best friend uncharacteristically bursts into tears, and, when asked by her concerned best friend if she's fine, refuses to talk about it?"

Lauren purses her lips. "Touché."

It's not the explanation I wanted, but at least now she knows I'm onto her.

"Come on." I shove the cookbook back in my bag, then loop my arm with hers. "I'll tell you everything. But we have to walk and talk, or I'll be late for work."

"I can't wait," she says giddily. "You met Hot Chef in the hot flesh!"

"At one point, I even held his hot hand."

She screeches, "Thea! What? How?"

I sigh as I hit the crosswalk button and glance her way. "You are truly never going to believe me when I tell you."

CHAPTER 6

NOW

July 16, seventeen days until "vacation"

I am splayed on my bed, sheets thrown off, hands tapping the mattress. I can't fall asleep. Last night went this way, too, which means I'm on track to spend hours counting the watermarks on my ceiling, reading a book I'm not invested in (if I read the one I *am* invested in, I definitely won't fall asleep), drinking a glass of water, and practicing meditative breathing . . . none of which will work. Then I'll finally succumb to sleep at an ungodly hour in the middle of the night and wake up a few hours later, the second the sun is up.

I'm exhausted. My mind is racing. I can't stop worrying. Something's off with Alex.

I felt the shift right after we agreed to the vacation, and since then, as we've texted, coordinating our schedules, figuring out how long we want to go and which days we can both get off. Alex has been quiet, subdued—very un-Alex.

And, like the scaredy cat I am, I haven't pushed, haven't pressed, haven't asked what's bothering him. Because I'm afraid what's bothering him is *me*.

I don't know why, can't put my finger on it. It's a gut feeling that something I've said—or haven't said—upset him. I could ask. I *should* ask. Maybe I'm wrong. But I'm terrified I might find out that I'm right.

I've spent enough time in therapy the past year and a half to know what Sue, my therapist, would say if I told her why I'm spiraling and how I'm handling it. She'd say my fear of talking to Alex about this is exactly why I should talk to Alex about this. Then she'd remind me that conflict avoidance does not equate to *consequence* avoidance.

"Dammit, Sue." I paw around my nightstand until I find my phone.

Before I can overthink it and talk myself out of texting him, I write the first thing that comes to mind and hit send.

You still awake?

I chuck my phone across the bed and pick up my boring book. I'm not going to lie here, staring at my phone, hoping Alex responds. Dreading how Alex might respond.

My phone buzzes. I drop the book, scramble for my phone among the sheets, and flop onto my stomach. I hold my breath as I read Alex's response.

Why wouldn't I be??

I squint at my phone's screen, registering the time. Huh. It's only ten p.m.

So, I type, somehow I missed that it's not the middle of the night.

My phone buzzes with his response.

Give yourself some credit. You're on a grandpa's sleep schedule, so thinking it's the middle of the night at 10pm isn't far off.

Relief whooshes through me. He teased.

I bite my lip, my thumbs hovering over the screen. Then I type, I really appreciate that you compared me to a grandPA.

Everyone knows it's only grandpas who go to bed at 8pm—Grandmas are the party animals.

I smile. You do realize not all grandmas are as cool as your mom.

Don't let Lydia hear you calling her a grandma. Mia's lucky she gets away with calling her Nones.

She won't hear it from me! I type. Well, not the grandma part. I've told your mom before and I'll tell her again, she's the coolest.

Eh, his text says. She's all right.

I roll my eyes. Alex's mom has him wrapped around her finger. Clearly, I type. "All right" is a solid basis for your delusional "party animal grandma" concept.

Fine, my mom's cool, he says, but I'm telling you, even boring moms turn into party animal grandmas.

I try to picture my mother, the serious, self-disciplined retired teacher who still goes to bed at nine and wakes up at the butt crack of dawn every morning, ever becoming a party animal.

I can't see it, I type.

Ted, grandmas are liberated women. They finally don't have to give a shit about everything they had to for the past thirty 5years. Find me a grandma who isn't living her best nightlife, now that she finally has that time to herself. No kids to put to sleep, no teenagers out worryingly late, no one's laundry to do, no meals to plan.

No grandpas to entertain, I add. Since they went to bed hours ago.

Exactly! he says. Which is why I call Mia's days with Jen my granny time.

A laugh jumps out of me. Look at you, a liberated woman!

I'd be able to enjoy it more, he says, if the Buccos weren't getting their asses kicked and I could figure out today's Wordle.

To your credit, I tell him, today's Wordle was hard.

Ted! he says. NO hints.

My smile squishes my cheeks up to my eyes. It's the blessing and the curse of my friendship with Alex. It's so easy talking like this. And it makes it that much harder when I need to talk to him about something that isn't.

Hey, I write.

I take a deep breath, rubbing where worry sits heavy in my chest. I want to talk to him about this. I want to know if he's okay, and if he's not, what I can do. But I can't text about it.

I type, then hit send before I chicken out, Tomorrow is our friendiversary.

The text shows as read. An ellipsis appears, telling me he's typing. It disappears. Appears again.

I push through the anxiety squeezing my insides and type, then hit send. How do you feel about grabbing our traditional celebratory gelato a night early?

Another ellipsis. Finally, my phone buzzes with his text.

Luna's is closed.

My heart plummets. Alex's family owns Luna's, and since becoming friends, the past two summers we've snuck in after-hours countless times for late-night gelato. This summer, we haven't, and I don't know why.

My phone buzzes again with another text from him. This time, when I read it, my heart soars right up to my throat.

Luckily, he says, I've got a key to a restaurant that stocks their gelato. Tell me when to pick you up.

I spring up in bed, tripping on the sheets as I climb out while typing, I can be ready in 5!

My phone buzzes with his response.

No rush on my end, gramps. This granny's got all night.

*

I should have pushed back on Alex's counteroffer to stop by his restaurant. But I didn't feel like I had the leverage. Now, I barely feel like I have a grip on anything.

Alex stands at one of the professional cooking ranges, backward ballcap on, apron strings tied tight, flipping a pan as heat dances beneath it. *A quick late-night bite*, he explained when we got here, and I swear it's because somehow he'd sensed I hadn't eaten more than peanut butter crackers for dinner. I was too worked up to try to cook something for myself from my small repertoire.

Now I'm biting my lip as I sit on a stool nearby, trying not to implode from lust as I watch him work.

I've seen Alex cook at home so many times, but watching him cook in his restaurant is new. It's tender, vulnerable. He's just dipping his toes back in the professional kitchen waters.

After a long stretch of silence, I ask him, "What's for dinner?"

"Chicken piccata," he says.

My heart jumps in my chest. That's one of my favorites. The first chicken dish he taught me how to cook. Sliding off the stool, I reach for an apron from a neatly folded stack. And then I walk over to the handwashing station. "Mind if I join in, Chef?"

Alex glances over his shoulder, and my breath catches. The sharp line of his profile, the furrow in his brow, the beads of sweat on his skin from the heat he's bent over.

A small smile lifts the corner of his mouth. "Wouldn't mind at all."

*

Bellies full of chicken piccata, gelato cups in hand, Alex and I stand at the intersection down the street from his restaurant, waiting to cross. The park we're headed toward technically closes at dusk, but there's a worn-smooth wood bench beneath a two-story birch tree at its entrance, waiting for us.

Alex nudges my shoulder with his. "Ted."

"Hmm?" My eyes are shut, tart-sweet key lime gelato melting on my tongue. "Time to cross?"

"Not yet," he says. "You take your lactase pill?"

"Yep." The pedestrian light flashes on, and we step out into the crosswalk. "Thanks for asking. I do feel like you missed an opportunity, though, to call me Gramps, with the lactase pill check-in."

"True." His gaze zigzags across the road, watching for cars as we cross. "Guess I'm not on my game today."

I glance his way, cataloging the visual confirmation that my hunch was right, that something is upsetting Alex—shoulders curled in, jaw tight.

We step up onto the curb, headed toward the bench.

"Hey." I nudge his shoulder with mine.

He doesn't look my way. He's stirring his zabaione gelato so vigorously, it's turning into zabaione soup. "Hmm?"

We drop onto the bench—which is more like a one and half seater than two—our hips, elbows, and shoulders pressed against each other. I swallow, nervous, and peer down at my gelato as I ask him, "What's wrong?"

In my peripheral vision, I watch him freeze, then slowly peer up at me. He clears his throat, then says, "What makes you think something's wrong?"

"I don't *think*. I know. I know you, Alex. I know when you're upset. What I don't know is the reason . . ." I bite my lip. "If it's my fault."

Alex freezes again, midstir. Silence stretches out in thick, slow seconds. He resumes stirring and says, "No, Ted. It's not your fault."

I hiss out a breath I didn't realize I'd been holding while waiting for him to answer. "Do you want to talk about it?"

"Nah." He tips back his cup of gelato soup and takes a swig. "Talked about it with Atlas."

"Oh." I shouldn't be disappointed. It's good that he talked to his therapist, that he had someone to help him work through whatever's upsetting him. But selfishly, now that I know I'm not to blame, I wish he'd want to share that with me, too. "That's good," I tell him. "Was it helpful?"

Alex sinks back into the bench, legs outstretched, and crosses his ankles. He nods. "Yeah. Talking to Atlas always helps."

I poke at my gelato. "I still can't believe you have a therapist named Atlas."

"I *chose* my therapist because he was named Atlas."

A laugh jumps out of me. I've never heard this. "Why?"

"It's a badass name," Alex says. "Did I picture my badass therapist named Atlas being older than my dad and fond of bow ties? No. But the guy's definitely delivered on the badassery."

"I mean, that's how I chose my therapist, too—badass-name vibes."

He snorts. "Nothing says 'badass' like the name Susan."

"Hey! Badasses," I tell him, "come in all shapes and sizes."

A soft laugh rumbles in his throat, and I smile reflexively. I love making Alex laugh.

Alex tips back another gulp of his melted gelato. I make a point of not watching his throat work as he swallows.

"You would pick a therapist named *Susan*," he says.

"She goes by Sue, I'll have you know. And she's *my* kind of badass. Calm and soft-spoken and unnervingly good at gently but firmly calling out my dysfunctional coping mechanisms."

He glances my way. "Yeah?"

I nod, spooning myself a mouthful of gelato. "Ohhh, yeah."

Silence settles between us. I swallow my bite, and when I peer up, I catch Alex looking at me, his expression tight. I hate that something's upsetting him, that I don't know what it is, that it seems like he doesn't *want* me to know.

I kick off my Birkenstocks and turn to face him on the bench, wedging my toes beneath his thigh. "Alex."

He holds my eyes. "Ted."

"No pressure, to talk about what's bothering you. But I *do* want to know, if you want to tell me. At any point. You can always talk to me."

A soft smile lifts the corner of his mouth. "Thanks, Ted."

"Of course," I tell him. "That's what friends do for each other."

He squeezes my ankle, but it doesn't linger, no thumb brushing my skin, no fingertips tickling the back of my leg. I try not to read into it. He says to me, "You're a good friend."

"So are you," I tell him. "The best there is."

"Wow." He reaches for his back pocket. "I'm telling Lauren."

"Don't you dare!" I grab his wrist. "I didn't mean it like that."

He lifts his eyebrows. "So I'm not the best?"

I groan. "You know I can't do this with you two. It's like asking a mom to choose which kid is her favorite."

"First of all," he says, "I don't appreciate that analogy's parentification of our relationship. Second, my mom absolutely has a favorite. All moms do."

"Let me guess," I say wearily, letting go of his wrist. "You're Lydia's."

"Obviously." Alex grins as he pulls out his phone, taps the screen, and proceeds to say to it, "Ted just told me I'm her favorite."

"Alex!" I yelp. "You did not just voice-memo Lauren."

He shrugs and pockets his phone. I'd be more annoyed if I wasn't so relieved that he's up to his usual antics, being playful. Smiling.

My phone buzzes in my shorts pocket. I sigh. "You *did* just voice-memo Lauren."

Alex sips his gelato. "Actually, I voice-memoed both of you. The good old group chat."

I pull out my phone as it buzzes again. I read Lauren's response and snort a laugh.

It's called Stockholm syndrome, ALEC. Just remember, I had to leave before she gave you the time of day.

Alex pulls his phone from his pocket again. He reads Lauren's text, and his smug grin morphs to a scowl. He hates when she calls him Alec. Pocketing his phone, he says, "That woman is a pestilence."

"Who just renamed our chat WHY IS ALEC STILL HERE." I laugh again as I set my phone on the bench. "She loves getting under your skin."

Alex glares at me.

That just makes me laugh harder. "Come on, you know what

she said isn't true. You and I got close before she moved away. And even if she hadn't left, we'd still be exactly where we are."

Alex tips his head. "You really think that?"

My smile fades. This is dangerous territory, the *what-if*s about us. What if we hadn't sworn to be only friends. What if we hadn't said things in those early days that allowed only for a path paved for friendship, when so much of what we said we wanted would cause a fork in a path paved for anything beyond that?

So often, when we get to this place of *what-ifs*, I divert us with humor, goofiness, whatever sends us back on the straight and narrow. But I can't tonight. Not when Alex is raw, when something hard is weighing on him, when I want him to know, as much as I can tell him, how much he means to me.

I wiggle my toes farther under his thigh, scooching close. "I *know* it, Alex."

Alex wraps his hand around my ankle again, and this time it lingers. Soft, steady sweeps of his thumb along my skin. His fingertips grazing up and down just a few inches of my leg, but it feels like it's everywhere, lighting me up.

His gaze is locked on mine. My heart pounds in my chest.

Slowly, Alex lifts his gelato cup and clinks it with mine. "Happy Friendiversary, Ted."

I clink my cup with his. "Happy Friendiversary, Alec."

"Not funny," he says.

"A little funny?"

He shakes head. "Nope."

I bite back a smile. "Cheers to . . ." I pause to do the mental math from the year of our fictional first meeting. "Twenty years? Is that right?"

A faint smile lifts the corner of his mouth. "That's right."

"Twenty. A milestone number. Should we take a photo? Make a little social media splash?"

His hand holding the gelato cup falters, like a plane bumping down with turbulence. His touch slips from my ankle.

My stomach knots. I feel like I'm right back where I was an hour ago, tossing and turning in bed. I believed Alex when he said it's not my fault he's upset, but I don't feel like I'm helping him *not* be upset, either. I keep messing up. I'm still missing something.

"Forget it," I tell him, smiling brightly. "Let's get back on track."

He rubs his shut eyes with his thumb and forefinger. "To what?"

"To us. To my toast." I clink my gelato cup with his again and say, "Cheers to two years of friendship that feels like twenty, and to many more to come."

I've barely finished my sentence when Alex tips his cup back, draining his gelato like he wishes it was something stronger. Following suit, I scoop up what's left of mine and shovel it in. The result is an unattractively large mouthful. When I try to swallow, I gag.

Alex's belly laugh rings through the quiet night air. He leans away from me, pulls out his phone, and snaps a picture.

"Awex!" I cover my chipmunk cheeks and glare at him. "No photos! And don't waff. Owww." I grimace, pressing a palm to my forehead. "Bwainfweeze."

"Poor Ted." Alex pulls me close, and my head falls into the crook of his neck. I sink into his touch, the heat of his body, the softness of his shirt, the warm spice clinging to his skin.

Alex rests his head on mine, then presses his thumb between my eyebrows. "Any better?" he asks.

I shake my head.

"Sorry I laughed," he says.

"And took a photo." There's still a frigid golf ball of gelato stuck in my mouth. I sigh through my nose.

"Sorry about that, too. Just not sorry enough to delete it." He adds, softer, "It sparks my joy, okay?"

I poke his side, and he catches my hand, then squeezes it. He curls my arm across his stomach, resting it at his waist, then sinks his hand into my hair and scratches at my scalp. My eyes fall shut. I turn to goo when he does this.

"Dat feels nice," I tell him. "But I'm stiw mad about da photo."

He laughs softly. "I'll keep it in my private folder—how's that for a compromise?"

I answer with a squeeze to his waist hard enough to make him curse under his breath. And then I tell him, "I wuf you, Awex."

He rubs his cheek against my hair and breathes in. "I wuf you, too, Ted."

CHAPTER 7

THEN

July 20, two summers ago

The windows are open to a muggy July night. The sun set hours ago, leaving behind a bruised blue-black sky. My third-floor apartment's temperature is earth's-core-molten. Or, according to my thermostat, eighty-five degrees.

I sit slumped against the refrigerator, taking in the state of the place—half-assembled IKEA bookshelves, stacks of books along the wall, too many moving boxes to count, my dog sprawled in front of my thrifted box fan.

"Well," I tell the dog, "I probably need to suck it up and call the property manager again about fixing the AC."

Argos lifts his head and makes one of his throaty almost-human sounds. Then he plops back down.

"Hey, now." I stroke my hand down his head. "A voicemail counts as a call. Did the property manager text or call me back last week to confirm he'd received that voicemail? No. But I still called."

Argos lets out another almost-human throaty noise. I reach for the fan to bring it closer, then slump sideways onto the floor beside him.

"The apartment looks like a bomb went off in it."

Argos whines and sets his paw on my hand.

"Good point," I tell him. "Before this evening, I'd hardly unpacked. So it might not be tidy, but at least I've gotten started, right?"

I pluck at my sweaty tank top plastered to my skin, my gaze wandering out the window. Across the street, two people sit on a balcony, shadowy silhouettes lit by a glowing waxing gibbous moon. I hear their laughter, the clink of silverware. Which makes me think of food. My stomach growls.

Argos lifts his head, eyes wide.

"Don't worry, pup," I tell him. "This is just what stomachs do when they're cavernously empty."

After I got off work, I came straight home, determined to actually get my apartment unpacked. With my work schedule the next few days, there is not a lot of time between now and Tuesday for all the zhuzhing I have left to do before Lauren comes over.

I told myself I'd stop once I'd tackled a few hours of unpacking. But then I got in the unpacking zone and before I knew it, five hours had passed. Now the time says it's too late for any kind of takeout dinner. Or gelato.

I am lightheaded, overheated, and extremely hungry.

"I think," I tell my dog, "now is when I scrounge around these boxes until I find the jar of Jif and gorge myself."

Argos drops his head on a distinct "harumph." Figures, the one truly human sound my dog makes is a sound of disapproval.

A buzz to my right makes me jump. In this hellscape of an

apartment, whose only and most important attractive feature is its dirt-cheap rent, I am prepared for the worst—murder hornets, rabid racoons, a plague of locusts.

But it's just my phone. I pick it up and then nearly drop it. Alex texted.

At risk of sounding like an absolute downer, is it just me or has this week been really bad?

I sigh as I type, The baddest.

Sorry it's been rough for you, too, Ted. How you hanging in? he asks.

I glance around my apartment, then type, Hanging in as well as could be expected for someone who's about to eat a jar of Jif for dinner. You?

Ted, he says. Not the Jif.

I'm still unpacking! And I don't cook. What else am I supposed to eat?

Literally anything but that.

Thing is, I type, Jif has more calories than air, which is my only other option, so I think I'm going to stick with the Jif. Also, you didn't answer my question—how are you?

Well, I was doing as well as could be expected for someone who's about to eat his feelings in the form of a giant tub of gelato. But now I'm anxiously pacing my kitchen because you're eating JIF for dinner.

"Alex has gelato?" I whine to Argos. "Salt in the wound."

Ted, he says, where do you live?

In a very small, unpacked apartment that's so hot I'm poaching in my own skin. Why?

Because I'm picking you up and feeding you. You can't eat Jif for dinner.

My stomach flips. It's midnight. Everything's closed.

Not when your family owns a pizzeria and gelato shop. After-hours Luna's is always open.

I nearly drop my phone again. I love Luna's. That's where Lauren and I had lunch yesterday. Are you serious?

I'm always serious about food, Ted. Let me know where to pick you up. I'm ready when you are.

Argos whines and nuzzles my elbow.

I send Alex my apartment's address and type, How does after-hours Luna's feel about welcoming a big, pea-brained yet adorable golden retriever?

After-hours Luna's feels like he can sit outside the kitchen where animals belong and enjoy the night air.

Argos harumphs.

I smile as I type and then hit send. We can work with that.

*

"You really were hungry," Alex says.

I come up for air from my perch on a prep table in the back of Luna's, cradling the bowl of lasagna I've mostly demolished. "I really was. Thank you again. I'll happily pay."

Alex looks offended. "You will not."

"Why?"

"First, because you're a friend, and friends don't pay. Second, because this food isn't Luna's. It's mine."

I blink down at the container. Then peer back up at him. "Wait, *you* made this?"

"I'm going to try not to be offended by how surprised you sound."

"No, no, I just assumed, when you handed it to me, that you'd gotten it from the kitchen fridge or something."

"I brought it," he says. "You must have missed me unpacking

the cooler when you were drooling over the gelato display and telling me the six-flavor combination you want."

"Excuse me." I stab another big bite of lasagna with my fork. "I was not drooling. But I absolutely did pick six flavors."

A smile flashes across his face, and for just a moment, I recognize the handsome, happy guy from the cover of the cookbook Lauren gave me. Heat hits my cheeks. I need to stop thinking about that cookbook cover. And Lauren calling him *Hot Chef*.

Alex's smile falls as he watches me take another bite of lasagna. He says, "I really wish you'd have let me heat that up."

"No heat," I mutter around my mouthful. "No more heat, never ever."

A frown tugs at his mouth, knits his brow. "Why's it so hot in your apartment? Is your AC not working?"

I shake my head. "Property manager is on it, though."

Hopefully.

"Will you and the dog be okay, staying there?" he asks. "While you're waiting for it to be fixed? Sounded like you were pretty miserable there, earlier."

"I was exaggerating about poaching in my own skin. I'll be fine. So will Argos. I have a giant box fan that keeps the air moving."

He narrows his eyes. "You sure?"

"Mm-hmm." I scoop up the last delicious bite, chew, and swallow. Then I tell him, "Thank you again, for the lasagna—that was incredible. So weird. I feel human now."

"Very weird," he says, "how eating *real* food does that to you."

I'm not taking the Jif bait. "Where can I wash this?"

"You can't." He pushes off the prep table he's been leaning on and takes the container.

I watch him drop it in the cooler at the end of the table, then cross the kitchen. He disappears into a walk-in fridge, then remerges with two giant bowls of gelato.

My throat thickens. I will not cry. "You didn't *actually* have to give me all six flavors."

He sets a spoon in each bowl and hands me mine. "I think we can agree it's been a six-flavors kind of week."

"Truth," I tell him. "So Alexander, want to talk about your terrible, horrible, no good, very bad day? Week," I amend. "I had to, though, because of the book. You familiar?"

His gaze narrows. "I hate that book."

I gasp. "Why?" *Alexander and the Terrible, Horrible, No Good, Very Bad Day* was a childhood favorite. I work it into the rotation every year at The Bookshop's StoryTime.

"Because," he tells me, "my dad always says it when I'm in a pissy mood—*Uh-oh, Alexander's having a terrible, horrible, no good, very bad day!*"

I bite my lip. "I think I'd really like your dad."

"Oh, I know you will," he says.

"'Will?'" I ask.

Alex looks my way. "My family is inescapable. If we're going to be friends, you'll meet them sooner rather than later . . ." He clears his throat and glances down at his gelato, scooping up a spoonful. "Maybe you've changed your mind about that, though. I shouldn't assume."

"I was going to say the same thing to you."

Alex frowns, peering up at me. "What?"

"You told me you had a bad week, and all you've done since then is take care of me." I glance down at my gelato, poking around it. "I don't want to have an imbalanced friendship."

"Hey." Alex settles on the table beside me. "We won't."

I give him a flat look. "What have I brought to this friendship so far?"

"Humor," he says. He sets down his gelato and extends one finger, then another, when he says, "Empathy. An equal fervor for gorging on gelato."

Argos whines outside the door.

Alex gives me a sidelong glance. "A needy dog."

I grimace. "I think he's developed separation anxiety since I left him with Ethan last week."

Alex glances at the kitchen door leading to the alley and sighs. "Mia's having a tough time with separation, too."

My heart aches. "I'm sorry, Alex."

"Me, too." He gives me a sad half smile. "It's rough."

"Is that part of why the week's been hard?" I ask. "You took her back to Jen?"

"Yeah, today was our custody-switch day, which was tough. And the past few days, Mia's been a ball of very big emotions. Understandably." He sighs, then has a spoonful of gelato.

"I'm sure it's a lot for her to try to make sense of. Hopefully, it'll get a little easier for her as it gets more familiar."

"Hopefully," he says, before another spoonful of gelato.

I take a bite, too.

Around his mouthful Alex says, "Divorce sucks."

"It sucks donkey dong."

He snorts. "Donkey dong?"

I laugh so hard, I almost spit out my gelato. "I overheard a kid say that to his dad at The Bookshop last week. I almost peed myself."

"Mia will be saying shit like that to me before I know it," Alex mutters. "That child is not afraid to speak her mind."

I smile. "I think that means you're doing something really right."

He's silent for a beat, then says, "I hope so."

I clasp his hand and squeeze. Alex stares down at my hand wrapped around his, and suddenly I'm self-conscious. It was an instinct, to reach out and comfort him the way I love to be comforted, but maybe Alex isn't a physical-touch kind of guy. Maybe his love language is words of affirmation or gifts or acts of service. I start to pull my hand away, but Alex turns his hand quickly and catches mine inside his, squeezing back. Even harder than I did.

His eyes meet mine as his thumb brushes my palm. It's only a small tenderness, yet heat bolts through me.

For a moment in Luna's kitchen, eyes locked with Alex as he held her hand, Thea felt a sun-warm wash of comfort sink through her skin, her bones, seeping deeper, until it settled in her heart, a glowing ember. She felt cared for. She felt desire. She felt hopeful. Maybe one day feelings like these wouldn't merely drift by but endure. Maybe one day she'd only feel battle-scarred, not indelibly broken. Maybe one day she wouldn't only hold hands with a kind, handsome man who made her laugh and made her feel safe —

Alex squeezes my hand again, wrenching me back to reality, before he lets go. He clears his throat as he scoops up another spoonful of gelato, then says, "How's your six-flavor combo?"

"So good." I shove a heap of gelato into my mouth, hoping it'll cool me down. "Yours?"

"Yep, it's good." He pokes around his bowl, then peers my way.

His gaze lingers long enough that I pause, spoon hovering in front of my mouth. "What is it?"

He's quiet for a moment, then says, "Been thinking about what you said the other night, you know, after we—"

"Told a huge vengeful fib to our exes?"

"That, yep." He clears his throat again. "I felt bad, after you left."

"Why?"

"Because you paid me a really nice compliment," he says, "and I was so caught up in my shitty feelings, I didn't do the same."

"Oh." I shrug. "I didn't expect you to."

Alex leans in. "That's not how this friendship is going to go, Ted. You hyped me up. I should have hyped you up, too. So now I'm going to do that."

"Oh, no, you don't have to—"

"You're beautiful." His gazes locks with mine. "And I've only known you a few hours, but I already know that you are a truly good person."

My cheeks are burning. "Um. Thank you," I say hoarsely. "That was profoundly inaccurate, but it's still a very generous compliment."

"Ted." He knocks his knee with mine. I peer up, and he holds my eyes. "Trust me. It's accurate."

Argos whines outside the door again. Alex tears his gaze away and stands, nodding toward the kitchen door. "Come on. Let's go check on the pea-brain."

*

Argos is much happier, now that we're together and it isn't in a sweltering third-floor apartment. He's on his stomach, chin resting on my feet, while Alex and I sit side by side on orange crates behind the restaurant's kitchen. Heads tipped back, we take in the cloudless night sky, a black plum speckled with sugar.

"So," I say, "Pittsburgh *does* have stars."

A faint laugh leaves Alex. "Sometimes."

"Didn't see it coming. When you picked me up, the sky looked like someone had thrown it a mean right hook."

He nods. "Yeah it was pretty rough. Which felt fitting."

Quiet settles between us. I glance over at him and ask, "Do you like to read?"

"Yep. Audiobooks are my jam. Why?"

I stare up at the stars again. "Moments like this . . . they feel like what I love most about books. These little reminders that we aren't alone."

Alex lets out a soft *hmm*. "You mean the stars showing up?"

"Yes. And us, too, showing up for each other. It . . . helps."

Alex peers my way. "Yeah, it does help."

"It'll get better, right?" I ask. "We won't always feel this messed up?"

A heavy sigh leaves him. "Honestly, Ted, a few days ago, I wouldn't have been able to tell you. But"—he nudges my shoulder with his—"feeling a bit more optimistic, now."

Warmth blooms through me. I nudge him back.

Alex peers down, deeply focused on his gelato. "Thanks, by the way."

"For what? Eating your delicious food? Gorging my way through thirty dollars' worth of your family's gelato without paying?"

He throws me a wry smile. "For listening. Being kind. Hoovering my cold lasagna like it's the best thing you've ever eaten."

"It *is* the best thing I've ever eaten." I pinch his elbow. "I did not hoover it, though."

"You did," he says. His smile turns wider. "Trust me, it's a compliment. Nothing strokes a cook's ego like watching someone tear through the food they've made."

"Well, then, please know I'll be happy to stroke it *any* time."

Once I say it, I realize how suggestive that sounds.

Alex pokes his tongue against his cheek. He's trying very hard not to laugh.

"You knew what I meant!" I shove his shoulder with mine. "Stop being juvenile."

"This coming from the woman who said earlier, 'sucks donkey dong.'"

A laugh jumps out of me. "True. But divorce deserved it."

His laugh is delightfully unexpected. Loud and deep, it echoes in the alley, melding with mine.

Alex stares at me, a crooked smile lifting the corner of his mouth. "I haven't laughed like that in fucking months."

"Me, neither," I say quietly.

I stare back at him, as the soft breeze rustles his hair and wafts my way a faint spice, a hint of citrus. I think it's his scent. And I think I like it.

I think I like *him*.

Argos whines from his mopey perch at my feet, his gaze fixed on Alex.

Sighing, Alex glances toward Argos and unearths a spoon from his back pocket. "Don't worry, pea-brain. I came prepared."

I watch Alex scoop a mound of vanilla gelato from his bowl and offer it to my dog, holding the spoon patiently while Argos licks it clean.

That's when it all begins, the first time it whispers through my thoughts.

I love him.

I wish I could say it was the last.

CHAPTER 8

NOW

July 22, twelve days until "vacation"

Happy Alex is back, and I couldn't be happier.

He's whistling in the kitchen—translation: a good cooking day—and when I showed up at the house a half hour ago, he hugged me in his Alex way, smooshed against his chest, his hand cupping my neck; then he handed me a plate of bucatini carbonara that smelled phenomenal and somehow tasted even better.

Alex's cheery whistle carries from the open kitchen window out to the backyard, where I'm hanging with Mia, sprawled on a lawn chair, my toes grazing cool pool water. Mia floats on her back in her beloved inflatable pool, wearing an oversized pair of white sunglasses and her favorite yellow polka-dot swimsuit. The air bubble she trapped inside her swimsuit at her belly looks the way mine feels, stuffed with Alex's delicious pasta.

I sigh contentedly. Then I steal a final surreptitious lick of my now-clean plate.

"I saw that," Mia says.

Not so surreptitious, then.

"Those celebrity sunglasses have to go," I tell her. "I never know where you're looking."

Mia lifts two fingers and points them toward her eyes, then me. I laugh, which makes Mia laugh, too.

"I don't *always* lick my plate," I explain. "Just, you know, in private. When the food is fantastic. So basically I do it a lot at your house."

Mia nods sagely. "Same. I always want to lick my lunch containers at school, on Dad days. But I don't, because Mommy and Daddy said it's not nice manners in public." She sighs. "Such a waste."

Another laugh jumps out of me. "I hear ya, kid."

"So you liked it?" she asks.

I smile. "Loved it."

"Dad!" Mia yells toward the kitchen. "Thea loves the bucatini!"

"Excellent!" Alex says from inside. "Because I do, too. Fucking finally," he adds quietly, but not quietly enough for Mia to miss it.

She grins. Then she yells, "I heard that!"

I hear Alex's groan through the kitchen window and watch his head drop back in defeat. He disappears out of sight, then a minute later walks out onto the back stoop and down the steps, three cake pops in hand. They're Christmas colors—red and green icing, dusted with white sprinkles.

He hands us each one.

"Thank you," we both tell him.

Alex sighs as he peers down at Mia. "I miss the days when I paid for my swears with a penny in a jar."

"I don't." She gives her cake pop a lick.

He laughs. "That much is obvious."

Mia says to me, "Give it a lick Daddy and I made them!"

"You don't have to lick it," Alex tells me. "You can just bite into it like a normal person."

"Who wants to be normal?" I lick my cake pop and smile up at Alex, squinting against the sun. "Mmm."

Mia asks me, "What do you think?"

"I think," I tell her, "this icing is *superb*."

"That's the part I made," she says proudly. "What's 'superb' mean?"

"It's a synonym for excellent."

She beams. "Got it! So like *really good*."

"Exactly."

"More words, Thea Thesaurus," she says.

This is a game we play. I frown, pretending to think deeply. "Synonyms for superb, okay." I tap my chin. "Horrendous. Atrocious."

She shrieks. "No, Thea! Those aren't cinnamons! They're Entenmann's!"

The day Mia stops calling synonyms "cinnamons" and antonyms "Entenmann's" will devastate me.

Alex shakes his head. "Ted, come on. Much better examples would be substandard, inferior—"

"Daaad!" Mia hollers. "Noooo!"

"What?" he gives her exaggerated deer-in-the-headlights eyes.

Mia slaps her hand to her forehead.

I frown and scratch my head. "Okay, okay, I've got it now. Despicable. Dreadful—"

"Thea!" Mia yells, brandishing her cake pop like a sword. "For real life now. More cinnamons!"

"For real life," I tell her, leaning in, elbows on my knees. "More synonyms for superb are: exquisite, outstanding, splendid."

Mia licks her cake pop and smiles. "Thank you." She turns toward Alex. "Daddy, lick your *splendid* cake pop, too!"

Alex lifts the cake pop, holding it up to the light, as if appraising it. He tips it side to side, brings it to his mouth, then bites off half of it.

Mia boos. I hiss.

Alex grins, then says around his mouthful, "So, how is Holidays in July Day treating you two?"

"Superb!" Mia says.

"Good," he says to her. He bites into his cake pop again and turns toward me. "How about you, Ted?"

I lift my clean plate in one hand, cake pop in the other, and sigh. "As you can see, I'm having a *terrible* time. *Lackluster* meal. *Horrendous* dessert. *Abysmal* company."

Mia nails me with a full icy stream from her water blaster.

I squeak. "Mia! I was just using antonyms again!"

She laughs around her cake pop, a golf ball tucked inside her cheek. "I know those were Entenmann's," she says. "I just wanted to get you anyway."

"You did, did you?" I reach into the pool and tickle her toes. Mia shrieks and kicks her legs, dousing me with pool water. I'm three times as wet as I was before the water blaster.

"Very effective revenge tactic," Alex muses.

I wipe water from my face. "It was actually quite refreshing."

A soft laugh leaves him as he peers back at Mia, who's lounging against the side of her little pool, hand patting her air bubble belly. She finally takes a small bite of her cake pop and says, "Wow. This is *outstanding*."

"Mia approved," I tell Alex.

He smiles at her, then turns my way. "And what's your verdict, Ted?"

I bite into my cake pop, too. Pillow soft, sweet vanilla cake. Rich, buttery icing that's only slightly, perfectly sweeter. An obscene moan leaks out of me.

"Thea approved, too!" Mia says.

Alex's gaze dips to my mouth, then darts away. He clears his throat. "Great." He turns toward Mia. "Think we should bring some to The Bookshop for the party tonight?"

Mia shoots her arms up into the air. "Yes!"

"Good. Because I made a sh—" He catches himself. "*Shoot* ton of these, also in Hanukkah and Kwanza colors, and they're taking up my entire freezer right now."

I poke his toe with mine. "Alex, I told you that you weren't allowed to make them! Coming up with a mess-free dessert idea was help enough."

"True." He gently tugs a corkscrew curl of my hair, then steps back. "But I couldn't say no when Fern reached out."

"Ugh." I scrub a hand across my forehead. "I get it. She's impossible to say no to."

"Actually," he says, "she offered me a ridiculous amount of money to make them. While also reminding me of how much she'd *invested* in me leading up to my first cookbook's launch."

"So she guilt-tripped you. Great."

"Nah. I only said yes because of the money. I found the guilt trip amusing, though. And I reminded her that the profit she's made from my subsequent cookbook's preorder campaigns, run exclusively through her store, have more than paid back her *investment*."

I squeak. Just the thought of talking to my boss like that makes me feel like I'm about to throw up. "You didn't."

"I did. You know me, Ted. I have no problem saying no if I don't want to do something."

"Truth!" Mia yells.

"Okay, smarty-pants," Alex says to her.

I sigh. "Well, I'm glad she paid you, but money or not, I'm still pi"—I stop myself, mindful of Mia—"*perturbed* that she bothered you in the first place."

"Perturbed," Mia says. She frowns. "That *sounds* like superb. But I don't think it *means* superb."

"Perturbed," Alex tells her, "means annoyed."

"*Very* annoyed," I add.

Mia frowns thoughtfully. Then she turns toward me, sliding her sunglasses down her nose. "Why are you perturbed?"

"Because I asked someone not to do something and they did it anyway."

Mia turns toward Alex. "Dad, when you make me go to bed at seven, I am *perturbed*."

"Which," Alex says, "leaves you well slept *and* well spoken. An all-around win."

Mia rolls her eyes as she sticks the cake pop in her mouth and slides her sunglasses back up her nose.

I say to Alex, "I'm serious. I am perturbed. I told Fern you were on deadline for your next cookbook and didn't need anything else on your plate."

Alex has even more than a cookbook deadline on his plate, but that's something he's asked me to keep private, so I couldn't tell Fern. Had I told her everything—that Alex has been testing recipes both for his cookbook and a menu revamp at his restaurant, while gradually easing into cooking again at the restaurant after stepping back four years ago to prioritize his mental health and his family; that he's not just juggling work-life balance in single-parenting and restaurant hours but also with the fear that he'll be unable to maintain that balance—she probably would have listened to me. I wish that my asking her to leave him be after he gave us the cake pop idea would have been reason enough.

Alex shrugs. "I can make cake pops in my sleep. It wasn't a big deal. Plus, Mia had a blast dying the icing."

I glare darkly at the cake pop. "I'm going to go throttle my boss."

Alex tips his head. "Throttle, huh?"

"Well." I wave the cake pop around. "Figuratively. And politely."

Fern, The Bookshop's owner, is the sweetest, gentlest woman on the planet on the surface, and beneath that a deeply stubborn, doggedly independent, set-in-her-ways business owner. That, paired with my still-in-recovery people-pleasing tendencies, means pushing back, holding my ground, and telling it to her straight are Herculean challenges for me.

"You haven't talked to her about your proposal yet, have you?" he asks.

I devote my attention to my cake pop, its sprinkles sparkling in the sun. "I'm still strategizing. These topics have to be approached tactfully."

Alex scrapes the last bite of his cake pop off its stick into his mouth and sighs.

"I did bring up vacation days, though!" I tell him.

He leans in and takes my empty plate resting in the grass beside me.

I'm washed in his familiar spicy scent, riveted by his profile—strong nose, dark lashes, lush mouth parted. He glances at me, and it's even worse now, as I'm pinned by his piercing gaze, the striking contrast of his deep blue eyes, his suntanned skin, his soft white tee and threadbare jeans draped over his hard, warm body.

I wedge my hands beneath my thighs. The urge to touch him, to rake my fingers through his dark messy hair, to grip his shoulders, draw him close, taste and touch and take what I want, is nearly unbearable.

"And?" Alex says.

I blink, dazed. "And . . . what?"

He arches back to dodge an incoming bee, revealing a sliver of his stomach. Tan, taut skin. Dark hair arrowing down to the waistline of his jeans, the muscles that form a V at his hips. My thighs clench against a sharp, pounding ache. My brain wipes clean.

Alex, thankfully, is too distracted by the bee to register my lustful crisis. As it zooms away, he straightens and his shirt mercifully drops. "You were saying you brought up vacation days to Fern?"

"Oh. Right!" I smile. "You're looking at someone who requested and was approved for seven straight days of vacation, starting August second. What do you think of *that*?"

Alex lifts the plate up to the sun, clearly noticing I licked it clean. He throws me a knowing grin. "I think it's a start."

I scowl as I watch him walk away from me. "I think it's a *superb* start!" I call.

Alex leans over the pool and tickles Mia's armpit, wiser than I was, positioned so he isn't splashed with water as she kicks her legs.

"Gotta clean up inside," he says to us. "I'll be back out soon."

"Let me?" I ask.

That's our routine—when Alex cooks, I clean up. I'm one of those weirdos who finds doing the dishes therapeutic.

"Nah," Alex calls over his shoulder. "I've got it. Thanks, though."

I frown, a bit put out by his rejection. I can count on my hand the number of times in the past two years Alex has turned down my offer to clean up after he's cooked, and it would involve raising one finger.

"Thea!" Mia says. "Is that your phone?"

I pat around my pockets, then the lawn chair, where I find it wedged behind my butt. Sure enough, my phone is buzzing. "Either my hearing is going," I tell her, "or yours is getting even better than it already was."

Mia points to her ears and says, deadpan, "I hear everything."

"Unnerving," I mutter. I tip my phone away from the sun's glare and smile when I see who's calling.

Lauren's face fills the screen, dark sleek hair brushing her shoulders, oversized black sunglasses hiding her eyes.

"Hey, Lo!"

"Hey!" she says. "Sorry I missed you last night. Client dinner ran long, and by the time we wrapped up it was one in the morning your time."

"That's okay," I tell her. "How are you?"

"Living the dream," she says.

I tip my head. "I can't tell if that's a serious statement, or—"

"Is that LoLo?" Mia yells.

Lauren smiles and hollers back, "Hey, Mimi!"

Mia paddles down the pool toward me and shoves her sunglasses up onto her head.

"Hi, LoLo," Mia says. "How ya doing?"

"Oh, I'm great," Lauren says. "How are you?"

"I'm splendid!" Mia yells. "Tonight, we're having a Holidays in July Day StoryTime party at The Bookshop, and I get to stay up late, and we're going to eat cake pops Daddy and me made and read holiday books and I'm going to wear a pretty red dress and my new gold sandals."

Lauren nods seriously. "Red dress, gold accessories, very chic."

Mia sighs. "Yeah, but I wanted to wear my new *white* dress that Ethan got me, and I wanted Mommy to wear hers, too, but Mommy said Ethan said we have to save our pretty white dresses for our special 'casion at our beach vacation. Mommy and Daddy and Ethan and Thea and Argos and me are going to the beach!" She spins and plunges back into the water.

My stunned brain chugs sluggishly along each word.

Special occasion . . .

New white dresses . . .

Oh, God. Ethan and Jen are getting married on our vacation.

Lauren says loudly, "Thea, what the *fuck*!"

Mia pops up out of the pool. "Dad! LoLo said a swear! I get another cake pop!"

Something slams inside the kitchen. "Dammit, Lawrence!" Alex yells.

I clap a hand over my face.

"*Another* swear!" Mia yells gleefully. "*Two* cake pops!"

Lauren leans in so close I can see her pores, which, for a woman who gets regular facials and has baseline flawless skin, is an achievement. She lowers her voice to a whisper. "Thea, what the hell is going on?"

A glowering Alex storms out of the kitchen, two cake pops clutched in his hands.

I tell Lauren, "It just happened, I swear. That's why I wanted to talk last night. Ethan and Jen invited us on a 'two-family' vacation in August, because they have something important to share with us that's going to 'impact Mia.' That's all they said. They've been very cryptic."

Lauren pulls back enough that I can see more than one eye and the bridge of her nose. "I don't like it."

"Neither do we. But Alex and I agreed whatever this 'important something' was, it was worth dealing with for Mia." I dart a glance at Alex, who's grumpily handing Mia her cake pops, then lean in and whisper, "I just realized that 'something important' is probably Ethan and Jen's beachfront wedding."

Lauren hisses out a faint, extended, "Shiiiit."

"It makes sense, right? White dresses? Special occasion? What else could it be?"

"Nothing. That has to be it." She leans in, too. "So are they expecting you two to be their witnesses? If so, that's . . . weird."

"I really hope not." I rub at my suddenly throbbing temple. "Can't wait to drop this bomb on Alex. He's seemed off since we decided to go, until today, at least. Today, he finally seemed happy."

"I *was* happy," Alex says.

I startle, nearly dropping my phone.

Alex crouches, meeting Lauren's eyes on my phone screen. "Until now," he says.

"Ale*c*," she says stonily.

"Lawrence." He narrows his eyes. "You cost me two more cake pops."

"You're welcome, Mimi!" Lauren calls.

Mia lifts both cake pops in the air and lets out a celebratory whoop.

Alex massages the bridge of his nose.

"So," Lauren says to us, "this vacation sounds like a nightmare."

Alex shoots me an accusing look. "You told her already?"

"Obviously," Lauren says. "She tells *me* everything."

A muscle jumps in Alex's jaw. He stands and tells her, "Later, Lawrence."

"Leaving so soon?" she asks sweetly.

"Staying," Alex tells her, "would risk more swears—and thus more cake pops—at which point my kid will be so sugared up, I'll have to peel her off the ceiling." He turns to me. "I'm going to finish cleaning up the kitchen."

I sigh, slumping back in my lawn chair. "Lo, do you *always* have to give him crap?"

"Yes," she says. "Now, tell me all about this vacation. Take it from the top."

"I'm not sure this is a quick FaceTime conversation topic. Maybe we can talk later, once you're done with work? I'll be up way past my bedtime anyway, doing cleanup after the event. That should line up well for you on West Coast time."

Lauren shrugs. "Now is fine, too. I'm flexible."

I blink, a bit stunned. "I don't think I've ever heard you say that about yourself. Outside of physical flexibility."

Lauren tugs her sunglasses down and smiles serenely. A tiki drink appears in her hand, which she takes a long tug of through a twirly straw. "At Frances the therapist's encouragement, I took the day off. No work for me today." She feigns two very unconvincing coughs. "I'm 'sick.'"

"Lo!" I beam at her. "I'm proud of you. And I like your therapist."

"I think I finally like my therapist, too. Now, fill me in." She settles deeper in her chaise and smiles. "I've got all day."

CHAPTER 9

NOW

July 22, twelve days until "vacation"

Tonight, The Bookshop has embraced its alter ego. The voices are loud, the vibes are chaotic, and the store's typical adults-to-kids customer ratio is fully inverted.

I love it.

When I pitched this Holidays in July event and one-day sale to boost The Bookshop's consistently subdued summer profits, I told Fern to picture the bookstore version of Narnia. It turned out more like Narnia's winter-wonderland wild-child twin.

"Good call on the earplugs," Dan shouts.

I wince at his volume, then tell him, "Glad they're helping."

"What?" he yells. He pulls out an earplug. "Sorry, I'm terrible at lip-reading."

"Just saying, I'm glad they've been helpful."

"Oh, definitely." Dan glances around the crowded store. "This might be the closest thing to a frat party that I've ever been to."

I tip my head, trying to figure that one out.

"But hey, people are buying books." He jerks his head behind him. "Boss seems happy about that."

My stomach drops. "Fern's here?" I crane around him, scanning the crowd. "She said she didn't think she'd make it."

I was *counting* on her not making it. I could tell even Narnia was a stretch for her comfort. Its winter wonderland wild child twin is going to send her into a full-blown panic.

Dan shrugs. "Guess she changed her mind."

I sigh. "Well, thanks for the heads-up. I'm going to go try to find her—"

"Thea!" Jordan yells.

I spin around. Jordan points to her watch. "StoryTime in five, right?"

I give her a two thumbs-up, then start wending my way through the crowd, on the hunt for Fern. "She just had to be diminutive," I mutter.

I'm so absorbed in searching for my five-foot-nothing boss in a sea of taller people that I miss what's in front of me, bumping hard into someone's chest. I yelp as I stumble back.

Alex wraps his hand around my elbow, steadying me. "You good, Ted?"

"Great!" I squeak.

His eyes narrow. "Ted?"

"Promise." I salute him. Because that's not suspicious at all.

He lifts an eyebrow. "Ted."

"Fern's here," I whine.

He leans in. "What?"

I press up on tiptoe and say right in his ear, "Fern showed up."

Someone bumps me from behind, which shoves me into Alex.

My hand slaps onto his chest. My nose smooshes into his jaw. My mouth grazes his neck. Alex clasps my waist, steadying me once again.

For a split second, my brain short-circuits, my senses telescoped to the warm, clean scent of his skin, the satisfying sandpaper scrape of his stubble, the heat of his hand gripping my waist. Every hair on my body stands on end.

I pull away, rubbing my nose. "Sorry," I tell him.

"All good." He squeezes my waist, then lets go. "You didn't know Fern was here?"

"She said she didn't think she'd make it."

He says, "You seem upset?"

I throw up my hands. "Of course I am! It looks like the Abominable Snowman threw up in here. She's going to freak!"

"She didn't seem freaked when I saw her."

I grab his arm. "She didn't? Where is she?"

"I don't know. It was a couple minutes ago." He pulls me into a comforting, smooshing Alex hug. "Take a breath, Ted."

I plop my chin on his shoulder and shut my eyes, drawing in a long tug of air, then blowing out.

"Good," he says.

I indulge myself, soaking in the comfort of his touch, take another deep breath, then step back. "Thanks. I feel better."

Alex looks at me like he doesn't exactly believe me. "I know you're anxious about everything going well tonight; you took a risk and pushed for this. Which I'm proud of you for, by the way."

"I hate risks," I say grumpily. "I hate pushing."

Alex bites his lip like he's fighting a smile.

I glare at him. "This is funny to you?"

"No. I just wish . . ." He clasps my arms, his thumbs running soothing circles along my tense shoulders. "I wish you could enjoy this instead of worrying about it. But I get why that's hard. Fern doesn't make it easy for you." He holds my eyes. "I will say, when I bumped into her, Fern said she's thrilled. Customers are buying the shit out of these books. You've got a reporter here, covering the event, and they are very happily eating their third cake pop while washing it down with a complimentary decaf cortado Jordan made them."

"Oh, thank goodness," I sigh. "If Dan had made it, we'd be cooked."

Alex smiles softly. "It's going great, Ted. Everything's going—" He does a double take suddenly over my left shoulder and freezes. "Shit."

"What?" I start to glance that way, too, but he squeezes my shoulders hard.

"Don't," he says urgently. "Don't look. Please."

"What's wrong?"

Alex steps close and whispers in my ear, "It's *Kate*."

It's hard to focus on what he's saying with his mouth brushing my ear, his familiar scent washing over me. I shut my eyes and force myself to process what he said. "Kate who?"

"Ted," he groans.

Hearing him say my name like that, low and rough, hot in my ear, I have to swallow a whimper. A flash of aching lust bolts through my body. "What?" I mutter hoarsely.

"It's *The* Kate. From the dating app—"

"Wait." I pull away, snapped out of my trance. "*The* Kate? From Kate Gate?"

"Kate-*Nate* Gate," Alex reminds me.

I whole-body shudder.

"Yes," he says darkly. "That one."

Kate-Nate Gate was the beginning and end of our foray into the dating apps. Alex and I agreed, after that night, to delete the apps and never speak of Kate-Nate Gate again.

"Dammit," he says, turning slightly, tucking himself against me. "She saw me. She *looked* at me."

"How threatening was the look?"

Alex scrubs his face. "I don't know, Ted." He peers up, then immediately looks down, swearing under his breath. "She's coming over."

"You want to make a break for it?" I ask.

"No, Jen isn't here yet. I have to keep an eye on Mia."

I frown up at him. "*Do* you have an eye on Mia?"

"Sitting crisscross applesauce in the kids' cozy corner. Reading *Miss Rumphius*, which I will buy, because it's covered in the sticky remnants of her fifth—God help me—cake pop."

"Wow. That level of awareness is . . ." *Hot*, I think. "Impressive," I say instead.

He nods. "Thanks. But can we come up with a solution for *The* Kate? Because she's definitely heading my way."

"Solution," I tell him. "Yes, I've got this."

I do not, but I want to. Alex is always so quick to jump in and help when I'm in a pickle—ready with ideas, offering solutions. I'm not a fast thinker like him, but I've read an astronomical number of novels, and somewhere in there has to be a character who's been in a similar situation.

"Romance, for sure," I tell myself. "Historical, maybe? Diverting an unwanted suitor?"

Alex, understandably, is perplexed by my muttering. "What?"

I snap my fingers as it comes to me. "Yes!"

"So confused," he says.

"Act like we're romantic," I tell him. "That's how we scare her off."

He rears back. "What?"

"What do you mean *what*? Did you not understand me?"

"No, I—" He shakes his head. "I meant, how *specifically* do you want to act romantic—"

Alex's voice cuts off as I throw my arms around his neck and press my body into his, hips against hips, my breasts smooshed into his chest. "Like this," I tell him.

I'm playing with fire, touching him like this. But I can do it. For Alex. Focusing on the task at hand—scaring off *The* Kate, I say to him, "Without looking, can you gauge how close she is?"

He swallows thickly. "It's blurry, in my peripheral vision, but she's closing in. Maybe five feet away?"

"Follow my lead, okay?" My fingers dive into his hair, and I tug a little bit. Alex's eyes widen.

"Okay," he says hoarsely.

"Babe." I say it louder than I normally would, but not so loud that it's obviously a performance. Hopefully.

Alex's mouth twitches. "*Babe?*" he whispers.

"I don't know!" I whisper. "It's the first thing that came to mind." Then I say louder, "This evening is going perfectly. I couldn't have done it without you."

Alex stares down at me, his hands, drifting down to my waist, tucking me closer. "Yes, you could have. But I'm glad I could help."

"You really did help," I tell him genuinely. "So much. Thank you."

"Ted." He reaches up and tucks a loose curl behind my ear. "Don't thank me."

"You sure?" I smile up at him, my gaze traveling over his face. "Because I was just thinking about how I can't wait to go back to your place and show you how *thankful* I am."

A swallow rolls down his throat. "Oh yeah?"

I nudge my hips into his. "Oh yeah."

My hands still in his hair, I draw his head down, like I'm about to nuzzle into his neck, and whisper, "She still there?"

"Hovering." His breath is hot against my ear. His lips brush my cheekbone. I fight a shiver as he says, "Very close."

"Squeeze my butt," I tell him.

Alex goes rigid in my arms. "What?"

"Squeeze. My. Butt." I nuzzle into his neck in earnest now. "Unless you'd prefer a reunion with *The*—" A squeak catches in my throat as Alex splays his hands wide and firm, one on each of my butt cheeks, and gives them a very enthusiastic grope.

I could not be more thankful that we're far from the kid's section and the store's crowd density hides what we're doing. The only audience I want for this is the woman we're trying to scare off.

Alex whispers, "She's clocked us." His lips graze the shell of my ear.

A white-hot ache pulses through me. "Great," I manage.

Something hard presses into my hip. My eyes pop open.

"Please try to ignore that," he whispers into my neck.

"Pretty big *that* to ignore," I whisper back.

"Ted," he warns.

"Sorry, just stating a fact!"

He groans. "I promise I'm trying to be as gentlemanly as possible."

I laugh hoarsely. "Rest assured, this is by far the most gentlemanly ass grope I've ever received."

Alex laughs, too. His hands slide up, settling at my waist. "She's stopped coming closer," he says quietly. "I think it's working."

"Of course it's working," I whisper. "Historical romance never fails me."

"Never would have thought an ass grope was de rigueur in Regency era ballrooms."

Another laugh jumps out of me. "It wasn't. But it was way too crowded in here for a waltz."

"Ah," he says. "It's all coming together now—ass groping, the modern equivalent of Regency England's waltz."

"Precisely," I tell him. "The waltz was considered downright scandalous when Germans introduced it to British society."

Alex gasps and pulls back, meeting my eyes. "You saucy Germans!"

I smile up at him. "Honestly, proudest part of my heritage."

Alex smiles back, and it hits me how it has too many times the past two years, in that way that makes it so hard to keep things in their safe friend place. Even the moments that start so wrong—awkward, tense, stressful—with Alex, they have this way of morphing into something that feels so right.

I clear my throat, then ask him, "What's you-know-who's status?"

Alex hazards a quick glance past me, and relief floods his face. His grip on my waist goes slack. "She turned around. We're good."

"Wait," I tell him, hands still locked around his neck. "Don't pull away yet. She might look back. We should make sure our . . . denouement is convincing, too."

"Good point." He meets my eyes, his mouth tightening in a

grimace. "Also, before we do, I have a minor problem to deescalate."

"What problem—" My mouth clamps shut when Alex shifts, I think, in an attempt to draw his hips away from mine. All it does is make even clearer, without my body pressed against his, that his "minor" problem is not so minor.

Heat floods my cheeks. "Ah. Right."

"I need you to say something really unsexy right now," he tells me.

"Okay. Sure." I rack my brain, then meet his eyes. "Did you pack any Gas-X? I forgot to take my lactase enzyme before I went to town on those olive and cheddar kebabs, and man, those cubes give me the toots."

Alex snorts, then drops his head to my shoulder on a pained groan. "Didn't work."

"What?" I am baffled. "Alex, lactose-intolerance-induced gas is *very* unsexy."

"But your toots are weirdly endearing? They sound like a tiny trumpet."

I glare up at him. "You know the rule. If I ever toot, no I didn't."

"Right." He schools his expression. "Of course."

"Daddy! Thea!" Mia barrels into our legs and smiles up at us. "Group hug!"

Alex's eyes meet mine. "Well. *That* worked."

I draw my body back from his immediately and settle myself into a respectable friend-hug posture. It's one thing for Mia to see Alex and me embrace as friends. It's another thing for her to see us tangled around each other like we just were. "I thought you had an eye on her," I whisper.

"I *did*." He scoops Mia up onto his hip and she throws her arms around our necks, squeezing tight. Alex tips his head away from her to my far side and whispers, "But then someone asked me grope her butt and started talking about the sensuality of the Regency era waltz."

I sigh as I wrap my arm around Mia and squeeze her back. "I should have seen it coming. The waltz always leads to trouble."

CHAPTER 10

THEN

July 25, two summers ago

It's a breezy Friday afternoon, I'm already off work, my apartment is no longer a disaster zone of moving boxes and partially assembled bookcases, and Tessa Dare's deliciously witty banter between the grumpy reclusive duke and the feisty wallflower who's crashed his castle is a much-needed distraction while I wait for Lauren to show up.

I haven't seen Lauren since our lunch at Luna's, and I haven't heard from her since she texted me on Sunday, asking if we could change her visit from Tacos and Tequilas Tuesday to Fried Food and French Wine Friday.

While I was suspicious last week at Luna's, I'm now sure something is wrong.

"No loitering," a gruff voice says. "It's right there, on the sign."

I peer up from my perch on my apartment's front steps, resting my finger on the line I was reading to mark my place. A smile breaks across my face. I recognize the owner of that gruff voice. "Mr. Fleischer, hi!"

Mr. Maxwell Fleischer, a regular at The Bookshop, is by far the crankiest man I have ever met. He's also my favorite. I've read too many books featuring lovable elderly grumps with prickly exteriors to take his surliness to heart.

He narrows his eyes at me, leaning heavily on a metal utility cart filled with groceries.

"It's Thea," I remind him. "From The Bookshop?"

"I know who you are," he grumbles. "What I don't know is why you're loitering on my stoop."

I blink. "Wait, you live here?"

"No," he says flatly. "I just schlepped all my groceries here and called it 'my stoop' for shits and giggles. *Yes*, I live here."

"So do I!" I peer over my shoulder at the building's multi-unit mailbox. "So *you're* unit two, 'M.F. NO SOLICITING!' I'm unit three, Theadora Meyer." I turn back and smile at him. "Right above you."

He scrubs his face. "Dammit."

"I promise, you've got nothing to worry about, I'm a model tenant."

"It's not that," he mutters.

"What is it, then?"

He tips his cart onto its back wheels and shoves it up the first step. "I was hoping you were a going to be someone cute."

I mime a dagger plunged into my heart. "Ouch."

He glowers at me. "Someone cute who's *my age*. Given the name, I had high hopes."

"Ohhh. Well, that tracks—I was named after my grandma." I stand up and reach for the bottom of his cart, lifting it up the last two steps as he pushes. "I'm sorry to have disappointed," I tell him. "If it's any help, I'm basically seventysomething inside?"

Mr. Fleischer gives me a withering look. "It does not."

"I understand; it takes me out of the running romantically, but just think, we *could* be friends here, too."

"'Here, too?'" His bushy white eyebrows shoot up past his black-frame glasses. "Toots, we are not friends *anywhere*."

"Now, I can take a lot," I say to him, holding the building's door open for him, "but I can't take your denying our friendship at The Bookshop. I don't sell a signed copy of Alexander McCall Smith's highly anticipated latest installment of *No. 1 Ladies Detective Agency* a week early to just anybody. And I know you don't split a blueberry muffin with any other staff member on their break."

He glares up at me. "That was one time, when I was very hungry, and *you* took your break with *me*."

I smile. "But what a delightful one time it was."

He pushes his cart inside, grumbling under his breath.

"Good to see you, friend!" I call from the threshold. "And neighbor!"

He waves a hand vaguely, then stops his cart in front of the elevator and presses the up button.

"Close the door!" he hollers over his shoulder. "You're air-conditioning the neighborhood."

"Ah, speaking of!" I let the door fall shut behind me. "My air-conditioning isn't working, and I'm having the hardest time getting through to the property manager about it. I thought I'd try the landlord, next. Any tips for how to reach him?"

The elevator dings, and its narrow door slides open. Mr. Fleischer turns, facing me as he backs into the elevator with his cart. "Yes," he says. "But be warned, he's a surly old sonofabitch."

I grimace. "Well, I'm sure he's got a lot on his plate. Landlording can't be easy, especially with a hard-to-reach property manager and an older building like this. I do need to get my AC fixed, though. It's so hot up there, my Jif peanut butter spread is currently more like Jif peanut butter syrup. I'll take any help I can get in reaching him."

The elevator door starts to close, but Mr. Fleischer juts his cart out in time to stop it. He sighs heavily and says, "Then consider it your lucky day. You just did."

In a truly epic exit, he yanks the cart back, and the elevator door slides shut.

I rush up the stairs as the elevator dings in the second-floor hallway, stopping when my face clears the floor to call through the railing rungs, "Just confirming, you're good to get the AC fixed?"

"No need to shout!" he shouts. "I'm old, not deaf!"

"Right, so—"

"Chrissake, yes, the AC will be fixed. I already texted my guy. He's on it. Now, would you leave a man in peace?"

"Great!" I tell him. "Thanks, neighbor! And friend!"

In answer, Mr. Fleischer's door slams shut.

"Can I just say," Lauren calls from the vestibule below, "I want to be that guy when I'm older?"

*

Lauren stands in the middle of my apartment, white-knuckling a frosty glass of French wine while trying very hard not to glare at my eyesore of a rainbow-sherbet kitchen—pea-green Formica counters, orange cabinets, vaguely coral vinyl floor tile.

"This," she says, "is delightful."

I sip my wine to hide my smile. "It's a dump, and you know it."

She spins my way, something fierce in her expression. "It is not. It's . . . vintage. And cozy."

I drop into a canvas director chair and gesture for her to sit in the other one. "Come on, Lo."

Lauren eases into the chair, then sets her glass of wine on the round, wooden coffee table between us.

I meet her eyes. "I feel like we have a lot to talk about, but first, I just want to address the state of the place, because I can tell you're freaking out."

"I'm not freaking out!" she says, plucking at her black tank top. "I'm slightly warm, that's all."

I laugh. "Slightly warm?"

"Fine," she says. "It's as hot as Satan's ass crack in here."

"It is. The AC is getting fixed, though, as you overheard."

"Good," she says. "How long has it not been working?"

I sip my wine again, buying myself time. "Since I moved here."

"What the hell, Thea? In this heat wave? Why didn't you say anything? You could have stayed with me."

"I've been fine!"

"*How*," she says emphatically.

I point to the two open windows letting in hot muggy air, the box fan that whirrs in one of them. "The cross breeze."

"What cross breeze?" she asks.

"Well, it's coming," I tell her.

"Coming?"

"It'll be here shortly."

She reaches for her wine and takes a gulp. "Thea—"

"I'm okay, Lo." I set my wine on the coffee table and lean in, elbows on my knees. "I know my apartment is underfurnished, undecorated, and extremely hot, and the kitchen is a midcentury design horror, but I'm okay with that.

"The AC's being fixed. I'm going to ask Mr. Fleischer if I can paint the kitchen cabinets something that works better with pea green, and replace the floor tiles with a design that ties those colors together. I don't have more furniture or any decorations because I'm taking my time and figuring out what I want." I smile, shrugging. "I'm going to make my living space look the way *I* want for the first time in my life."

Lauren smiles, too, and lifts her wineglass. "Cheers to that."

"Cheers," I say, clinking my glass with hers, "to a home that isn't wall-to-wall greige."

"Ethan and his *fucking* greige," she mutters into her glass.

"So." I ease back into my chair. "Are you going to tell me what's been going on?"

Lauren pauses midsip, then slowly lowers her glass and sets it on the coffee table. Groaning, she slumps back in her chair, then frowns up at the ceiling. After a beat of silence, she asks, "Am I having a stroke, or is the overhead lighting cutting out every three seconds?"

"It's the lighting," I tell her.

I tip sideways on my chair to reach the wall switch and flick it off, leaving the room bathed in molten evening light, gilded dust motes dancing in the air.

Turning toward her, I say, "Lo—"

"I know, I know, I'm being avoidant." Lauren groans again as she sits up. "Okay."

I nod. "Okay."

"Okay. I'm going to tell you two things I've been . . . holding on to."

"Okay?" I say quietly.

Lauren springs up, dashes over to the fridge, and pulls out the Viognier she brought. After topping off our glasses, she says, "First." She wedges the cork back in the bottle and sets it on the coffee table. "Just going to leave that there. We're going to need it—"

"Lauren."

"Okay! Sorry!" She takes a gulp of wine, then blurts, "I hate my birthday."

I ease back in my chair, perplexed. "Okay?"

"Okay," she sighs. "We have to stop saying 'okay.'"

"Sure," I tell her. "Let's try, 'Why?'"

"Yes. Why." She draws in a deep breath, then blows out. "Because," she says quietly, staring down at her wineglass, "my birthday is my mom's death day."

"Lo," I whisper. Tears fill my eyes. "God, I'm so sorry."

A sigh leaves her. "Yeah, me too." She takes a gulp of her wine. "And now you know why I get trashed on my birthday."

I absorb that, silence lingering between us.

Lauren gives me a pleading look. "Say something? Besides that you're sorry for me."

I open my mouth and shut it. This feels fragile. *Lauren* feels fragile, and she's never felt that way to me. I have no idea what to do.

"Thea," she says, her pitch almost sharp. She looks desperate. "Anything, seriously, whatever is in your head."

I rear back. "That's a dangerous demand, Lo. You know that. My mind is a strange, unfiltered place."

Lauren picks up the bottle of Viognier and sloshes wine into her glass. I have a feeling she plans to fill it to the brim.

I jerk forward and pluck the bottle from her. "Okay, fine, I'll say something!"

Lauren meets my eyes, her grass green gaze glassy with unshed tears. "Thank you."

"Don't thank me yet," I mutter, as I pour wine into my glass, then set the bottle safely beside me. I swig some wine then say hastily, "You told me your mom was 'out of the picture.'"

Lauren gulps some wine. "Well. Death does take you out of the picture."

"Right, but obviously I interpreted it more literally. As in, alive but absent, and thus villainous."

She glances out the window, toward the sunset, and a heavy sigh leaves her. "It would be a hell of a lot easier, if she had been."

I turn and peer out at the sunset, too, thinking of my mother. Of how I both love her and hate how she's made me feel most of my life. Of how strange it would be, losing that anchor, the person who brought me into this world, the grief that might come both for what we never had and for what we did. I wonder if I'd feel guilty or relieved, to be free of knowing only love laced with disappointment; if it would finally ease the ache that's never left to be someone worth loving for who I am, not who someone wants me to be.

Lauren reaches for my hand and clasps it, squeezing tight. Her gaze stays fixed on the sunset as she says, "I'm sorry I lied to you."

"It's okay, Lo." I squeeze her hand back. "I'm sorry she's gone. But I'm glad she was someone worth grieving."

Lauren swallows thickly. "Me, too."

For a moment, we sit in silence. Then Lauren reaches for the wine bottle. "Time to finish this sucker off."

She pours our wine truly to the top, and we both take a few

spill-preventing sips, watching the sunset dip lower on the horizon.

"I just remembered," I say to her, "that you said there were *two* things you'd been holding on to."

She swallows slowly, and when she speaks her voice comes out thick. "Yeah. I did."

"It can wait," I tell her. "If that'll help. If today's been enough emotions. I mean, it probably shouldn't wait *forever*. But maybe you could tell me sometime this month, say, by the time we go to Savoureux for your birthday?"

Lauren freezes, mid-sip, then lowers her glass. She looks my way, and her eyes are filled with tears.

"Lo." I clasp her hand. "What is it?"

Lauren stares down at our hands. "It's going to have to be sooner than that." She bites her trembling lip as she meets my eyes. "Because, in a month . . . I won't be living here anymore."

CHAPTER 11

NOW

July 25, nine days until "vacation"

I feel like I've been hit by a truck. I haven't slept well the past few nights, since the Holidays in July event. It's taken me an eternity to fall asleep, and once I do, I've managed only a handful of hours before startling awake from a deeply hot sex dream about Alex, heart pounding, drenched in sweat, my body on the sharp-sweet edge of release.

After three days of this nonsense, I am wiped out and on frazzled, and not even being at The Bookshop today can make me happy.

Ro, a fellow staff member, comes in through the back door wearing a blush that jumps against their freckled skin and a dreamy smile that tells me their lunch break second date went just as well as their first.

When they see me, the smile drops from their face. "You're *still* here?"

"Nice to see you, too," I tell them. Shifting on my desk chair in the staff room, I wince. Everything hurts.

Ro rakes back the short-cropped strawberry-blond curls that fall into their eyes. "You said you were going to go home to rest."

"After I got this under control," I tell them. "Almost there, and then I'll be gone, promise."

Ro sighs. "I'm sorry I panic-called. I feel awful that you've spent the entire day here, and you weren't scheduled to."

I glance their way. "Don't be sorry, Ro. That's on me—I didn't walk you through what to do when this happens."

"Yeah, but I could have called Fern instead of bugging you."

The desktop dings with another disgruntled customer email. I click it open and start to type my now-memorized response. "Good luck getting ahold of her," I mutter.

Ro frowns. "She has been, like, *oddly* absent lately, hasn't she?"

It's comforting to know that it's not all in my head, that I'm not the only one who's thought Fern has been scarce. She hasn't shown in the office since the event, hasn't reached out or said a word about it. Even before that, over the past month, she's been dodgy about coming in or talking on the phone.

I should reach out to her and check in—about her absence, the event, the business proposal I've been waiting for the perfect time to put on her desk. Except between the tension with Alex and this impending "vacation" and my horrible sleep, I'm so fried and anxious, I have no confidence I'll do any of those things well—most of all, the business proposal—and there's a lot riding on my doing that well.

And Alex, the one person I want to talk to about it, is being just as elusive as my boss.

I expected that, after our flirty antics done in the name of scaring off Kate. That's what we do, when we veer off the friendship-only path—we go quiet for a couple days, or we stay chatty but avoid the topic.

Or, in my case, have highly detailed, very horny dreams three nights in a row inspired by our latest inadvertent, dangerously lusty detour.

Ro opens their locker and drops their belt bag and Bike da 'Burgh water bottle inside. "Do you think Fern's sick or something?"

I freeze, hands hovering over the keyboard. That possibility never occurred to me. I'd just assumed I'd done something—or hadn't done enough—to inspire Fern's distance.

"I hope not," I finally manage.

"Yeah," Ro says. "Me, too." They shut their locker door gently, then head out of the staff room to the front of the store.

Another email featuring a grumpy customer headline pings the inbox. The vision for how my day was *supposed* to go flits through my mind—curled up with Argos on his fluffy doggy bed and Charmaine Wilkerson's new release.

I sigh heavily. "I need a *real* vacation."

Hailey, our fresh-out-of-college new hire and the reason I dragged myself to work today rather than curled up on my couch with a good book, pops her head into the staff room. She's still humming with nervous, guilty energy.

"How's it going?" she chirps. "Need another coffee?"

"Going okay. And no, I'm all caffeined out. Thank you, though."

Her nervous gaze darts between the computer and me. "Need anything else?"

"Nope. I'm heading out for the day. But if Fern comes in before closing, would you text to let me know?"

Color drains from her face. "*Is* Ms. Holloway coming in?"

"No that I know of," I tell her, eyes back on the computer screen as I crank out one last email response to a disgruntled customer. "Just wanted to be notified if she does."

Hailey nods. "Okay! Of course!"

Once she's gone, I let out a heavy sigh, stand, and stretch. A miserable groan leaves me.

I'm halfway to the staff door exit when my phone buzzes. I pull it from my overalls pocket, glance at the screen, and smile as I answer.

"That's a pretty fancy outfit for a run, Lo."

Lauren's behind the wheel of what looks to be the latest rental sports car, in her usual corporate-chic attire. Hair swept up into a tight chignon, eyes hidden behind Manhattan sunglasses, her look today is very Audrey Hepburn in *Breakfast at Tiffany's*. If Holly Golightly had road rage.

Lauren slams on the horn and yells, "Asshole!" She darts a glance my way, then back to the road. "Sorry about that. As you can see, I'm running late for our buddy-run. Why are you in real clothes? Are you at work?"

"Not anymore." I shut the staff door behind me and start across the gravel parking lot.

"I thought you were off today."

"I was."

Lauren glances my way again, a notch of concern in her ordinarily wrinkle-free brow. "I feel like there's a story there."

"A long one."

"Want to talk about it?"

"Maybe once we start our run, if I can talk while running, which, knowing the pace you make me run, I probably won't."

She grins evilly. "You like my grueling pace."

"Oh sure. I love it. Maybe I'll get started on the run now so I can take it easy but still finish when you do. I probably could run in what I'm wearing."

"Let me guess," Lauren says. "Stretchy overalls and Birkenstocks."

"Bingo."

She sighs. "One day, I'll get you to wear more flattering footwear."

"You'll never take away my 'stocks."

Lauren smiles. "At least I convinced you to invest in decent running shoes."

"Which I've broken in nicely the past couple months. If I wasn't so sleep-deprived, I'd say this three-miler is going to be a breeze."

"That, and it's eighty-five-percent humidity in Pittsburgh right now. This swamp weather makes runs miserable."

"Way to sell it, Lo." I frown. "Wait, how do you know it's eighty-five-percent humidity here?"

Lauren pauses for a beat, then says, "I checked the weather app. Drink lots of water before you head out, young lady."

I roll my eyes. "Long-distance friendship has turned you into such a mom."

"Deal with it," she says. Then she blows me a kiss. "I'm going to sign off so I can focus on getting around all these slowpokes. Good if we push back our run by a half hour?"

"Perfect." I mime starting to jog slowly. "I'll get a head start. And you'll drive safe, right, speed demon?"

She cackles deviously. "Please. That's as likely as your giving up Birkenstocks."

*

I'm hiding in a patch of shade as I stretch my quads, on the edge of the pedestrian and bike path beside PNC ballpark, my usual starting point for my runs along the Allegheny River.

"This," I tell Lauren, "is going to suck." I try to wedge my earbuds in tighter. They already feel like they're about to slip out, I'm so sweaty.

"It's disgustingly humid," she agrees.

I frown. "In San Francisco?"

"Nope," she says.

Squinting, I rub my forehead. I could have sworn she was still in San Francisco, dealing with the new client from hell. "Then where are you?"

"Surprise," she says coyly.

My head snaps up, searching the path, just as a woman rounds the bend. Short dark hair tugged back. Long, willowy limbs. A wide, bright white smile.

I run toward Lauren, screaming so loud, the geese perched on the grass nearby startle into the sky.

*

"Oh my god," I pant. "I'm gonna die."

"Mm-hmm," Lauren says, fiddling with her fitness watch, "me, too."

I stumble onto the grassy hillside in front of the ballpark and flop down, our vicious three-mile loop complete. "Did I hallucinate you? You look real, but you're not even winded, which is impossible."

She rolls her eyes. "I'm not a hallucination. I'm here, in person, because my best friend's having a tough time, and I now have enough professional boundaries to take a day off and fly in so I could be here for her."

I pat her foot. "You're the best. And the worst. You made me run so fast."

"It's good for you," she says, eyes back on her watch.

"At least," I tell her between gasps of air, starfished on the grass, "I think I'll finally sleep well tonight."

Lauren peers down at me, head tipped in concern. "You sound like a dehydrated camel."

I lift my middle finger to the air.

"Come on," she says, offering me a hand. "I'm parked in the lot right up those steps. I have a bottle of water in the car."

I slap my hand into hers and let her yank me upright.

Lauren says as we walk, "So, you're not sleeping well."

"Too much on my mind. Weird dreams. I keep waking up after four, five hours of sleep."

"Sounds like you need to get laid."

I glance at her sharply. "Lauren. I've told you, unless you live through what Alex and I did, you will never understand why it will be a cold day in hell before I ever use a dating app again."

"There are other ways to get laid." She lifts her hands. "And I *won't* bring up the obvious solution of banging the Hot Chef. There are lots of scenarios that could lead to hookups for casual sex."

"Not for me. I'm a homebody bookworm whose social life consists of Banjo Night at the Elks and monthly euchre tournaments with my ladies' choir."

"Once again, my deepest grief that you are straight. If you

weren't, that would be incredibly fertile ground for sapphic hookups," Lauren says.

A sad laugh leaves me. "True."

"So what's going on?" she asks.

"Oh, I don't know. I'm still sitting on the business proposal for Fern. I'm willingly going on vacation with Alex and our exes. I keep having horny sex dreams about Alex, set in the bookstore of my dreams. I don't think we need Sue to break this one down for me—I am stuck between what I have and what I want, personally and professionally, and I'm miserable."

Lauren's quiet for a beat. "And until that changes, you're probably going to stay miserable."

I sigh heavily. "Yeah, probably."

"So . . ." She glances my way. "What are you going to do?"

"I don't know." I point at Burgatory across the road. "But I think gulping down a milkshake the size of my head might help me figure it out."

"Hell, yes." Lauren says. "I missed the fuck out of those milkshakes."

*

Lauren stirs her straw around her strawberry milkshake, watching me closely.

I swallow a cold peanut-butter-chocolate gulp of mine and say to her, "You flew across the country for me."

She smiles. "Sure did."

"You didn't need to do that, Lo."

"I know I didn't." Her smile fades as she stares at me. "But I wanted to. You've sounded so stressed lately."

"I have been," I admit.

"Talk to me about it," she says. "Work, Alex. Whatever you need to get off your chest."

I groan, stabbing my straw into my milkshake. "I've been sitting on the business proposal for Fern, because it never feels like the right time to give it to her. Lately, she's been so scarce, I couldn't give it to her even if it did feel right."

"Hmm." She sips her milkshake. "So she's the owner and store manager, right?"

"Technically. After she promoted me, we're comanagers."

"Except she's never there to comanage."

"Not lately, no. It's been a gradual ghosting, now that I think about it. She's been showing up less and less."

Lauren nods. "So is that why you were at work today, when you'd said you were going to take off?"

"I did take off, but then there was a crisis, so I had to go in."

"What was the crisis?"

I tell her the CliffsNotes version, that this morning, Hailey received a new highly anticipated title releasing next week and put it out on the floor, which, for a lot of books, isn't a big deal. This title, however, is embargoed, meaning that if it's put out for sale before its laydown date, the store risks losing future early-receiving privileges, and even being fined.

Lauren groans. "Shit."

"Oh, it gets worse," I tell her. "She not only put it on the floor—she also sent the email I'd drafted to notify customers who'd preordered it that it was available for pickup. I had to take all the books off the floor, then contact everyone she'd emailed and say, 'Hey, just kidding, that book we told you was ready for early pickup isn't out for another five days, so please don't come in and try to pick it up, because we can't sell it to you.'"

"That," Lauren says, "sounds like a nightmare."

"I had so many customers show up and ask for their book today, I was thinking of turning it into a drinking game."

Lauren laughs.

A laugh jumps out of me, too.

Our laughter fades, and after a beat Lauren says, "Thea, can I ask you something?"

I nod as I suck down another gulp of peanut-butter-chocolate milkshake.

"You said you've been dreaming about banging the heck out of Hot Chef, owning and running a bookstore exactly how you want, and you told me that means you're stuck." Lauren leans in, eyes holding mine. "What I'm wondering is, *why* do you feel stuck at work, and with Alex, when you have choices you could make that would change things?"

The milkshake feels too thick as I swallow. I clear my throat. "Because I'm scared."

"Of what."

"That wanting more could cost me what I already have. Fern might reject my business proposal. She could be deeply offended by my ideas. She might fire me, and then I'd lose my job, that community, my happy place."

Lauren stirs her milkshake with her straw, eyes still holding mine. "And Alex?"

I stare back at her, my throat tight. I've never told Lauren how much I love Alex, how hard I have to work to keep that love from tumbling over, spilling out, risking our friendship. Because to tell her, I'd have to face it myself, feel something I can manage only in my dreams.

But she knows, I think. She has to.

"I'm scared I'll lose Alex," I tell her, "if we become anything more than friends. If we tried being romantic and things fell apart, it's not like we could go back to being best friends—"

Lauren clears her throat.

"*Local* best friends," I amend.

"Thank you."

A weary laugh jumps out of me. "You're ridiculous."

She grins. "You were saying, about your friends-to-lovers dilemma with Alex?"

Just the thought of it makes my chest ache. "If we fell apart romantically, I'd lose him, and Mia, and . . ." My eyes well. "I'd be devastated. That's why I'm stuck. Because there's no safe way to grow beyond where I am. It's too risky."

"Have you considered," Lauren says quietly, "that you're already losing, by staying where you are?"

My heart twists. "Yes. But then I tell myself to be grateful for what I have instead of pining for what I don't." It's an easy and familiar response, what I grew up hearing when I wanted and dreamed and reached.

"Thea, I think that's bullshit—you can be grateful for what you have *and* want more. Sure, at one point, you were happy with where you are, comanaging The Bookshop, just being friends with Alex, but you're not there anymore, not here.

"You keep saying you can't change things because of the risk. But Thea, I think you know in your heart that change has already happened in you. I think that's why you're miserable—because you're fighting it. It's like trying to shove your feet into a pair of favorite shoes you already outgrew. They used to fit you perfectly. They made you feel like a million bucks at one point. But they don't fit anymore, and no amount of shoving yourself into them is going to make them feel how they used to. It's just going to hurt."

I swallow against the lump in my throat. "You would use a shoe metaphor to talk about feelings."

Lauren smiles wryly. "I got that from Frances, actually. She figured out that shoes are the way to my heart. Therapy now consists of a *lot* of shoe metaphors."

I laugh. "She sounds like a great therapist."

"She is. Not many therapists will do daily sessions, let alone speak my love language of shoes."

"Daily?" I blurt.

"Daily," Lauren says, before ducking her head to suck down a gulp of milkshake. "Not all the time, just when I'm struggling to stay on track. Because while I'm a strong, statuesque boss bitch on the outside, inside I'm a high-maintenance toddler who requires an enormous amount of positive reinforcement and frequent reminders not to ingest toxic substances."

I smile. "You are not. Inside, you're a high-maintenance kindergartner."

Lauren barks a laugh. "So *that's* why Mia and I vibe so well."

"That and your keen fashion sense."

Her smile deepens, and our eyes hold. Lauren leans in. "I know you're scared, Thea. But I also know you're brave. And I know you've read enough stories to understand that being brave doesn't mean you're not scared; it means, even though you're scared, you fight for what's right anyway."

"Yeah," I whisper, poking around my milkshake.

She takes a deep drink of hers. Then she frowns down at her glass. "Wait. Didn't these used to be boozy?"

"They can be." I slurp a mouthful and swallow. "You asked for the regular ones when we sat down, and I was fine following your lead. I figured, given what you've been working on with Frances, that was intentional."

"Wow, that's scary," Lauren says, a little wide-eyed. "I didn't even think about it."

I smile. "Frances and her shoe metaphors must really be working."

"A little *too* well." Lauren scowls down at her milkshake. "Non-boozy milkshake. What's even the point?"

CHAPTER 12

NOW

July 23, seven days until "vacation"

The first winter after I met Alex, he started a tradition of walking me to work on the days he didn't have Mia, calling me on the days that he did. I knew I shouldn't let him, that it was too much to take from a friend, but it was so comforting to walk alongside him, or to hear his voice in my earbuds, as I trudged through the dark, cold mornings, and be reminded I wasn't alone.

I tried so many times to say he didn't have to, it wasn't necessary, but every time, he'd tell me, *Three sisters, Ted. I've got three of them, and if they were living alone in a city, walking to work before the sun was up, I'd want their friend to see them safely there, too.*

The sister angle was my loophole. I could accept Alex's chivalry because it was brotherly, because in his explanation for his generosity and protectiveness, he'd essentially labeled me a fourth sister, and that made his chivalry safe.

When the outer door to my building comes into view, I miss

a step and nearly slide down the rest of the way. Argos looks up at me white-knuckling his leash, fighting for my life on the stairs, as if to say, *Would you get a grip?*

"How," I ask my dog, "am I supposed to do that when he's out there waiting for me. And looking like that?" I point to where Alex stands outside my building in a backward Pens ballcap, a faded heather gray T-shirt, hands in his jeans pockets, staring at the sunrise bathing him in a soft peachy glow.

Argos harumphs.

My heart rate doubles.

As I push open the door, Alex turns and smiles. "Morning, Ted."

I can't help but smile back. "Morning, Alex. What . . ." I let the door fall shut once Argos decides to cross the threshold. "What's up?"

Alex reaches out a hand toward Argos's leash. "I'm taking the dog today, aren't I?"

I nod. "Yeah, but I thought you'd meet me at The Bookshop."

Alex's hand curls around mine before he slides the leash up onto his wrist. "And I thought we could walk and talk."

"Okay," I say quietly.

Argos takes the lead, tugging toward the crosswalk. Alex and I fall into step behind him.

"I'm sorry," Alex says, "that I've been quiet the past few days."

"You don't need to be—"

"Ted."

I glance over at him.

Alex's eyes hold mine. "I'm sorry. I got all in my head about going back to the restaurant full time, and I had to lock down and get myself straightened out before I got back in touch. It had nothing to do with you, but it affected you, and I wish it hadn't."

An odd, awful pain stabs through me. I was disappointed that Alex dropped off the radar when I thought it was to reset after our flirty nonsense at The Bookshop. But I'm devastated that he went quiet and it had nothing to do with me, or us.

I shouldn't be. I should be relieved—it means that our friendship is solid, that we're safe, that he wasn't spiraling about how good it felt to be that close when we were scaring off Kate, touching, whispering, moving together—

I shake my head, snapping myself from my thoughts. Then I take a step closer to Alex, so our arms brush, so I can feel his warmth. "I'm sorry I wasn't there for you. I thought you wanted space."

Alex shrugs. "You didn't need to listen to my anxiety spiral about work-life balance and potentially ruining my relationships and losing myself in my job again."

I slide my fingers into his hand that isn't yanking Argos back and squeeze. "No, I didn't *need* to," I tell him. "Just like you didn't *need* to walk me to work."

We come to a stop at the crosswalk, waiting for the light. I lean my head on his shoulder. "But I *want* to," I say quietly. "Just like you do. Because that's what best friends do for each other. Right?"

Alex doesn't say anything. But he turns his head and plants a kiss on my hair.

*

We're almost to work when I finally get the courage to blurt out, "I think Ethan and Jen are getting married on vacation."

Alex nods. "Yep, me, too."

I come to a grinding halt. "You do?"

"Well," he says, "Mia told me about the white dress Ethan

bought her that matches Mommy's and that has to be saved for a special occasion on our beach vacation. Seemed pretty intuitive."

"Why didn't you say anything?"

His eyebrows shoot up. "Seriously?"

"Right, fair." I adjust my bag on my shoulder. "I didn't say anything, either."

Alex's gaze dips down to the sidewalk ahead, then back up to me. "How do you feel about it?"

A sigh leaves me. "Honestly, I don't even know. It just feels weird—like a weird thing to do, roping us into it."

Alex grunts.

"How do you feel about it?" I ask.

He shrugs. "Same as you."

After a beat of silence, I say to him, "And speaking of weird, is it just me, or is it odd that we've heard nothing else from Ethan or Jen about this vacation, and we're a week away from the trip?"

Alex frowns in concentration, gripping Argos's leash and leaning back to hold my dog steady as a flock of pigeons settles on the sidewalk ahead of us. It makes my heart squeeze, that this is automatic to him, that he knows doggy training taught my goofy pup to sit, wait, and not bark when commanded, but it never managed to train the "Get the birds!" out of him.

"Part of why I wanted to walk you to work," Alex says, "was to talk to you about that." He whistles sharply, scattering the pigeons, then, as they shoot skyward, eases up on Argos's leash. "I've been emailing with Ethan about logistics."

My head snaps his way. "You two have been *emailing*?"

He shrugs. "Better than talking in person. That way I don't have to constantly suppress the urge to shove my fist down his throat, just the urge to end every email with 'Fuck off and have a terrible day.'"

I snort. "Understandable."

Alex smiles my way. "Haven't heard that snort in a while."

We stop at the light, waiting to cross, and Argos sits like I've taught him, peering up at me with those big brown eyes, long pink tongue lolled out, eager for praise. I bend and give him a smooch on his head. "I don't *snort*," I tell Alex. "I chortle adorably."

"You snort," he says as the crosswalk sign flashes on. "And *that's* adorable."

Pleasure zings through me. I try to brush it off, to not tuck it tight in my heart. I've already hoarded too many moments like this, the past two years, shoved them behind a door that creaks with the pressure of so many dangerously tender, meaningful memories, feelings, desires.

Alex clears his throat. "Anyway, Ethan and I have been emailing about the trip, and so far, we've discussed a tentative menu, conditioned on what's available locally, our arrival time, and who's driving with whom, but I obviously wanted to get your input. He's getting Jen's."

I shrug. "You know I'm up for anything, menu-wise."

"Even oysters?"

I gag reflexively. "Nope, not those."

Alex *tsk*s. "I'm gonna do it, Ted. One day, I'll find an oyster recipe that you like."

"No amount or combination of butter, lemon, herbs, wine, or anything else I love will ever make a sea booger taste or feel like less of a sea booger."

Alex belly laughs. "You know that just makes me want to try even harder, right? I love a challenge."

I smile. "I know you do. What about arrival time? They'll be there already, right? So it's just a matter of when we get there."

He shakes his head. "They nixed the two-week stay. Between us being able to take off only a week and Jen saying it's too much time away when she needs to prep for the start of school, Ethan decided he'd 'accommodate our schedules.'"

"How magnanimous of him," I say dryly.

Alex grins. "He said we should aim for the ass crack of dawn Monday morning, which, annoyingly, I agree with. I haven't been to Bethany, but whenever I've gone to Ocean City, summertime traffic was hellish any time past sunrise, with how many people were driving inbound for their rentals. I realize we're getting there Monday, so it probably won't be as bad, but I figure, better safe than sorry. Unless you tell me that when you used to go, it was on a Monday, and it wasn't bumper to bumper. Maybe Ethan's just fucking with me."

As we stop in the gravel parking behind the store's staff entrance, I turn to face him. "I wouldn't know."

Alex frowns. "What do you mean?"

I shift the strap on my cross-body bag where it's digging into my shoulder, then fiddle with the buckles, even though I know they're secure. "He never took me to the beach house."

A thick, charged silence stretches out between us, like the uneasy hush that falls right before the skies open up. I don't have to look at Alex to know he's furious on my behalf. I try to push past it, because the last time Alex got fired up for me, I told him I loved him, and I definitely said it in a way I shouldn't have, while *feeling* a way I shouldn't have, either.

Who knows what I'll do this time, if he goes on another one of his protective, impassioned tirades.

"I've actually never been to the beach before," I babble, because anything is better than this silence. "At least, in person. Been to some pretty beautiful beaches in my reading adventures, though. I'm excited to see the real thing!"

I throw my arms around Alex's neck, quickly hugging him goodbye, then springing away. "Thanks for walking me to work." I bend to kiss Argos's head. "And for walking this goofball to doggy day care. I'll pick him up after work; then we'll get a good walk home. See you tonight!"

I rush toward the door and immediately curse myself for not having remembered that the staff entrance lock sticks so badly; I have to wiggle my key in it for half a minute before it gives. Needless to say, my entrance to work will not be a swift exit from this conversation, and I really wanted it to be.

Suddenly, a warm hand wraps around my elbow, spinning me around. I bump into Alex's chest and wheeze out air as he curls his arm around me in a wonderfully strong, bone-crushing hug. And then I melt into him, like the sucker that I am. My head plops onto his shoulder.

Alex rests his head against mine. I feel his heart thundering in his chest.

I lift my head, looking at him. Alex looks at me, too, his nose brushing mine for a moment, before he eases back, but only a little. It's not enough. Want hums through me: in my fingertips, aching to sink into his hair; my lips, desperate to taste his; every inch of my body pressed close against Alex, begging to press even closer.

My body, my heart, they're a magnet to his. Every time we come close, it's closer. And every time it's harder to pull away. I overpower the impulse to give in by reminding myself of the first time we kissed, how dangerous that was, and pull myself back, putting enough distance between us that I'm capable of thinking straight.

"You've really never been to the beach?" Alex asks. "He never took you?"

I shake my head.

"Why didn't you tell me?"

"Didn't seem like something to bring up."

Alex is quiet for a moment, his jaw tight. "Well," he finally says, "now that I know that, I'd say we have our decision on who's driving with whom."

"Oh?"

"You, me, Argos," he says. "Ethan, Jen, Mia."

"Really? You know Argos has noxious nervous-car-ride farts."

"Exactly," he says.

"I don't understand."

"Everything I've suggested, Ethan's countered with the opposite. And this time, I'll graciously give him what he asks for."

I bite my lip. "That is devious."

His hand skates up my back, a soothing, gentle touch. "That is the least he deserves."

He lets go, then steps past me, sliding Argos's leash higher up onto his wrist. I watch him grip the doorhandle and lift up as he turns the key I'd abandoned in the lock. They key wrenches smoothly left. He just . . . opened it.

"What the heck?" I ask.

Alex shrugs. "The restaurant's back door lock has always stuck like that, too."

I take the key from him, peering down at it. "Thanks," I tell him quietly.

He brushes his knuckles along my arm. "You okay?"

"Yeah, I'm okay." Sighing, I meet his eyes. "I'm going to ask Fern for a meeting before we leave for vacation. I'm nervous about asking her. And I'm terrified of the meeting. But I'm going to do it."

Alex smiles so wide, it makes my heart skip a beat. "To go over your business proposal?"

My smile's reflexive. "Yes."

Alex yanks me into another hug, crushing me to him. "I'm proud of you, Ted. You deserve to go after what you want."

I smile against his shoulder, wrapping my arms around his waist. "Thanks. I'm proud of me, too."

"Good," he says into my hair. "Because what you're doing takes guts."

"You'd know, wouldn't you, Chef?"

"It's not the same." Alex lets go of me and steps back. "I'm not head chef at the restaurant again."

I clasp his hand in mine and squeeze. Alex has been dipping his toes back into working in the kitchen at his restaurant over the past year, on the condition that his former sous, Olu, remain the head chef. I know he's scared to throw himself back into work there full time—so much so that even the limited number of hours he's been putting in feels like playing with fire.

"No," I agree, "you're not head chef right now. But you're working your way there." I squeeze his hand again. "That takes guts."

"Well, that's true," he says. "Olu is a fucking drill sergeant. An absolute nightmare to work under."

I roll my eyes.

Alex grins, taking a step back. "Hope it's a good day at work, Ted."

I smile as I watch him start to walk away.

"Alex!" I call.

He turns around, facing me.

"Hope it's good for you, too," I tell him.

Alex tips his head. He looks confused. "Hope what's good?"

"A good workday," I explain.

His expression clears, then brightens. "Oh, it will be." He starts walking backward, wearing a sly smile that means he's up to no good. "Even while Olu's yelling at me for how poorly I prep mirepoix, after I send that email to Ethan, I'm going to be riding a real high."

"Do *not* sign your email to Ethan with 'Fuck off and have a terrible day!'"

"I won't," he says. "But I am going to derive an immense amount of satisfaction from the mental image of his choking on Argos's noxious flatulence for six straight hours."

A laugh jumps out of me. "Haven't you heard, schadenfreude isn't good for the soul?"

"Whoever said that," Alex tells me, "never met Ethan."

CHAPTER 13

THEN

July 28, two summers ago

I make it three days before I cave and text Alex.

I held it together on Friday, after Lauren told me she was moving away and we talked about what the next few weeks would look like over a bottle of Cinsault rosé and a truly obscene amount of fried food; when I hugged her goodbye and watched her drive off, thinking that soon I'd be waving goodbye to her , except that time she wouldn't be coming back. I held it together while I buried myself in work through the weekend and today. Until I came home after work, desperate for a cuddle with Argos, then remembered he's still at Ethan's.

That's when I fell apart.

I'm clutching my phone to my chest like it's a lifeline when Alex shows up outside my apartment building looking windblown, rain splattered, and slightly winded. I push open the door to let him in. I'm trying very hard not to cry.

The door falls shut behind him, and as he gets a good look at me, Alex says, "Oh, shit."

Which is when I burst into tears.

"Hey," he says softly. Alex takes a step closer, his toes bumping into mine. "Can I hug you?"

I answer him by throwing myself into his chest. His arms wrap around me, and like it's the most natural thing in the world, he rests his cheek against my head. His hand traces circles on my back. "It's okay," he whispers. "You're okay."

"Thanks for coming," I choke out. "I'm sorry for the fairly unintelligible SOS text."

"The text was fairly unintelligible," he admits. "But I got the gist."

"I tried to work with autocorrect, but autocorrect did *not* work with me."

"Autocorrect can get fucked," he says. "Or, as autocorrect would suggest, 'get ducked.' Which is why autocorrect can get fucked."

"Thank you. What good is a spellcheck function when it can't fix my inebriated ramblings?" I sigh against him. "I haven't had any wine today, actually. I'm just so sad, I'm incoherent."

A sob bubbles out of me.

Alex squeezes me against him. "Shh, it's okay. Come on, let's get up to your place."

I nod against his shoulder. But I don't move.

Alex peers down at me. "Do you need a piggyback?"

I laugh hoarsely. "You couldn't carry me."

"First of all, that's insulting; I'm a very strong manly man. Second of all"—he shrugs off his backpack and slides it up his arms so it's on his front, turns, grips me by the thighs, and hoists me onto his back, making a yelp jump out of me—"challenge accepted."

"Okay," I concede as he walks us up the stairs. "You are a strong manly man."

"Thank you," he says. "You may now praise my superior physical fitness."

"You've gone up one flight of stairs," I point out.

"After I ran here," he says.

"You *ran*?"

"Car's in the shop. I'd just missed a bus. It was only half a mile. Running was by far the fastest."

Something warm stirs in my chest. He *ran* to me.

"Running with a bookbag," I tell him, "sounds unpleasant."

"Nah," he says. "You know how many mornings I ran to school with a thirty-pound book bag on my back to make it on time, because my uncle beat my ass whenever I was late?"

"Your *uncle*?"

"School principal," he explains, like this is an actual explanation.

I frown. "That seems like a very good reason he *shouldn't* have been beating your ass."

Alex shrugs. "Point is, I'm a running-with-backpack pro."

"This is me." I slide off his back and jimmy my key in the lock until it finally gives. "Welcome," I tell him, as I open the door, "to my shoebox."

Alex takes in my apartment, shutting the door behind him. He shrugs off his backpack, steps out of the same beat-up Nikes he was wearing when I met him. For the first time since he got here, I notice what he's wearing. Black sweatpants with what looks like a burn hole in the upper thigh. A Pitt T-shirt that's the same blue as his eyes, so threadbare in places, I can see a hint of his skin. House clothes, my mom would call them—the stuff you change into after a long day, when you're in for the night.

Maybe Alex goes out dressed like this, but I don't think that's the case. Even on the day I met him, when he was clearly having a tough time, his white T-shirt was thick cotton, bright, with no stains. His basketball shorts looked new, no holes in sight.

Which makes me think that these are his house clothes, that he was settled in for the night. Until I texted him. And then he ran here.

The warmth that spilled through me creeps up my cheeks. I turn away and, as I encounter a stark reminder of the state of my apartment, flush for a different reason—profound embarrassment.

"Please ignore the wine bottles," I tell him. "And the used tissues." I pluck up the empty bottles littering my kitchen counter, the wadded tufts of Kleenex scattered across the floor like dandelion fluff. "I was going to clean up, but you got here a lot faster than I thought you would."

I chuck the wine bottles in the recycling bin and do a very unclassy step into my trash can to smoosh down the mountain of tissues I just dumped into it.

Alex still hasn't said anything.

He stands with his back to me, facing my bookshelves, his head tipped slightly. When I walk up to him, I see he's smiling.

I glance between my bookshelves and him. "What is it?"

"That's an impressive wall of bookshelves."

"You think?" I move so that I'm standing beside him, shoulder to shoulder.

"Very impressive," he says. "Organized by genre. *Alphabetized* within genre." As his gaze travels the bookshelves, his smile deepens. "If I was a betting man, I would have made a lot of money tonight."

"Meaning?"

He peers over at me. "Meaning, I would have gone all in on this being exactly what your place looked like. A few pieces of unassuming, practical furniture; wall-to-wall shelves with a library's worth of books."

"Well," I say. "Good to know I'm so predictable."

"Nah." He nudges my shoulder with his. "Not predictable. Relatable." He's quiet for a moment, then says, "When I moved into my new place, the first thing I did was set up my kitchen. I slept on a mattress on the floor the first night I stayed there because I hadn't put my bedframe together, but my kitchen looked like I'd lived there for years.

"The way you talk about how much you love books, how much they matter to you—you talk about them the way I feel about cooking. It makes sense, that this is what you'd prioritize, what would make you feel most at home." He shrugs. "Your books."

My heart's pounding as I look at him. I am an emotional disaster. Grieving my friend's impending move. Recognizing I need to put on my big-girl panties and face my postdivorce life head-on all on my own. And there's a very beautiful man standing in my apartment who appreciates my alphabetized, organized by genre, thousand-plus book collection, talking to me like he gets it. Like he gets *me*.

I'm unfortunately one of those women who gets horny when she's sad and being comforted. I want to curl up like a cat in his lap and feel his hands run soothingly over every inch of me; listen to his warm, deep voice tell me everything's going to be okay; then I want him to throw me onto my bed, sink into me, and make me *feel* like everything's going to be okay, too.

Alex senses my internal meltdown. "Ted? What's wrong?"

I shake my head. My eyes well with tears.

He wraps an arm around me, holding me to his chest. "You want to talk about it?"

"Yes," I tell him. "But first, I want to wine."

"Whine?" He asks. "Or wine. As in, drink wine."

"The one," I tell him, "that involves alcohol."

He reaches for his backpack. "Thankfully, I came prepared."

*

A fuzzy number of hours have passed since Alex got here. It's late, past midnight, I know that much. Traffic is finally quiet but for the occasional car that rolls by, the city bus that hisses to a stop outside my building every twenty-some minutes. The sky is pitch-black outside my windows, and my apartment is dim, lit only by a cone of butter-yellow thrown by my nearby reading lamp. The wine has left me pleasantly mellow-brained and loose-limbed. Telling—well, sobbing at—Alex about Lauren's upcoming move, has left me drained yet peaceful, that specific kind of relieved exhaustion that comes after a good, hard cry.

Finally, a breeze billows through the windows, stirring my newly sewn field of dandelion tissue balls. Two bottles of wine sit empty on the coffee table, while Alex and I lie sprawled on the floor, staring up at the ceiling.

"I'm sorry," he says.

"It's okay," I whisper through the tears I keep wiping away. "I'm sorry for being such a mess."

"You're not a mess, Ted. You're going through messy shit."

"No difference."

"Big difference." He props up on an elbow, staring me down. "I'm right about this."

"How do you know?"

"Because my therapist said so. And my therapist, annoyingly, is always right."

I sigh and go back to staring at the ceiling. "Sour Patch?" I reach into the bag and offer him one.

"Nope. Those things fuck with my palate."

"And cigarettes don't?"

He scowls at me. "I never said they *didn't*. I just said they were a vice. And that I'm quitting them. Which I've done a great job of, so far."

I raise a hand, and he slaps it for a high five.

"And how," he says, "are you doing on your gas station hot dogs, Ms. Sodium Nitrates?"

"Haven't even walked into a 7-Eleven for a whiff of one."

Alex tips his head. "Not there yet. I'll walk through a cloud of smoke anytime I can."

I grimace. "Well, I might have actually walked into a 7-Eleven for a whiff of one yesterday. But it was a *rough* weekend." I toss the Sour Patch in my mouth and chew. "I probably need a therapist."

Alex seems unphased by my topic jump. "You ever had one before?"

"No." I feel around the Sour Patch bag but come up empty. "They scare me."

"Why?" he asks.

"Because from what I understand, going to therapy is paying someone to make me do my least favorite thing ever—deal with conflict, sadness, disappointment, fear; pick a negative emotion, I don't want it."

Alex pulls a Twizzler from the bag between us and bites into it. "I get that. I avoided it for years for the same reason." He shoves his hand into the bag again, pulls out another Twizzler, and offers it to me.

I lift my head enough to bite into it and flop back down. "What eventually made you decide to go?"

"Mia," he says. "She wasn't born yet, but she was due soon, and one night, right in the middle of dinner service, I just lost it. Full-on panic attack. Things weren't good with Jen. I'd been running myself into the ground, working obsessively at the restaurant. I was constantly anxious about becoming a dad, because I wanted to be a good one, and I had no confidence I could do that. Everything I'd relied on in life to avoid all the shit I never dealt with stopped working. So I figured, if I had no choice but to deal with the shit, I might as well talk to someone who could help me actually *deal* with it.

"Full transparency," he adds. "I did not happily skip off to therapy after the kitchen panic attack. It took me a couple weeks, and a couple more episodes, to finally schedule an appointment. I knew I needed help, but I was scared to admit it. Because my whole life, I've told myself 'I can'—that's how I got through things. So when it finally hits you, when you realize 'I *can't*,' it's hard to wrap your head around it, let alone your heart. When 'I can' is how you've always told yourself you're 'fine,' or you will be, it's terrifying to face 'I *can't*,' because then how do you know you're going to be fine? When it's never been okay to not be okay, admitting you're not okay and you can't make yourself okay like you always have is an existential fucking crisis." He bites into another Twizzler. "At least, it was for me."

I sit up slowly and face him. "I think . . . the past few days have been . . . that for me."

"I'm sorry, Ted. That you're in that place." He scrubs a hand down his face. "And I'm sorry I talked *so* much."

"You talked *deeply*. You're a philosophical drunk, and I like it."

He boops my nose with a Twizzler. "Don't be nice right now."

I grab a Twizzler and boop him, too. "Don't tell me what to do."

He seems self-conscious, eyes down, his hand fiddling with the Twizzlers bag. "I really am sorry, if everything I said, if that wasn't the vibe you needed. 'Cause if it wasn't, I just brought a lot of that vibe. I talk too much when I'm drunk."

I set my hand on his. "You didn't talk too much. And that was exactly the vibe I needed. I'm an amplified drunk—whatever I'm feeling just feels bigger—and the past few days, I've been feeling really bleak. What you said," I tell him, "it helped me. A lot. Thank you."

Alex peers up at me, and there's something so exposed, so vulnerable in his expression. "You sure?" he asks. "Because if it actually was too much, if I went too far, you can tell me that. I *want* you to tell me, Ted."

I remember what he said the night we met, out on his stoop, what he called his fatal flaw. *I do that a lot, dial myself up to an eleven.*

And I remember telling him my fatal flaw, too. *Mine is dialing myself down to a one.*

"I'm sure," I tell him. I take his hand in mine and hold his eyes. "Do you know why I asked you to come over tonight?"

A swallow works down his throat. "Because the other person here that you'd talk to is the person you're really upset won't be here in three weeks?"

"No. Even if this wasn't about Lauren leaving, and I was this upset, I wouldn't have texted her." I peer down at his hand, turning it so I can see his palm, his fingers, the lines and scars carved into them. "Because I didn't know how to deal with it. And I *want* to. Which meant I needed to talk to someone who'd go there with me. Lo and I, we love each other, and we are good friends to each other in many ways, but not in this. We don't talk about tough things," I admit.

Alex says, "Sounds like she could use a therapist, too."

A laugh jumps out of me.

"The wine," he groans. "It obliterates my filter. Sorry."

"Don't be. That's what I'm getting at. Even though I suck at it, I like that you talk about hard things, Alex. That's why I texted you tonight, I wanted your 'dialed up to an eleven' to put a fire under me. Maybe the same way you've reached out to me because you wanted my 'dialed down to a one' to bring you some comfort."

I peer up at Alex and tell him, "I guess, what I'm trying to say is . . . I think we're really good for each other. Flaws and all."

Alex is quiet for a moment, his gaze fixed on mine. "You're right. I have reached out to you, in part, because of that. But Ted, I *never* want you to dial yourself down to a one for me."

My heart aches in my chest. "I haven't."

"Promise?" he says. "And promise you never will."

"Promise. And I promise I never will—no lower than a three."

"Six," he counters.

"I'm not even dialed up to a six for *myself*, my dude. Don't push it."

He sighs. "I never want to dial up to an eleven on you, either."

"You haven't," I tell him.

"I won't," he says. "I promise."

I squeeze his hand in mine. "I trust you."

He squeezes my hand back. "Thank you." His mouth twists to the side. He looks away. "For saying that."

I lean in, wrapping my arms around him. It is, I'm realizing, the first time I've hugged Alex. I've thrown myself into his arms before, initiated a hug. But I did that for me. I've never done it because I knew *he* needed it. Until now.

Alex sinks into my hug, and, unprepared for that, I fall sideways, bringing him down with me on a loud *thump*.

"Ouch," he says into the floor.

"Alex!" He rolls toward me onto his side. I reach for his face, searching it for a bruise. "What hurts?" I ask. "Your nose?"

He shrugs. "It's taken harder knocks before."

"I'm sorry. I wasn't braced for all your muscly manliness. You are not light."

"That hug felt so good," he says, "I kind of forgot about holding up my own body."

I smile, my hands cradling his face, curved along his jaw. "I like that you forgot. Because that means you think I'm someone you can count on to catch you. Which I will," I add. "Next time. Because I'll be prepared."

Alex smiles, and I feel his cheeks lift beneath my palms. "I'll try not to go timber on you too often."

Silence settles between us, and the air thickens—charged, humming.

I pull my hands away and sit up. Slowly, Alex sits up, too.

Diving into the Twizzlers again, I take in the room. "You know what this place needs?" I ask.

"A kitchen that isn't frozen in 1963?"

I chuck a Twizzler at his head. "Yes, but not what I was thinking. It needs more empty wine bottles."

Alex scrapes a hand through his hair. "Thing is, when I drink, I want a cigarette. And I've downed a bottle of wine, so . . . I *really* want a cigarette."

"I want a gas station hot dog in the worst way," I admit. "But we're sticking to our resolutions. Which means no more drinking. We'll do something else fun and escapist."

Alex glances around my apartment.

I glance around, too.

"Okay," I tell him, "I don't have much to do here. Yet. I need to buy some board games, a deck of cards. A TV. Just haven't gotten there."

"That's okay," he says. "Let's see what we can come up with." He pulls out his phone and starts typing.

I shove another Twizzler in my mouth and lean in, peering over the top of his phone. "Whatcha doing?"

"Googling," he says. "'What to do for fun when you're divorced.'"

"And with a friend," I tell him. "Add that."

"And. With. A. Friend," he says, thumbs moving across the screen. He hits enter. A frown tugs down his face. "What the fuck, Google."

"What?"

"Get on *dating* apps?" he hollers at the screen. "That's your number one recommendation?"

He chucks his phone away, I think intending it for the nearby director chair. Instead, it threads the gap between the back and seat, which means his phone soars *through* the director chair, across the room. Miraculously, it lands on Argos's dog bed.

"Phew," Alex says. "I thought that phone was toast."

"You do strike me as someone who should invest in a quality phone case."

Alex gives me a scathing look as he eases upright, then crosses the room to scoop up his phone. "I'm going to take that as a compliment: you think I enjoy such a vigorous and active lifestyle, I need a phone case to see my phone safely through all my fearsome escapades."

I snort. "You're also a *funny* drunk."

A smile spreads across his face. He bows theatrically. "Thank you."

"Google really said we should get on the dating apps?" I ask.

His smile dissolves. "You had to bring that up."

"It didn't happen all that long ago. I thought I was just picking up where we left off before you launched your phone across the room."

Alex flops down beside me again, flat onto his back, and sighs. "You're right. I sidetracked us. Yes, Google said that. I just really don't want to get on the apps."

I peer over at him. "Ever or right now?"

Alex is quiet for a beat. "I don't know, Ted. Sometimes I wonder if I wasn't just bad at being married to Jen. Maybe I'm just bad at being married."

"Why?"

"Because I'm intense, and historically, when I get passionate about something, it eclipses everything else. From the moment I opened it, my restaurant was everything to me, and I couldn't see that I'd sidelined my marriage until I was about to be a dad, and by then, it was too late." Alex glances at me. "I don't work at the restaurant anymore. That was my Hail Mary, to try to salvage things with Jen. I quit, left it in the very capable hands of my former sous, Olu. The only work I've done since then has been on my cookbooks. I haven't gone back to work at the restaurant since."

I turn on my side, elbow tucked under my head, and face him. "What's your restaurant's name?"

His brow furrows. "Everything I just said, and that's your question?"

I nod.

He smiles faintly, his look quizzical, then tells me, "Squisito."

"That's Italian?" I ask. At his nod in response, I add, "Italian for . . . ?"

His gaze travels over me. "Exquisite."

Heat flushes through me. I know he wasn't talking about me, when he said it, but he was looking at me when he did. My brain understands the difference. My body does not.

"I'd like to eat there sometime," I tell him.

"You have, in a way. The lasagna I fed you, when we went to Luna's—that's one of my recipes, a favorite at Squisito."

I smile.

"What about you?" he says.

"What do you mean?"

He turns to face me, too, elbow tucked under his head, mirroring me. "Do you want to get on the apps, at any point?"

I stare at him, my heart's pace picking up. "I don't know. I think, before I figure that out, I have to figure out myself better. Everything feels jumbled right now. I feel disoriented, and . . . bruised."

A soft grunt leaves Alex. "Bruised is a good word."

For a moment, we just look at each other, no sound but the hum of cicadas, the box fan whirring in my window.

"So that's that," I tell him. "We won't get on the apps. Maybe one day, but not today. Today, we'll . . . do the Wordle."

He snaps upright. "Connections?"

"The Spelling Bee?"

"Strands!" we say at the same time.

He sighs. "My god, Ted. We were made for each other."

Affection curls around my heart. Alex opens his arm wide, and I scooch in, resting my head on his shoulder. His arm comes around me snug, a comforting weight, and he brings his phone close so we can both see it. His head nestles against mine. We both sigh with contentment.

Alex opens up the *New York Times* games app and asks, "What should we do first?"

I tap the Spelling Bee. "We'll go in order."

"Which would mean starting with the Crossword?"

I peer up at him, and my heart skips. Our mouths are very close. For the first time, I think about kissing Alex. And I wonder if maybe Alex is thinking about kissing me, too.

He drags a curl back from my temple and asks, voice soft, "Where'd you go?"

"I was just thinking . . ." A swallow works down my throat. "We're way too drunk to do the Crossword."

"Good point," he says. "We can do it in the morning."

A surprised laugh tumbles out of me. "Planning to stay the night?"

"Sure, sounds good." He taps the Spelling Bee to open the game, slides his thumb across the letters, and spells S-A-G-E.

I poke his side. "I was asking *if* you were planning to."

"Well, I wasn't," he says, "but then you invited me." He nods toward the far end of the room. "Argos's dog bed looks decadent."

I glance over at the dog bed, which I can admit is ridiculously plush and oversized, a gratuitous splurge. "You might actually fit on it. Be my guest."

"I'm teasing, Ted. Give me thirty to sober up, then I'll head home."

"Don't," I blurt. "I mean, don't head home unless you want to."

He peers down at me, searching my eyes. After a moment, he seems to find whatever he was looking for, because he settles back into place, resting his head against mine. "I'll stay."

I slide my finger across the letters on his phone and spell P-A-G-E. "Because you want to?"

"Because I want to," he says. "And also, because that dog bed looks cozy as fuck."

CHAPTER 14

NOW

August 2,
one day until "vacation"

In my five years at The Bookshop, I've pushed for two things, and they are the two things I'm most proud of—StoryTime on Tuesday morning and Saturday afternoon, and our monthly book club that I started, which, to my profound embarrassment, Fern referred to on our website and our in-store flyers as Try It with Thea.

The first time I griped to Lauren about that, we were out for Fried Food and French Wine Friday. She laughed so hard, she snorted champagne up her nose, which felt, frankly, like justice had been served.

Try It with Thea, which runs in addition to our main book club (this one, of course, enjoys an innuendo-free name, Fiction with Fern, focused on new release literary fiction), is a concept I came up with for people who are still figuring out what they like to read, or who, like me, love to read multiple genres but can get overwhelmed by their options.

When I first started the book club last year, I both loved and hated running it. I mostly loved it, and for many reasons. I started to make friends among its members. I had a time and place to spend with people who enjoyed reading as much as I did and see slivers of them peek through their thoughts and feelings on what we read; what they related to or what they didn't; what they felt was unjust or, conversely, justified; and which characters they rooted for as well as which ones they couldn't wait to see vanquished.

And I, somewhat, hated it. Sometimes, the monthly pick was a flop, even for me, and our discussion was lackluster. Then I felt like a failure who'd picked a dud of a book and disappointed everyone and waisted two hours of their lives, plus their reading hours. It made my people-pleasing skin crawl. Which was why, according to Sue, it was a very worthwhile thing for me to continue doing.

Sue was right. I've stuck with it long enough that I don't hate any part of book club now, besides the name. I don't love when a book is a flop, but I don't want to curl up and hide when it happens, either.

I'd like to say I've arrived at that same level of comfort with discomfort, when it comes to calling meetings with my boss. But I haven't at all.

Fern walks in through the staff room back door at exactly seven-thirty, half an hour before other staff members will get here to prep opening the store for the day, and for a moment, I'm so nervous, I'm sure I'm going to puke.

"Good morning, Thea." Fern sets down her thermos of coffee and tucks her usual flowy linen dress, this one in moss green, beneath her as she sits. Her eyes crinkle behind a pair of half-moon gold wire-rim glasses, and her white hair is, as always, swept up into a small chignon on her head. A cloud of patchouli floats around her.

"Morning, Fern." I sit down across from her, holding the manila folder that contains everything I've been dreaming of, working toward, hoping for. My hands are shaking so badly I nearly drop the folder.

Fern reaches across the table and rests her hands on mine. I try to smile, to look calm and poised for what I'm about to do.

Slowly, she draws her hands back, across the table, and with them the manila folder. Wordlessly, she opens it, her gaze darting down the first page. Her expression is unreadable, her ever-present serene smile giving away nothing.

My stomach knots viciously.

Fern peers up at me over her glasses. "It's your meeting, Thea. Take it away."

"Right." I clear my throat. "So, having looked at page one, you'll see first on my proposed agenda is . . ."

She flicks the manila folder shut, still smiling.

My gaze darts from the folder to her. "Why did you close the folder?"

"I'm not interested in reading an agenda. I'm sure you've included valuable data points, all the necessary numbers, but I can look at those later." She leans in, elbows on the table, and holds my eyes. "What I'm interested in is hearing what *you* have to say."

I dart another glance at the manila folder. I'm terrible at presenting, unless I'm talking about a book I love. I was planning on walking Fern through each bullet point, clinging to the order and magnitude of the proposal.

But that's not what she wants. And if I want *this*—my dream for this store, for my future—I have to at least try to wing it her way.

Drawing in a deep breath, I shut my eyes. I picture what I've let myself want and hope and reach for.

Thea Meyer stood outside The Bookshop, drinking in the sight of it—the tall, colorful shelves teaming with book; the stands of local artists cards, stickers, candles, bookmarks; the patrons sipping coffee, plucking a book from the shelf, turning it over to read the back copy, smiling to themselves. Falling leaves drifted from the tree above her, morning sun warm on her face, as she felt a tug in her heart, a quiet voice inside her growing louder:

You could do more than love this place; you could pour your heart into it.

This place has made you happy, but you could it even happier.

You could make something good and strong and beautiful even more so.

I open my eyes, meet Fern's gaze, and take the leap.

*

My meeting with Fern this morning is taking up 98 percent of my brain space, and only the last 2 percent is left for my last task before vacation—book club tonight.

I'm replaying Fern's response as I drag chairs into a rough horseshoe shape in the middle of the bookstore and members start to trickle in, ordering from the coffee bar an herbal tea, an evening decaf, a cookie, a muffin.

You've given me a lot to think about, Thea. Let's talk once you're back from your trip.

"She hates it," I mutter to myself. "I'm going to get fired, and then I'll be stuck at a job I hate, scrubbing toilets without the perks of pushing books to compensate for that misery."

"Who's scrubbing toilets?" Mr. Fleischer asks, those bushy white eyebrows darting up above his thick black-frame glasses.

I jump and spin around, clutching my chest. "No one." I frown at him. "How did you even hear that?"

He taps his ear. "Hearing aid tune-up this morning. Now move."

I step aside to make way for him. He's leaning heavier on his walker these days, moving slower. I've offered every book club since we started to drive him, and every time he's refused me. I'd take it personally, if I didn't know I'm still his favorite neighbor *and* favorite Bookshop employee.

"Quite the selection this month," he says.

"Quite the selection?"

He grunts.

"What is it with my favorite old people giving me cryptic responses today?" I join him in the next chair over as he eases himself down.

"Fine," he says. "I'll put you out of your misery. It was gritty and moving and, most importantly, feminist as fuck." He leans in, voice lowered. "Which means Archie's going to *hate* it."

Archie Burton is Mr. Fleischer's opposite. He's all smiles and chummy small talk, but beneath the surface, he's a creep of a guy who manages to keep his comments just below the level of inappropriate that would give grounds to kick him out, and I think he does that very much on purpose. I'd be lying if I said I haven't picked some titles largely in the hopes that they'd be "woke" enough to scare him off. So far, I haven't had success.

I smile at Mr. Fleischer. "I'm not actually counting on Mr. Burton showing up for discussion tonight." I lean in, too. "And by that, I mean, I really hope he doesn't."

"He will," Mr. Fleischer says, groaning as he leans back in his seat. "Just for the pleasure of pissing on our fun."

"You think it'll be fun tonight?" I ask.

There's an energetic twinkle in Mr. Fleischer's eye that I haven't seen in a while. It loosens my worry for him a little, as he pats my hand. "Oh, it's gonna be lively, toots. I can feel it."

My phone buzzes in my pocket. I pull it out and smile as I open up the message, a selfie of Lauren holding *The Grace Year,* her face turned toward it, a smooch pursing her lips. Below it says, Give Burton hell for me! Wish I was there!

"Who's that texting you a message?" Mr. Fleischer leans in. "Your beau?"

"My *friend*," I emphasize, "Alex? No."

He rolls his eyes. "Right. Your *friend*, Alex. Who comes over all evening and cooks for you and walks your dog, and drives me to my doctor appointments because *someone's* too busy being Ms. Important Bookstore Manager."

"First of all, that's what friends do," I tell him. "They visit each other and cook for each other, and walk each other's dogs and drive each other's curmudgeonly neighbors places."

"Uh-huh." He rolls his eyes again.

"Second of all, I've *tried* to take you to your doctor appointments, but you keep blowing me off because you want to hang out with Alex while he drives you around, which, you know, ouch. But I get it, he's a likable guy."

"And your car is a death trap," he adds.

"It is not!" I glare at him.

He ignores that. "Who's that message from," he says, leaning toward my phone, being his nosy self. "Oh, the shrew."

"You hush." I bite back a smile. "Like you and Lauren aren't both cut from the same cloth."

"God help me if we are!" He hacks a phlegmy cough.

"Alex has been talking smack about her, hasn't he?"

He shakes his head. "Nope."

I don't buy it. "You can't take him literally when he does that. It's just a petty game between the two of them. He doesn't *actually* dislike her."

Mr. Fleischer gives me a long stare. "Theadora. He's *wildly* jealous of her. He's jealous of anyone he thinks gets more of you than he does."

My heart skips a beat, then jolts back into rhythm. "That's not . . . I don't—"

"Bah." He waves his hand. "Forget it. Just answer the shrew."

I falter for a moment, thrown by his words, before I steady myself. "Only if you take a selfie with me to send her."

He folds his arms across his chest. "Absolutely not."

I sigh, turning to my phone, responding to Lauren. I heart the photo she sent, then write, Wish you were here too! Hoping Burton doesn't show, but if he does, I'm ready to rumble. Did you like the book??

My phone buzzes with her answer. I. LOVED. IT.

My phone buzzes again. SO. FUCKING. MUCH. THE ENDING!!! *SOBS*

I turn my phone toward Mr. Fleischer. "Lauren loved the book, too."

He sneaks a glance toward my screen, then leans in. "Well," he grumbles. "At least she has good taste in books. Swears like a sailor, but—"

"Coming from you!"

"I," he says archly, "am old. Which means I get to be a hypocrite and not a damn soul gets to call me out."

I smile. "Is *that* what it means?"

"One day, toots, when you're shriveled up into a pruney version of yourself, like me, you'll understand. Hopefully, you'll have pulled your head out of your ass by then."

I gasp. "About what?"

"Just take the selfie, already." He leans closer, pressing his temple to mine. I hesitate for a moment, smarting a little from what he's said, but then I lift my phone, angle it down, and take the picture. I send it to Lauren and text her: Mr. Fleischer loved it, too!

My phone buzzes. Tell that old coot he has good taste in books. But he still needs to get his eyebrows waxed.

I do *not* tell him that. But Mr. Fleischer's leaning in already, squinting at my screen before I can exit out of our message.

His laugh is loud and hoarse and delightfully unexpected. He dabs the corners of his eyes. "'Old coot.' God, she's a pill."

My phone buzzes with another text from Lauren. You doing okay, after your meeting with Fern?

Mr. Fleischer's sharp tone pulls me from our text conversation as he says, "Who the hell are you?"

"Mr. Fleischer." I squeeze his hand gently, pocketing my phone with the other. "That's no way to greet first-timers." I peer over my shoulder, gearing up to apologize for our one-man unwelcoming committee, then freeze. "Jen?"

She's smiling, but I can see nervousness turning it tight at the edges. Her hands are clasped in front of her. "Hey, Thea. I . . . hope it's okay for me to be here?"

I shoot up out of my seat. "Sure. Yes. Of course. Absolutely."

"Please keep going," Mr. Fleischer quips. "I need to brush up on my affirmative synonyms."

I shoot him a warning look. "You need a cookie to perk you up, Mr. Grumpus. I'll have Ro bring one right over."

He narrows his eyes at me. "Fine. But make sure it's oatmeal raisin."

"Nothing but the grossest for you, Mr. Fleischer."

"Okay, butterscotch breath." He points a finger to his open mouth and mimes an overdramatic gag. "Talk about gross."

"Those butterscotch chocolate chip cookies are divine, and I will hear no slander!"

"Yeah, yeah." He waves his hand. "Get on with attending to the interloper."

I spin back toward Jen, who's standing there still, her smile a little more relaxed. "Sorry about that," I tell her. "Mr. Fleischer keeps me on my toes."

"I can see that," she says, her gaze darting from him back to me. She clears her throat. "Sorry for . . . springing this on you. It was a spur-of-the-moment decision. I've been on the hunt for Mia's white-knit cardigan, to pack it for the beach, and Alex said he thought she might have worn it here last week, for the Holidays in July event. Maybe she'd left it here? I figured I'd come by and try to find it, so I looked up the store hours, then I saw there was a book club discussion tonight for *The Grace Year*, which is . . ." She sighs, setting a hand on her heart. "It's one of my favorites. Fingers crossed, eventually they'll let me add it to the seniors' English curriculum."

My stomach twists, hearing her say that, seeing her here.

Over the past two years, Jen's never seemed too keen to talk, so she and I haven't interacted much beyond pleasantries. I've been okay with that, keeping her at arm's length, never close enough to let proximity kick up all sorts of painful questions I know will only lead to bad feelings: what Ethan saw in her that made her worth throwing out his "reconnect with himself" reason for our divorce; her status as a mother not being a deal-breaker, despite his "not being ready for kids" decade-long explanation for keeping motherhood from *me*; what made her someone whose ex-husband at least tried to win her back, to fix things with her, when mine couldn't even be bothered to go to one session of couple's counseling, who quit on me when I simply asked him to *try*.

I know all these thoughts and the feelings underpinning them are distorted, a reflection of my broken self-image that I'm still piecing back together, after growing up the way I did and spending a decade and a half with a man like Ethan.

But they are thoughts I still have every time she comes into my orbit.

So of course, of all nights—when I've just taken the biggest risk of my professional life; when I'm days away from spending a *week* with her; when the old wounds from recognizing how little I inspired in Ethan that he never, not even once, wanted to take me to this treasured family vacation home of his, are fresh in my head; when I'm about to lead a book discussion for a book I loved but to which I am very unsure how other people will respond—she's here.

At least, I tell myself, she loved the book.

"Why don't you grab yourself something from the coffee bar," I tell her. "On me. I'll go look for Mia's sweater."

"Oh no, I'll buy it," she says quickly. "You don't need to—"

"I insist," I tell her. "On me, please."

I smile at Jen the way I have smiled at so many people so many times before. Not quite meaning it, but trying to trying to muster up warmth and kindness when I feel anything but.

As she smiles back, wide and genuine, relief loosening her shoulders, I'm reminded, in the same way my "make myself small" sometimes does something good, makes space for someone who needs that, this "fake it till you make it smile" can do something good, too—show someone warmth, give them kindness, when they dearly need t.

Which, as I head toward our box of lost and found, on the hunt for Mia's sweater, makes me wonder, with her beachfront wedding just days away, her happily ever after stretched out before her, why Jen, of all people, seems to have needed just that.

*

To my relief, the book is not a flop. It leads to an intense conversation at points, but overall, our book club agrees *The Grace Year* was well written and thought-provoking. Jen is quiet during our discussion, so much so that by the end of it, I'm surprised to see she's still here.

By the time most members have left, I finish folding and stacking chairs. Ro is closing down the coffee bar, and Hailey, who worships at my feet since I managed to contain the damage on her embargoed book flub, is sweeping the floor. Jen lingers nearby with Mia's sweater in hand, talking to Kat, a smart, friendly member around Jen's age who also has a kindergartener. Jen glances my way as Kat calls goodbye before heading out the door.

Then she walks toward me.

"Can I help with anything?" she asks.

I smile. "That's nice of you to offer, but no, we're basically done, right?" I turn to Ro.

They wave me off. "Yep! All I have to do is close up. Get out of here."

"Thanks, Ro." I turn toward Jen, who's still standing there, a growing sense that there's something she wants to talk about, something she has to say to me.

Maybe she's just going to come straight out and tell me about the surprise wedding we're in for this week. I can't think what else it would be. Whatever it is, even though I'm dreading it, I say to her, "I'm going to grab my bag, if you want to walk out with me."

"Sure!" she chirps. She sounds even more chipper than Hailey, which I didn't think was possible.

Her enthusiasm spikes my anxiety. I head through the store, leading us down the back hallway to the staff room. My heart knocks hard against my ribs.

It's awkwardly silent as Jen hangs in the doorway while I pack up my bag, slip it over my shoulder, then power down my computer for the night. Relief whooshes through me as I spot the small stack of books that I'd set aside for Mia—some early reader copies, some damaged final ones the store won't put on the floor. I scoop them up and turn to Jen with the books in hand.

"Can I send these with you?" I ask. "I figured Mia might enjoy some new reads on the drive to the beach."

I hold my breath, remembering what Alex said earlier today, his reverse-psychology plan to trick Ethan into driving my dog, who suffers from car-ride-induced flatulence. Maybe it worked, or maybe it backfired and Mia will be driving with Jen and Ethan after all.

Jen hesitates. "Oh. Thank you, but . . . Ethan said Mia is riding with you and Alex."

Said. The word hangs in the air, souring my stomach. Ethan *said*, not *asked*.

When Alex sought my thoughts on who should ride with whom, he told me Ethan was asking Jen for hers.

Sounds like Ethan did *not* ask.

Sadness seeps through me. Because that sounds very much like the Ethan I knew, the Ethan I was married to . . . the Ethan whom Jen is about to marry.

"Are you okay with that?" I ask her.

Jen shrugs, smiling faintly. "Sure. She'll have more fun in the car with you two, anyway. I need to make some tweaks to my lesson plans before the school year starts, so I'll do that while Ethan drives."

"Oh," I say. "Well, that's good, at least. I forgot you'd be getting prepped for the school year already."

"Mm-hmm." She sniffs, her mouth suddenly twisting. "Thanks for finding her sweater. Mia said she had a lot of fun at the event."

"Good." I smile. "She seemed to. I . . ." My words die off, as I falter, surprised by what I'd been about to say next, what I genuinely felt, remembering Mia, who kept glancing toward the door, hoping her mom would show up. "I'm sorry you couldn't make it," I tell Jen.

"Me, too," Jen says hoarsely. She bites her lip. Which I realize is trembling. Her eyes are growing wet. Mine widen with alarm. Because, unless I'm way off, I think Jen is about to cry. Hard.

"Come on." I tip my head toward the hallway, and Jen follows as I lead her to our back door staff exit.

After Jen steps outside, I follow her and shove the door shut behind me. As it lands with a *thud*, Jen bursts into tears.

For a second, I freeze, rooted to the ground.

She's curled in on herself, shoulders rounded, hands covering her face.

I spring into action, stepping close, setting a hand on her back. "Hey, what's wrong?"

She shakes her head. I glance around, spotting the pair of wrought iron chairs chained to the trunks of two twin willows Fern planted behind the store when she opened it, and tell Jen, "Come on, sit down."

Jen lets me guide her to the chairs, dropping onto the edge of one. "I'm so sorry," she whispers. Her hands fall from her face to her lap. Tears stream down her cheeks.

I set a hand on her knee, gentle, tentative. "You don't need to be sorry."

She shakes her head, sucking in a breath as she sits up, composing herself. I watch her wipe her cheeks, dab beneath her eyes. "I'm okay."

I'm quiet for a moment, hesitating, before I tell her, "You don't have to be."

Her chin wobbles as she glances my way. "You were really good tonight."

I'm a bit thrown by the turn in conversation. "Oh. Um, thank you."

"I know I was quiet, but I was just . . . really impressed. I was taking it all in—how well you moderated the discussion, encouraged curiosity, engaged people's perspectives. And when things got heated, you reined it in, moved everyone forward, guided the topic into less amped-up territory." She smiles tearily. "Command of the classroom is what we call it in teaching circles."

"I'm familiar," I tell her. "My mom was a public high school teacher for thirty-five years." For the first time I make the connection—both Jen and my mother are high school teachers, both mothers to exuberant daughters.

I wonder if, at some subliminal level, that's why I've kept my distance from Jen the past two years. Because I was afraid I'd see my dynamic with my mother played out again and hurt for Mia, or I'd see something better, something kinder and hurt for myself.

"Really?" Jen's smile deepens. "Me, too."

I nod. "I know."

"Not for thirty-five years, of course," she says quietly. She peers down at Mia's sweater in her hands, then opens it up from the ball she'd crumpled it into and folds it neatly. "That's a long time."

"Especially given she taught *math*." I shudder.

Jen laughs faintly. "I could never."

"Me neither, but she loved it. I think she would have kept teaching until she kicked the bucket, if they let her."

Jen swallows thickly, smoothing her hands along Mia's now-folded sweater. "Maybe I'll feel that way one day. But right now, I feel like I can barely manage it. Being a mom and a teacher is . . . a lot harder than I expected." She dabs beneath her eyes again. "Teaching took a lot out of me before I had Mia, and I figured it would be more demanding after she was born, but I had no idea . . ." She huffs a breathy, sad laugh. "I had *no* idea."

It feels like raging inside me is one of those tornado warnings that was a staple of my life growing up in the Midwest, one that built in volume as it slid up in pitch, a harsh, wailing siren.

Jen glances over at me. "Maybe your mom's told you that, too?"

I shake my head slowly. "My mom and I . . . don't talk much. And when we do, we don't talk about the past."

"Why?"

I almost tell Jen that's none of her business. But something stops me.

"Because the past wasn't great. Because I was a handful; and she was drained after pouring so much into her teaching, her students; and my dad wasn't very present, so she basically had to raise me on her own, and that made for a not-so-fun first eighteen years of life with Thea Meyer."

A pinched sound catches in Jen's throat. "That's what I was afraid you'd say."

I tip my head. "What do you mean?"

She peers up at the darkening sky, her chin trembling again. "I feel like I'm getting it all wrong. Like I'm failing Mia. Like I don't have enough for her. I don't know how to do my job other than how I did it for fourteen years before I had her, and how I'm doing my job is . . . demanding.

"I have so many students who are dealing with so much at home, in their communities. They need me to teach them, but they also need me to listen to their feelings, to be patient with them when they're dysregulated, to believe in them, to push them toward their potential, to comfort them—"

"To be a mother to them," I say softly.

I've only ever read about riptides, but this feels like one that just yanked me out to sea. A minute ago, I was safe at shore, water up to my waist, feet firm in the sand. And now I'm half a mile out in the ocean, disoriented. Floating in a vast, terrifying possibility.

Jen is doing a daunting, overwhelming job because she's doing it with her whole heart, the only way I could ever stomach doing my work—pouring myself into it, giving it my best. And I have no idea what it looks like to be torn between giving my work my best and somehow safeguarding, preserving enough *best* for my child.

That wave of sympathy submerges me in the truth, then wrenches me back up to the surface, and now I see it, *feel* it. The possibility that, like Jen, like me . . . my mom was doing her best. And no, it wasn't good enough, wasn't enough for what I needed, but . . . maybe that wasn't all her fault, or even my dad's fault; it definitely wasn't mine, I know that the way I know Mia's needing her mother's presence, patience, affection, and guidance would never be Mia's fault. Maybe it was really very much the fault of a much bigger, broken system.

My eyes well with tears.

Jen glances my way, her expression scrunching as she sees I'm crying, too. "Thea?"

"Are you doing the best you can?" I blurt.

Jen searches my eyes for a moment, then slowly nods. "Yes."

"Right," I tell her, trying to steady my voice. "And you're sitting here, crying to someone you hardly know, because you're so torn up after reading a book about a broken world and wounded daughters and oppressed mothers, and your heart went straight to what matters most: your daughter.

"You're worried that you're failing her, and to me means you are absolutely *not* doing that, or if you are, in this moment, you're not going to *keep* doing that. You're going to look at what you have and what you need. So you can find a way to give your work all that you need to and give Mia what she needs as well. I know you love her enough to figure that out."

Hitching yourself to my self-centered ex, I want to say, *is probably not going to give you what you need.*

But it's not my place to tell her that. And maybe, just maybe, Ethan's going to be better to her than we was to me. I pull my hand from her knee and sit back.

Jen says quietly, "I'm worried it's too late."

"Mia's six," I tell her. "And I know those first six years are pretty important ones, but so is the rest of her life."

She nods. "True."

"I'm not a mom. I have no idea what you're going through, but I am a daughter whose mom made mistakes. And that's okay. She was human; humans do that. That wasn't how she failed me, Jen. She failed me because... she never faced her mistakes. Because she taught me not to ask her to face them, either, taught me to bury my hurt and hide what I needed. That's what went sideways—not the mistakes, but how she handled them. How she *didn't* handle them.

"Mia's not me, and you're not my mother, but I can tell you, if mistakes had been handled rather than avoided, even if all those mistakes still happened, I know I'd be talking to my mom a lot more."

It sinks in, as I say it, how true that is. How much it would mean if my mom were to call me and we *did* talk about the past, even now. It would hurt that it had taken this long, come so late. But it wouldn't be *too* late. It wouldn't fix the past, but it could help me heal from it.

Jen peers over at me. "Thank you."

I swallow, blinking away tears. "I probably just said way too much."

"No. You said just the right amount." Smiling, she reaches for my hand and squeezes. "You're a good person, Thea. I'm really glad you're in Mia's life."

With those words, Jen stands, hugging Mia's sweater tight to her chest, and walks across the parking lot.

For a while, I sit there, my chest tight, tears blurring my vision.

And then I fumble for my phone, texting my therapist. Sue's reminded me regularly, if I ever have a rough day and need support, to reach out; if she can give me a call, talk me through it for a few minutes, she will. I've never taken her up on that offer before tonight. I've wanted to a few times, but I always worried I'd be imposing; I talked myself down, told myself it wasn't that serious, that it could wait until our next session.

This cannot wait.

After sending my text to Sue, I shove my phone away, wiping frantically at the tear tracks on my cheeks. I tell myself there's a good chance Sue will be unavailable, that her work phone will be powered off for the night.

While I wait, I think about calling Lauren, who's still on the West Coast. But it's only five there, and she'll be working for hours before she can call back. Even if I did text or call Lauren, it doesn't feel right to bring up my mommy problems to someone who's had to say goodbye to hers.

My phone buzzes in my lap, and my gaze snaps down to the screen. It's Sue.

Hi, Thea. Of course. I have about 15-20 minutes now, if that works for you. I'm ready when you are. Just let me know when to call.

I stumble upright, hiking my bag onto my shoulder as I text Sue, thanking her and telling her that I'm ready to talk.

She calls a minute later, as I'm starting my walk to Alex's, her voice warm and familiar and, I'm not ashamed to admit, comfortingly maternal. Tears fill my eyes, and my throat thickens. I don't know that I'm going to be able to talk to my therapist so much as cry at her.

Like always, Sue asks me how I'm doing, what I need to talk about.

This time, for the first time, I tell her what I need even though I *really* don't want to need it. My voice wobbles, but I don't wait until it's steady or hold back what might unsteady it again. I don't keep a single thing inside.

I tell her everything.

CHAPTER 15

THEN

August 2, two summers ago

I'm sitting at Alex's kitchen table, sipping a very good, very strong cup of coffee as Friday morning sun spills in, warm and buttery, through the windows. Alex sips his coffee, then sets it down, turning back to the stove, where he's making the breakfast he invited me over for. He's moving around . . . stiffly.

"Something hurting?" I ask.

"Better question would be, is anything *not* hurting."

"What happened?"

He seems to hesitate, then says, "A cascade of events."

"Beginning with?" I watch him wince as he shifts his weight, tensing his shoulders, his lower back arching in.

"Ah. Well." He leans over the pot on the stove and winces again. "Your floor."

My mind flashes back to the other night, the two of us lying on the floor, Alex's arm still curled around me. My eyelids growing heavy, telling Alex, *we should go to bed*, immediately realizing how that sounded, about to clarify what I meant, then being answered with a snore, his heavy arm curling tighter around my shoulders. Then early the next morning, when I woke up the moment the sun hit my eyes, like I always do. For a few minutes, I watched him sleep, cataloged his features. The tips of his dark, thick lashes burnished bronze by the morning light. His bittersweet-cocoa bed-head hair, indecisive curl-waves stuck out in every direction. The dark stubble darkening his jaw right up to his cheekbones. How beautiful I thought he looked. And thought about kissing him again.

Heat rolls through me.

I clear my throat. "Next time," I tell Alex, "you should definitely try the dog bed."

A soft laugh rumbles out of him. "My back still would've been fucked up. I went too hard on the rowing machine, trying to work out the knot. Then I overdid it on the stationary bike."

"I'm sensing a theme," I tell him.

He sips his coffee. "Yes. I can get a little . . . overzealous with things, including, but not limited to, workout machinery, but it's that or smoke to deal with stress, and we have an agreement, don't we?"

"Haven't even looked at a gas station hot dog stand in weeks."

He grins. "Look at us, staying strong."

"Does anything help?" I ask. "With the pain."

"Nah, I just have to wait it out. Stay active and do my stretches. Sleep on my absurdly posh ergonomic mattress and take ibuprofen and look forward to waking up not feeling like I'm eighty."

"How old are you, actually?"

"Fifty," he throws over his shoulder.

I nearly spit out my coffee. "You are *not*."

He has his back to me, mostly. I can see only a sliver of his profile, but it's enough that I catch the corner of his grin, the deep dimple it sets in his cheek. "The men in my family age really well—what can I say?"

"Alex."

"Thirty-five," he says. "Thirty-six in November."

"Uh-huh. A Sagittarius."

He glances over his shoulder. "How'd do you figure that? Aren't most November birthdays Scorpios?"

"Yes, but you are one hundred percent a fire sign."

He laughs, then gingerly glances at me over his shoulder. "You?"

"Textbook Libra."

"Noted," he says, "but I meant your age."

"Oh. Thirty-three. Thirty-four in October."

He grins. "Spring chicken."

"Tell that to my ovaries. Because they're telling me, I'm a ticking clock."

"Nah," he says gently. "You've got time, Ted. You'll get your babies."

My heart pinches. "You really think so?"

"Know so." He turns off the burner, then carefully scoops out four poached eggs. "Until then, I've got feisty four-year-old you can have *whenever* you want."

I laugh. "Mia is a blast."

"She's a goddamn handful," he says affectionately. "Also a fire sign."

"Aries." I'm confident of this.

He smiles. "Textbook Aries."

As I see him start to plate the food, I jump up, rummaging around his kitchen for silverware, napkins, place mats.

When I take my first bite, a whimper sneaks out of me, then a deeply appreciative, "Holy shit."

Alex's mouth tugs up at the corner. "I hope that's a good 'holy shit.'"

"It's a euphoric 'holy shit.'" I dive into another bite, sweeping a piece of crisp toast through sun-gold yolk and glossy burnt-umber sauce. "What is it?" I ask.

"Oeufs pochés en meurette," he says, "á la Chef Diane."

"Chef Diane?"

"My mentor," he says. "She hated how the original recipe made the eggs turn purple; it calls for poaching the eggs in burgundy wine. So instead, she taught me to poach the eggs in water, then make a sauce with the wine, said it made everything about the dish better. And she was right—it's better like this, in every way."

"Well, I have nothing to compare it to, since this is my first time having . . . what was it again?"

Alex smiles. "Oeufs pochés en meurette."

Desire hums in my veins. I did forget what it was called, but I asked him to repeat the dish's name mostly because Alex speaking French is hot as hell.

"Yes," I manage hoarsely. "That. It's phenomenal. So please thank Chef Diane for me."

"I would," he says, "but she's dead."

I nearly choke on my food. "Oh my god, Alex, I'm so sorry."

A chuckle tumbles out of him. He sighs as he cuts into his food. "No need. Sorry I said it that way, but I had to. That was her condition, when she told me she was sick, that whenever I talked about her, I had to tell people she was six feet under the way she would have—bone dry, all in for the shock value. Except Diane wouldn't have broken as fast as I did. She would have given you this flat stare for five seconds that felt like five minutes. *Then* she would have laughed."

I smile. The way he talks about Diane reminds me of the way I talked about my namesake, Grandma Thea. Respect, deep gratitude, even deeper admiration. "She sounds like she was special."

"Yeah," he says quietly. "She was."

"That's who your first cookbook is dedicated to, isn't it?"

Alex peers up at me. And now I realize I'm busted.

I caved this past week and scoured The Bookshop for Alex's cookbooks, learning he's published two—first, *Come Viene, Viene*, the one Lauren gave me, which came out four years ago, and second, *A Tavola, Non S'invecchia*, which came out last year. I bought the second cookbook and, on my lunch break, flipped through both of them—more beautiful, mouthwatering photos (of food *and* Alex); more scribbled-in-the-margins notes.

He tips his head and says, "So you *do* know who I am."

"I *do*," I tell him. "You're my first celebrity best friend."

He groans, letting his head fall back. "I didn't say it like that."

I drop my voice and do my best Alex Bruscato: "*So you do know who I am.*"

Alex belly laughs. "Okay, I said it like that."

"I'm teasing," I tell him. "One hundred percent teasing. I knew what you meant. And I actually didn't know who you were, when we met."

"Okay, that's what I thought," he says.

"Why?"

Alex is suddenly deeply interested in his food. I lean in, enjoying this. The fun of talking, teasing, this innate comfort I feel around him to be playful. "Why, Alex?"

"People just . . ." He takes a bite, chews, swallows, then looks at me like he's hoping I'll have forgotten where we were in the conversation. I smile, eyebrows lifted, so it's clear I haven't. "They act a certain way, when they know. They're different."

I set my chin on my hands, laced together. "So you really *are* a celebrity."

"Eat your damn breakfast," he grumbles.

I laugh. "No, I'm serious. I've read six celebrity autobiographies, and they all said that—there's this feeling you get when people know. They change around you."

Alex shrugs. "I'm not a celebrity. I'm just . . . recognized in the foodie space. And when that damn cookbook took off—"

"Oh, the hardship! A bestseller!"

He stabs a piece of bacon from my plate and pops it in his mouth.

I gasp. "How could you?"

"Smartass tax," he explains.

I try to stab a piece of bacon from his plate, but his fork parries mine, pinning it to his plate. I drag away my empty fork, moping.

"Three sisters, Ted. I have a lot of practice defending my food."

"Three?" I sigh. "I always wanted sisters."

"No, you didn't."

I laugh. "I did! All I had was a brother eight years older than me who found me deeply exasperating. Probably because I was."

"You? Exasperating?" He shakes his head. "Nah."

"So rude!"

Alex grins, then takes another bite of his food. "So, just one brother for you?"

"Yep. Just three sisters for you?"

"Three is plenty. What about the rest of your family?"

I shift in my seat, poking at my food. "My parents are retired, moved to Columbus."

"*To* Columbus?" he asks.

"Yep."

"Who retires *to* Ohio?"

"Apparently, their post-retirement dream life was one surrounded by fields of corn. And both their families are there."

Alex is quiet, watching me, like he's waiting for me to say more about them. I don't.

"Getting the sense things aren't . . . great with your parents?" he finally hedges.

I shrug, trying to ignore the dull, familiar ache in my chest. "They're not great. But they aren't terrible, either. That's sort of it in a nutshell. We're just . . . not very close."

Alex nods. "Parent shit is hard."

I peer up, surprised by that. Alex so far has given me tight-knit, we-love-the-heck-out-of-each-other, big-happy-family vibes. Going by his knowing tone, maybe I was wrong. "Yeah, it is. Nothing about my upbringing was *bad*. It just . . . wasn't . . ."

"Good, either," he says.

I nod. "My parents were tired. I was an oopsie. My mom was my age when she had me, my dad was . . . well, your age. They thought they were done having babies, after my brother. Dad's was in car sales, and the commission life is stressful. He was either gone all weekend and I missed him, or he was home on weeknights and grumpy, and then I wondered who I'd been missing in the first place. Mom was a dedicated public-school teacher, and her students and her teaching were what she poured herself into. By the time she'd come home to me on weeknights or handle me on her own all weekend while dad had his big sales days, she didn't have much left. Neither of them did.

"To be fair to them, I think I was a handful. I talked a lot, asked a lot of questions, never slept in, never stayed put in my seat. I always asking for some new *something*—a toy, a game, an adventure, pushing for more than what was right in front of me. I didn't make it easy for them to . . ."

Love me, I think. "Enjoy my childhood," I tell him.

Alex gently knocks his knee with mine under the table. I glance his way but find it hard to meet his eyes, self-conscious.

I have no idea why I just told him all that. I never told Ethan all of that. It was too embarrassing, too humiliating, to admit that my parents never made me feel unloved, but they never made me feel particularly loved either, and for a long time I've yoyoed between whether that was my fault or theirs, but whosever fault it was, I knew it wasn't something you broadcast to the guy you hoped was falling in love with you. No matter who was at fault, it didn't paint me in a flattering light.

"You sound like Mia," Alex says.

There's such affection in his voice for his little girl, whom I know from her StoryTime visits to be a ball of curious, precocious, talkative, always-moving exuberance—a little girl who reminds me a lot of the little girl I used to be. A lump settles in my throat.

"Well," I tell him, "then may I recommend, if you get to the point where you've been poked and pleaded with so much you feel like you're about to lose your mind, that you shove a stack of good books in her hands."

Alex tips his head. "Is that what your parents did? Gave you books?"

"My mom did," I tell him. "I think she was at her wit's end. She took me to the library, told me that it was where I could find everything I was looking for, that reading a book was like getting to live another life. That sold me. I fell in love with reading. I mean, I became *obsessed*. I tore through the entire kids' section, then every middle-grade title at our local branch."

Alex smiles.

"I didn't love every book I read, but I loved even that experience. Knowing if one wasn't my favorite, I'd find one that was. And I did. I found *so many* favorites. And once I did, I started wanting to reread them, missing my favorite characters like they were friends who'd moved away, so eager to revisit their worlds, feel that magic again, and I'd have these meltdowns when I realized I'd returned a favorite book and couldn't reread it. I got so sad that I couldn't highlight my favorite passages, doodle hearts and thoughts throughout the best chapters. Dad figured out the solution to that part. He took me to the nearby secondhand bookstore, because we were always on a budget. I found so many of the ones I loved. And we bought so many books, we had to ask for boxes to carry them out. I'd never been so happy in my life."

His smile deepens. "And now you're a bookseller."

"Now I'm a bookseller," I tell him.

"Is that the dream for you?"

I'm taken aback by his question. I can't remember the last time someone asked me what my dream was, for myself, my future.

"Yes," I tell him. "And no."

He tips his head. "Go on."

"I used to dream about opening up my own bookstore when we lived in St. Louis. Well, it started in St. Louis. I got a job at a local indie bookstore there when my publishing job in New York didn't happen. Back when we were in college, Ethan told me he planned to build his consulting career for a few years in St. Louis, then take it to New York, which lined up perfectly with my professional hopes. While I waited for him, I got a job at the bookstore in St. Louis, and then he kept delaying the move to New York, until..."

"He said, 'Just kidding, let's go to Pittsburgh instead'?" Alex offers.

I nod.

Alex's jaw tightens. "And he had no qualms about crushing your career aspirations?"

"I wasn't too disappointed by the time he told me about Pittsburgh. I'd fallen in love with bookselling, and I'd started dreaming about how I could open up my own place one day. Then we moved to Pittsburgh, and I got a job at The Bookshop to build my network here, and instead of dreaming up my own store, I realized I wanted the one I was working in."

His eyebrows lift. "As in, you want to own it?"

"One day," I tell him. "If it works out. Fern, the owner, she's built something incredible in that store for the past thirty years, but... it's also frozen in time in some pretty major ways—. I have ideas, plans, tools for expanding it physically, online, through social media, with in-person and online events. The Bookshop is great as it is, but it could be incredible. There's so much that's possible that I'd love to do to make the store a knockout."

Alex smiles. "Sounds like that's the dream."

"Operative word being *dream*," I tell him. "For now. What about you?"

"My dream?" he asks.

"And your background, your family. Same as I told you."

Alex drains his water like he wishes it was something much stronger. "Well, I come from a dysfunctional Italian restaurant family. Lots of yelling. And good food. And big fights. And great music. Too much churchgoing. Not enough therapy."

"Ooh." I lean in. "I read a book about a family like that."

He leans in, too. "Sounds like the last kind of book I'd want to read."

"Tell me more."

While we finish our breakfast, he does. I hear all about Alex growing up in Luna's kitchen, napping on benches during prep hours when he was too young to be in school. Learning to cook from his parents, aunts, and uncles. Earning his place in the kitchen first in the grunt work of peeling, chopping, washing dishes. Then, finally throwing himself into cooking, driven to be the best, to make a place for himself among what sounds to be a very intense, very large extended family and three formidable sisters.

"For a long time, I hated it," he says, sitting back in his chair. Our plates are empty. My belly is deliciously full.

"Why?" I ask.

"Because it was so consuming, chaotic, volatile. I felt . . . trapped in a world I didn't ask to be brought up in." He peers down at his plate, arms folded across his chest, as he says, "But then I realized, I didn't have to feel trapped. Or even stay stuck. I could be so fucking good, I'd blow right out of there. And for a while I did. I made a name for myself, worked at some of the world's best restaurants. Then I came back here when my dad had a heart attack scare, met Jen through a friend of a friend. Stayed for Jen. Opened my restaurant, became obsessed with my restaurant. You know the rest. Broadly, at least."

"I do." I lean in, elbows on the table. "So after all that, what's the dream for you?"

He peers down at the table, runs his finger along a mark in the wood. "I'm not sure, honestly. In another life, in which I wasn't tethered to Pittsburgh, I'd leave, open up a new place in another city, not because Pittsburgh's a bad place; it's a great city in lots of ways—affordable-ish housing, already strong and growing stronger food scene, tons of green space, a culture of hard work and humble beginnings. It's just that staying here, when so many people here know me, Jen, my family, it's like the narrative's already written for me, which makes it tougher to envision how I can evolve, change, be inspired. It feels . . ."

"Limiting?" I offer.

He nods. "Yeah."

"I get that," I say quietly. "Do you . . . resent Mia for that? Tethering you to Pittsburgh?"

Alex smiles softly. "Nah. Staying here makes some parts of my life feel harder, but . . . she's worth it. She's worth everything."

My heart clutches. My throat feels suddenly thick. "So . . . with the life you have, the one you're living right now, what's the dream?"

"Right now." He tips his head, narrows his eyes. "I'd say the dream is be a good dad and crank out this final cookbook I'm contracted to write, then figure out if I can ever work at the restaurant again without losing myself to it." After a beat, he says, "I don't know if I'm capable of dreaming without going too big, too hard."

He slants a glance my way. "Don't celebrity tease me right now, but you really didn't know any of that? You didn't Google me?"

"I did, yes."

He seems to brace himself. "And?"

"And I remembered the internet can be a dumpster fire of misinformation. I typed in your name, then immediately closed out of the browser before I could read a thing."

"Why?" he asks.

"Because I didn't want to learn the internet version of Alex

Bruscato. I wanted to learn this one, the real one, in front of me. You." I lean in, wiggling my eyebrows. "Besides, it's not every day you become IRL besties with a chef prodigy."

He hollers, "I said no teasing!"

"You said no *celebrity* teasing. And did I say that word? Besides just now," I clarify.

He narrows his eyes at me, but he's fighting a smile.

I pick up his dish, then stack it on mine. "Come on, Chef. I'll clean up, and you can tell me more about your rise to fame."

*

I'm wrapping up the dishes while Alex wipes down his range when he asks me, "So how did you eventually figure out my . . . background?"

I smile over at him. "Your first cookbook, it was an apartment-warming gift from Lauren. The best friend who's moving," I remind him.

"Ouch." He slaps a hand over his heart. "That hurts."

"What?"

Alex throws the towel he was using over his shoulder and leans in. "*I'm* your best friend, remember? Your oldest, dearest friend?"

"Ah, of course. And my first love!"

"Damn right." He snaps the towel at my butt, making me yelp. Our eyes meet, wide with mutual shock.

"Shit," he says, "I'm so sorry. Why did I do that? I don't know. God, it's so weird. Sometimes I forget we barely know each other—"

I cackle. "Your face!"

He whips the towel at my butt again. "You're a menace!"

"I'm the menace? You just towel-spanked me! Twice!"

Alex throws the towel over his head. "I'm the menace."

"Maybe we're both menaces." I lean in and drag the towel off his face. And suddenly he's there, much closer than I realized, and I'm staring at him. Our mouths only a few inches apart. A swallow works down my throat.

Alex lifts a hand, sweeps his thumb across the edge of my mouth, along my bottom lip. Every nerve in my body crackles. "Egg yolk," he says. "You had some there."

Embarrassment sweeps through me. I scowl up at him. "You're *just* telling me?"

His gaze dances across my face. "Honestly, I didn't notice, until you were this close."

I realize I *am* close to him. Too close. I step back. Alex does, too.

For a moment, it's awkwardly silent in the kitchen. Alex takes the towel from my hand, sets it aside, then steps beside me with a clean towel, drying the pans I've washed.

"I feel like we were talking about something," he says. "But I've completely forgotten what that was."

"Before my egg-yolk face distracted you?" I say tartly.

He glances my way. "Are you embarrassed?"

"Obviously!"

"Why?"

"Because I had egg yolk on my face! And you had to wipe it off!"

"It was endearing," he says.

"Endearing." I roll my eyes. "Sure."

"Ted, can I inform you of something?"

"Inform away." I pick up the last pan in the sink, add a squirt of dish soap, and start scrubbing.

"I am a physically affectionate guy."

I fumble with the pan. "Not terribly Sagittarian of you."

"Cancer moon," he explains.

I peer up at him, genuinely surprised. "You are the first man I've ever met who knows this much about his star chart."

"Trust me, I didn't learn it voluntarily. My sister, Ari, went through an astrology phase. A *very* intense, impassioned phase."

I smile. "Intense and impassioned, huh? Real surprised she's related to you."

Alex looks at me steadily, undeterred by my teasing. "Physical affection is big for me. And it has been pretty scarce for . . . quite a while."

"I get that," I tell him quietly. "Me, too."

He holds my gaze for a beat longer. Heat creeps up my cheeks.

Slowly, he turns back to the pan, eyes on the towel as he dries it. "So something like egg yolk on your mouth, I don't see it how you do, as something to be embarrassed about. I'm too busy being greedy for the chance to touch you. Because it feels good. Because you seem to like it when I do, and that makes me feel good, too. So if it really is just embarrassment that makes you regret a moment like that, I hope you know, on my side of things, that's not where my mind is. But . . . if it's because me touching you makes you uncomfortable—"

"It doesn't," I blurt.

Alex glances my way, his expression tense, wary.

"It doesn't," I tell him, my voice calmer, meeting his eyes. "I do like it. It . . . feels good to me, too. Very good."

His gaze holds mine. "I haven't been friends with a woman in a long time. And you're really fucking good at putting me at ease." He clears his throat. "See inappropriate towel spanks from five minutes ago."

My heart's thudding in my chest.

"So," he continues, "just . . . please tell me, if at any point I'm going too far, touching too much, okay?"

I nod. "I will. And same, with me? I know I hug. A lot. And that can be . . . a lot."

Alex smiles slowly.

"What?" I ask.

He shrugs. "Just realizing, you *are* a bit of a cuddle bug."

I set the pan down in the sink with a *clunk*. "Based on what?"

"On how you were snuggled up to me when I stayed over at your place."

"You"—I point the scrubber at him—"were just as snuggled. You had your *arm* wrapped around me Wednesday night."

"You," he says smugly, "were *glued* to me Thursday morning."

Fresh heat slams through my body. "Not when you woke up."

His grin deepens. "Not when you *thought* I woke up."

My jaw drops. "You menace!"

"That's it!" He stabs a finger in the air. "That's what we were talking about!"

Surprising myself, I have this urge to *push*. To demand. Why did he pretend to be asleep? Why did he let me lie there, glued to him (I was absolutely glued to him), staring at him like that?

Oh god, does he know I was staring at him? That thought wipes away any interest I had in pushing the conversation further.

"We were talking about," he says, "being vengeful menaces."

I turn the spigot on, rinsing the pan. "Vengeful? Us?"

Alex darts a smiling glance my way as he picks up another pan and starts to dry it. "What I was thinking about, then—"

"Before or after the towel spanks?"

He nudges me with his shoulder. I set the rinsed pan on the

drying rack and turn off the water. "Sorry. You towel-spank when people are saucy. I get glib when they're sincere. It's a bad habit. Can I have a dish towel?"

"To spank me?"

"To dry the dishes," I say neatly.

"Fine," he sighs, then tosses me a towel. "I was just thinking, for how much getting back at our exes was the reason we started spending time together, we haven't spent much time talking or thinking about them. It's not what I expected, but . . . this feels way better. And I don't mean just the touching."

Touching. It's an innocuous word but not the way he says it. Goose bumps bloom across my skin. I try to hide the shiver that ripples through me by reaching for a pan, then starting to dry it.

"What were you expecting from our hangouts?" I ask. "Toxic vent sessions in which we'd vilify our exes and judge them for jumping into a new relationship before the ink had dried on our divorce decrees?"

"Hmm." He tips his head. "That *does* sound appealing."

I laugh. "Yeah, that's sort of what I'd expected, too. And I imagine a time will come for that. But for now . . ." I nudge his shoulder with mine. "I like this. It's nice, to just push them, the sadness, all of it, out of our heads, and feel . . . almost happy?"

"Happy-ish," he says.

I smile. "That," I tell him. "Happy-ish."

CHAPTER 16

THEN

August 9, two summers ago

"Were you not just telling me the other week," I say to Alex, "that you *hate* street biking?"

We're walking down the sidewalk leading to my apartment, under the cool comfort of shade cast by the tree tunnel overhead. I have Argos on his extendable leash, ten feet ahead of me, with Mia half riding her balance bike, half clutching his leash. She wanted to hold his leash herself, but Argos gets too excited about birds to be trusted not to take off if one shows up and send Mia and her balance bike flying off with him.

"I hate street biking because of the cars," Alex says, "which tend to drive not around cyclists but *at* them."

"Right," I say slowly, then sip my coffee. "And this cycling event you're talking about in city streets . . . *doesn't* involve cars?"

"Nope. That's the beauty of it, Ted." He peers over at me, his eyes shadowed by his ball cap's brim. "There are *no* cars. They close down parts of the city for a four-hour stretch to form a route, and anybody can bike through the streets."

"Huh." I smile. "That sounds fun."

"It is," he says. He has as swig of coffee from his cup. "I've been doing it with Mia since she was a toddler. You should come."

"If I have off work, or if I can get off, I'm in. When is it?"

"In an hour."

I balk. "An hour? Why are you just mentioning it?"

Alex tugs at his ball cap brim, then lifts it off, scraping back his hair with that hand, before he tugs it back on. "I forgot about it until this morning. Jen texted to ask if she could take Mia so *they* could do it." His jaw works. "Even though it's always been my thing with Mia. I asked Jen why she wanted that, when it's my weekend, and historically my thing, and she said, 'Ethan and I are going to ride. I thought it would be a good bonding opportunity for him to hook up her buggy to his bike and get a ride together.'"

"Oh, hell no."

"Right. First, because that's our thing, and second, she now rides a tag-along bike attached to mine, not a *buggy*."

He reaches into the bag he's holding in the same hand as his coffee cup and unearths a very wonderful-smelling pastry. "So," he says, "I asked you if you wanted to take a walk, picked up blackberry streusels, and decided I'd try to butter you up into going with us. Because . . . *they're* going to be there. Jen wants to get to ride along with Mia for part of it, at least, she said."

I lean in and bite off half the streusel he holds out, then say around my mouthful, "The pastry's great but superfluous. I was in the moment you suggested it involved outbiking our exes."

Alex frowns. "Did I suggest that?"

"No. But I have a hunch it's going to get competitive between us."

Alex pops the other half of the pastry in his mouth. "Nah, I don't think so."

*

We spot Ethan and Jen a block away, straddling their bikes, and suddenly, I have no idea why I said I'd do this.

It's one thing to logically understand that my ex is a self-preoccupied, self-absorbed manchild, and that he did me a favor in showing me that. It's another thing to truly feel that, down in my bones. In my heart. Looking at Ethan, I know I'm not there yet.

I don't miss him. I don't want him back. I'm not even jealous of Jen, that he wants her. I just . . . ache. This is the man that I spent a decade and a half of my life with, and I'll never get that time back. This is the man I grew up with, built a life with. And now, looking at him, he feels like a stranger.

It isn't, I realize, Ethan whom I've been missing, whom I'm aching for, as we draw closer, walking our bikes toward them. It's the peace, the confidence that I was where I was supposed to be, with the person I was meant for. I miss believing in that, trusting in it. It feels like there's a crater in my chest, still smoking from the impact of learning that lesson, a crater that, even when it cools, will leave me marked, changed forever. I will never look at love the way I used to. And maybe that's a good thing; but all I can think about is how scary that is, what that leaves me with—no confidence in recognizing what love *is*, only a handful of pain-riddled takeaways on what it *isn't*.

Alex snorts beside me, jolting me from my thoughts. I glance his way. "What is it?"

"Ethan. He looks like he's vacuum sealed himself into that getup."

I follow his line of sight to my ex, who's wearing one of his black cycling bib shorts over a gray sleeveless sweat-wicking crewneck. The ensemble, unpleasantly, leaves *nothing* to the imagination.

My stomach feels like lead. "I hated those bibs."

Alex peers my way, his amusement dissolving as he looks at me. I must be wearing everything I'm feeling on my face, because he clasps my fingertips, squeezing briefly. "Go ahead," he says.

I tear my gaze away from Ethan, meeting his eyes. "Go ahead and what?"

"Roast him," Alex says. "It'll feel good. You're too nice about him, Ted. And nobody can *actually* be that nice toward a tool bag like him, which means you're just burying it, and that is not good for you. So get it out." He leans in, drops his voice, his breath warm against my ear. "Fucking roast him."

"He looks like a Barnum and Bailey strongman who forgot his handlebar mustache," I blurt. "*And* his muscles."

Alex chuckles. "Good start. Keep going."

"Guys like him are the reason for evolution deniers—'two billion years, and this is all the further we got?'"

"Oh!" Alex nudges my shoulder with his, making me crack a smile. "On a roll now!"

"He," I say through gritted teeth, "is the human equivalent of menstrual cramps."

Alex whistles appreciatively. "As a brother to three sisters, I just want to say I recognize that roast for what is." He offers his hand for a high five. I meet it with a slap.

"What about you?" I ask Alex. "How you doing?"

Alex slants a glance at Jen, then back to me. He clears his throat, then says quietly, mindful of Mia, who's happily pedaling along, on her tag-along bike connected to the back of his. "It's different between us. I'm the one who fucked up."

I tip my head. We haven't talked about this—what exactly what went wrong in our marriages. It's been nice, avoiding it. But maybe it would feel even nicer, having gotten it out there.

"I was a workaholic," Alex says. "I acted like my first love was my kitchen, my restaurant, my career, rather than her. I hid *why* that was—because my pristine, perfectly run kitchen, my rising-star status, made me feel like I was in control, and I was desperate for that, because inside, I was spiraling out.

"When Jen told me that she was unhappy, that she didn't feel like I loved her, instead of telling her how much I was struggling, how poorly I was handling it, that it wasn't that I didn't want to love her, it was that loving her didn't give me the relief that being in the kitchen did, I pointed to every reason she *should* feel loved."

My chest aches.

"I fucked up," he says quietly. "And by the time I understood that, it was too late."

"Why?" I ask him. "Why too late?"

"Because," he says steadily, "she couldn't forgive me when I tried to fix it."

I can barely wrap my head around the concept of a husband who actually tries to fix your broken marriage. Ethan tapped out the second I raised the possibility that there *might* be something broken between us. And yet, when Jen's husband tried to fix it, that wasn't enough.

"I'm sorry," I say quietly.

He shrugs. This story is older to him than mine is. Less shocking, more familiar. I can tell there's pain he still carries, but the wound isn't raw like mine, doesn't sting how mine does every time I encounter Ethan or anyone whose story brushes against the pain of mine.

I stare at Jen, as that wound stings sharply. Unlike her, my husband quit. Didn't care enough even to try. And when hers did, it wasn't enough. It's hard not to judge that, to not want to grab her shoulders and shake her, and say, "At least he gave a shit!"

But maybe Jen's judging me the same way. Maybe, after hearing how Ethan tells it, she sees me as a hypercritical, ungrateful woman who couldn't be happy no matter what, who had to find *something* wrong, and Ethan had to save himself from my *toxic negativity*.

Maybe, in some way, Ethan was right; I could have been more grateful, made peace with what we had, rather than grieve and long for all that we didn't. Maybe Jen wasn't completely wrong to feel that her hurt ran so deep, her unwillingness to forgive was justified.

But maybe I was right, too, to want something other than a marriage that *was* disconnected and often hurtful, and a different man would have heard that for the plea it was to become close, been grateful for the chance for better—really, *any*—intimacy. Maybe Alex did everything he could to make it right when he could, poured all his heart into his work on healing, being vulnerable, repairing what was broken, and to someone else, that would have been more than enough to heal together.

Maybe, when it comes to telling the stories of our failed relationships, the wounds they inflicted, there are only unreliable narrators, too much hurt warping our perspectives, thwarting any chance to land on the truth of what went wrong.

Maybe, instead of asking, *What went wrong?* we should ask, *When did we stop telling the same story?* Maybe if we could try to figure out when the tugs of our experiences became so distanced, they tore that shared story apart into two stories whose plots couldn't be reconciled, conflicting characters as perpetrator and victim, irreconcilable portrayals of what hurt was premeditated and what was incidental, we'd actually get somewhere.

Because then it wouldn't be all about figuring out, blaming, or exonerating who was wrong or right. It would be about figuring out what kind of story you'd hoped to tell, the story that got away from you; what kind of journey you want to take as you pick yourself up and start to stumble down the road again, the story you want to find yourself in.

As we come to a stop in front of Ethan and Jen, I'm exhausted from everything that's been running through my brain.

Alex reaches out, sensing I've gone quiet, his fingers brushing mine.

"Hey," he says softly.

I peer over at him. "Hey."

He threads his fingers through mine, and in answer, I squeeze, holding his eyes.

"Mommy!" Mia yells.

We pull our hands away, drawn into the inevitable, what we've managed to avoid since the awkward exchange between the four of us on my old porch, what started all of this.

"Hi, baby!" Jen crouches to hug Mia, who runs toward her.

I am *not* jealous of Jen's fabulously ample, lifted derriere, accented by her spandex bike shorts and the deep squat she effortlessly completes to hug her daughter.

Self-conscious, I check the drawstring on my running shorts; the last thing I need is for them to, by contrast, slide down my nonexistent pancake ass.

Ethan throws me a glance, raking his gaze down my body. "You've lost weight," he says to me. "But then I guess that makes sense, since you're probably not eating much. You lost your personal chef, didn't you?"

"Did you lose yours, too, Ethan?" Alex asks. He dips a chin, nodding at Ethan's lean biceps. "Or have you always been that meager?"

Ethan's eyes flare.

I squeeze Alex's fingertips with mine, biting my lip. I don't subscribe to any one idea of what makes a man attractive, masculine, "man enough," and under any other circumstance, Alex giving Ethan hell for his lean physique would have left a bad taste in my mouth.

But this isn't any other circumstance. Ethan hit a nerve he's hit before, critiquing my body, reminding me of my uselessness in the kitchen. It was a low blow. Alex went just as low, defending me, and far from leaving a bad taste in my mouth, this revenge is *sweet*. Because I know Alex didn't do it for himself; he did it for *me*.

Thankfully, Jen and Mia haven't been tuned in to this, but as Jen stands with Mia, it's evident that there's tension between us.

Jen darts a nervous gaze at Ethan, then Alex, then me. "Nice... day for a bike ride," she offers.

"Very nice," I tell her.

"Glorious," Alex says dryly, as Mia launches herself toward him. He scoops her up, tossing her high, making her squeal.

Ethan's jaw clenches as he watches. Alex's arm muscles, as he tosses his forty-pound daughter up into the air, do *not* look meager.

Jen's watching the two of them, something pained in her expression, some ache I can't name. It makes me ache, too. Sadness, chased by a pinprick stab of jealousy.

"Well," Ethan says tersely, straddling his bike, "were we planning on actually getting a ride in?"

"Yes!" Mia says, taking his words, in that beautifully pure, endearing way kids have, completely literally. She leaps into a starfish stance, legs wide, hands wider and yells, "Let's gooooo!"

I jump into the same stance and join her, yelling, "Let's goooo!"

Mia shrieks with laughter.

Alex is smiling as he crouches, checking her helmet straps, helping Mia to steady herself on her tag-along bike seat. I try and fail not to stare at his thighs, as his shorts ride up enough to reveal a stark tan line, a dusting of dark hair, leg muscles flexing as he shifts in his crouch, then stands.

An ache curls through my body as I look at him, as I replay how quickly he came to my defense. I'm having very lusty, very unfriendlike thoughts about my *friend*.

Turning away, I pluck at my tank top and try to fan my well-on-their-way-to-tomato-red cheeks. My hair is frizzing out in response to the humidity in the air. My skin feels sticky. I already have boob sweat. Nice day for a bike ride, my butt.

"Ready?" Jen calls, leading us out onto the road.

Alex and I mount our bikes, then meet each other's eyes. "What do you say, Ted?" he asks. "Ready to kick their ass?"

A zing of pleasure snaps through me. I tear my gaze away and shout, "Ready!"

*

I have never been this close to death. My thighs tremble, my lungs are heaving. We're so close to the end of this wonderful, hellish, exhausting bike ride, and I am determined to win.

The route is a loop, the first half of which was an indeterminable climb through downtown, up into the Hill District, past the hockey arena. Ethan and Jen easily beat us up the hill, with my lackluster fitness and Alex hauling a kid weighing down the back of his bike. The second half, which is all downhill, is another story.

By the time we're back in Downtown's Market Square, we've caught up to them, Ethan looking smug, Alex fuming, Jen and I similarly winded but determined to keep pace with the guys.

Alex and I finally pull ahead on the downhill side of the bridge stretched across the Allegheny River, leading to our neighborhood, the North Side. As we rounded the bend of a small side street past the Clark Building, the last tiny hill leading up to our starting point, I know we're going to beat them.

We *have* to beat them.

Alex glances my way, eyes bright, a near maniacal gleam in them that I know I'm mirroring right back at him.

Then we face forward, lean into it, and fly up the hill.

As we crest the top, we turn onto the road leading toward the local community college and Gus and Yiayia's, the rainbow-umbrellaed snow-cone truck that was our meeting point, coming to a screeching halt seconds before Ethan and Jen soar up behind us.

I wobble off my bike. It takes three shaky tries to engage my kickstand.

Alex dismounts, too, and knocks down his kickstand, looking only slightly steadier than me. Mia hops off and races toward the snow-cone truck. "I want a large!" she bellows.

Alex and I follow after her, breathing heavily, wiping sweat from our faces.

"That," Alex says, "was a damn satisfying victory. A petty victory, but a satisfying one."

"Thankfully," I tell him between heaving breaths, "pettiness is our brand."

Alex laughs hard, straight from his belly, as we fall into the Gus and Yiayia's line, holding Mia's place while she stands right by the cart, eyeing the flavors.

We turn, facing each other, and suddenly Alex yanks me into a hug. I sink into it, plastering my sweaty body to his, squeezing him tight.

"That felt so good," he mutters.

I nod. "That felt *amazing*. At least, psychologically. My body says that it felt like death."

He laughs again, squeezing me to him, so nothing's between us. Hips pinned to hips, my breasts smashed against his chest, sweat-slick thighs sticking as his hands curl around my waist.

We both pull back after a moment, looking at each other, chests heaving, sweat dripping down our faces. Our eyes lock, and some unknowable force seems to tug us closer, closer, until our noses brush, until I can almost taste him, almost feel his lips brushing mine.

Heat coils through me. My nipples harden. A sweet ache throbs between my thighs. My tongue darts out, wetting my bottom lip, as Alex rakes his teeth over his.

We are dangerously close to an endorphin-soaked kiss.

"Where's Mia?" Jen asks.

We snap apart.

"Exploring her options, right by the cart," Alex says, turning enough to point to his daughter, exactly where he said she was.

Jen glances between us, once again, something written on her face that I can't place. Ethan saunters up to us, looking and sounding the least winded of all of us. "I thought that would be a bit more challenging," he says offhandedly, before taking a not-nearly-desperate-enough drink of water from his bottle. "I hardly broke a sweat."

Alex and I glance at each other—winded, flushed, soaked through with perspiration. I think with anyone else, Ethan's dismissive dig, his pointed reminder that we might have narrowly won the race but it cost us, that if he'd tried as hard as we had he probably would have beat us, would have crushed the euphoric joy of this moment.

But I'm not with anyone else. I'm with Alex. My petty vengeance coconspirator. Fellow gelato-gorger. Great hugger. Even better listener. *New York Times* games buddy. Honest and kind and in my corner. My friend.

Like they're nothing, like they're meaningless, Ethan's words slide off me, gone as quick as the rivulets of sweat sluicing down my body, evaporating in the pressing heat.

That is the real victory. Not the petty one. Not the one Ethan tried to undermine. The win he can't take away. The win I'm most proud of.

Eyes locked with Alex, I smile.

CHAPTER 17

NOW

August 3, first day of "vacation"

I can't see the ocean yet, but I can sense it. In the warm breeze wafting in through the car's open windows, different from the oppressive humid heat of Missouri, the summertime stormy mugginess of Western Pennsylvania—salt-sticky damp, the briny tang of fish and sea creatures that's almost pungent, almost off-putting, yet it makes me breathe deeper, draw it in, taste it on my tongue.

"Ted," Alex says quietly, hands on the wheel, eyes on the road. "You're seriously going to leave me hanging there?"

I lower *The Ministry of Time*, which I've been reading to him in a hushed voice for the past five and a half hours. "Didn't mean to," I tell him. "I just got my first whiff, and it distracted me."

"First whiff of what?" He rubs one eye with the heel of his hand, then reaches for the thermos of coffee we've been sharing since we pulled out of Pittsburgh in the nighttime darkness, a sleepy Mia buckled into her car seat, tucked in with blankets and her favorite lovey, a battered stuffed panda bear she delightfully named Polar Bear.

"The sea," I tell him, watching Alex take a deep gulp of coffee.

He briefly glances my way, then back to the road, fumbling with the thermos as he tries to wedge it into the cupholder. I reach for the thermos, taking over the task, and our fingers brush. I try to push away the pleasure of that sensation, the heat of his skin, the calluses I graze as I pull back, but Alex catches my hand and clasps it, settling it on the console armrest between us.

"I'm still pissed he never brought you here," Alex says, his thumb sweeping over my hand. "But I'm happy I get to be the one who does. That I'll be there when you see the ocean for the first time."

I stare at him, my throat thick, and squeeze his hand. "I was going to say the same thing."

*

We've beaten Ethan and Jen to the house, judging by the empty gravel lot we pull into. We don't give the house a second glance. The white cedar shingle bungalow is the least compelling feature of this "vacation." It's Ethan's; it was never mine, and it never will be. That could haunt me, if I were to let it, but I won't. This week isn't going to yank me back into the pains of the past. I'm going to keep my gaze on what's ahead.

I pop out of the car as Alex scoops up a sleepy Mia from the back, tucking her head on his shoulder, her legs draped down his torso, her feet swinging past his hips. She's getting so big, the last traces of baby-ness that clung to her round cheeks and dimpled thighs when I first met her suddenly gone, stretched out into a knobby-kneed, long-legged six-year-old snoring on Alex's shoulder. I wrap the blanket around her, pinning it beneath Alex's arm, and on her other side, beneath Mia's, a little quilted cocoon.

Alex smiles down at me, purple smudges of fatigue shadowed beneath his eyes. He looks a little rumpled, a little weary, a little like the man I met two years ago. But mostly, he looks like the man I know now. The man more familiar to me than anyone else. There's a light burning in his blue-flame eyes now, a warmth in his smile that wasn't there, as the sea breeze whips his dark hair and he whispers, "Ready?"

I nod, then shake my head. I tell him, hushed and hoarse from hours of reading aloud, "I'm nervous."

He tips his head. "Why, Ted?"

"Because what if it isn't like what I've imagined? What if I don't feel the way I have when I've been there in my books? What if—"

"Ted." Alex smiles softly, his fingertips grazing my collarbone, then my neck, whispering along my jaw, as he sweeps my frizzy curls from my face and tucks them behind my ear, safe from the wind. "It won't be like what you've imagined. And it won't feel the way it has in books. But that's a good thing. Because that means, now, it's *real*."

He curls an arm around my shoulder, drawing me close. "It doesn't belong to someone else's words, someone else's story anymore. It gets to be yours." He presses a soft kiss to my hair and says, "That's why it'll be even better."

I curl my arm around his waist, blinking back tears.

"I love you," I whisper.

He stares down at me, his eyes searching mine. "I love you, too."

I love him. Those words echo inside me, as powerful as the ocean's roar on the other side of the dunes, the wind whistling it as it carries the gulls overhead. The truth glows in my heart, like the sun creeping up on the horizon, brightening each second, illuminating everything.

I shut my eyes, as it washes over me, what I've been running from for so long.

I can wrap my love for Alex in *friendship*, *closeness*, *platonic affection*, in whatever *safe* name I want, but when all the pretty paper, tidy folds, smooth corners, sturdy tape is ripped away, what's beneath it is still what's beneath it, and it is undeniable: I love Alex, and I love him in a way that I know all too well, it's the kind of love that is anything but safe.

For two years, I've held that love in the same place I've held my ache to see the ocean, in the security of an idea, a vivid theoretical, in the safety, the secrecy of my mind.

But Alex is right. That's gone now. All that's left is what I'm both dreading and desperate for. Because it's unknown. Because it's risky.

Because it's *real*.

I peer up at him as our gazes hold. Alex searches my eyes, and I wonder if he sees it, what's happened inside me, the ripped remnants of my fear scattered around me; what's left, what's been beneath it for so long, finally exposed to the elements, exquisite and terrifying.

I set my hand on his heart and feel it pounding beneath my palm. "I'm ready," I tell him.

For a moment, he keeps staring at me, something fierce infusing his expression, his touch. But then he eases his grip, tears his gaze away toward the ocean, and says, "Then let's go."

We cross the dunes, squinting into the sunrise, the light glancing sharply off the water.

My breath catches as I get my first glimpse. I squeeze Alex's hand as he stands, quiet beside me, keeping vigil as I drink it in.

My heart unfurls and stretches as wide as the ocean, spilled out in every direction, a shimmering blanket whose colors feel familiar, woven from what I know—woodsmoke and rock moss, the steely blue of a thunderstorm sky. And yet it's so much more. More than what I wished for, wondered, feared, more than what I built up in my mind from pieces of what I knew to a composite of what I didn't.

Alex's thumb sweeps across my hand, grounding me to the moment. The sea air wrapped around me. The waves' *crash* and *draw*, roaring in my ears. My heart pounding in my chest, longing like a pulse thundering through me, filled with love that I finally understand isn't a composite, either; isn't built from the shattered fragments of my past, the charred remains of everything that went wrong, that could collapse around me again.

Everything, in that moment, is devastatingly vast and mysterious and beautiful, like nothing else I've ever known. Because it's real.

Alex is right. It's *better*.

CHAPTER 18

NOW

August 3, first day of "vacation"

We can't get into the house until Jen and Ethan are here, so while we wait, I soak up the ocean view with Mia, who's happy digging in the sand while Alex does some self-admitted snooping around the property.

The moment Jen and Ethan pull in, Mia sprints toward their car.

Alex turns toward me. "What do you say we get out of here?"

I laugh. "A great way to kick off our 'two-family' vacation."

"Mia's happy," he says, nodding toward the car, which Jen has just stepped out of, scooping Mia into her arms. "That's what matters."

Jen waves at us. We wave back.

"How about this, Ted." Alex steps closer, smiling down at me. I turn my hands into fists so I won't reach for him. "I'll make up an excuse for us. We have to dash into town, grab groceries for dinner tonight."

I glance over at the car again as Ethan steps out, in one of his preppy pink polos. Just the sight of him nauseates me. "I can work with that."

"Great," he says, already tugging me by the elbow around to the other side of the house.

"Where are we going? The car's that way."

"I thought," Alex says, "we'd go for a little bike ride."

I gasp. "Alex Bruscato, *voluntarily* street biking?"

He throws me that smile that's just for me—annoyance tangled with affection. "Bethany Beach, I'll have you know, is a very bike-friendly town."

*

I thought I loved city biking. Now I know what I love best is beach-town biking.

A bracing sea breeze snaps through my hair, the sun pouring down on us.

"Look at us," I call over my shoulder, "biking like pros!"

Alex grunts but says nothing else. He's too busy white-knuckling his bike handles and glaring down every driver on the road.

"Alex," I yell against the deliciously bracing wind, "relax! These bike lanes are wider than the roads back home! You can ride a bike without treating these cars like they're assassins until proven innocent."

Alex hollers, "There is not a strong enough Xanax in the world for that to ever happen!" before he flips off the car passing us and yells a colorful Italian insult in its direction.

To be fair to Alex, the driver steered their car right to the edge of the bike lane. To be fair to the driver, they would have had to give us so much space they'd be driving into oncoming traffic to satisfy Alex, and even then, he still might have threatened to make meatballs out of them.

"This was your idea, remember!" I call over my shoulder.

"I thought," he yells, "it wouldn't still feel like we were gambling with our lives!"

We come to a pause at an intersection as opposing traffic cruises by, Alex rolling to a stop beside me. "I'm just teasing you," I tell him. "We can turn back and get the car."

He throws me an exasperated sidelong glance. "I'll be fine, Ted. I can do hard things."

"I know you can. But some things can feel too hard, and that's okay,. For instance, I cannot drive to a big box, everything-under-one-roof store, you know, like the massive chains that stock your cookbooks that you refuse to look at and sign. It's too hard."

Alex mutters something under his breath as he reaches for his water bottle, then takes a long drink.

"Thank you for asking," I tell him. "I would love to explain. So, to start, I acknowledge that, in plenty of ways, I am a weird woman." I catch a small grin tugging at his mouth as he bends and shoves his water bottle back in its holder. "But when it comes to shopping," I tell him, "I'm as basic as it gets. You know why I never drive Old Reliable when shopping?"

Alex leans over his handlebars, placing his sweaty forearms right in front of me. "Because," he says, "every ride in *Old Reliable* could be its last, and you'd sooner read a pirated e-book than say goodbye to your somehow-still-running 1997 Buick Regal."

My eyes trail across his sun-goldened, sweaty skin. He's sweaty everywhere. Forearms, biceps, throat, all of it dripping. Alex straightens, lifting his shirt at the collar, using it to wipe sweat from his eyes, which exposes at *most* two inches of tan, taut skin at his stomach, yet a bolt of heat crackles through me.

I tear my gaze away, squinting against the sun. Hopefully, it looks like I'm watching the traffic light instead of trying to briefly blind myself so I can't ogle him anymore.

"First of all," I say. My voice comes out a high-pitched squeak. I clear my throat and try again. "I would *never* read a pirated e-book. I would read an e-galley provided by the publisher, or a legally borrowed library copy. Second of all, I no longer drive Old Reliable to go shopping because I learned the hard way that when I know I have four passenger seats' and a trunk's worth of space, I walk in for bodywash, seltzer, and a new pair of sunglasses, and walk out having bought half the store."

He tips his head. "What do you *buy*?"

"Yummy-smelling candles. More pajamas that I *don't* need. Cute but overpriced sweatshirts. And sweatpants. And slippers. Nail polish that's the slightest shade different from a color I already have but somehow cannot leave behind. Sour Patch. More Sour Patch. Seasonally scented hand soaps. Too many boxes of fruit tea. More toys that Argos will immediately destroy . . . Don't make me keep going."

Alex's mouth tips into a grin. "Sounds fun."

"It is not," I tell him. "It's chaos. And it's terrifying to lose all grip on my self-control. Because after the thrill of impulse shopping, regret hits me like a receipt longer than my inseam. And I have *long* legs."

His grin deepens. "I'm aware." He wraps his finger around the handlebars and leans in, holding my eyes. "I still think, deep down, when you've let loose, you didn't actually regret it, Ted. I think you just *told* yourself that you should."

My heart thuds in my chest. I don't know what we're talking about anymore—the dicey times in our friendship I've gone Full Wild Thea, or my two hundred dollar impulse shopping sprees.

"Well." I straighten my shoulders. "Regret it, I did!"

Why I said it like Yoda is beyond me. Alex bites his cheek, fighting a smile. He looks like he's wondering the same thing.

Thankfully, the light turns green, giving me a swift exit from that land mine of a conversation.

"A shit liar, you are!" Alex calls.

"A flat tire?" I yell back. "Not me!"

*

Alex grabs a few groceries at the market in town to give our fib some backing, and then I drag him to where I really want to go—the local indie bookstore.

As the door falls shut behind us, Alex says, "Any word from Fern?"

I peer over at him. "She said we'd talk after I was back."

He's quiet for a moment as we wander around the table display of new releases. "You could follow up before that," he says.

I straighten a crooked book on its stack. "That would be pushy."

He shrugs. "Maybe she wants you to push."

"Why would she want that when she told me we'd talk when I came back?" I hear the defensiveness creeping into my voice, but I can't help it. Just giving her the proposal in the first place, I've already stepped so far out of my comfort zone. Now Alex wants me to go even further?

"Because maybe she's testing you." Alex picks up a book, skimming the back. "That's what I would do when someone told me they wanted to buy into my business—I'd want to know that they were really invested, that they were hungry for it."

I frown. "You would?"

Alex sets the book down and meets my eyes. "When it comes to relationships, passionate people want to see passion in others."

I blink, my heart starting to beat double time. "Professionally?"

"Of course. And personally," he adds, drifting toward the kids' section. "Before you ask, I'm *not* going down the cookbook aisle."

I catch up to him, spin around, and give him sad-puppy eyes. "But I'm *passionate* about my best friend seeing his cookbooks in person."

He comes to a stop, eyebrow arched, and says, unmoved. "No."

"Pleeeease." I lean in, hands clasped, and throw in a hearty bottom-lip-out pout. "I just want to walk by and look at them. If you do that much, I'll consider calling Fern while we're on vacation to follow up on my business proposal."

He hesitates for a second, the sighs heavily. "Fine."

I beeline to the cookbook aisle, find Alex's books on an eye-level shelf, and silently scream. "It never gets old."

He rakes a hand through his hair and tugs. "Okay, we saw them. Let's go."

"Just give me a minute." I straighten out the copies, making sure they look their best.

"Ted." He sounds exasperated. And also, just a little endeared by my antics. It makes me smile. This is Alex and Thea solid ground.

"One last adjustment," I tell him, scooching his second cookbook half an inch to the right. "All set."

"Great," he says, gripping me by the hand, "Now let's go—"

"Alex?" a voice calls from the other end of the aisle.

We both spin around, facing a woman in a sage-green romper and coordinated Birkenstocks walking briskly toward us. Long brown hair streaked with subtle sun-kissed highlights, a heart-shaped face, kind blue-green eyes. The closer she gets, the prettier she is.

Alex drops my hand. It shouldn't sting, but it does.

"Andi?" he says, sounding genuinely surprised. *Pleasantly* surprised. "What are you doing here?"

"I'm here with the kids! Our annual beach vacation. What about you?"

"Same," Alex says. "On vacation with Mia." He's conveniently left out being here with Ethan and Jen. And me.

"What a small world." Andi flashes Alex a megawatt smile. Alex smiles back.

My gaze snaps to her bare ring finger, the trace of a tan line where a ring used to live. Fear wriggles through my heart. There's a warmth, a familiarity between them. And with Andi's ring-free finger, there's nothing stopping it from becoming *more*.

Their conversation seems to fade as my heart pounds in my ears. The chiding voice of reason in my head reminds me, *This was inevitable. He's never been yours to keep.*

When we made our friendship pact, rationally, I accepted that, eventually, Alex would fall for someone, and I was going to have to smile my way through it. Or, if I couldn't, pack up and move. Probably out of the country. Brush up on my German, push books at an indie store in Köln.

Not a viable solution anymore. Not if Fern says yes to my business proposal, if The Bookshop isn't just hers anymore but ours, and one day, when she's ready to sell her half of the ownership to me, mine to love and grow for a very long time.

Not when I love Alex and Mia and this life I've built as deeply, wildly, and fully as I do. Shock slams through me.

Even before I faced what I want—who I want, I'd already anchored myself to Pittsburgh. In my business proposal, my book club, my promises to Mr. Fleischer about the genre for next month's pick, my plan for this fall with Lauren to take her to Alex's restaurant. I *want* to anchor myself there. To the life I've built—and at the heart of that life is Alex. What would I do if I lost him to someone else?

It's always been theoretical—a far-off terrible *one day* that I pushed away, told myself I'd deal with when that day came. Otherwise, I'd make myself sick. But now, it's horribly real.

I stand rooted beside him, watching Andi and Alex beam at each other, battling the urge to clasp his hand and yell, *Mine!*

"Thea." Alex's voice wrenches me from my spiraling thoughts. He turns toward me, and says, "This is Andi."

"Hi," she says warmly.

I shove down my possessive thoughts and tell her just as warmly, "Great to meet you."

"Same!" Her smile deepens, its wattage somehow doubling. "*So* great to put a face to a name—I've heard *so* many wonderful things about you."

That takes me by surprise. "Really?"

Alex says quickly, "Andi is Marlowe's mom."

My smile holds, but as everything slots into place, it feels like a rictus on my face. Marlowe is Mia's kindergarten best friend. Mia spends a lot of time with Marlowe. For many of those playdates, Alex and Andi have probably shared conversation over drop-off and pickup; talked and gotten to know each other while the kids ran around the playground; spent time together at Marlowe's birthday party this past winter at the ice rink, where Alex said he met a few "not totally annoying parents," which meant he actually really liked them.

I see how it could all unfold from here. Grabbing coffee after the kids are in school, exchanging numbers, going on a no-kids-night date—

I blink, stopping myself. "Marlowe!" I say brightly, hoping I haven't taken too long to respond. "She's such sweetie."

"Aw, thank you." Andi squints a smile. Even her eye crinkles are cute. "I love her and Mia's friendship. They're two peas in a pod. Which, speaking of *peas*," she says, reaching past Alex toward the shelf that holds his books. "I've heard a certain *someone's* first cookbook has a pasta with peas recipe that will entice even my picky I-hate-peas eaters. I came here just for it." She throws a guilty glance at her heaping basket of books and games, and grimaces, gorgeous even in her self-deprecation. "Not that you can tell. Local bookstores are my Achilles' heel!"

Crap. I think I like her.

"You really don't need to buy it," Alex tells her, looking pained. "I have an obscene number of copies sitting at home. My publisher sends them to me, and I don't know what the hell to do with them. Let me bring you one, next time Mia and Marlowe have a playdate."

Andi hesitates, still hovering at the shelf. She drops her hand. "Are you *sure*?"

"Absolutely," Alex says.

She bites her lip. "Well, only if you promise to sign it for me."

A stripe of red creeps along Alex's cheek. He's standing in profile to me, but I know his other cheek is turning red, too. My stomach sinks. She made him *blush*. It takes a lot to make Alex blush—I've seen it happen twice in our entire friendship.

"Consider it done," he says.

Andi flashes that megawatt smile his way again and clasps his wrist. "You're the *best*, Alex. Thank you!"

"No problem," he says.

Andi takes a step back, reaching for her cart. "Well, I better get out of here, before I do any more damage."

"The struggle is real," I concede.

She smiles my way. "It was so great to meet you, Thea, and great to see you, Alex! Text me! We should totally get the kids together while we're here."

"For sure," he says.

"Bye!" she calls.

We both watch her brisk exit toward the cashier. I turn toward Alex, whose gaze has darted up to the ceiling. "Inspecting the fluorescents?" I ask.

"Yep," he says, without missing a beat. "Trying to figure out why they make Mia have to drop a deuce every time."

A laugh jumps out of me. "I want to ask how you came to this conclusion that the fluorescents are at fault, but I also don't know if I *want* to know the answer."

"You don't," he says, then glances down at me. "If you're done giving me that smug smile, I'd like you to buy whatever book you want so we can get out of here."

"Smug?" I blink. "Me?"

"Smug. You." He clasps my hand again, but this time, he

threads our fingers together. Pleasure and pain twist through me. I love when he does this. I don't want to give it up. I don't want there to be someone else whose hand he holds.

My heart's racing. Sweat pricks my skin.

"You okay, Ted?" he asks. He knows me too well. Alex can spot my panic from a mile away.

I squeeze his hand in mine. "I'm fine. Just thinking, maybe we should swing by the sunglasses first and grab you a pair, so you can shop incognito. Seeing how much you blush you get when accosted by a fan."

"Ha!" he says loudly. "You're! So! Funny!"

I smile wide. "Oh, I know."

Alex rolls his eyes. "Come on, smart-ass. Let's get your book and get out of here."

"No sunglasses, really?" I ask. "Not even to combat the fluorescents?"

He peers down at me with that familiar irked but delighted smile. "Unlike Mia," he says, "the fluorescents don't have that impact on me." Then, after a beat, as we wander out of the cookbook aisle, "Well, at least not since I hit middle school."

*

I'm looking both ways, leading us as we ease out into the bike lane, when Alex says, "So are you really okay with this weird, likely beachfront wedding for Ethan and Jen happening? Are you okay with the idea of them getting married?"

"I am," I tell him. "Why?"

"Beyond the obvious, that it's awkward and manipulative for them to trick us into attending and thus supporting it?" He's quiet for a moment, then says, "Because maybe it . . . kicked up feelings for you."

I slam on my brakes.

Alex swerves around me. "Jesus, Ted!"

"Sorry! Come on, let's pull over." I walk my bike next to him, and we both walk our bikes up onto the sidewalk, then past it, to a stretch of grass on the other side, beneath the shade of a tree. I set my hands on my hips, straddling my bike. "Alex, are you seriously asking me if I still have feelings for Ethan?"

Alex scrubs his face with both hands. "Yes. No. I don't know. Not like, *feelings* feelings, just . . . feelings about him, you know, getting married again."

I scrunch up my nose. "No. I don't have feelings for Ethan, at least, not any positive ones. Those are long gone . . ." I peer out toward the water just a few blocks away, beyond the dunes, and remember the sun glinting off of it, the incessant wind curling through my hair. I take a deep breath. "The only thing I feel is . . . concern. For Mia and Jen. Because nothing I've seen from Ethan the past two years makes me think he is any better of a man than he was when I was married to him. Jen's saddling herself with that. And Mia . . . she's going to grow up seeing that. Seeing her mom love someone who acts that way. You can't be happy about that, either."

Alex nods, eyes down on the ground, hands planted on his hips. "I'm not. But there's nothing I can do about it."

I know how deeply that has to pain Alex, how hard he's struggled and worked to learn how to cope with the parts of life that he can't control. I can only imagine how difficult that surrender is when it comes to his child.

I tip my face toward the wind as it picks up, a soothing juxtaposition to the hot sun beating down on us. "Maybe," I tell Alex, "hopefully, he's changed. Maybe he's become somebody who deserves them both. I hope so."

Alex's jaw tightens. "I still want to shove my fist down his throat every time I see him, so I don't think so."

I laugh. "You're always going to want to shove your fist down his throat."

"Because he hurt you," Alex says. "Because he didn't even try to do better by you. And you deserved that, Ted. You deserved his very fucking best, even if it turned out to be too late."

Alex glances out toward the ocean, silent for a moment, before he says, "Sometimes, I tell myself, I have no place to judge Ethan, to hate his guts for what he did. I fucked up in my marriage, too. It doesn't matter that Jen and I were never going to work in the long run; I still regret that I hurt her, when I didn't fix my shit fast enough, that I made it impossible for us to end well.

"I wish I could say I never hurt her the way Ethan hurt you, but I can't. What I can say, though, is that when I realized what I'd done, when I finally pulled my head out of my ass and got help and listened to Jen, I tried to make it right. I fucking fought for us. And that, right there, is the point at which I tell myself, I have every right to judge and hate Ethan, because that's the ground I have to stand on, that he doesn't—you deserved to be fought for, Ted, to be brave for. And he fucking blew it."

Tears streak down my cheeks, but I'm smiling. "I love you."

I say it how I always have, but it doesn't *feel* how it always has. It feels the way it did just an hour ago, on the beach, strangely wild and wonderfully surreal, like there was a muzzle on my heart that's vanished , and now, finally the truth has broken through. A wild, untamed creature released from captivity after so long, it doesn't quite know what to do with its freedom.

Alex leans toward me, tucking a curl behind my ear, beneath my helmet strap. "I love you, too, Ted."

Thea gazed at Alex, lost in him. His fingertips as they grazed her throat. His eyes locked with hers. The heat and scent of him, the familiarity of his old Buccos shirt and black basketball shorts. The mystery of everything beneath that, hard, and, firm, and warm, divots and muscles, scars and birthmarks. She wanted to touch them, see them, learn them. She wanted to tear off her clothes and show him every mystery scattered across her skin and beneath it, in her heart, her mind.

She wanted to kiss him so badly, she could barely stand it.

My phone buzzes in my pocket, startling me from my reverie. I pull it out unsteadily, peering down at the screen, then smile.

Alex sighs. "What does Lawrence want."

"How did you . . ." I frown up at him. "How did you know it's Lauren."

"You have a specific smile for her. Which, pettily, I resent."

Mr. Fleischer's words rattle through my brain. *He's wildly jealous of her. He's jealous of anyone he thinks gets more of you than he does.*

I've always told myself Alex is being playful when it comes to the way he gripes about Lauren. I know he loves that I have her friendship, because he sees how happy she makes me.

But . . . what if Alex gets jealous, too? What if he feels about Lauren the way I felt around Andi? If I were him, I'd have lost my mind by now.

Alex leans in, looking genuinely concerned now. "Everything okay?"

I peer down at Lauren's text. ANY WORD FROM FERN GULLEY? If not, call her!! Tell her she'd be a schmuck not to say yes to you!

I pocket my phone and sigh. "Everything's fine. Just Lo telling me the same thing you did, about reaching out to Fern."

Now it's Alex's turn to look smug. "I like Lawrence when she agrees with me."

"Of course you do."

Alex grins, then suddenly steps onto his pedals and rolls out into the bike lane.

"Last one home has to make lunch!" he yells.

As un-Alex as he could ever be, he takes off into the bike lane, sending a thrill through me.

CHAPTER 19

THEN

August 16, two summers ago

I have three missed calls from my mom, but no texts, which means it's not urgent, but it is uncommon enough to put me on edge. I'm annoyed that I'm distracted by this, that she can call a few times, not leave a voicemail, and still tug on my heart, thread it with worry, despite how little connection we share.

The last thing I want to be is distracted tonight. I want to be fully present. Even though tonight is bittersweet.

"Hot Chef did this," Lauren says over her menu. "Didn't he?"

I smile at her from across our two-top at Savoureux, shrugging. "What can I say? I've got friends in high places."

She shakes her head. "Of all people to befriend a culinary star, Our Lady of Chef Boyardee."

"Listen here. I don't *love* eating garbage processed food. I just have to sometimes, so I don't shrivel into dust."

"You could," she throws out, "do this thing called 'learn to cook'?"

I glare at her. "I'm aware."

Lauren beams. "I'm teasing."

"Kind of," I tell her.

"Kind of," she admits.

"Sort of like you were 'joking' about dragging me into going on runs, then you actually regularly dragged me into going on runs. Or when you were 'just playing' about giving me nearly all of your furniture when you moved?"

Lauren breaks first, laughing hard, her chin tucked to her chest, but I'm close behind her, head thrown back, elbows on the table, manners be damned, trying and failing not to snort.

As our laughter fades, the mood turns somber for the first time since we sat down to dinner—her goodbye dinner, before she flies out tomorrow to her first consulting job in Chicago, until the next client takes her somewhere else.

Over the past week, Lauren's condo has been emptied, too much of its beautiful furnishings and art foisted on me, sticking out like swanky sore thumbs in my dingy shoebox apartment, a few treasures put into storage, left to wait for the day when Lauren's job isn't constant travel.

And now, tonight, on our last French Wine and Fried Food Friday until who knows when, it's time to say goodbye.

I've been trying to stay upbeat, and Lauren has been, too. But we both know what's coming, and the weight of that can't be entirely ignored.

"I've been pushy," she admits. "I know I've heckled you about the shit you eat. And I dragged you on runs. And I foisted a lot of furniture on you."

"A *lot*," I agree. "I'm going to have to plastic wrap it all so Argos doesn't destroy it."

"Ah, he can fuck it up. I don't care. I don't want it back—I told you that. It'll be out of style by the time I own a home or condo again, anyway."

"Then I graciously accept your generous gift of someday-unfashionable furniture, Lo."

She smiles, but it's strained. "I just want you to be okay."

"I'll be *fine*, Mom." I roll my eyes like a moody teenager.

It makes Lauren's smile deepen before it fades. "I'm not mothering you. I'm best-friending you."

"Well," I tell her, "remember I have another BFF food snob now. So don't worry, okay? He'll already just as pushy as you about making sure I periodically eat better fare than SpaghettiOs and Lean Cuisines."

Her mouth twists. "That's good."

I clasp her hand across the table and squeeze. "He'll never be you."

She peers up. "And I'll never be him."

I pull my hand away slowly. "That's . . . true. But I'm not sure what it means."

"I know, Thea." She smiles. "And now that I'm about to get out of here and we are solid in our friendship, I'll illuminate you. The first day we met, and I asked if you wanted to grab a glass of wine?"

I nod.

She leans in. "I was hitting on you."

I grip the table like the world just tipped sideways. "Oh my god."

Lauren sets her chin on her interlaced hands, batting her long dark eyelashes. "Mm-hmm."

"Oh my god," I say again. "How did I miss that?"

"Well, sweets, it probably has something to do with what I figured out five minutes into our wine meetup—that you are extremely heterosexual. It didn't even occur to you that I'd see you that way because *you* didn't see *me* that way."

I set my hands on either side of my face, full-on *Home Alone*. "I feel like a jerk!"

"Don't," Lauren says. "I wasn't hurt at all or even particularly surprised. I had meager hopes—with your worn-down bronze Birkenstocks, mustard-yellow stretchy overalls, wild hair, and 'I like everybody' energy—that you might be a delightfully chaotic bisexual, but it turned out you were just a delightfully chaotic *straight*."

"Lauren," I say between my self-imposed squished cheeks. "This is so embarrassing."

"Why?" she asks. She's smiling, completely unflustered. I couldn't feel more flustered.

"Because I might have hurt you—"

"I just told you that you didn't," she says patiently.

"Yeah, but I wasn't *aware*. Why wasn't I aware of that?"

"Listen, I've been around enough to learn that there are some people don't pick up on the cues that other people are attracted to them," Lauren says. "It's nothing to be ashamed, of Thea. Honestly, it's endearing. Also, very badass. Think of all the broken hearts you've left in your wake and you never even knew!"

"I need a drink." I glance around. "Can we get some more wine? What kind of service is this?"

"The kind that isn't rushed," Lauren tells me, "and which starts with a small complimentary pour of blanc de blancs, which is lovely by the way."

Wistfully, I watch Lauren sip the last of hers in its delicate glass flute. Mine's long gone. I drained it the moment our server brought it by.

I sigh, meeting her eyes again. "I feel bad, Lo."

"Thea, please don't." She sets down the flute. "I told you because I wanted it to be out there to be put behind us. And so you'd understand that, while I've known you long enough to recognize you and I would be a *terrible* romantic pairing—"

"*Terrible*? I'm a little hurt," I tease.

She levels me with an *I'll indulge your nonsense* look. "Thea. I'm a controlling, neurotic, hypercritical, vain, deeply opinionated woman, and you are literally none of those things, besides a woman. We wouldn't have lasted a week."

"Okay, fine," I sigh. "You're right."

"I always am," she says. "What I keep trying to get at is that this new BFF of yours . . . I'm not sure I'm ever going to be one hundred percent happy about him. Even if he is the Hot Chef who pulled strings and used his in to get us this reservation before I left. Because, doomed romantic potential aside, Thea, I love you so much. And you've been my number one since the day I met you."

My vision turns blurry as tears fill my eyes. "Dammit, Lo." I take a slow breath, trying to steady my voice. "You've been my number one, too."

She smiles as she reaches across the table, her shiny red nail polish, the delicate gold rings on her tan fingers, glinting in the candlelight. I take her hand and squeeze.

"Love you, too," I tell her.

A bottle of blanc de blancs settles on the table beside us, and our hands come apart as we ease back into our seats. We peer up at our server, perplexed.

He smiles. "From Chef, on the house," he explains, drawing the cork out of the bottle with a cheery pop. "Chef said to tell you she's glad to have you here and please come back any night; a table will always be available. Any friend of Chef Alex's is a friend of hers."

Lauren's eyes roll up to the ceiling as he fills her flute, then mine. "Of course there'll be an always-open table," she mutters, "now that I'm *leaving*."

"All the more reason for you to come back and visit." I lift my flute and tell her, "Cheers to wishes coming true . . . better late than never?"

Lauren sighs as she clinks her flute with mine. "That goddamn Hot Chef."

*

Our meal is divine, at least by my humble standards. What makes me happiest is that Lauren thinks so, too. When we order dessert and ask for the check, we're told it's already been covered. *On the house*, we're told again.

But I have a hunch that while *Chef* might have been kind enough to gift us a bottle of wine, she would not have comped a three-hundred-dollar meal.

Alex did this.

While Lauren's in the bathroom, I text him from beneath the table, You're in trouble.

My phone buzzes in my lap, and I peer down. Wouldn't be the first time.

I smile as I type, Being serious, thank you, Alex. For the reservation. For the meal. That was incredibly generous. TOO generous.

When it comes to good food, there's no such thing. You deserve a damn fine send-off for your friend. Now enjoy it, Chef's orders. Bon appétit.

Before I can form a meaningful response, Lauren's back from the restroom. I tap a heart on the message, then hide my phone. Determined to enjoy this bittersweet night as much as I can.

Bellies and hearts full, we linger at our table, the last pour of dry, sparkling white fizzing in our glasses as we pick at the lemon mille-feuille on a plate between us.

"J*esus*," Lauren mutters around her bite. "This is decadent."

I nod, eyes shut, savoring the flavors on my tongue. Buttery puff pastry, tart-sweet lemon curd, rich pastry cream. "I love it," I whisper.

Lauren snorts. "I can tell."

A loud familiar blast of a laugh echoes through the restaurant, rupturing my happy bubble. My eyes snap open, focused toward the source of the sound.

And then I drop my fork. It lands quietly on the tablecloth, drawing no one's attention except Lauren's. She glances over her shoulder, in the direction I'm staring, then freezes. "What in the ever-loving *fuck* is that chode doing here?"

Ethan sits with a group of eight, three tables over, his back to us, his arm stretched out along the chair beside him, where I see warm-honey-blond hair, a familiar petite hourglass silhouette . . . Jen.

"What in the ever-loving *fuck* is *she* doing here?" Lauren hisses.

I knock her knee with mine under the table. "Lo."

She glances back at me, rage in her eyes. "What."

"It's okay," I tell her. "It was bound to happen." I shrug, hoping I seem fine, observant and unemotional. "Life in a midsize city, ya know?"

Lauren drains the last of her wine, then sets down the flute. "That fucker is just hanging out already with all your old friends and *her*—"

"They were never *my* friends, Lo." I sip my wine, trying to calm my racing heart. "They were his friends from work and their wives, and we never meshed. I wasn't their type."

"Boring jerks with sticks up their asses?" she offers.

I smile. "We were just different."

Lauren seems to hesitate for a second, then leans in. "*Do* you have other friends here, Thea? Am I stranding you with Hot Chef?"

I was about to cry a second ago, but now all I can do is laugh. *Hard*. So hard that Ethan and Jen and Ethan's buddies and their wives are probably looking over at me now, as I make a scene.

Lauren starts laughing, too, covering her mouth as she snorts. I wheeze a laugh, fold forward toward the table.

We are embarrassing. And I couldn't care less.

I finally settle down enough to dab my eyes and take a long drink of ice water. "Yes, Lauren, I have other friends, here. Mostly through work and the library."

"So . . . *book* buddies," she says as she dabs around her eyes, too. She sounds concerned.

"I met them through the bookish community, if that's what you mean. We're not *close*, but I'd consider them friends." I shrug. "I don't know. I used to have more close friends, back in St. Louis, but then, the last couple of years before we left, they all started having babies, and understandably their lives changed so much. I plugged in how I could, but they were in a new chapter of life, making new friends . . ." My voice wavers. "*Mom* friends."

Lauren reaches across the table and squeezes my hand. "And you wanted to be one of those mom friends."

I nod. "Obviously, when we moved here, I understood those already-dying friendships weren't going to last long distance. So I threw myself into finding a job I loved, which I did, and getting settled into the house and exploring the city. And then I met you."

Lauren grins. "And then I completely monopolized your time for three years."

"Wouldn't have had it any other way."

Ethan's loud braying laugh rings out in the restaurant again. It's impossible not to look over. When we do, Ethan glances over his shoulder right at me, curls his arm tighter around Jen, and smirks.

Lauren glares his way. "I'll fucking end him."

"Lo," I chide.

She slants me a look of pure frustration. "You're too gracious toward him. Villainize him, Thea. Hate his guts. He was a piece of shit to you."

"In some ways, yes," I tell her, "he was. But I'm tired of being mad, Lo. I don't want to waste any more energy on being mad at him."

"I agree," she says. "Channel your energy into brutal premeditated vengeance."

"Lauren."

"For instance, while he's got lil Ms. Tinkerbell here over at *your* house that the fucker took"—she points her fork my way—"you take a shit on his porch, then ding-dong-ditch him."

A laugh jumps out of me in spite of myself. I adore Lauren—her honest irreverence, her fierce love, her unapologetic vindictiveness. I clap my hands over my face and muffle the sudden sob that bursts out on the tail end of my laughter.

"Sweetie," she whispers, leaning in. "I'm sorry. I shouldn't have said that." She's silent for a beat, then tells me, "I should have said, '*I'll* take a shit in a bag, light it on fire, leave it on his porch, then ding-dong-ditch him.'"

Another gunky laugh jumps out of me. "I'm going to miss you so much, Lo."

"I'm going to miss you, too." She sniffs, straightening her shoulders, then leans in as she says, "The jackass clocked us again. And can I just say, you look slammin'?"

"*You* look slammin'," I tell her. "You always do."

Lauren scowls at me. "So do you, you turd nugget." She picks up her phone, unlocking it, then turns it my way.

I blink, startled to see a photo of me in profile, candlelight soft and flattering to the angles of my face, accentuating the summertime freckles scattered across my nose and cheeks, drawing out the amber in my brown curls that spill to my shoulders, calling out the gold in my hazel eyes. My head's bent from peering down at the menu, but my eyes are up, my lips pursed in a pout that accentuates their fullness, something I've been self-conscious about for as long as I can remember.

"Go ahead," Lauren says. "Look at this hot-as-fuck photo of you and try to tell me *I'm* slammin' while implying you're not."

"Okay." I grin. "I look slammin' tonight."

"Hell, yes, you do!"

I hear the click of another photo being taken and groan, "Lauren!"

"What?" she says. "I needed a photo of you smiling, too, not just giving me bedroom eyes."

I snort. "Bedroom eyes."

Lauren takes another bite of dessert, then licks her fork clean. "Ethan's still watching us. So is Tink."

"Jen," I remind her quietly.

"Really don't care about getting her name right." Lauren leans in, a sudden sinister grin on her face, and says, "What do you say I kiss the hell out of you and give them something to be jealous of?"

I smile as I lean in, too, and say, "No."

Her grin dissolves. "Why the hell not?"

"Because I don't want to ruin tonight by about making it about anything other than our friendship. And I don't want to have to learn that, in addition to running, cooking, personal style, and general badassery, kissing is another thing you're better at than me."

Lauren narrows her eyes. "You're so full of shit."

"I'm no,!" I tell her. "I really don't want to make it about . . . *him*. Or her."

"That part I believe," she says. "But the rest of it, stop knocking yourself down, Thea." She clasps my hand inside both of hers, then says gravely, "If you do one thing for me once I'm gone—"

"You're not *perishing*, Lo. You're relocating for work."

"Still," she says. "Do this for me, at least, if at first you can't do it for yourself—be *big*, Thea. Take up space. Do whatever the fuck you want, because you can, and because, once I'm out of here, there will be a significant deficit in Pittsburgh's collective boss-ass bitch quota. But most of all, take care of yourself, so I know you're okay. All right?"

I smile softly and tangle my hands with hers, clasping them together. "I'll try my best. To be a big, space-taking, boss-ass bitch. And I *will* take care of myself. I'll be okay."

Lauren nods, her eyes searching mine. Then she leans in again and says, "Sure you don't want to kiss my face off and make them insanely jealous?"

"Come on, Lo. Let's get out of here."

"Fine," she sighs.

I stand, purse on my shoulder, stretching out my hand to Lauren. She stands, too, and takes it, letting me lead her in a winding path out of the restaurant.

Outside, we're welcomed by the warmth of a balmy summer night, a rare clear sky smattered with dazzling stars.

Lauren turns toward me, our hands drawing apart. The playfulness from inside has evaporated. Now it's only the quiet night, the hum of crickets, and the steady rumble of cars and buses rolling by. The background noise for our goodbye.

"Nightcap back at my place?" I ask, my voice thick, knowing I sound a little desperate. "I've got a very cute postage stamp of a backyard, with string lights and a café table and chairs, thanks to this pushy friend I have who foisted them on me."

"And strung up the lights?" she adds. "In the perfect zigzag pattern because your efforts looked like they'd been woven by a drunk spider?"

A laugh jumps out of me. I brush away the tears. "Yeah. She's a good friend."

Lauren dabs at her nose, peering down the road. "Your offer is tempting," she concedes, "but I think maybe your friend needs to head back to her mostly empty condo and collect herself."

"I get that," I whisper. "It's a tight fit back there, anyway. Two five-foot-eleven women in that postage stamp, feels like we're sitting in the lawn version of a too-tight tub."

She laughs roughly. "It's a microscopic yard. I think my condo closet was bigger than that."

I *know* her closet was bigger that backyard. "Maybe a smidge."

She snorts loudly. Then she glances toward a car rolling toward us, another one behind it, both pulling to a stop.

"Separate cars?" I ask.

She nods. "For separate ways."

I blow out an unsteady breath, then I launch myself at her, hugging her hard. My chest aches, my eyes burn. I squeeze Lauren tight and tell her hoarsely, "It's tight quarters, but that postage stamp will always be waiting for you. String lights. Café table and chairs. A cold bottle of white with your name on it." I pull back and hold her eyes. "And a friend who wants to share it with you."

"Sounds perfect," she mutters, wiping at her cheeks. She holds my eyes for a moment, then curls her arm in mine, guiding us toward our cars. "Just think, after I get my footing in this job, months of hotel living under my belt, I'll be even more accustomed to close quarters by the time I visit your postage stamp again."

Months. I won't see Lauren for months.

She stops at my car, then yanks me into a fierce hug. "Miss you already," she says.

I squeeze her back, hard. "Miss you already, too."

She pulls away abruptly, putting distance between us as she walks to her car. No gentle, slow extraction. Very Lauren, ripping off the Band-Aid.

I call to her, "Come visit the postage stamp soon, okay?"

Lauren opens her car door and grins. "You know I will, as soon as I can. At which point, between hotel living and our postage-stamp wine nights, if you finally take me up on my offer to kill Ethan, prison will feel spacious!"

"Lauren!" I shriek. "No jokes about homicide!"

Cackling like a gorgeous villainess, she slips into her car and slams the door shut.

I force myself into my car, my hands shaking as I buckle myself in, tears blurring my view out the window as the driver pulls out.

I feel so impossibly sad.

But I feel something else, too, as I stare up into the cloudless night. Inside my heart, my own finally clear sky, glittering with tiny pricks of hopeful light.

Tonight, I told Lauren I'd be okay. And tonight, I finally know I meant it.

CHAPTER 20

THEN

September 13, two autumns ago

Fall isn't here yet, but there's a tinge of crisp cool in the air that makes me eager for it. It's been five weeks since the endorphin-soaked almost-kiss, and I can't stop thinking about it. Every time I see Alex, I find myself staring at his mouth, asking myself, *What if?*

I have to stop. I just don't know how to.

I try to line up my hangouts with Alex so that they're on Mia days. It's easier to trust I won't throw myself at him and do something reckless with his daughter around. But even that isn't helping as much as I'd hoped.

Because watching a man be a good dad—especially when your dad was largely absent and when present didn't seem particularly happy about it—is deeply attractive.

Today, though, it's a even easier than normal not to think about kissing Alex, to watch him as he pushes Mia in her swing and not feel that sensual tug drawing me toward him. Because today, I'm pathetically sad.

No Fried Food and French Wine Friday with Lauren will happen tonight, not even via FaceTime. Lauren is spending her birthday, and the anniversary of her mother's passing, without cell service, at an on-site consult for a cutting-edge one-with-nature home design project somewhere in the Southwest. I still sent her a Happy Birthday text followed by what I hoped was a few comforting words about missing her mom today.

The texts haven't shown as delivered. I keep checking my phone, hoping they will.

"Everything okay?" Alex asks.

I shove my phone back in my jeans pocket. "Yep."

He's looking at me closely, still somehow perfectly timing his pushes on Mia's back to send her soaring up to the sky in the basket swing she crammed herself into. "You sure?" he says.

"It's Lauren's birthday today," I admit. "And the anniversary of her mom's death."

His eyebrows shoot up. "Shit."

"Daddy!" Mia yells. "Bad word!"

"Sorry, honey" he says.

"Gotta give me a pennyyyy!" she yells, the last word stretching out until it morphs into a shriek of delight as he sends her flying upward again.

"Add it to my tab," Alex tells her. Then he says to me, "So you reached out to her?"

I nod. "She's somewhere for work with no cell service, and it makes me antsy. I want to be sure she gets my messages."

"She will," he says. "And even if she doesn't today, she knows you love her, Ted."

My nose stings. I will not cry today. "How do you know?"

"Because, based on everything you've told me about your

friendship with her, Lauren would have no reason to question how much you love her or that you're thinking about her today, even if you can't reach her. Because, since I've met you, all I've seen is that you show the people in your life how much you care about them. There's no room for doubt. Your coworkers. Your friends from the library. That crank who owns your building—"

"Mr. Fleischer," I tell him.

"Mr. Fleischer, that's right." Alex smiles. "That guy is a *trip*."

"He's lucky he's cute," I mutter. "And a decent landlord, now that he knows it's me upstairs and I keep him well stocked with baked-good leftovers from the store's coffee bar."

"Why's that?" Alex asks. "The lucky-he's-cute part."

"The man listens to the TV in his living room, right beneath me, so loud that I can hear the newscasters *breathing*."

Alex laughs. "My dad's like that, too, with the morning news. He's not even that old or hard of hearing, either. I think he just does it because it gets my sister out of his hair every day from eight to nine."

I smile. "Which sister?"

"Sophia. The oldest. She lives with my parents, and she's always on Dad about taking his meds and busting him sneaking—" He mimes drawing on a cigarette, as he pushes Mia up into the air.

"Thea!" Mia yells.

"Mia!" I yell back.

Mia smiles my way, a web of dark waves cast across her face. "Push me!"

"Please," Alex reminds her.

She rolls her eyes. "Daddy, I *know* that."

"Mia." He tickles her as she drifts back in her swing. "So *say* that."

She wriggles in her basket swing, shoving off his tickles as she shrieks, "Thea, *please* push me!"

"Gladly," I tell her, stepping in as Alex moves aside.

We're quiet for a minute, except for Mia, whose happy squeals ring out in the air. I glance over at Alex and catch him staring at me.

I must be staring back at him, too, because suddenly Mia's swing is about to barrel into me. I leap back just in time not to get clobbered, pushing her up in the air again.

Alex asks, "What's your favorite food?"

I do a double take his way, but I'm careful this time to bring my gaze back to Mia. "I don't know," I tell him.

His brow furrows. "Why not?"

"Same way I don't know what my favorite book is, either. I'm not done yet. How could I know what's my favorite, before I am?"

The furrow deepens. "But when you're done reading or . . . eating, won't that mean you're dead?"

"Yep!" I tell him.

"Ted, that is morbid."

"I guess. But I can't stand the idea of saying something's my favorite, that this is the best a book can be, when there's so much left to read." I shrug. "Same with food. Actually more so, with food. I've eaten a lot less great food than I've read great books."

He watches me for a beat, then says, "I know a guy who could fix that."

"Fix what? The existential bleakness underpinning my philosophy on favorites?" I shake my head. "I'm way too German for that to ever be fixed. It's hardwired in my DNA."

He cracks a smile. "I meant, the part where you said you've eaten a lot less great food than you've read great books."

"Oh." Warmth spills through me. "You don't have to do that."

"Why wouldn't I?"

I turn back to Mia, pushing her again, higher, like she asks. "It just seems like a lot of hassle."

"Ted." He laughs dryly. "Cooking is my passion. *And* my job. Which means, sometimes, I lose all passion for it and hate that it's my job. Basically, it's already a hassle. Cooking for the people I care about . . . helps."

I glance his way. "How so, Chef?"

He leans against one of the metal poles anchoring the playground swing set, arms folded across his chest. "Why do you give me books, Ms. Bookseller?"

My cheeks heat. "I've only given you a couple."

"Even higher, Thea!" Mia yells.

"Please," Alex reminds her, but his eyes stay fixed on me.

"Please!" Mia shrieks.

Dutifully, I give her a strong push, sending her flying up, squealing with happiness.

"Because I love reading," I tell him, "and I love that it's my job to help the right book find the right reader, but sometimes my job is also a bunch of other grubby tasks that make me love my job a lot less and feel . . . distanced from what got me doing that work in the first place . . ."

"And?" he prompts.

A shiver runs down my spine. Sometimes I feel like Alex can read my mind, like he knows exactly where I'm going when I'm talking to him, almost before I do. Or maybe it's that he listens closely, in a way I've never encountered in anyone else before, intensely focused, tracking every word. Maybe it's simply unfamiliar to me not only to be listened to, but to feel heard.

"Giving books to people I care about," I tell him, "it's . . . a way to show people I care, that I'm thinking about them and hopefully giving them something that makes their lives better, even if only for a couple hundred pages. And maybe it's selfish, but it helps me . . . fall in love again." A beat passes, before I realize it's probably best if I clarify. "In love with *reading*. Again."

"So," Alex says, "what you're saying is, when you share your gift with the people who matter to you, it reminds you why you loved that gift in the first place. Is that right?"

"Yes," I tell him quietly.

Alex pushes off the swing set, his gaze holding mine. "Then let me cook for you," he says. "Because I care about you. And because . . . it'll help me fall in love, too. With cooking. Again."

Maybe he's teasing me a little, mimicking my words, but it doesn't sound like teasing. It sounds there's something deeper beneath the surface of what he's said; it *feels* that way, as he steps closer, until we're shoulder to shoulder.

For a moment, we stand there, side by side, watching Mia, wild-haired, legs kicking, full of joy, swinging up into the sky.

Alex glances my way and says, "Please?"

"Well, all right." I lean into him, just the slightest, my shoulder pressed to his, and smile. "Since you asked nicely."

*

My body is that delicious strain of sleepy from a taking a little too much sun and eating a little too much good food. I sit, elbows on Alex's kitchen table, a handful of playing cards fanned in front of my face as I stare at Alex across from me.

Mia's snores through the baby monitor, and I smile behind my cards. Her first snore was halfway through my first verse of the "I Am Here" StoryTime song.

"That kid was worn out," I tell Alex.

"Took her long enough," he says. "I spent so much energy wearing her out today, *I* am worn out."

I laugh. "Same. I'll bring Argos next time. They can wear each other out instead."

"Deal," he says.

"Thanks again," I tell him, "for dinner."

"Thanks for doing all those dishes," he says appreciatively.

"Happy to."

He shakes his head. "You don't mean that. No one is happy to do the dishes."

"I am," I admit. "I find it relaxing."

He leans in, eyes wide, cards pressed to his chest. *"Relaxing?"*

I lean in with my cards against my chest, eyes wide, mirroring him. "I am just as incredulous that you find cooking enjoyable."

"Strange," he says.

"Agreed."

We both sit up, eyes back on our cards. Alex just explained the rules of two-person euchre to me five minutes ago—for the second time—and I've already forgotten them. Other thoughts have been bouncing around my mind tonight, loud and insistent, taking up so much space that I can't hold on to anything else.

Maybe it's the whisper of change in seasons that's turned me pensive, but ever since we were at the playground this morning, I've been thinking about this summer. While Alex and Mia and I soaked up this sunshiny almost-fall day, filled with her bubbly laughter, the wind in my hair, kicking a soccer ball in their backyard, reading books with Mia while Alex cooked, then tucking her in, I kept thinking, I feel such a comforting happiness when I'm with Alex.

I needed this gentle summer, when so much else was abrasively painful: divorcing, moving out of my home, saying goodbye to Lauren. And I'm grateful for what my gentle summer with Alex gave me.

But I also know this isn't real life.

With the exception of the infamous, near-death experience of our bike-ride race, Alex and I have insulated ourselves from our exes, from the bigger picture of what brought us together, steered our conversations clear of the topic of our divorces, when the fact is our exes are still here, weaving in and out of our lives. In conversations about plans and logistics for Mia, handoff and pickup days for Argos. In unexpected moments, because I swear there's something about this city that keeps wrenching people from your past onto your path, when, either alone or together, we've spotted Ethan or Jen or Ethan *and* Jen, and it's been a bucket of ice water dousing me head to toe, every time.

I've been rereading some of my middle-grade favorites the past few weeks, most of them Karen Cushman titles—*The Ballad of Lucy Whipple*; *The Midwife's Apprentice*; *Catherine, Called Birdy*. Stories of young girls on the cusp of womanhood, not fully on their own, physically, at least, but very much on their own within themselves, thrust into often harsh, daunting circumstances. I loved those stories when I was younger, because they felt true. Because I often felt alone even when I wasn't, and there was something inspiring about their courage; they didn't try to deny what they were up against, more or less entirely on their own, and they didn't buckle, either. They faced it, leaned into it, stretched, and grew.

I know why I've been rereading them. Not for nostalgia, but

for the reminder. That's who I wanted to be when I grew up—a brave, resilient woman who forged a life of her own.

But somewhere along the way, I lost sight of that *want*. Or maybe I stopped fighting for it. I let Ethan's want be the louder one, the want that steered my path. Then I met Lauren, when I was so lost and she was so sure, and I often piggybacked on her wants.

Now, I have Alex. And Mia. And it's so tempting, the thought of throwing myself into *their* life, telling myself it's some platonic-version redemption of the story I'd wanted with Ethan. A man in my life who's kind and playful and cooks before I do the dishes, a sweet little girl to tuck in at night, a deck of cards and a bottle of wine between the two of us, after she's fallen asleep.

Rereading those books, I've been reminded that while that path is tempting, it isn't what I want—to keep turning to someone else's wants to guide me, rather than search myself for those answers, even if I'm not sure yet what that want is.

I still have a lot to figure out, but I know this: I want to stretch and grow. I want a life that isn't a rebound from the shattered one I had with Ethan or a replacement for the one that plugged into Lauren's.

I want a life that feels new, and strong, and true to me, built from the foundation of what I want. A life that's *mine*.

Possibilities flash in front me, all the things I could learn, try, do on my own; the ways I could make myself bigger, like Lauren said.

As I look at Alex, one clear idea pops into my mind.

"Would you teach me how to cook?" I blurt.

Alex lifts a card from the middle of his hand, moving it to the end, unphased by my outburst. "Sure," he says.

Sure. Just like that. Like I asked if it's September. If it's Friday. No hesitation.

I never tried to ask Ethan if he'd teach me. I knew, if I did, he'd laugh, or worse, if he did say yes and try, it would have turned out like it did when I was younger, with my mom—strained patience, taking over the moment I messed up or lost focus, far away in my vivid imagination, interrupting with questions that only elicited a weary sigh.

Thea knew she could be hasty when doing tasks. And while she'd learned not to interrupt with questions, she was still insatiably curious. She struggled to follow directions that weren't written down, and even then she had to reread them. She always managed to keep up with life's logistics—homework and soccer practice and piano lessons as a kid, the bills and the laundry and the doctor appointments as an adult—but it was never easy, and sometimes she let things go too long because she couldn't figure out which task to start, when her brain felt so loud and dizzyingly noisy. And even when she'd done it all well, it was exhausting, a tenuous juggling act riddled with anxiety, teeth-clenched, dreading the moment she'd finally drop a ball.

She grew up observing those idiosyncrasies frustrate her already impatient mother, then, later on, irking her husband who'd turn sharp and short. Trying loving the people she was supposed to love best, trying to please them, she learned to make myself small as a girl and as a woman to stay that way. Being her full self only led to hurting and being hurt. Now, she'd begun to think, that hurting and being hurt had happened because she'd tried to do a good thing in a bad way, in a way that cost Thea her true self. Now, she had a promise to keep—to Lauren and more importantly, to herself. She was going to be big, to learn to love herself, to learn from and love only people who wanted all of her.

People like Alex.

"You daydream a lot," Alex says. "Don't you?"

I blink, snapped from my thoughts. A blush creeps up my cheeks. "It's a bad habit," I tell him.

Alex shakes his head, a soft grin tugging up the corners of his mouth. "I don't think so. Not when it makes you smile like that."

Setting my hand on my warm cheek, I feel the truth in what Alex said. I am smiling.

Even so, I feel vulnerable, exposed, asking Alex for what I have. To learn from him. To make mistakes in front of him. To trust him to be patient with me while I do.

"You really want to teach me to cook?"

His grin deepens. "I'd love to teach you to cook."

My heart trips, then warms. "Just the fundamentals," I tell him. "Nothing extensive or demanding. We can keep it to basics, so I won't take up too much of your time. Doesn't even need to be lessons, really. We could just do it when we're hanging out and you're cooking meals. I can be your sous, learn from working beside you."

Alex holds my eyes. "We could do it when we're hanging out and putting together meals, sure. But I'd also be happy to make dedicated time for it."

Butterflies race through my stomach. "I realize this is like asking Lisa Leslie to teach me how to shoot layups."

"That flattery"—he says, eyes back on his cards—"will get you somewhere."

I laugh. "What can I do to . . . I don't know, compensate you for cooking lessons? Babysit Mia? Be your scullery maid?"

"You already are my scullery maid," he says mildly, his mouth tipping at the corner. He's teasing. It makes me smile.

"I do the dishes after you cook for me, that is *not* being your scullery maid. I'm serious Alex, what can I do, to return the favor?"

His gaze slides up again and locks with mine. He's quiet for a moment, then says, "Would you read to me, sometimes, when I'm cooking, maybe, or when we're just . . . hanging out?"

My heart sprouts wings, beating wildly in my chest. "Sure. What kind of books?"

"Ideally," he says, "the books you love and think I'd love. Or not. It can be whatever you want. Nothing extensive or demanding, though, so I don't take up too much of your time."

I sigh. "Message received. I cheapened it by making it transactional. And I made it sound like I'd be twisting your arm."

"Bingo." He sets down his cards.

"Actually, we're playing euchre."

He gives me a quelling look.

As I bring my cards up to hide my face, his deep belly laugh echoes in the kitchen.

Alex curls his fingers around my cards, lowering them, then setting them gently face down on the table. He's close, leaning in on his elbows. His warm spicy scent washes over me.

I take him in for a moment, my eyes traveling his body because I can't help it. He's in another old T-shirt, heather gray with a vintage Penguins Hockey logo across the chest, hints of skin peeking through where it's so threadbare it's almost sheer. He's slightly sunburned on the bridge of his twice-broken nose, on the tops of his cheekbones above the shadow of his stubble. His eyes are deep, midnight blue.

"I think," he begins, "that you know me well enough by now to believe me when I say, I won't tell you I want to do something if I don't want to do it. And I want you to be just as honest with me, Ted."

"I know," I tell him. "I am." And I mean it, which feels . . . strange. And good.

I always thought holding in the truth, when I knew it might bristle or challenge, was an act of protective care for the person you loved, for your relationship. I'm starting to understand it actually did the opposite. Because a lie of omission is still a lie, words empty of true meaning. And empty words are flimsy things on which to build a relationship. What I thought threatened love is actually what shores it up most.

"You promise?" he says.

"I've been honest with you, and I'll keep doing that. Promise."

Eyes on his cards, he smiles. "Good. Now, let's play some cards."

CHAPTER 21

NOW

August 3, first day of "vacation"

On second thought, the house we're staying in probably should have been of more interest to us. Had we explored it when Ethan and Jen got here, before taking off on our impromptu bike ride, we would have been better prepared for what we're facing now:

Our bedroom. *Our* bedroom, which has only one bed.

I stare at the tiny folded card sitting on the dresser, bearing our names in Jen's pretty teacher's cursive.

Thea and Alex

"Um," I say unhelpfully.

Alex turns, facing Jen and Ethan, who stand in the doorway, Mia behind them, sprawled in the living room, her head propped up on Argos, who's happily dozing, no qualms about playing his frequent role as her pillow. She has her headphones on, eyes glued to her iPad as she watches *Bluey*.

Jen smiles at us brightly. She's honestly glowing. Ethan's expression is unreadable.

"Not to sound ungrateful," Alex says. "Would there, uh"—he clears his throat—"happen to be another room that has *two* beds?"

"Yes," Ethan says. "But Mia and Jen are staying in that one."

I glance to Jen, who's still smiling, like none of this is weird, let alone bothering her. She and Ethan are about to get married—not that she knows we know that—and she's going to have a sleepover with her kid all week, instead of cozying up in this massive bed with her soon-to-be husband?

"Is there another room?" I ask, finally finding my voice.

"No," Ethan says, looking at me like I should know this, before realization clears his expression. I think he's only remembering now that he never brought me here. If he feels guilty about that, he doesn't show it.

"It's an old home," he adds after a beat of awkward silence, sounding a little defensive. "My great-grandparents built it, and they only had one child, my grandfather; and then he only had one child, my father. No need for more rooms than those two."

I don't state the obvious, that this means there were no guest rooms. Seems antipathy for hospitality runs in Ethan's family. I always wondered if Ethan kept our socializing largely out of the house because he didn't want to bring people into the space that, despite his largely successful greige aesthetic, I managed to clutter up with books, flowers, houseplants, and as much colorful art as I could. In my low moments, I worried that he didn't want people in a space that, to him, felt too much like *me*. Now I'm realizing, he probably just didn't like hosting and came by it honestly.

I expect to feel relief as I put the pieces together. But I don't, like glancing down, expecting to see a scab you're so used to still being there, only to realize it's vanished, already healed.

"Where are you sleeping, then?" I ask him, genuinely curious.

"The pullout sofa," Ethan says.

"How noble," Alex mutters.

Jen gives him a chiding look.

"Not *that* noble," Ethan says breezily as he steps back, then turns toward the living room. "I personally find that mattress the comfiest in the house."

Alex and I look at each other, biting back laughter as we smile.

This sleeping situation is a disaster. But if we can laugh about anything, it's about my ex being a consistently douchebag human being.

"Alex!" Ethan calls from somewhere deep in the house.

Alex's smile dissolves before he calls back, "Ethan!"

"Your help in the kitchen?" Ethan drawls.

I stare at Alex, who glares out the doorway, that jaw in his muscle working overtime.

"Alex, I—"

"Don't apologize for him," he says, reading my mind. He tugs me into his arms for a hug. "I can handle him. Go enjoy the beach, soak it up."

"You don't want me to stay? Be your kitchen backup?"

Alex nuzzles into my hair. "Nope. This way, if I kill Ethan while he tries to boss me around the kitchen, you won't be an accessory to murder.'

I squeeze my arms around him. "You and Lauren joke too much about homicide."

"When it comes to Ethan," he grumbles, "there's no such thing. Lawrence would agree with me."

He pulls away and leaves me in our bedroom, battling a delirious blend of laughter and tears. The laughter wins out, though I muffle it in a bed pillow.

Because he's right. Ending Ethan is one thing he and Lauren definitely agree on.

*

We've almost survived our first night of "vacation." Dinner was served without Alex ending Ethan, and it was delicious—fresh-caught pan-seared fish; grilled peach, goat cheese, and arugula salad; and a summer risotto that Alex whipped up that had me fighting hard to keep my foodgasm noises to myself. They're funny when it's just Alex and me. With Ethan and Jen, it would have been beyond awkward.

Mia's in bed, her snores carrying through the living room, with the door left cracked open, per her request.

I'm finishing the dishes while Alex does his usual full wipe down of the appliances. It makes my heart twinge, seeing him do that. He has every reason to leave Ethan's family's kitchen grease splattered and fishy. But he won't. Because this is what he does, his routine, a matter of pride and discipline, to respect the tools that allow him to do his craft.

Jen finishes gathering up Mia's toys from the middle of the living room, then tiptoes over to the bedroom and carefully eases the door shut.

Ethan is nowhere to be seen.

He always made himself scarce during after-dinner cleanup, and if that isn't a big red flag that I took way too long to recognize, I don't know what it is.

Alex pulls a seltzer from the fridge, offering me one. I take it, setting it on the counter beside me while I finish drying the last pan.

"Jen?" Alex says, extending a seltzer to her, too.

She startles, hearing him say her name. "Oh." Jen smiles, a little tentative, as she takes it. "Thanks, Alex, yeah."

He nods, then shuts the fridge door.

Jen cracks her seltzer. Alex cracks his. I set down the pan, then crack mine. The room is an awkward almost-silent, the only sounds our seltzers' fizzy carbonation and the faint roar of the ocean at night.

"I think I'll pour some wine, too!" Jen says, rounding the island.

"I've got just the thing," Ethan says, making us all jump.

He shuts the door behind him that leads to the lower level, which I saw only in passing when we first came inside from the beach. It struck me as a pretty typical man cave—a den with a bar, an extensive wine collection, a big TV, and a deep-cushion leather sofa, which I'm assuming is the extremely comfortable pullout couch Ethan is planning to sleep on.

Ethan turns the bottle, facing it out to us. If it weren't so unique, I probably wouldn't have recognized it, let alone remembered it. But it is, and I do. Slim neck, tapered green glass, a label painted with watercolor flowers.

That's the bottle his parents gave us on our wedding. An extremely nice bottle, Ethan had explained. I asked him, on a couple anniversaries in the early years, where it had gone. Now I have my answer. It ended up here. He kept it for himself.

Maybe it's like his hosting—maybe there's a less hurtful explanation, same as with hosting. Maybe he was saving it for some special anniversary that we never got to.

I find myself suddenly exhausted, not just from the all-nighter we pulled to get here. But from doing this—exerting energy to somehow finally make sense Ethan, to figure out what he's really doing and why. I want to know for Mia's sake. Hell, even for Jen's. Because I want him to be better for them than he was for me. I want to find proof that I can hope he'll be good to them.

He's so closed off, so inscrutable, that feels damn near impossible.

I glance toward Alex, who's been watching me. He peers at Ethan, who's watching me, too.

I turn toward Jen and say, "I'm wiped from the drive, but what do you say? One round of euchre?"

Jen looks to Ethan, who's opening the wine, to Alex, who's made no move to do anything, watching us closely. Then she smiles at me. "Well, one game wouldn't hurt."

*

We've played two games, and we're halfway through our third, after Alex and I beat Ethan and Jen in the first game, and Ethan decreed another game was in order. Ethan and Jen won the second one. At which point, both Alex *and* Ethan decreed a rubber match was necessary.

Alex turns down the ten of spades on top of the kitty, which is a relief. I have a handful of hearts and diamonds. Next up is Jen.

"Pass," she says.

I pass, then Ethan does. Alex calls hearts trump, and *my* heart does a little leap. I'm so tired, but I'm not too tired to want to win, even if the prospect of victory isn't quite as gripping as it seemed when we first decided on this vacation and I made Alex promise me we'd crush them.

Jen leads with a king of clubs. No clubs in my hand, I can ruff it. I throw off a queen of hearts, so Alex knows I have a decent bit in my hand, and hopefully so that Ethan, if he's also out of clubs, can't outtrump my trump.

Ethan has clubs, and Alex throws off a low diamond, letting my trump win the trick for us. Alex sweeps up the cards, setting them beside him with a snap, and nods my way.

Just as I'm about to lead with an ace of diamonds, Jen blurts, "Ethan and I have to tell you something."

Alex and I peer up, glancing from her to Ethan. Ethan's looking at her with an expression I've never seen on him before, can't put my finger on, a soup seasoned with so many flavors that nothing's discernible.

Jen glances between us. "We asked you to come here because . . . we're going to get married this week on the beach."

Ethan's still watching her, saying nothing.

I stare at him, searching for some clue to guess what he isn't saying, what's happening in that brain of his.

Jen smiles at him, then at us. "We haven't told Mia yet. Just that we're going to have a special day and wear special dresses."

Alex draws in a breath, looking over at Jen. "When *are* you going to tell her?"

Jen looks to Ethan.

Ethan finally speaks up. "We thought the night before would be wise. To diminish the . . . anticipation? Mia doesn't seem to handle waiting for things very well."

Alex throws Ethan a scathing glare. "You mean she 'handles waiting' like a kid who gets excited about the things she's looking forward to?"

Ethan shrugs. "Sure."

I rest my bare feet on Alex's below the table, then hug his calves between my ankles. Touching to touch. Telling him I'm here,. Reminding him that Ethan isn't worth getting fired up for.

Alex meets my eyes and exhales slowly, then turns to Jen to make it clear he isn't speaking to Ethan as he says, "Thank you for telling us."

My heart clutches. He said *us*.

Jen glances back and forth between Alex and me. "You don't seem . . . surprised? Not that I wanted you to be, I just . . ."

"Mia," I explain. "She was very excited about her new white dress and the 'special occasion.'"

"Oh." Jen smiles. "I should have thought about that, that she'd be eager to tell you. Would you please keep this between us," she says to me, then turns to Alex. "Until I tell her?"

"When do you plan to tell her?" Alex asks again.

"The night before," Jen says, smiling over at Ethan. "Thursday night. We'll get married on Friday morning."

Ethan smiles, reaching across the table, clasping her hand. "Friday morning," he says.

Alex and I meet eyes across the table, feet still touching beneath it. He throws me a wink that reminds me of his dad, that makes me smile. I wink back the only way I can, a clumsy double blink.

Alex grins, then peers down, focused on his cards.

"Your lead, Ted," he reminds me.

I throw out the right bower, the jack of hearts, so he knows I have it and he doesn't have to worry about Ethan or Jen having it in their hands. As I do, I sense it in him, despite his excellent poker face, the relief, the confidence. With this trick in the bag, he knows, based on his remaining cards, that we're going to take a third trick, get the point we wanted, and with that, win.

I should be thrilled, vengefully satisfied.

But all I can think about are his legs, tangled with mine below the table. The sight of him across from me, windblown and tan, seawater in his hair turning every rebellious wave into loose curls that kiss everywhere I've dreamed of kissing—his temples, his ears, the nape of his neck.

About the room with one bed, waiting for us down the hall.

CHAPTER 22

THEN

November 13, two autumns ago

Fall shows up and saves the day. I haven't figured out how not to want Alex. The only solution I came up with was to see less of him, which I knew would hurt him and crush me, and then Alex would notice I'd pulled away, none of which I wanted.

Thankfully, I didn't have to figure out an alternative. Fall busyness did it for me.

The last weekend of September, I went to bed with a belly full of chargrilled corn and sun-warm tomatoes, windows open to the breeze, my dog at my feet, then woke up the next morning, shivering at the chilly damp blowing in, Argos curled up beside me for warmth, desperate for the comfort of a hot breakfast and a hotter cup of coffee.

When I got out from beneath the covers, tugging on two pairs of socks because I had no idea where my slippers were, I saw that, after a month of playing phone tag—the game: keep missing each other, leave no voicemails—Mom had finally texted me.

Please call me when you can. I'll be sure my phone is on ring so I don't miss you.

Knowing I'd been avoidant long enough, I made myself a cup of coffee, found my slippers, and called Mom, who answered on the first ring and told me what the past month's missed calls had been about . . . Dad needed an angioplasty.

I drove to Columbus, spent the week of my birthday getting up to speed on what I'd missed, helping around the house, cleaning and running errands, then drove back to Pittsburgh. Since then, I've been drowning in work as we prepare for our busiest, most profitable time of year—the holiday season.

With school back in session and Jen teaching, Alex has shifted from being a fifty-fifty custody parent to the primary daytime weekday parent, dropping off Mia and picking her up from three-day-a-week pre-K. He also started work on his third cookbook.

We've been lucky to manage seeing each other every two weeks, and that includes Alex stopping in with Mia for StoryTime every other Saturday. Texting has become the backbone of our friendship—the occasional gripe about our exes or the overcast weather, but mostly, it's talking, being close, with the perk that, because we're not seeing each other in person, I don't have to expend a massive amount of mental energy on not staring at Alex's mouth and thinking about kissing him.

Alex
thumbs up, thumbs down: pumpkin

Thea
in a pie/muffin, thumbs up! Double thumbs up if there's cream cheese frosting involved.

Alex

k . . . what if the pumpkin item *didn't* include a shit ton of sugar?

like, for example, if was used to make tortellini

maybe there's sage, garlic, brown butter, ricotta, pecorino cheese involved

hypothetically

Thea

hypothetically? that sounds like an ALL the thumbs up.

but, I can't be *sure*. I think that's probably something I need to eat 5 to 10 lbs of before I can tell you definitively.

Alex

Ted, that's a lot of homemade pumpkin tortellini

Thea

you're right, but someone has to be brave and make the necessary sacrifices for culinary greatness.

I volunteer as tribute!

Thea

Hey. So. That Gillian McAllister thriller I gave you, didn't see it coming, but it's a wee bit emotional, so maybe don't read it unless you want to sob every twenty pages.

Alex

TOO LATE YOU EMOTIONAL SABOTEUR

Thea

ALEX!!!! IM SORRRYYYYY!!!

Also, "saboteur"?! Talk about an epic Scrabble word. Duly impressed!

Alex
Thank you. But I'm still mad about the book. No more pumpkin tortellini for you!

Thea
I DIDN'T KNOW, OKAY?

I was crying so hard, reading it on the bus, the driver kicked me off at the next stop, which was outside Jeni's ice cream, so then I ate my feelings in a triple scoop of way too much rocky road and now I have a belly ache

IN SHORT I'VE PAID FOR MY CRIMES DON'T TAKE MY PUMPKIN TORTELLINI TOO

Alex
FINE.
Now stop texting me. I have the last 15% of the audiobook to finish while I knock out food prep.

Thea
so . . . maybe don't try to cook while listening to that last 15%?

Unless you want the number one ingredient of whatever you're making to be your tears

Alex
DAMMIT, TED, IT'S GOING TO GET WORSE? I'M ALREADY A MESS

Thea
How about I pick up Mia from preschool today?

Give you a bit of time to collect yourself?

And make more pumpkin tortellini?

Alex

You, my friend, are a bold woman.

Thea

is that a yes?

Alex

Yes, now LEAVE ME TO MY EMOTIONAL DEVASTATION

Alex

Mia told me at bedtime tonight, I "moosh" Thea.

Took me a minute, but I figured out she was saying, "miss"

Thea

well, now I'm crying

WHO'S THE EMOTIONAL SABOTEUR NOW

Alex

Um Mia?

Thea

sure, blame the kid.

or you could admit that this is payback for the tearjerker thriller

Alex

you DO deserve payback for putting me through that book.

but it was just an honest update

Thea

tell Mia I moosh her back?

Alex
Will do

Thea
And Alex, honest update,
I moosh you, too

Alex
And I moosh you, Ted.
Lots.

By the time we're trudging through November, life isn't any slower, but there's still a faint glow from our gentle summer, warm in my heart, as if what Alex and I have figured out, the ways we've managed to connect through the busy autumn, are like two hands cupped around that flame, keeping it alive.

For the first time in six weeks, I'm sitting in Alex's kitchen. Instead of summer sunshine, we're lit by dim recessed lighting as we sit down to play after-dinner cards. Alex's threadbare T-shirt has been swapped out for a faded, butter-soft hoodie, one of its drawstrings clenched between his teeth. The living room fireplace pops and hisses as it burns, echoing summertime's woodsmoke-grill scent, wisps of charred hickory curling through the air.

I stare at Alex, whose hair is longer, indecisive curl-waves falling onto his forehead, around his ears, brushing the top of his hoodie. His five-o'clock shadow scruff has grown into a beard. He looks different. But he feels the same. Comfort. Playfulness. Warmth.

His socked feet drag along mine beneath the table, no steady pattern or rhythm to their movement, just touching. Touching to touch. I don't even think he knows he's doing it.

I'm an affectionate guy.

I remind myself, this is a quality of Alex, not of our relationship—our *friendship*. It's not special just to us. I have to remind myself of these things, not just because I want to kiss him, but because when I look at him now, especially given how much less I've seen him the past few months, it happens again. I think and feel what I thought and felt that first time at Luna's.

I love him.

I'm too raw from my divorce, too jaded by what happened, to worry that this love is anything close to the romantic kind. But it's *a* kind of love, and it just might scare me more than it would if it was romantic. Because it's different. Because I can't put my finger on why that is. Because it feels like something that's seen and seeped through more of my honest, messy self than any love before.

If Alex picks up on my mental spiral, he doesn't show it. He's relaxed, slouched in his chair, chewing on his hoodie string, eyes on his cards. "Ted," he says, "how's your timer?"

I peer down at my phone, grateful to have somewhere else to tell my eyes to look. I have to stop staring at him. "Two minutes left."

He nods. "And what's up next?"

"Pull the crèmes out of the fridge. Sprinkle with a light layer of brown sugar." I smile devilishly. "Then I get to *torch* them."

Alex bites back a grin. "*Slightly* concerned about how fire-happy you are."

"It makes me feel so powerful, wielding fire!"

"Yeah, maybe we'll torch the crèmes outside," he muses, turning over the top card in the kitty.

"Pass," I tell him when I see what he turned up.

He turns it over, too. Before he might call trump, I say, "Alex?"

"Hmm?" His eyes are on his cards, rearranging them.

"Why did you say yes when I asked to learn to make crème brûlée?"

"Why wouldn't I?"

"You don't think I need to learn other things first?"

"You *have* learned other things," he says.

"I helped you make wedding soup," I point out. "And asked you to show me how to make homemade pasta. Then tonight, I asked to learn how to make crème brûlée. I've been a chaos demon, and you haven't held me back."

He peers up at me. "Did you want me to hold you back?"

"No," I tell him. "Unless... you think holding me back would have been better for me, for teaching me how to cook."

Alex sets down his cards. "Before Mia, I would've told you that you had to learn other things first. I would have walked you through what they teach at culinary school, in that same order, by increasing degrees of difficulty and skill. I would have been an uncompromising, exacting hard-ass who made you do the same thing over and over until you perfected it, before I let you move on."

I hear regret in his words. It makes my heart ache.

"But then I had a kid," he says, "and I stepped away from the restaurant. And I started raising someone who learned best when she was personally invested, when she had a *relationship* to what she was learning, when she could be curious and explore. When she didn't feel like what mattered most was pursuing a perfect outcome but instead figuring it out along the way. Because that brought her joy. Even though it wasn't how I was taught to learn or how I'd taught others, she learned everything she needed to.

You were invested in helping me make soup, then learning how to make homemade pasta and crème brûlée. I could tell you were excited about them. That's why we started there."

"So what you're saying is, I have a childlike disposition?" I tease.

"I'm saying," he tells me, "you have *joy*, Ted. And the last thing I'd ever want to do is dim that. I've done enough dimming for one lifetime."

Alex tears his gaze away, back down on his cards. "Your timer's about to go off. Sugar's on the counter."

I push up from my chair, then circle the table. "Cards abreast!" I warn him.

Alex slaps his cards down on the table, brow furrowed as he watches me come closer. Standing behind his chair, I bend low enough to wrap my arms around his shoulders and chest. I set my chin on his shoulder.

"Ever read *The Life-Changing Magic of Tidying Up*?" I ask.

Alex's head lists toward mine. His temple settles, snug against my cheekbone "No. But I've heard about it."

"What have you heard?"

He wraps his hands around my wrists, his thumbs grazing my pulse points. "The gist. You get rid of stuff you have no use for. Keep what you do. Then organize it in a way that you can find and use what you've kept. Basically, how I keep my kitchen."

I smile. "Right. There's a phrase she uses to guide that discernment process. You only keep what 'sparks joy.'" I squeeze him tight. "For me, you spark joy."

Alex is quiet for a moment, then says, "So that means . . . you'll keep me?"

For as long as I can.

"Yep," I tell him. "But it also means you spark joy."

Alex's grip slides up my arm, tugging me around the chair, toward him, onto his lap. I land with my hands on his shoulders to steady myself. His hands settle on my waist, thumbs brushing my hip bones.

Our eyes hold. And then he pulls me down, wraps his arms tight around my waist. I curl mine around his neck and breathe him in. Warm skin, clean spice.

My phone's timer goes off, but neither of us move.

His voice is hoarse, so quiet, I almost miss it. "You spark my joy, too, Ted."

*

"This crème brûlée," I tell Alex, "sparks my joy."

"Your 'crème brûlée sparks my joy' noises," Alex says, "spark my joy."

I peer over at Alex beside me, both of us stretched across the floor in front of the fireplace, heads propped on Mia's gigantic beanbag. The spoon slips from my mouth. "Oh no. Was I making foodgasm noises again?"

Alex coughs, I'm pretty sure to hide a laugh, then scrunches up his face. "Nah. Not at all."

"Ughh." Mortified, I tug up the hood on his sweatshirt that I borrowed and yank the drawstrings tight, until all that's left is a small circle that I can barely see out of.

A second later, I hear his phone's shutter-click sound.

"Alex!" I yell.

"No yelling!" he whispers. "Mia's sleeping."

I hiss back, "Seriously? A picture?"

I reach for his hand holding his phone, but with my limited vision, I end up half-punching the ceramic ramekin he's holding in the other.

Alex yells, "Back off my crème brûlée!"

"No yelling!" I parrot in a whisper. "Mia's sleeping."

Alex snorts. "You honestly could yell, I've got her sound machine blasting, and once she's out for the night, she's out. I was just trying to sidetrack you."

I growl in frustration, lunging for him again. "I want that photo deleted!"

"It sparks my joy!" he yells. "That means I should keep it!"

I yank at my hood to widen my field of vision, set my ramekin on the floor beside me, then dive onto him.

"Ted!" he wheezes as I throw myself across his body, reaching for his phone. "Hold on. Let me—"

He turns enough to set his ramekin on the ground, and as he does, I get a good grip on his phone, then yank it out of his hand.

Alex is breathing heavily as he rolls toward me, his hair poking out everywhere from wrestling against the beanbag. He props himself on an elbow, takes his phone back, unlocks it, then hands it back to me. "Go on," he says. "Delete it. Unspark my joy."

And then he casts a forlorn glance to the ground. He looks like Argos, after he's been caught chewing up one of my Birkenstocks. But somehow, even cuter.

I groan, flopping onto the beanbag. "Fine." I drop the phone on my stomach. "You can keep it. *If* you also have a not-terrible picture of me, too."

"I already have lots of those," he says.

I peer slowly his way. I've never once been aware of his taking my picture.

Alex opens his mouth, then shuts it, then says, "That sounded really creepy."

"Yep."

"I'd like to address that."

I tell him, "I'd like that, too."

"Mia," he says. "She takes your photo when you're around. Like, every time."

My heartbeat stutters. "What?"

Gently, he lifts his phone from where it rests on my stomach and navigates to his photos, down to Albums, where a rounded rectangle says on the right, *Thea,* my smiling face on the left side.

I scroll through the album, laughing. Many of these photos are objectively unflattering, taken beneath me, from her four-year-old height. Even so, they make my heart pinch. Mia wanted my picture.

Some aren't unflattering, at least. My goofy smile as I'm juggling her size-three soccer ball in the backyard. My who's-a-good-pup look I give Argos, as I cup his face and pucker up to kiss his head. My upside-down grin as I hang from the playground bar, jazz hands out, my hair frizzy and wild, nearly brushing the ground.

"Why?" I ask Alex.

He eases down beside me on the beanbag, opening an arm. An invitation. I roll toward him, setting my head on his shoulder, and his arm curls around me. He holds his phone above us in both hands, just like he did that first night at my apartment, as we Wordled and tore through mini crosswords.

"She has albums for her special people," he tells me.

I watch him swipe through to his Albums, catching fragments of faces and names. Jen's face on an album named *Mommy.* An older couple, head-to-head, that I think might be his parents; a man with Alex's vivid blue eyes, a woman with his dark waves and curls hair. Another older couple who might be Jen's parents, based on their looks. Three women, one after the other, who have to be his sisters.

"No Album for Ethan," I observe. I am vindictively pleased.

Alex frowns down at me. "*Hell* no."

"You wouldn't let her make one?"

Alex grins. "Even better, she didn't *ask* to make one."

I try to hide my glee, the delirious grin squishing up my cheeks.

Alex lifts his eyebrows. "Wow," he says. "Now *that* sparked your joy."

CHAPTER 23

THEN

November 28, two autumns ago

"Ted," Alex says. He rests his hand on my bouncing knee. "What's up?"

"I'm nervous."

He glances my way briefly, brow furrowed, then back to the road. "Why?"

I huff out a breath, staring ahead. "I don't know."

"If it helps, I'm nervous, too."

"*You're* nervous?" I peer over at him, surprised. "You look completely chill."

"Chef face," he explains. "I've mastered looking chill on the outside while losing my shit on the inside."

I wrap my hand around his, where it rests on my knee. "Want to tell me?" I ask.

"First big holiday after being divorced," he says. "I only saw Mia for a couple hours this morning, and now I'm showing up at my parents' place without her."

He swallows thickly. I lean across the console and set my head on his shoulder. I don't have words of comfort. I can't imagine how awful it feels to spend the holiday away from your child.

"I miss her," he says. "And it feels wrong, to be without her. All of this, first-time stuff, after divorce, it feels . . . weird."

"Yeah." I stare out the window. "It does."

"There's another feeling," he says. "I don't know exactly what it is. I feel sad. And a little guilty because I'm also . . . relieved? *This* sucks. But this time last year sucked, too. I was miserable. Jen was miserable. We were still hiding that from everybody, putting on an *everything's fine!* performance, even though we both knew we were headed for divorce. I felt so fucking lonely, carrying that inside me, no one else knowing. It was awful."

My mind drifts to Ethan's and my last Thanksgiving. He flew to his parents' home in D.C., and I stayed home because I was going to be working all day Friday and Saturday, in preparation for and then during Small Business Saturday at The Bookshop. I FaceTimed my parents with Argos on my lap and wished them Happy Thanksgiving, and caught a peek at the spread of Thanksgiving classics filling the table, my extended family milling around in the background. I didn't want to be there, with a bunch of people I wasn't close to, in a home that wasn't the one I'd grown up in. But I didn't want to be alone, either.

When I hung up, I curled myself around Argos and cried until Lauren called me from her sister's in St. Louis, a little drunk and talking very fast as she explained I was her phone-a-friend for family trivia, and she had ten seconds to name the third sister in *Little Women*.

I smile, remembering her yelling, after I told her, "*That's* it! I knew she was an anemic invalid played by Claire Danes, but I couldn't remember her name for the life of me," before she bellowed even louder, "IT'S BETH! How do you like *that*, Carl!"

Carl, Lauren's brother-in-law, to whom, when he asked for Lauren's blessing to marry Gina, Lauren said no one would ever be good enough for her baby sister. Carl, whom Lauren secretly adores, because in response, he told her she was right, but he wanted to spend the rest of his life trying to be.

I feel a pang of sadness—missing Lauren; wishing I had a family I felt like I belonged to; grieving, as silly as it sounds, the home I left Ethan, which I loved to decorate for the holidays. It isn't mine to decorate anymore, and it never will be ever again.

And then, weaving through that sadness for what's gone, what never was, the thinnest thread of hope—for a future that I will one day look back from, to a past that is this moment, the moments since the divorce, the moments ahead, and maybe then, that past will be something I remember with pride, contentment, maybe even happiness.

I thread my fingers through Alex's and squeeze tight.

"Bittersweet," I tell him. "That's what that feeling is."

He glances my way, then draws my hand up, pressed to his cheek. "Bittersweet," he says. "Yeah. That's it."

*

"Um." I stare, dumbfounded, at the banner stretched across the doorway leading to his parents' kitchen.

HAPPY DAY, THALEX!

Alex stares at it, too, unblinking, as he mutters, "Jesus Christ."

Before we can unpack the banner any further, a literal dozen people descend on us. Alex makes introductions over the growing buzz of voices. Lydia, his mom. Nick, his dad. Aunts, uncles, a handful of cousins whose names fly by me, his sisters, Sophia, Ariana (Ari), and Catalina (Lina), whose names I'm confident I'll remember but not which faces they belong to.

I'm hugged, kissed on the cheek, spun around, hugged again, and oohed and aahed over. It is *a lot*.

Alex lets out a shrill whistle, startling everyone into taking a step back. "Let her breathe!"

His mom smacks his arm, muttering something in Italian under her breath that would make me nervous it was critical, if it weren't for the warm, pleased smile playing on her mouth as she looks at me. She's short and curvy, with caramel-brown eyes and Alex's dark, thick hair threaded with white piled up on her head. Her apron has a picture of Mia in her little soccer uniform, tiny cleated foot propped on a soccer ball, then below it, *Mia's #1 Fan*.

I want her to hug me again already.

"Welcome," his dad says, clasping my hand in his. He's a smidge taller than me, a smidge shorter than Alex, his hair silver and styled short, parted neatly. Alex has his deep-blue eyes but not much else. He smiles, inspecting me. "Theadora," he says, in a thick accent I can't place. "Good *Greek* name. Like *Alexander*."

I dart a glance at Alex, whose eyes widen. "Oh my god, Dad—"

"Enough with the *Big Fat Greek Wedding* shtick," Alex's mom says, taking my hand from his.

"I'm sorry," Nick says, the faux Greek accent vanished. He winks. "Great to meet you, Thea. Welcome."

I smile, remembering what I told Alex when he described his dad that first gelato night, what Alex told me. I was right, and he was, too. I like his dad already.

"You had me there for a second," I tell Nick. "But I have

watched that movie an inadvisable number of times, to the point that I have it memorized."

"A fellow *BFGW* fan! I love her!" Nick yells, wrapping an arm around me. "What about *Mamma Mia*?"

"Obsessed," I admit.

He slaps a hand over his heart. "I'm a goner."

Gently, Lydia draws me out of Nick's adoring clutches. "Come on, Thea," she says. "Let's get you a glass of wine."

I follow Lydia into the kitchen, glancing over my shoulder at Alex, who seems to be bickering with his dad and one of the sisters, pointing to the banner.

"You're not together, are you." Lydia says. A statement. Not a question.

"Um, no?" I glance over my shoulder again, hoping I'm not messing something up. Alex would have told me if he wanted me to lie to his family about us being a couple.

"Ariana was positive you were. Apparently, you're a prominent feature in Alex's social media," she explains.

My cheeks heat. After the petty bike race, Alex and I decided we'd start posting photos of each other on our feed. Nothing overtly romantic, more of a statement. The longer Jen and Ethan last, the more, it seems, we both want to prove we're lasting, too, even as something different. Something that, in my mind, is infinitely better. Because it's safe and solid. Because Ethan and Jen could break up tomorrow, hearts freshly shattered. But Alex and me? No such risk.

"We're just friends," I explain. "Our exes are together, and we sort of bonded over that at first. But now . . ." I shrug, smiling, nervous. "It's a friendship of its own. A good one."

Lydia smiles. "That sounds very healthy. I have no ill will toward Jen, because she's the mother of my granddaughter, so please know I'm not judging her, but I have no idea how she could jump right from one relationship to another. Heartbreak needs time to heal. And the people who hurt each other need time to figure out how that happened, what role they played. That way, when they want another relationship, they don't just do it all over again, repeating the same mistakes."

I blink, a little taken aback. And . . . maybe a little encouraged by it. Could that happen for me? After enough time has passed, might there be a day when I trust that I *could* pursue romance again without holding my breath, terrified for it to implode on me?

Lydia sets a glass in front of me, then points to the bottles lined up on the counter. "Red, white, or rosé?"

In the chilly months, I love red. But that bottle's not open. "I like it all," I tell her.

"But which would you *love*?" she asks, smiling up at me.

"Oh. Um." I clear my throat.

"I'm going to open them all for dinner," she says, leaning in. "So don't you worry about asking for an unopened bottle."

She reaches for the red, cuts across the seal, twists the corkscrew in, then yanks the cork out with a pop.

"How'd you know?" I ask.

"Your eyes," she says. "They lingered."

I make a mental note to be sure my eyes linger nowhere else tonight that Lydia might notice. Say, on her son, who, despite the bushy fall beard he's grown, I still very much want to kiss.

Lydia pours me a glass of red as she says, "I'll get Ari to take down the banner."

We both dart a glance toward the entryway, where Alex and the same sister—Ari?—and his dad are still going at it. Lydia peers back at me, then nods toward the counter, where a bowl of fishy-smelling mollusks sit. "Ever shucked oysters before?" she asks.

I shake my head. "Never eaten them, either. But I'm happy to try."

"Excellent." Lydia takes a sip of her wine. I take a sip, too. "While we shuck, you can tell me all about yourself. Your background. Your family. Your divorce. I want to hear it all!"

When she turns toward the oysters, I take the kind of sip I really need.

A deep, bracing gulp.

*

A game of Pit dominates the dining room table. It's loud and hot. My cheeks are flushed, my hair sweat-frizzed and tugged up onto my head. Alex's body's has brushed mine with every movement of the game. Which means, it's been constant.

Named the winner, Alex raises his hand in a magnanimous wave. We all boo and hiss. His sisters frisbee cards at him.

This, I think, *is family*.

I glance across the table at his mom as she stands and says, "Cake time!"

"Can I help?" I stand, too, but I'm yanked down by the belt loop of my jeans, bumping into Alex as I land in my chair. "What was that for?" I ask him.

Alex leans in, turning toward me, his shoulder like a shield that blocks the noise and attention of the table. For a moment, it's nothing but his face close to mine, his flushed cheeks, bright blue eyes, the scent of his sweat mingling with the spicy clean that clings to his clothes. He sets his hand on my back, threads it around my waist and draws me closer. His mouth brushes my ear as he says, "Remember the banner?"

I pin my thighs together beneath the table as a sweet, hot ache crushes through me and settles right *there*. "Hard to forget the banner," I say as steadily as I can.

Alex says, "It was for both of us."

"I mean, I figured. It looked sort of like a 'ship name. Thalex."

He groans. "I'm really sorry. Apparently, because I didn't scream at my family that we *weren't* dating, they assumed we were."

"I don't care, Alex. I actually think I'm kind of attached to it? *Thalex*. It sounds like *something*. Not sure what. It'll come to me, though."

Alex's expression turns serious. "Ted, remember when you were gone for your birthday?"

I spent the week in Columbus while Dad had his angioplasty after the series of ministrokes my mom had decided she'd wait through a month of telephone tag to tell me about. My birthday was the day of his surgery, and I didn't expect anything, of course. But Mom didn't even say anything—not the day of, the day before, the day after, the whole time I was there.

I pulled out of my parents' house and held off the tears until I'd made it to the highway. Then I sobbed off and on the whole six-hour drive home.

"Yes," I tell Alex. "I remember."

"We never celebrated *your* birthday."

"You called me," I remind him. "You and Mia left me a voicemail singing me 'Happy Birthday.'"

I saved that voicemail. I'll have it saved forever.

"But we never celebrated," Alex says. "It's my birthday tomorrow, and you're getting to celebrate with me now, so it's only fair."

"What's only fair?"

He eases back, revealing two cakes heaped with white icing, flickering with candles on the table in front of us.

"It's only fair," he says quietly, "that we get to celebrate *you*, too. Homemade birthday cake and everything."

My throat is thick. "So . . . that was the 'happy day' part of the banner?"

Ari—pretty sure it's Ari—pops her head in, on the other side of my shoulder, making me jump. "I called in a favor," she explains, "to whip up this banner real quick, with my buddy, Knox, but we didn't have great service over the call—his shop's in a service dead zone, so I think maybe a few words cut out on him, plus I told him I was on a budget and he charges per letter, soooo . . . this *was* supposed to say, *Happy Birthday, Thea & Alex*, and we ended up with *HAPPY DAY, THALEX*. Wish I could take credit for the creative genius of 'Thalex,' but I can't."

I smile up at Probably-Ari. "Thank you—that's really sweet of you to include me."

Alex playfully nudges Ari back, then grips my chair and draws me closer, until we're shoulder to shoulder, staring down at our cakes.

Everyone starts to sing.

My eyes burn. My chest tightens. I don't want to cry. But I think I'm going to.

"Say something funny," I mutter to Alex out of the side of my mouth, all while smiling at his family.

"Thalex," he whispers in my ear, curling his arm around me. "I figured out what it sounds like."

"Mm-hmm," I squeak.

His family are a bunch of yell-singers, horribly off pitch. It might be the best sound I've ever heard. "Happy Birthday, dear Thalex..."

Alex flips them all the double bird, making them cackle, his mom loudest of everyone, then says to me, soft in my ear, "It sounds like a prescription."

I turn toward him. "Ooh, *yes*, that's it!"

"For erectile dysfunction," he whispers.

A laugh wheezes out of me. "That sparked my joy!"

"Good." His gaze settles on my smile. "Because that laugh sparks my joy."

I clutch his hand beneath the table and force myself to look away, to meet his family's eyes, these people who hardly know me, so willing to show me love.

Alex threads our fingers together and squeezes. "Happy Day, Ted."

I glance his way and squeeze back. "Happy Day, Alex."

When I bend over my cake to blow out the candles, I catch a whiff of sweet-spiced pumpkin, rich-tart cream cheese. A fresh wave of tears threatens to spill. He remembered what I said about pumpkin. He told them. And they made this cake, for me.

I shut my eyes, draw in a breath, then blow out, in one long grateful, gust, every candle on my cake.

CHAPTER 24

THEN

December 31, two winters ago

I started therapy the first week of December, and it sucks.

Alex reassured me it gets better, after a while. He said it's like prep for cooking, arduous and frustrating, seemingly busywork, feeling like too much effort for not enough reward. But you have to do it, because in the end, the meal you sit down to is only as good as everything you put into giving it a strong foundation.

I want to believe him. I'm hoping I won't have to believe him, that soon it'll know it for myself. Right now, though, it's hard.

It probably doesn't help that this is the busiest, most stressful time of year at work and also the start of cold and flu season, so all month, staff has dropped left and right with various illnesses, and I've been constantly scrambling to cover for that. Then, of course, there's the fact that I just weathered my first divorced Christmas. Usually, I love the holidays. This year, I've felt like a Scrooge.

"Another one?" the bartender asks us.

I look to Alex, sitting beside me on the neighboring barstool. He turns to the bartender and says, "Very much, yes."

I laugh a little. We're both tipsy. Exhausted. Spent. I drove to Columbus for Christmas mostly out of guilt. My dad hasn't fully bounced back from the angioplasty, and I pictured my mom stressed by caring for him, doing everything herself, because for some reason, she'd insisted on hosting Christmas, not just Thanksgiving, too. Then my brother texted to say he'd be there. If Matt was coming, I knew I was, too.

Alex had Mia Christmas Eve, at his parents', where Jen apparently came for a visit that wasn't too strained. After Mia told them it made her sad they hadn't been together at Thanksgiving, they decided to make an effort to share the holiday for her. Christmas Day, Alex dropped by his old house and watched Mia open presents, then made a brief appearance at Jen's parents', where things were slightly more strained, thanks to Ethan's presence.

We talked on the phone for hours Christmas Eve and Christmas Day nights, and when I told Alex it was the only good part of the holiday for me, he said, "Yeah, Ted, me, too. Well, with the exception of Mia tearing open her presents. She was feral. And we definitely did a divorce guilt amount of gift giving, so there was *a lot* of carnage."

I laughed when he said that. I think it was the only time I laughed all December, before tonight.

Alex, like me, does not look like he's been feeling the holiday spirit, either. He's slumped over the bar, shoulders rounded.

Above us, strung across the ceiling, is truly an astronomical number of colored string lights, and dangling from them, dozens of oversized Christmas ornaments. It's karaoke night at Bob's Garage, and a couple on the other side of the room are singing

"What Are You Doing New Year's," only slightly off key but with so much heart and mutual infatuation it makes me want to throw up. Or throw something.

I glance around and sigh. Everyone around us does not seem to have gotten the memo that it is not the season to be merry.

"Why did we come here again?" I ask.

Alex swings his head my way. "Because we were trying to cheer up and not spend New Year's Eve wallowing in self-pity?"

"That's right." I drop my head on his shoulder. "I don't think it's working."

"It's not," he admits.

The bartender slides our whiskey sours right into our hands, giving us a sympathetic glance. "On the house," he says. "You two look like you could use it."

"Thanks?" Alex says.

"Sympathy drinks." I snort a laugh, folding my arms on the bar and dropping my head into them. "We're *that* pathetic."

Alex straightens and swivels on his barstool toward me. "Come on, Ted. We're not pathetic."

I peer up from my arm cave, frowning. "We aren't?"

"We aren't," he says. Alex's lifts his glass into the air. His hand wavers for a moment, like he almost doesn't have it in him to keep holding steady, like even just a perfunctory cheers is too much cheer to manage.

Guilt slugs me as I look at him. He's trying so hard. And I'm not.

I sit up, too, sweeping my drink off the bar and clinking it with Alex's, a bit more forcefully than I meant to.

"Shit," Alex mutters, before licking along his wrist to catch the whiskey sour sliding toward his sleeve. I'm sad-horny again, and a flicker of lust catches to a flame inside me as I watch him.

"Sorry," I tell him sheepishly. "Want me to help?"

Alex laughs faintly. "Help yourself, instead. You're just as bad as me."

I peer down at my hand, the whiskey sour covering it. "Huh. Guess you're right."

I lick at my wrist, too, and our eyes catch. Alex snorts. I snort louder. Then I cackle. Alex's belly laugh jumps out of him, seeming to surprise him as much as it surprises me.

We lick our way up our hands, still laughing, as I tell him, "We look like two sad tiny kittens, bathing ourselves."

"Oh." Alex's expression crumples. "That image is so sad. It does *not* spark my joy."

My chin wobbles dangerously. "Shit. Me neither."

Our laughter, the momentary spark of happiness, evaporates into at bleak, empty silence.

Alex throws back half of what's left of his drink, and I follow suit. We set down our glasses, whiskey and tart-sweet citrus burning down my throat. I shake myself and straighten my back. We were just getting somewhere good, and I brought us back down.

"Why is it," I ask, trying to sound perky, "that it's called sad *puppy* face? Aren't sad kitten faces just as pathetic? Maybe even more so? They're so tiny and fluffy, and they have such tiny paws!"

Alex frowns in thought. "I think it might be because, between cats and dogs, dogs are definitely the dumber and thus more innocent creatures. A kitty is arguably as cute as a puppy, but the kitty's going to grow up to be a vengeful, furniture-shredding, bread-stealing—"

"Bread stealing?"

"Figaro," Alex mutters darkly, "stole more toast from me than my own sisters managed to."

I tip my head. "Have I met Figaro?"

"Ted, I'm thirty-six. I haven't lived at home since I was eighteen. He'd have to be immortal to still be around."

"Rest in peace, Figaro," I say solemnly.

"Try rest in perpetual *anguish*," Alex says. "He was a demon in black-and-white furball form."

"Wow." My eyes widen.

Alex hangs his head and mumbles, "I really liked my toast."

I set my hand on his arm, squeezing. "It was homemade-bread toast, wasn't it?"

He nods sadly.

"Well, now I get it," I tell him. "Because I would do violence to anything that tried to come between me and Bruscato homemade-bread toast. Fuck Figaro."

Alex peers up at me, smiling faintly. "Did you grow up with dogs? That why you got Argos?"

"Yeah. I badgered my parents for a dog for years, and they finally caved when I was in seventh grade—a golden retriever named Bailey. She was my cuddle buddy. I wasn't *technically* allowed to have her on my bed, but she ended up there every night. I took such good care of her. Groomed her, walked her every day. It was, according to my mother, the first time I showed her 'the capacity for consistent responsibility.'"

Alex makes a face like he just smelled something stinky. "I don't think I like the sound of your mom"

I laugh a little. "She was worn out. And grumpy."

"Who could ever be grumpy with you?" Alex asks. He leans in, cupping my face. I think maybe Alex's caution around not drinking much so as not to crave cigarettes has left him with a slightly lower tolerance than me. His thumbs stroke up and down my cheeks. "You're so beautiful. And kind. And patient. And funny. Who wouldn't want to love the shit out of you?"

I bite my lip, fighting a smile as I set my hands over his. "I think this is the whiskey sour goggles talking."

"Goggles don't talk, Ted." Alex hiccups. "They *see*."

"You're right." I draw his hands down from my face, because I can't take the torture. He's drunk, and I'm tipsy. He's saying sweet things to me, and I've wanted to kiss him for three and a half months and nothing's made that want fade.

Alex keeps his hands tangled with mine, setting them on my lap. He leans in. "What were we talking about? Before I told you how pretty you were?"

"Sad-kitty versus sad-puppy face," I remind him. "We got on the subject of your demon childhood cat, as evidence that cats grow up to be domesticated furball psychopaths."

"Yes!" He leans in, eyes wide. "So that's my answer. Why it's sad-*puppy* face is because kitties grow up to be cats who are sinister as fuck. Dogs are just big puppies. They stay dumb and cute, and that never changes. So sad-puppy face, which tugs on your heartstrings, has to evoke pure innocence. Not demonic, needle-clawed animals who steal your toast."

"To be fair," I say, "I have met some really sweet cats in my day."

"Where?" Alex says, like this is ludicrous. "*Where*, Ted!"

"The shelter," I explain. "When I was a teenager. I was bored and lonely a lot on the weekends. So I volunteered at the animal shelter. Played with the dogs and cats to help them stay socialized and as happy as possible. It's a tragic, self-fulfilling prophecy. Shelter animals have this bad rap as mean, unlovable creatures, but they're not. They just get grumpy because they're stuck in a cage, and then no one wants them when they seem grumpy, but they never asked to be put in that cage. It's terrible—"

"Ted!" Alex wails. "This is *not* sparking my joy!"

"Sorry!" Now it's my turn to cup his face. "Alex, look at me."

He opens his eyes. They're wet, like he was actually about to cry. "What?" he whispers.

I slowly cross my eyes, dragging my right eye toward my nose. Then I cluck my tongue when I've gone as far as I can, sending my left eye pinging away, like an eight just struck by the cueball.

A laugh wheezes out of Alex as he drops forward, his forehead bumping into mine. "I love you," he whispers.

I blink, stunned. And then I immediately talk myself down. He means friend love, of course. Alex is as affectionate with his words as he is with his touch.

"I love you, too," I whisper. "You're the bestest friend."

He doesn't say anything for a moment, but then he slowly pulls away, meeting my eyes. "Better than Lauren?"

"Lauren's not here," I hedge.

He leans back in. "But if she *was*."

I bite my lip, torn. "It's different. We're *different* kinds of best friends."

"Hmm." Alex narrows his eyes and reaches for my phone.

"What are you doing?" I ask.

"Sending myself Lauren's contact info."

"Oh, hey now—"

"Shh," he says magnanimously. "Don't worry, I've got this."

"Got *what*?" I'm half exasperated, half amused, a reversal of our usual roles.

Alex leans in, curls an arm around me, and lifts his phone for a selfie. "Smile, Ted?"

There's just the slightest upswing in how he says it, an unsureness that I hate to hear. I lean in, pressing my temple to his, and smile wide.

The photo's a little blurry. Our smiles are wide but our eyes look a little sad, smudged with shadows beneath them from not enough sleep and too much booze. In my black boatneck long sleeve, Alex in his charcoal-gray thermal shirt, we both look like we're headed to a funeral, entirely out of a place in this festive, explosion-of-color bar on New Year's Eve.

But something about the photo makes me smile. Because it's honest. Because it's real.

Because it's us.

Alex hunches over his phone for a second, grinning while his thumbs fly across the screen. A second later my phone dings.

I reach for it on the bar and groan. Alex sent the photo to Lauren and me, then below it, HAPPY NEWSYEAR SIEVE FROM THEDA AND HER BESTEST FREND ALEC.

Lauren responds immediately. Who the hell is this and what have you done with Thea? Thea, if you're there against your will, send the knife emoji!

Alex frowns at the text. "That's rude of her. Why would she think you're here against your will? I'm a nice guy."

"You're the nicest guy," I soothe him.

I sigh as I type, Lo, I'm out with Alex, very much of my own free will. We're both a little tipsy, and Alex got excited about sending you a photo.

My phone pings, a separate text from Lauren only to me. WAIT, THAT'S THE HOT CHEF?

Lauren's been so busy with work, and I've been so busy trying to keep myself afloat the past the months, I've hardly managed to talk to her, and when I have, I've kept conversation to other parts of life. I already think about Alex too much. I didn't need to bring it into my rare phone calls with Lauren, too.

His name is Alex, I type, and we hang out sometimes.

"Hang out sometimes?" Alex glances from my phone screen up to me. He looks completely stricken. No, worse. Gutted.

I drop my phone. "Alex—"

"I thought we were *friends*," he says, a little sloppily. "Bestest friends!"

"We are!" I'm panicking, because Alex is giving off strong vibes á la kid at The Bookshop who just dropped their hot chocolate and is about to *wail*.

"Not according to your text with *her*," he says, clearly wounded.

I grasp his arms, drag my hands up his shoulders, ducking to meet his eyes. "I haven't told her about you because I didn't want her to know how much I like you. Because I don't really know what to do with how much I like you, Alex, so just talking and thinking about it more than I already do is not helpful."

"Wait." Alex blinks, then frowns, his brow furrowing with an adorably deep crease. "You really *like* me?"

I swallow nervously. I hope that he's as drunk as he seems, that he won't remember any of this tomorrow. "Yes, Alex, I really like you."

His breaks into a smile, wide and deep-dimpled. Utterly beaming. "I really like you, too, Ted."

My phone dings with a text from Lauren. I steal a quick glance, but that's all I need to read it and immediately want to puke. Hanging out with HOT CHEF and not a word about it?! You've been holding out on me, ma'am, and You! Are! In! Trouble!

"Ted," Alex says.

I tear my gaze away from my phone and meet his eyes. "Yes, Alex?"

"Can we go home"—he hiccups violently—"and cuddle?"

I open my mouth to make up an excuse, a detour—anything to keep us from going back to his place and snuggling on the couch when we're both varying degrees of intoxicated, sad, and lonely.

But then the song for whoever's next up on karaoke starts to blast over the speaker, and after four notes, I know exactly what we're in for. Listening to happy people sing happy holiday music was a downer. But there is something even more downer-inducing than that, and it is 100 percent Joni Mitchell.

I'll figure out how to redirect the cuddle session eventually. Right now, I have to focus on us making a quick exit. Because Alex needs me to have my shit together, and if I stay and listen to this song, I absolutely will not be able to.

"Let's get out of here." I slap down a twenty on the bar, then slide off my stool.

Alex glances from me to the money, then back to me. "That was fast. You really want to cuddle, huh?"

I throw a thumb over my shoulder. "'River,'" I tell him, then add, to emphasize the point, "Joni Mitchell."

Alex jolts on his stool like he's been electrically shocked. He suddenly seems halfway to sober. "Oh, *fuck* no."

As he slides off his stool, we find each other's hand, fingers locked tight, and shove our way through the crowd, straight toward the door.

*

Even though I'm the one who's felt sick to her stomach since that text from Lauren, Alex is the one who pukes, thankfully *after* our driver drops us off in front of his house.

"I never liked that rhododendron anyway," Alex mutters as I unlock his door.

He makes it to the powder room toilet just in time for round two, and I follow him, rubbing his back, pausing while he retches again. I hesitate at first, but then I figure maybe it'll put him at ease if I just keep talking, if I don't make it some big deal. Once he's done, the toilet flush's echo faded from the bathroom, I ask, "Why didn't you like the rhododendron?"

"It didn't bloom," he says, sitting slowly back on his heels. "I did everything I was supposed to, and it still didn't bloom. Mia was so disappointed."

My heart twists. I glance out the window at the rhododendron peeking above it, rubbing his back again. "Maybe it needs a partner plant."

Alex stands, then ambles over to the medicine cabinet. He pulls out a toothbrush, lines it with toothpaste, and starts to scrub. "A partner plant?" he asks.

I shrug. "Rhododendrons don't technically *need* a mate plant, but . . . it can help to have another plant nearby. Cross-pollination," I add, at his blank look. "It increases the chances of a flower."

Alex peers at me as he scrubs his teeth, toothpaste foam gathering at the corners of his mouth. "A partner plant," he says again. He smiles.

And I can't help but smile back.

I step aside as he bends over the sink, spits, then rinses, taking time to make sure his scruffy beard is clean, too, then turns toward me. His eyes are clearer, back to their deep-blue brightness. I think he's pretty much sober now.

"Sorry about that," he says quietly.

I shake my head, threading my fingers through his. "Don't be. Happens to the best of us."

"Didn't happen to *you*," he says, slipping past me, taking me by the hand out of the bathroom and toward the couch.

"That's because," I explain as I drop on the couch with a plop, "I've been drinking more than you. My tolerance is higher. That isn't a good thing."

He's still standing, looking unsettled as he scrapes a hand through his hair. His gaze darts away then back to me. "Would you say you're sober, then?"

I squint. "Ninety-five percent. You?"

"About the same. That puke did me good."

After a beat, I say to him, "Why do you ask?"

Alex clears his throat, hands on his hips. He's staring down at the ground. "Because back at the bar is a little fuzzy, but . . . I think I remember asking you to cuddle and you being up for that, and I uh . . . I wouldn't want us to do that if we weren't both clear-headed. That is, *if* you were still up for cuddling."

I told myself I wouldn't let us cuddle not because I don't want to, but because I don't think we should. But after this past miserable month, and before that, a fall spent barely seeing Alex, I simply can't make myself care right now about doing what I think we should. I want to do what I want. What he wants.

Standing from the couch, I wrap my arms around his waist and set my head on his shoulder. "I'm up for cuddling. Very much, yes."

He laughs. "I do remember saying that."

My heart rate doubles. "Do you remember after that?"

He's quiet for a moment, then rests his head against mine. "Not much, beyond that I was glad I was with you. I'm still glad about that."

My pulse slows, relief unspooling through me as I tell him the truth. "I'm glad I'm with you, too."

Alex pulls back enough to look at me, his eyes clear and bright, sparkling in the glow from the twinkly lights strung around his Christmas tree. "I'm always glad when I'm with you, Ted. Even when everything is shit."

He curls his hands around my neck, his thumbs sweeping along my jaw, and I list toward him. Heat curls through me. "I... feel the same way." I can barely form a sentence. My whole body is a live wire.

I slide my palms up his chest and press myself against him. I wish I could blame the drinks or the depressing reality of my first divorced Christmas, but I can't. I'm touching Alex because I'm desperate to.

His hips rock toward mine. His gaze drops to my mouth. "Ted," he whispers roughly. There's an edge in his voice, a plea.

"I'm sorry." I try to pull back. "I shouldn't—"

"You should," he mutters, dragging me back against him.

It's the only permission I need, before my body finally gives in to what it's been fighting for over half a year now.

I press up on tiptoes, so we're eye to eye, sink my hands into his hair, and brush his lips with mine, so faint, I'm not sure it happened, but then Alex leans in and meets me, his mouth brushing mine, too, minty warmth gusting over me, and I know it's real. A whispered, frightened, momentary kiss.

My nose grazes his. Our foreheads meet. Silence hangs in the room.

Kissing Alex felt so right. And yet suddenly, I'm petrified it was the wrong thing to do.

Alex curls his hands around my waist, tucking his head into the crook of my neck. "Ted," he whispers.

My heart's pounding in my ears, and maybe it's warped my hearing, but I don't think so. He sounds like he regrets it.

We shouldn't have. We're *friends*. Friends don't kiss. They can't. Not if they want to stay friends. And there is nothing I want more than to keep Alex Bruscato as my friend.

"Night, Alex." I hug him as platonically as I can, then wrench myself away, throw open the door, and start power walking home.

My phone buzzes with a text two minutes into my walk. It's from Alex.

Let me know when you're home safely?

I feel like I just swallowed a rock. I should be relieved—on the rare occasion he hasn't walked me home in person or on a call, this is what friend Alex has texted his friend Thea. He's being a good friend to me.

Why then, am I so sad that he's given me exactly what I want?

CHAPTER 25

NOW

August 5, third day of "vacation"

The first night of vacation, the one-bed situation led to a one-bed argument, a not-too-pleasant hiss-whispered debate in our bedroom, after beating Jen and Ethan at euchre. I reminded Alex he gets an eighty-year-old's back when he doesn't sleep on a good mattress. Alex countered that the mattress seemed like shit anyway. I argued that I'd be sleeping on the floor if he tried not to sleep in the bed. Alex threatened to chuck me in the bed if I tried it, which did my raging lust for him no favors whatsoever.

Eventually, we compromised—after everybody went to bed, we'd steal the couch cushions from the living room sofa, put those on the floor in our room, and take turns sleeping on them, then wake up early enough to put them back before anyone else was awake and could notice. I slept on them the first night, after winning rock paper scissors to decide who got the floor. Alex slept on the cushions on the floor last night.

And today, I can tell he's still paying for it.

I doubt anyone else can tell. He's been kicking a soccer ball with Mia across the sand, and half an hour ago, he was lifting her above the waves. Now they're crouched at the surf, poking around for sea creatures. Lines of pain bracket his mouth, and there's a notch carved between his eyebrows.

But he's toughing it out, for Mia.

A wave of longing tugs at me with a force that feels as elemental as the waves receding from the shore. Alex being a good dad is so damn hot.

I force those lusty thoughts away, as I remind myself I'm sitting feet away from his ex-wife and my ex-husband. Then I refocus on Mia and Alex, the joy that creeps across Mia's face as she shows him something, when he meets it with curiosity, energy, just as much enthusiasm as she gave him.

I'm watching them behind my sunglasses, over the top of my book, when Mia turns, then yells, "Mommy! Come here! I found something!"

Jen peers up from her book, smiling. "Coming!" She drops her book, tugs at her sarong, making sure it's tight at her waist, and crosses the sand toward Mia.

When Jen joins Mia and Alex along the water's edge, Alex makes no move to leave. They don't act how they often have the past two years, like it's a game of tag, one parent in, one parent out. My heart squeezes as I see Mia smile up at both of them, tugging Jen down to her and Alex's level.

Maybe I shouldn't look, maybe it's private, but I can't help but watch and admire. I have no idea what it's like to sever every fiber of your relationship while having a kid who still weaves you together. I've watched the past two years as Alex and Jen have tried to stitch parts of their lives back together, for Mia's sake—Christmas that first year, then Easter, then a joint birthday party, as well as Thanksgiving and Christmas last year. I've seen them both at more of her soccer games this past spring. Even talking outside for a few minutes, exchanging notes, getting up to speed on everything Mia, on custody-change days.

And I've seen Mia drinking it all in, soaking it up.

I don't know what's ahead, how this is going to go, when I finally work up the courage to talk to Alex, but a rush of peace courses through me as I realize, whatever he wants from me, whatever way I can share life with Alex, I'll never wish Jen wasn't part of it—because Mia needs her. She needs her parents, together, kind and loving, whenever and however they can be.

A shadow over me drags me from my thoughts. I peer up, shading my eyes. "Hi, Ethan."

"Thea." He lowers to the sand beside me, flips open the cooler lid, and pulls out a water. He doesn't offer me one. But I didn't expect him to. Cracking the lid, he squints as he watches Mia, Alex, and Jen down on the wet, packed sand. After two long gulps, he sets the water bottle back in the cooler, then turns and looks at me. "Doesn't it bother you?"

"Doesn't what bother me?"

He nods toward them, the breeze ruffling his hair, his eyes narrowed behind his round tortoiseshell sunglasses. I experience that odd, surreal feeling that comes over me sometimes, when I'm around Ethan for more than a few passing seconds. How bizarre it is that he was someone I swore my life to, someone whose body I drew into mine. Someone I peed in the same bathroom with while he showered, drove to the hospital when his appendix was about to burst.

And now, he's a stranger to me. Cold and closed off.

"Doesn't it bother you," Ethan says, "that no matter how far back you and Alex go, *they* will always have this, something they share in a way you can't. Their daughter."

For a moment, pain knifes through me. Probably not as Ethan intended, not for some jealousy or desire that I could be Mia's mom instead of Jen. But because *I* wanted to be a mom. I wanted to have kids. And I have none.

I glance away from him, back to the water, where Mia stands, holding hands with Alex and Jen, as they lift her above a wave, then send her splashing down into it, her head thrown back in laughter, pure joy on her face. Jen smiles at Alex, who meets her eyes, and just briefly, his mouth lifts in a smile, too. The next moment, their eyes are down, but their smiles stay, because of where their eyes are, what they're focused on. Mia.

Ethan leans in a little, his voice softer, and says, "Think about it, what that means, what she'll always remind you of—those two, together. Making her, loving each other when they did. Every milestone, every big moment, you'll have that right in your face."

Mia shrieks with joy as they lift her over another wave.

I smile as I swipe a tear from my cheek, my gaze fixed on her. And I tell Ethan, "Yes."

"Yes, *what*?" he says.

I turn and stare at him. "Yes, I've thought about that. And yes, that will be right there, in my face. I hope it'll be in my face even more, each year." I wipe away another tear, turning to face him fully.

Ethan looks at me like I'm speaking gibberish.

"It isn't about us, Ethan. And it isn't about Alex and Jen, either. It's about *her*—about the fact that the kinder her parents are toward each other, around her, the better off she is. It's about her needs, as a *child*." A sad laugh tumbles out of me. "But you can't see that, can you? Because you're just a child yourself."

Ethan's shoulders roll back. He stands suddenly, hands shoved in the pockets of his swim trunks, and says, "Come at me all you want, but ask yourself—is this what you really want for the rest of your life?"

"Yes," I say simply, standing with my book, pinning my hat to my head with one hand against the wind. If I stay here a minute longer I'm going to wallop Ethan with one or both of those items. "And if it wasn't what I wanted for the rest of my life," I tell him, "I wouldn't deserve a life that had them in it."

CHAPTER 26

THEN

February 14, two winters ago

Alex and I haven't talked about the New Year's Eve kiss. I'm grateful for it, because I need our safe, familiar friendship, the comfort of our now-standard wintertime-evening hangout positions, cuddled up on the sofa.

Cuddled up *platonically*, of course.

Sure it's Valentine's Day, but we've agreed to ignore that. I had an early shift at The Bookshop, came home, walked Argos, and changed into comfy clothes. Alex picked up a pizza and tubs of gelato from Luna's and brought them to my place for dinner. We gorged ourselves on pizza, and now we're working our way through our first tub of gelato and the *New York Times* games.

It's only five o'clock, but it's been dark for an hour. It feels like midnight.

We're lounging in shorts and T-shirts, because the heat hangs in my third-floor apartment, rising from the units below, to the point that I have my heat turned off, a window in the living room cracked to let in a frigid sliver of winter air.

I frown up at the Wordle on his screen, only two guesses left, as Alex holds his phone above us. My head rests on his shoulder. His chin nuzzles into my temple. "What the *hell* is this word?" I ask.

"If I knew that," he says testily, "We'd be doing the mini by now."

His surly response surprises me. Very un-Alex.

I turn my head and ease off his shoulder, onto his upper arm, meeting his eyes. "You okay?"

He stares down at me and sighs. "No. I'm sorry I snapped."

"I wouldn't say *snapped*," I tell him. "*Grumped*, maybe?"

I turn so I'm sideways, and with how narrow Lauren's hand-me-down midcentury sofa is, I have to wedge my leg over his so I don't fall off. I try to keep my thigh as low as possible, barely brushing his knee. As far as possible from his groin. Cuddling with Alex like this is torture enough—wonderful, terrible torture. I'd stop doing it if I didn't feel so desperate for the closeness, the comfort of touching and being held. I keep telling myself that I'd want this with anyone, that I'm just starved for intimate touch, for sex. But I know why I keep cuddling up to him, even when, after every time we break apart, I walk away from it keyed up and aching, every nerve a live wire—because I want to feel this close to *him*.

And this is as close to physical intimacy as we can have. As close as it can get.

In part, I'm sure I'm suffering so badly because of how long it's been since I've had an orgasm by anyone's hand except my own. And also because the winter weather here is *the* worst; I need all the happy brain chemicals I can get, and cuddling offers those in spades.

For as lovely as I find Pittsburgh's sunshine-while-sprinkling-rain fairy-tale springs, its grand tapestry of amber, bronze, and crimson foliage lanced by gold-sun autumns, even its summers, which, though often humid and riddled with storms, are growing on me, for how lush they turn the grass, the trees, the flowers; I cannot find a single thing to like about its winter. Bleak, gray, frigid, weeks of hardly any sunshine, months of icy wind and tiny icebergs of dirt-streaked grimy snow clinging to parking lots and sidewalks. To me, it is absolutely miserable. I have yet to meet a Pittsburgher who feels any differently, which makes me feel a bit better about my annual three-month-long bad attitude because of it.

But even though misery loves company, it doesn't help me make it through any better. I have yet to get a straight answer out of anyone here on how *they* make it through any better. I'm starting to wonder if that's because the answer isn't necessarily something you share with a casual friend or the staff at the bookstore you're visiting. I'm starting to think the answer lies in how many fall birthdays belong to my StoryTime attendees.

Each StoryTime, I ask if anyone has a birthday, so we can sing to them, and then I can read one of my rotation of birthday-themed children's books. September through November, over half those kids' hands shoot up.

In short, I think Pittsburghers of childbearing years and childrearing inclination make it through winter by cuddling up and making babies.

The making-babies part is off the table for Alex and me. But the cuddling, I have been wholeheartedly leaning into.

Alex shifts a little underneath me, stretching to set his phone on windowsill behind him. "I grumped," he admits.

"What's got you grumping?" I ask.

He stares at me. "Well, it's February, and we're in Pittsburgh."

"Good point." I brush a clump of Argos fur off his shoulder. "Anything else?"

He shrugs, setting his fingers in my hair, brushing the curls off my face. "I'm . . . lonely."

"Lonely?" I ask quietly, trying not to sound hurt.

Even though I am. What he's said pokes an old wound, a deep one, a hurt I'm trying to heal with Sue in therapy, but that's taking a lot longer than I'd like.

You're not enough.

"Ted," he says, peering down at me. "I don't mean . . . emotionally. I've got you. My family. My buddies."

I smile faintly. I met his "buddies" early in the new year, when Alex invited me over for the birthday party he was hosting for his friend Mike. They're good guys, playful like Alex, friendly and warm, some of them married, some not, some of them in the food scene, others from his pickup basketball league, even some from high school.

"So if not emotionally," I say. "You mean . . . physically?"

A swallow works down his throat. "Aren't you?"

Suddenly, I am deeply aware of every part of our bodies that is touching. My leg on his, my pelvis against his hip. My breasts pressed into his ribs. Heat creeps up my cheeks. "Yes."

He sighs, easing away from me slightly. "It's getting distracting."

I sit up, suddenly self-conscious and guilty. Maybe I've been torturing him with all this cuddling. Then again, he's the one who asked for it, who set this precedent. But even then, just because he started it, that doesn't mean he has to want to keep going. I can be the one who stops, or who at least offers to.

"What do you want to do?" I ask.

Alex groans as he sits up, too, raking his hands through his hair. "I don't know."

I bite my lip, warring with myself. The thought of nudging Alex toward finding someone new, someone who'd take my place, someone he'd share *everything* with, selfishly makes me feel ill. But the thought of seeing him miserable like this, just so I can keep his friendship, keep loving him in this way that's safe and sure, makes me feel even sicker.

Maybe there's a compromise. A middle way. A reasonable first step that will scratch the itch for Alex without forcing me to let go of him entirely.

"What about . . ." I reach for his phone, then mine, setting them on our laps. "The apps."

Alex blinks at me. "The *what*?"

"The dating apps. I know Google pissed you off when it suggested it, but . . . that was seven months ago. We're on the upswing, right? New year, new . . . journey? I don't know . . ." I swallow my fear and dig deep for courage. "And I'll do it with you."

Alex stares down at his phone, then peers out the window, quiet for so long, I start to wonder whether he's fallen into some fugue state. But then he turns back toward me, rolls his eyes, and says, "Oh, why the hell not."

I leap up, grabbing the second tub of gelato. While we eat, we create our accounts, make our profiles, and offer each other some mutual editing. Opinions are given on which photo to use as our main picture, how much to say: Do we mention divorce? Does Alex say he has a kid? Do I mention I own a dog?

We go with short, witty—we think—bios, and after rather extensive debate, decide to include the less-witty but salient details. The divorces, the daughter, the dog.

"We're not looking for anything serious," Alex says as he adds in that information. "But why would we want to even *casually* date or hook up with someone who thinks divorced people are fuckups. Or someone who hates kids—"

"Or dogs," I add. "Which means they are *soulless.*"

"Or allergic," he provides.

"Well, yeah, that, too. But even so, between Argos and some casual fling, I'm going with Argos every time."

"Fair."

Alex and I sit back on the couch together, legs on the coffee table.

Not cuddling.

We stare at our profiles, then look at each other.

"Well?" he asks. "Ready to start swiping?"

I groan. "I kind of feel like I'm going to puke."

"That might be all the gelato we just ate," he says.

"Yeah." I stare at my phone. "But I also think it's because I'm thirty-four and on a dating app for the first time in my life. Why don't people meet in person anymore?" I whine.

"Because modern Americans live highly insular, digital-forward existences, and their experience of community is largely virtual, rather than in person."

"Thanks," I say tiredly. "That was uplifting."

Alex shrugs. "Just speaking the truth."

"Well, then, here we go."

We look at each other one more time, turn back to our phones, and start to swipe.

*

Fate is either fucking with us or finally being kind, because in the first hour of our swiping, we both match with people who, at least judging by their profiles, seem pretty promising. It's either a good outcome or too good to be true.

We're about to find out.

"Are we being smart," Alex asks, as he pulls his car into a space outside the indoor adult-only Putt-Putt golf spot. "Or are we being really dumb?"

"A little bit of both?" I peer over at him and try to bury the ache that stabs through me. He looks handsome. *Really* handsome. He's trimmed his beard a bit, put some kind of product in his hair, giving his wave-curls lush definition. His deep-blue sweater brings out his eyes, and the stretchy camel-colored hybrid jean-chinos he's wearing hug his thighs.

His brow furrows. "What's wrong?"

"Nothing," I say, the closest to a lie I've ever told him. "Just nervous." That, at least, is the truth. I am nauseatingly nervous.

Alex reaches for my hand, threading our fingers together. "We don't have to do this. If you're not comfortable—"

"I'm good." I squeeze his hand. "Promise."

He searches my eyes for a beat, then lets go of my hand. "Okay, then let's do this."

We throw open our doors at the same time, me hugging my coat around my body, Alex seemingly impervious to the brutal cold, leaving his jacket in the back seat.

Huddled together, we rush onto the sidewalk, then up the steps. The Putt-Putt place looks lively, vibrating with music as we near it. It's in The Terminal, a place in The Strip District, where I've gone with Alex to visit his favorite spot for cheese and cured meat, Pennsylvania Macaroni, and dozens of other specialty-food stores. The Terminal, Alex explained, used to be the place where all the grocers and suppliers docked and unloaded their goods. Now it's been "revitalized" or, probably more accurately, gentrified, filled with upscale restaurants and vendors that appeal to the twenty- and thirtysomethings who've filled the new condos on the other side of it, along the Allegheny River.

When we matched with our dates—Kate, for Alex; Nate, for me—Alex suggested we offer to meet them at the same spot; that way, if I got a bad vibe from the guy, he'd be nearby, ready to whisk me away. I tried to point out that this might harsh the potentially *good* vibes with Kate, but Alex only waved a hand and said, "If that were to happen, and she couldn't be cool with my being there for my best friend, then she's not worth it."

"Maybe," I told him, "don't lead with the fact that your best friend is female. Could be a deal-breaker."

Alex just frowned and said, "Maybe I should have put *that* in my bio, too."

He turns toward me now as we stand outside the door. I'm shivering from nerves, from the cold. "You sure you want to do this?" he says.

"Yes!" I try to infuse as much enthusiasm as possible in my voice. "It'll be a good time. We'll flirt and have fun, play Putt-Putt and maybe *putt* out, if you know what I mean."

Alex shakes his head, fighting a smile. "I'm the one who's supposed to be cracking dumb-dad jokes."

"You really do not deliver on that front," I tell him as he opens the door. "I'm just making up where you fall short."

"My most heartfelt gratitude," he quips, setting his hand on my back, guiding me in. Just that momentary touch, the heat of his hand seeping through my coat, sends a wave of calm rushing through me.

As soon as we step inside, he drops it. I feel like I've been thrown out in the middle of the ocean without a life raft. Which isn't fair. I encouraged this. I *led* us here.

Time to put on my big-girl panties and find a life raft of my own.

Alex leans in as we stand behind a group of people who can't seem to make up their mind about where they're going or what they're doing. "Ted," he says quietly.

I peer over at him. "Hmm?"

He smiles softly. "You look smokin'. Just so you know."

Pleasure spills through me. "I was thinking that about you, in the car."

His smile deepens. He rocks back on his heels. "I thought so."

I smack his chest. "Smug is not a good look on you."

"But a sapphire-blue crewneck sweater is, isn't it?" he teases.

I roll my eyes but can't help the smile that tugs at my mouth. "Yes, it's a *very* good look."

His smile fades. "Remember what I said—just text if you feel uncomfortable, if you need anything, okay?"

Surrounded by the crowd, hidden from Kate and Nate, who might be here, I clutch his hand with mine and squeeze. "Thanks. You, too, okay? I took, like, two sessions of karate, twenty years ago, and I'm not afraid to use what I know. I will defend your honor, if called upon."

Alex squeezes my hand hard, then presses a kiss to my hair, the first he ever has. It unravels me.

"Good luck, Ted."

His hand slips from mine and he wends his way through the crowd.

*

Nate is a nice guy, if a little handsy. Then again, I did say in my bio that I was here for a good time, not a long time, which Alex warned against, so maybe I'm just getting back from the universe what I put out.

Which, speaking of, as of right now, I do *not* plan to put out.

Still, I'm trying to roll with it. I haven't gotten a text from Alex, and I can't see him right now, around the Putt-Putt setups, the countless heads filling every free space around them. I'm going to hang in there. For Alex.

And probably because this will make Lauren laugh when I call her and tell her about it later.

"So Thea," Nate says. He's leaning against the small bar staked at the entrance of every Putt-Putt station, his gaze raking over me. "Talk to me about what you're looking for."

I'm focused on my putt, adjusting my stance, trying not to spend too much mental energy attempting to reconcile the not-red-flag bio and photos in his profile with the man standing a little too close me.

And now, behind me.

I angle myself away, resetting my stance. "Oh, you know," I start to say, not really knowing where I'm going with this. "I'm looking for fun. Something low-key and chill."

That sounds plausible. If a little floozy.

Not that there's anything wrong with being floozy. I'm just not sure *I'm* feeling floozy. All the lust that's plagued me for months seems to have shriveled up the moment I saw Nate and he drew me into a very enthusiastic, near-butt-groping hug hello.

"Gotcha," he says. His gaze dances away, lingering somewhere for a moment, then back to me.

"What about you?" I ask, before I swing. The ball sails up the ramp, then down, headed straight for the hole, but then a windmill blade knocks it away. I groan.

"Same." Nate steps closer. "Low-key and chill."

I hand him the club, which Nate takes. Then he opens his arms and says, "Why don't you and I putt this one together."

My eyes widen. I can picture exactly how that setup is going to go, Nate bent over me, caging me in. I don't like that picture at all. "I couldn't take your putt!" I wave him forward. "It's all you."

Nate gives me a coy look, like he thinks this is some game we're playing, like he thinks I'm actually enjoying it. "You sure?" he says. "I mean, I find that, when it comes to this stuff, the *more* the merrier. Makes it more *fun*. What do you think?"

I tip my head, trying to parse his emphasis, but coming up short. "Um . . . in some situations, definitely. A good, you know, group effort, can be a game changer. But, with Putt-Putt, I think it's pretty much a solo gig."

He grins. "Solo gigs can be solid foreplay," he concedes, before turning to putt.

I dive into my skirt pocket, then pull out my phone. At first, I'm relieved to see there's a text from Alex, but then I'm not. Because the text just reads SOS.

My head snaps up, and like I've conjured him, Alex is right

there, staring at me, wide-eyed, like a deer in the headlights. On his arm *hangs* a woman who is either well on her way to shit-faced or deeply disinclined to stand on her own two feet.

"Kate!" Nate says, chucking the club aside. "Great to see you! Who do we have *here*?"

"This," Kate says, "is Alex." She swivels my way, her gaze raking down me. "And who is this?"

"Thea," Nate says proudly, like I'm his to introduce.

"Well," Kate says, "isn't this fun!" She detaches herself from Alex long enough to attach herself to me, curling her arm through mine. "You are *adorable*."

Nate sets his hands in his pockets, glancing between Alex and me, looking pleased. I have no idea what's going on. I turn to Alex, who's searching my eyes wildly. I widen mine. *What is it?*

He widens his. *What is going on?*

I realize that Alex doesn't know I was about to send an SOS myself. Which means, I think, he's sticking with this totally weird situation because he's assuming I'm somehow interested in it.

I extract my arm from Kate's carefully, lifting my phone. "Sorry, I tell her, "just need to check in on the dog with the sitter."

"Take your time," Kate purrs.

I type SOS TOO to Alex, then hit send.

"So," Nate says to Alex, "how long have you two been on the scene?"

Alex frowns as he feels my text reach his phone, buzzing in his pocket. "What scene?" he asks.

Kate laughs and throws herself at him again, slowing his progress as he pulls his phone from his back pocket. "I love it when they act innocent. It's totally my kink."

Nate glances from me to Alex, then grins. "Mine, too, babe."

"Babe?" I blurt, my gaze darting between them. "Did you just call her babe?"

"No need to get jealous," Nate says, easing toward me. "There's plenty of lovin' to go around."

Everything clicks in a millisecond. "Oh shit."

"We're out of here," Alex says, wrapping an arm around my shoulders and dragging me with him.

"No need to be shy!" Kate calls. "Though, really, that's a kink of mine, too."

"Alex," I gasp as we rush toward the door. We're practically jogging. "They're swingers!"

"No shit," he mutters, nearly shoving someone aside, out of my way.

"They, like, planned that!"

"Yes, Ted."

"How!" I yell as we stumble out into the biting-cold air outside.

"In the past ten seconds that I've had to try to come up with an answer," Alex says, rushing us toward his car, "I've only come up with one possibility. Your picture."

I frown up at him. "My what?"

"The picture," he says, "that you included in your profile? The one with all my family and me at Dad's birthday party in December?"

We throw ourselves into the car. My door's not even fully closed before Alex starts to peel out.

"I don't get it," I tell him. "Why would that—ohhhh."

"I was in it," he says. "And I have my arm around your shoulders."

"We agreed that would inspire a healthy, nontoxic level of advantageous jealousy in a prospective suitor."

He lets out a little disbelieving, high-pitched laugh. "Why are you talking like that?"

"I don't know, I read a lot of historical romance! That's beside the point. So you're saying they work together—"

"They're swingers, Ted, not hit men. But yes, they strategized, and based on our bios, I guess assumed we'd be up for some . . ."

"Group effort," I say miserably.

Alex glances my way. "Yeah. Pretty much. You okay?"

"Nope. I am not. I mean, he didn't do anything gross. But I just . . . wow. How are you? Are you okay? Kate seemed *really* handsy."

Alex shudders. "I don't want to talk about it."

I bite my lip, adrenaline starting to ebb in my body, the comforting hum of the car rolling down the road, Alex's familiar scent suffusing the air. "That was a disaster."

"Yep," he says.

"No knocks on swingers," I tell him. "Because, you know what, everyone deserves to have consensual fun and intimacy however works for them."

"Yep," he says again.

"So I'm not disparaging their *lifestyle*," I add. "But I am saying, I don't think I want to use the dating apps until I figure out how to *not* have that happen again."

Alex snorts as he guns it through a yellow light. "Good for you. I, however, don't plan to use the dating apps *ever* again."

"What about your . . . loneliness.?"

"Oh, that won't be a problem for quite some time," he says. "Kate made sure of it. I think my balls hid so far from her groping hands, they're somewhere up near my tonsils. Who knows if I'll ever get them back. They might be lost forever."

A laugh bursts out of me. I slap my hands over my mouth as I blink over at Alex.

He peers my way, a crooked smile tugging at the corner of his mouth. His Thea smile. Part exasperation, part affection, all love.

Friend love, yes. But it's *his* love for *me*.

That's all I need. All I want from him.

And I'll hold on to it with both desperate hands, until the shock fades, until the loneliness comes back, until Alex once again realizes he wants more than what we share, more than I ever want to take a chance on us becoming, all the *right* it could cost us if being more than friends went wrong.

But I won't think about that down-the-road day today, or tomorrow.

I won't think about it for as long as I possibly can.

CHAPTER 27

THEN

July 17, one summer ago

For the first time since I met him, Alex gets bad haircut.

He walks through the back door of his parents' house into the open-concept kitchen and dining room, where his mom and I sit, blowing up birthday balloons for her party tomorrow. Lydia doesn't seem peeved that she's the one filling her house with hot-pink helium balloons for her own party, and when I asked her why, she told me, "It's what I want, and I don't mind making sure I have it."

I filed that away. Something to aspire to. Something that, in addition to her long hard hugs, her delicious homemade birthday cakes, her fierce love of Mia, and a hundred other little things she's done and been since I met her last Thanksgiving, makes me love her even more.

Lydia and I pause, mid–balloon tying, staring at Alex.

"Madonna Mia," Lydia mutters, crossing herself.

Alex sighs and heads straight to the fridge, pulling out a beer. "Thanks, Mom."

"What did he do to you?" she says. "And on the day before *my* birthday!"

"He gave me a bad haircut," Alex says flatly.

"It's not *that* bad," I tell him.

Alex levels me with a look that says, *Liar*, then takes a long pull from his beer. "It's that bad," he says. "I'm aware of it."

"Is this your first time?" I ask. "Getting it cut . . . wherever you went?"

"No," Alex says calmly. "I go to Ray's once a year, to get a trim."

"A *trim*!" Lydia yells. "You look like a lamb shorn in the spring. By a drunk, senile grandpa who has no business cutting hair anymore!"

I nudge her foot under the table. Lydia throws me a *What? It's the truth!* look that's a dead ringer for Alex, then swivels back to her son.

"Why are you still going to Ray?" she demands.

"He's still alive," Alex says.

"A miracle," Lydia mutters. "No, a curse."

"Mom!" He throws up his empty hand, taking another hefty swig of his beer from the other. "I've been going to him my whole life. I can't *not* go to him. It would break his heart."

"I should have him court-martialed," Lydia grumbles.

"Though Ray *is* a veteran," Alex says, dropping onto the chair beside me, "I don't think that's a viable option."

"It'll grow back," I tell Alex. I'm telling myself this, too.

His luscious curl-waves have been clipped so short, there's barely enough left to even curl, which is a rather tragic shock. Even still, it's the facial hair that's the most startling.

Maybe striking?

I tip my head as I stare at him. "Bear with me," I say to them both, "but I *think* I like the mustache."

Lydia throws up her hands and storms off, leaving Alex and me alone in the kitchen, surrounded by fifty hot-pink balloons floating across the ceiling, seventeen left to go. One for every year of Lydia's vibrant, hot-pink life.

Alex looks over at me wearily. "Hey Ted."

I suck in a mouthful of helium from the balloon I haven't tied off, then say, in a truly perfect munchkin voice, "Hi, Alex."

A belly laugh jumps out of him. My heart skips as I watch him throw back his head, smiling, all tan skin and bright white teeth, the sharp line of his jaw, his Adam's apple. I haven't seen any of that for almost a year, while the scruffy beard hung around. Maybe I love the mustache. Maybe I love that I can see his face again.

Maybe I just love *him*.

I push the thought away, buried where it belongs. I'm sitting in his parents' house, my dog running around outside in the backyard with Mia, blowing up his mom's birthday balloons, savoring the comfort and sweet-warm joy of belonging, and a huge part why I can savor it is because I know it's secure. Because we aren't in a wobbly romantic relationship, some unsure thing; we're friends, *best* friends. And that's the only way I know I get to keep this—a family I feel a part of, a friend to trust and rely on, who relies on and trusts me, a love that, for the first time in my life, feels safe.

Alex takes the balloon from me, sucks in a mouthful, then says in a similar, though slightly deeper, munchkin voice, "Happy Friendiversary, Ted. Aren't you happy to be best friends with a guy who looks like Tom Selleck's much-less-attractive Italian doppelgänger?"

My laugh wheezes out of me, high and ridiculous. "Tom Selleck!" I munchkin-shriek.

Alex belly laughs, sucking in more helium, then says in his munchkin voice, "Mia told me I looked like a bison."

I snort, then burst into laughter so all-consuming, there's nothing left do but slide down my chair onto the floor.

Alex follows me, sliding down his chair and landing beneath the table with a thump. We're both so tall, we have to hunch not to hit our heads.

"This is the part," he says in a less-munchkiny voice but still not fully his own, "where you tell me I'm *hotter* than Tom Selleck and I *don't* look like a bison."

My laughter fades as I look at him, in our shadowy cave beneath the table. I lean in, cupping his cheeks with my hands, tracing the mustache with my thumbs.

My heart is pounding, each thud like a drum beating out the rhythm, the words, the truth.

I love him.

"Alex," I tell him, in my almost-normal voice. "You are *way* hotter than Tom Selleck. And you definitely don't look like a bison. And I'm so, so glad you're . . ." My voice catches.

Because it almost feels like I'm about to lie to him. And I told myself I'd never do that.

But as I sit there, staring at him, I realize what I was about to say isn't a lie. I *am* so, so glad he's my best friend. That is true, even when, in weak moments, I wish he was more, that I could be brave enough to take that chance.

Mia shrieks outside, chased by Argos's happy bark, then Lydia's warm voice, her words indiscernible, only the joy and love woven through them reaching us. The sounds of a little girl I love, a woman I admire. It would break my heart to lose them.

The love that lets me keep them and never risks my losing them has to be enough.

"I'm so, so glad you're my friend," I say quietly, battling to keep the sadness from my voice.

Alex wraps his hands around mine, pinning them to his cheeks. "I love you, Ted."

I bite my lip, holding back the longing that's begging to be let out, to be named, to be known. "I love you, too, Alex."

"How?" he whispers, his eyes searching mine.

My chin wobbles. I swallow thickly. "I love you so much, I could never stand to lose you."

He takes my hands from his face, cradles them inside his, staring down at them. "Meaning what?" he asks quietly.

"Meaning, there are some loves that end and some that don't—" My voice catches again. I clear my throat, folding over until my head rests on his hands. "I never want to love you in a way that could end. That could hurt us. That could hurt Mia. If I—"

"Shh," Alex says, easing down to the floor beside me, turning me until I'm tucked inside his arms, our familiar cuddle position. "I understand," he says quietly. "You don't . . . you don't have to say any more."

I sniffle, curling myself against him, clutching at him. I feel carved down the middle, like my heart's being shredded. Because, though I've wondered, hoped, in those weak, foolish moments, I've never been sure that Alex loves me the way I love him. Until he asked how I loved him. Until I saw his eyes brighten, then dim, because of *me*.

Until now.

It's thrilling. It's heartbreaking. It makes staying the steady, safe course infinitely more difficult.

But if I've learned anything this year, it's that I can do hard things. And maybe, one day, I'll be able to do something even harder, face how much I love him, be brave enough to tell him, trust that it would be worth it, even knowing everything I'd risk one day losing.

But not today. Not any time soon, judging by the way I shiver and cling to him, like a small, frightened child.

I have growing up to do, work to put in.

I have a long way to go.

I rub a hand over his heart, circling it gently. "Alex?"

"Hmm?" he says quietly, nuzzling his nose into my hair.

"You seemed sad when you came in. And not just about the haircut. It was almost like the haircut was the least of your worries."

He sighs. "Jen took Mia to kindergarten orientation this morning, without me."

I lift my head, anger rolling through me. "What?"

His fingers play through my hair. He's staring up at the ceiling. "It wasn't that big of a deal."

"Yes, it was. You're her *dad*. You belonged there, too—"

"Jen said she thought she'd forwarded me the email," he says. "From the school. Which she had not." He shrugs. "An honest mistake."

I set my head on his chest, my hand still circling his heart.

"You really think it was an honest mistake?" I ask quietly.

Another heavy sigh leaves him. "I want to. I *need* to. Because otherwise, she's still angry with me, still punishing me sometimes, and I have to believe she wouldn't use Mia to do that."

I think about the number of times the past year I've picked up

Argos from Ethan's house, how obvious it's been that he hasn't been exercised enough or fed his normal food, hasn't been given the cuddles and pets he needs, and how little sense it makes to me that Ethan would do that, unless he was trying to hurt me. It has to be infinitely more painful to consider, for Alex, for his child to be used like that.

But then I think about how I was raised, not terribly, but not well. I think about all the ways I've seen people, in their weak moments, be selfish, vindictive, hurting so badly all they could do was lash out at others and hurt them, in a wasted effort to alleviate their own pain.

"Maybe," he concedes quietly, "she was punishing me. Because I've been . . . happy . . . ish."

I smile sadly. "Maybe. I think maybe Ethan has been punishing me, with Argos. Keeping him, and not taking great care of him, when he couldn't give a crap about him before the divorce."

Alex hugs me tight. "Sorry, Ted."

"I'm sorry, too. It's infinitely more significant, what she's doing with Mia."

"Possibly," he adds.

"Possibly."

"I guess I find it hard to believe," he says. "Why would Jen want to punish me? Why would Ethan want to punish you? Wouldn't that mean, in some way, they're still hung up on us? *They're* the ones who divorced *us*. They shouldn't give a rat's ass about our happiness, let alone make an effort to shit on it."

I sit with that for a minute, staring up at the bottom of the table, the names carved in it—Alex, Ari, Lina, Sophia. More names I don't know, some I do. A family heirloom, treasured so much, everyone wants to leave their mark on it.

"I think," I tell him, "even though they're the ones who ended it with us, that doesn't mean they stopped feeling anything about us. It just means divorce is how they handled what they felt."

"So what do I do with that?" Alex asks.

I shrug. "I don't know. Talk to Jen? Ask what's going on?"

"She'll lie," he says. "She'll just apologize, say she messed up, and then for a while, she'll try to be nice, cooperative, communicative. It's been the pattern. What about you and Ethan?"

"I'm keeping a journal, taking him to my vet friend—she's on the first floor in my building. She's been giving Argos regular checkups documenting neglect. It's not so bad that I'm worried he's being hurt, but it's enough that hopefully I'll have a strong case and a paper trail to eventually shove in Ethan's face when I say he has to give me the dog, or I'll report him for animal cruelty."

"Damn, Ted, well done."

I smile, but it's sad, and it fades fast.

"Yeah," I tell Alex. "I think maybe it's time for us to punish them a little, too."

"Ted," he says warily. "I don't want to play Jen's game, if that's what she's at. I don't want that to happen to Mia any more than it already possibly has or will in the future."

"I know." I nestle into him, tracing with my finger a heart over his heart, again and again. Telling him I love him, *really* love him, in this way that I can.

"I do want to punish them," I say quietly, angrily.

I know my anger is bigger than our exes; it isn't all their fault, by a long shot, but it feels so *good* to have someone to blame, someone to point the finger at. Divorce has made me doubt myself, doubt love, doubt people's goodness. It's made me feel broken and skittish and bitter. Not always, not even most of the time anymore, but it's still there, lying in wait. When that wound is jabbed just right, it hurts terribly, and I want a guilty party for the sharp, bruising pain.

I want someone to blame for why I'm so scared to grab the love that's in front of me. And I know, even while I crave a villain, it doesn't matter who gets or takes the blame for my pain; it matters that I deal with it. It's up to me, to heal myself.

"I want to punish them," I say again, softer, calmer, "by being even better best friends than they are romantic partners. I want to outlove the *hell* out of them."

Alex is quiet for a minute, then he says, "What if . . . we're just the best of friends we can be to each other, because that's what *we* want to be. Maybe that's the best revenge of all—letting go of the need for it."

My heart clutches. "You are wise, Alex Bruscato. And I don't like it."

"Sometimes." I hear the smile in his voice. He presses a gentle kiss to my hair. "And yes you do. You like my rare bouts of wisdom. And you like me."

I squeeze him hard. "I do."

"Even with my Tom Selleck mustache?"

I peer up at him. "Maybe *especially* with your Tom Selleck mustache?"

A laugh rumbles in his throat, shaking his chest and me, too. "I know I already said it," he tells me quietly, "but I sounded like a munchkin when I did, so I'd like to say it again." His thumb sweeps tenderly down my cheek. "Happy Friendiversary, Ted. Divorce is the worst fucking thing that's happened to me, but it gave me the best thing in life, besides Mia . . . you."

I smile as I blink away tears.

"I'm real lucky," he says.

"I am, too," I tell him. "Happy Friendiversary, Alex. I honestly can't imagine life without you, and I never want to. Cheers to a year spent being the best of friends, and to another ahead, being even better ones."

He smiles, his gaze tender. "Cheers to that."

So that's what we do, for a whole year, spend it as the best of friends.

Only friends.

Until the email. Until "vacation."

That's when everything changes.

CHAPTER 28

NOW

August 5, third day of "vacation"

"You were quiet tonight," Alex says. He's rubbing a towel over his wet hair, his threadbare shirt sticking to his skin in places where he missed it when drying off.

I ease onto the bed and slip beneath the sheets. "I'm sorry."

"Don't be," he says. "That's not why I brought it up. I was just . . . worried about you. Quiet isn't really your thing."

I narrow my eyes at him playfully. "Coming from you."

He eases onto the edge of the bed, the far side. It's not far enough. It's infinitely too far away. "We're two Chatty Cathies. Part of what makes us good friends. Never a quiet moment. Or a dull one."

I smile as I roll toward him beneath the sheets and clasp his hand. "It made me happy," I tell him, "seeing you and Jen spend time together with Mia today."

Alex is quiet for a moment, turning his hand inside mine, rubbing our palms together. "It made me happy, too. We should have been doing more of that all along. It . . ." He blows out a breath, clears his throat. "It means a lot to Mia. That's what we should have been focused on—her, not us."

"Yeah," I whisper. "But you were both hurting. Healing takes time."

He nods, staring down at our hands. "We had a good talk tonight. About trying to do more of that when we're back home. Just, you know, brief outings. A meal here and there, taking her to activities together at school."

I squeeze his hand. "That sounds amazing, Alex."

"You think?"

I smile. "I know."

He smiles, too, and then his gaze drifts toward the sliding doors leading out to the small balcony off the bedroom, the dark sky, the ocean rolling beneath it. "Don't think Ethan will share your enthusiasm, but he can get fucked, as far as I'm concerned."

I roll onto my back, anger churning through me.

Alex glances back at me. "What?"

I shake my head.

"Ted." He leans in, then winces.

"Lie down," I tell him, lifting back the sheets. "Please?"

Alex searches my eyes. "You sure?"

"Very much, yes," I tell him.

A spark of light hits his eyes, a flicker of joy. So many shared memories between us.

He eases down, carefully sliding his legs beneath the sheets. A long, relieved sigh gusts out of him. Alex peers over at me, lifting his arm. "Cuddle talk?"

I scooch toward Alex, careful not to jostle him as I settle in, as I rest my head on his shoulder. His hand finds my hair, fingertips grazing along my scalp like he's done so many times before. "What's going on, Ted?"

"Ethan," I say quietly. "He really pissed me off today."

Alex freezes. "What did that fucker do."

"Relax."

"I'd prefer to know what he did first. Then I'll decide between relaxing in this bed or sharpening my knives."

I roll my eyes. "No jokes about homicide."

"Disagree," Alex says.

"He said some shitty things. Unsupportive things," I say quietly. "Things that make me worry he won't be supportive of what you and Jen are trying to be better at, for Mia. He feels . . . threatened by that, I think."

Alex is quiet for a moment. "Ted. I'm sorry he upset you, that he burdened you with that. But, it's . . . not your burden to carry."

I sit up suddenly, staring down at him. "Why not?"

Alex looks up at me, a little wide-eyed, surprised. "Because that's for Jen to deal with and, at worst, for me to step up in support of her."

"It is my burden to carry. Because it's about Mia. And I love her. Because, if Ethan keeps being fucking Ethan, with his shitty attitude toward her and you and Jen trying to be together more as parents for her, he'll *hurt* Mia," I say thickly. Suddenly, my vision is blurry. Tears swim in my eyes. "You don't know what it's like, growing up around people who make you feel like your existence is a nuisance they'd rather not deal with. It's terrible, Alex; she doesn't deserve that—"

"Hey." Alex yanks me down, grunting with pain as he does. He crushes me inside his arms, holding me tight as I cry quietly at first, then harder, turning to muffle my face against his chest.

Everyone's in bed, but it's a small, echoey house. I don't want Mia to hear me.

"Ted," he whispers, kissing my hair.

I scrunch my eyes shut at the pain-pleasure of it. He doesn't do it often, but whenever he does, it makes me ache so fiercely I feel like I'm going to collapse in on myself.

"Ted, it's okay."

"It's not okay," I say hoarsely.

"It *will* be," he says. "Because I'm going to talk to Jen. And we're going to hold Ethan accountable. He won't hurt Mia. I promise."

"You swear?" I pull back far enough to meet his eyes, clutching at his shirt.

He smiles softly, tucking a curl behind my ear, his gaze roaming my face. "I swear."

Relief washes over me. I trust Alex. I know if he says he'll do something, he'll do it. I don't know how exactly it will play out, what it will take, but I know he'll make sure Mia's safe, that she's protected, that no one will get to make her doubt she's loved.

"Thank you," I whisper.

Alex turns slowly, curling me in his arms so we're both on our sides, face-to-face, heads resting on the same pillow. For minutes, we just look at each other, nothing but the roar of the ocean filling the room, the sounds of our steady breathing.

"Ted," he says quietly, his fingers drifting through my curls. "I hate when you cry."

"I know," I tell him. "But you've never told me not to."

He nods. "It kills me when you're hurting, though. I want to go whip up a cake or a plate of pasta, put a smile on your face."

"No more cooking for you," I tell him. "You're hurting, too, in case you think I didn't notice."

"Nah."

I poke his stomach. "Honesty," I remind him.

"Yeah," he sighs, deflating. "I'm hurting."

"Can I rub it?" I ask.

Alex bites his lip. I roll my eyes. "You really are a twelve-year-old inside."

"Eternally," he admits.

"Your *back*," I meant.

"That's all right."

I prop myself on one shoulder, looking down at him. "Would it help? Honesty," I remind him again.

Alex peers up at me, something tight in his expression. "Yes. And no."

My heart stutter as I stare down at him. "Why?"

Alex searches my eyes. Long silent seconds stretch out between us. "You sure you want me to answer that? Because we've gotten this close to it before, Ted, and every time you turned me away."

"Turned *us* away," I say quietly, fresh tears pricking my eyes. I pick up his hand and bring it to my cheek. "I know. I'm sorry."

"Why?" he asks quietly, turning his hand inside mine, cupping my cheek. "Why did you?"

"I was scared," I whisper hoarsely. "I was scared of anything that could take us past where we were, because where we were was so good. And anything beyond that good . . . it could become bad. Friendships last, Alex. Relationships . . . they end."

Alex says gently, "Friendships *are* relationships, Ted. And those can end, too."

"Not ours," I whisper. "We'd never let it."

"No?" he says, tipping his head. "How would it play out then, when you found someone, or I did? You're telling me we'd just keep on doing what we've been doing—"

"No." I shake my head wildly, pinning his hand to my cheek. "I couldn't think about that—"

"Exactly," he says softly, tenderly. "And why is that?"

I stare down at him, shaking with the fear of it, the magnitude of it inside me, years of love and longing denied and buried, pushed down over and over, screaming to be let out. "Because *I* want you. And I don't want anyone else to have you."

Emotion tightens his face, air gusts out of him. "God, Ted."

I'm crying, trembling as I cling to his hand, to *him*. That'll I've done for two years—cling to him, to what made me feel safe, to what gave me enough love to live on without living in constant fear that I'd lose it.

"I've been so selfish," I whisper.

He shakes his head, blinking rapidly. His eyes are wet. "No, you haven't. You've been scared, Ted. I was scared, too."

I search his eyes. *"Was?"*

He smiles crookedly, his thumb sweeping over my cheek. "A man has needs. And eventually, those needs become much louder than his common sense, or any kind of life lesson. I want you, too," he says roughly. "But I wanted *you* more than that want, and I knew that meant I had to take you the way you'd let me have you. You made it clear, last year, that's what you wanted. But the other day, when you first saw the beach, when you looked at me, it felt like . . . maybe that had changed, or that . . . it *could* change. One day."

I nod as I turn my face and kiss his hand. "You're disturbingly good at reading my mind."

"Sometimes," he concedes. "But in some ways, I have very much been stumbling around in the dark. *This* place," he says, "most of all."

"Because I kept you there." I feel so guilty, so ashamed.

Alex tugs me down into his arms, holding me close. "I don't fault you for that, Ted. You needed the time you needed. I was always going to be here, waiting for you on the other side of that."

I bury my face in his neck, careful not to squeeze too hard, even though I want to, even though I'm dying to pour out, to show him how much he means to me, how much his love, his patient, steady love means to my battered heart.

"Always?" I ask quietly. "How long are we talking?"

"As long as my right hand kept working," he says dryly.

I snort. "Fair." I stare at him, my humor dying away. "Maybe... maybe I can make up for lost time? Give your right hand a break?"

Alex stares down at me, a wry smile on his mouth. "If we did, I'd prefer if it was a mutual makeup."

I audibly gulp. "I wouldn't be mad about that."

"But first," he says quietly, so hushed I can barely hear it, "I'd want to kiss you."

My heart clangs against my ribs. My mouth tingles, anticipation humming through me. "I'd want that, too."

He draws me closer, grunting with the effort, until I'm flush against him as we lie on our sides, one hand cupping his cheek, the other curled around his waist, gently kneading at his lower back. His eyes flutter shut. "Hold that thought," he says. "Please."

I still my hand.

He smiles. "I just want to be entirely focused on the kiss."

I lean toward him, but he pulls back, out of reach.

I give him my best pout, making a soft laugh rumble in his chest. "I've waited years to do this, Ted. You think I'm gonna just let you plant one on me, after all that?"

"I wish you would," I grumble. "Besides, we've kissed before."

"Not the way I wanted to kiss. That was a tease, a hint, a *torment*." He curves his hand around my jaw, my cheek, his thumb brushing my lip. "I've thought about this so many times," he mutters, his gaze roaming my face. "In pure times and in impure times," he admits.

Heat rolls through me.

"It was pretty great, each time," he says.

"Alex," I plead.

"Now it's your turn to wait," he tells me. Gently, but firmly. It makes want tingle through my limbs, reverberating like a plucked string.

"When you told me the other morning that you were worried the ocean wouldn't hold up to all you'd imagined it to be, that it might let you down, and I told you it wouldn't because it was yours, because—"

"It was real," I tell him.

He nods. "All I could think was, that's how kissing you would be—better than the best thing I could imagine, more satisfying than I could have ever fantasized. So . . ." He leans in, eyes on my mouth, "I'm going to prove myself right."

For a moment it's nothing but silence, not even the ocean's roar reaching my ears, and I wonder if time's stopped, just to torture me.

But then he's there, his lips brushing mine, warm, firm, air gusting out of him, washing over me, and I gasp, like I've been revived, shocked back to life.

It's nothing like our first, fearful kiss. And yet I can't help but think that somehow it's tethered to it, that this kiss now, like the many ways we've loved each other, is inextricable from where we started.

Alex deepens the kiss, opening his mouth, groaning into mine, a slow, savoring stroke of his tongue that makes my hips arch into his, heat pool molten between my thighs, where he presses into me, hard and thick. I crush myself to him, so desperate for every part of my body to feel every part of his, licking into his mouth, earning another groan from deep in his throat. His stubble scrapes my skin as I kiss him frantically, sucking at his bottom lip, tasting his cupid's bow. I'm wild with want.

"Ted," he rasps, squeezing me against him, rolling me onto my back.

I barely muffle a cry at the pleasure of feeling him over me, his body pinning mine to the mattress. My breasts ache where his chest rubs against them. My hips arch up, chasing relief for the pounding throb between my thighs.

"Tell me to stop," he whispers. "If you want, okay? We don't have to—"

"I want to," I gasp, running my hands up his shirt, madly tugging it off. "I want to so bad."

He helps me, yanking off his shirt, but then his back twinges; I can see it, and he grimaces.

"Alex, lie down." I guide him off of me gently, settling right against him as we lie how we started, side by side, face-to-face.

Clumsily, I tug off my shirt and chuck it aside. "Let's . . ." I can't believe I'm saying this, but I know it's the right thing. That Alex has waited for me, wanted me, and I have made him wait long enough. Now it's my turn to be patient.

We could make it work tonight—people have sex in all kinds of positions, with all kinds of bodily needs and limitations, and I have no doubt it would be wonderful.

But I know Alex. I know how he wants this—he wants to take me, have me, and feel like himself when he does, not held back by pain. I don't want the first time we do this to be tinged with his hurt.

"Let's touch each other," I whisper, drifting my hand down his chest. His stomach jumps, his hips buck as I sweep my finger along the waistband of his shorts. "And sleep in this bed, *together*," I tell him. "And after a muscle relaxer, and a good Thea massage, and a night in a decent bed, we can do . . . everything else."

Alex looks tortured. "I hate past Alex."

"Why?"

"Because he stupidly slept on the floor, and if he hadn't, he'd be doing everything tonight."

I cup my hand around his cheek, kissing him softly, wondering at the sparks that dance across my skin, the desire that hums through me from just this, the faintest brush of lips.

"I love past Alex," I tell him, before kissing him softly again.

Alex melts against me, groaning as I open my mouth, as he skates his hand down my back, then over my ass and wrenches me against him.

"I love present Alex," I whisper.

His hips rock into mine as I reach between us and wrap my hand around him through his shorts. "I love all the Alexes you've ever been and ever will be."

"Ted," he gasps, reaching between my thighs, stroking over my sleep shorts.

I whimper as he drags two fingers over me, then rubs, a swift, sure circle.

I'm so close, already, stars dance in the edge of my vision. "Alex—"

He crushes his mouth to mine, pulling me tight against him, as our hands fumble and learn, stroking, caressing, hard, then soft, fast and slow. "I love you," he whispers, his voice breaking as his hips falter, as he holds my eyes.

I arch into him, shaking as release slams through. "Love you," I gasp. "I love you."

He takes my mouth, his tongue plunging into me the way I know he wants to with his body, the way he will, soon, and, I hope, over and over for a very long time after that. For as long as we have.

I'm panting into his mouth, soaking up his grunts, his ragged breaths, the need trembling through his voice as he says my name over and over, until he buries his face in my neck, biting down as he comes with a pained groan, spilling hot and long, seeping through his shorts, to my hands. I stroke him, drawing it out, until he reaches down, takes my hand, and brings it to his pounding heart.

I hold his eyes as long as I can, as I lean in and kiss him, gentle, savoring,. He sighs into our kiss, drawing me with him, as he eases onto his back, and I curl around him, hiking my thigh high over his, splaying my hand over his heart where it slams against his ribs.

"You were right," I say. "It was better."

He sighs sleepily, turning to kiss my hair. "I know."

I laugh, dazed, incandescent. I kiss right over his thundering heart. "Want me to get you that muscle relaxer?"

He shakes his head slowly. "Nah. This?" He swats my ass, then yanks me close, plastering me to him. "Did the job even better."

"Better," I tell him, "seems to be our theme tonight."

"Even better than that," he says drowsily, kissing my forehead. "*Best*."

CHAPTER 29

NOW

August 6, fourth day of "vacation"

When I imagined a day at the beach, this is *almost* what I pictured.

The real thing, quite on theme, is even better.

The lemon-yellow sun, its zesty rays sprayed across the cloudless aquamarine sky. The sea-glass ocean, tumbling in, crashing into frothy white waves, spread like lace on the hot sand. I'm hanging out with Mia, who's starfished on the blanket beside me, taking a sun break under the umbrella.

Alex and Jen are on a walk, having their talk about what I told Alex last night, about what Ethan said, the harm I'm worried he could do. And hopefully, even more than that, about how things can be better, friendlier, for Mia.

Ethan, thankfully, isn't around. He drove off an hour ago, I assume on some beach-wedding-eve errand.

"Hey, Mimi."

"Hey, *TheeThee*," she says.

I laugh. "Never heard that one before," I tell her.

"Just thought of it," she quips, wiggling her eyebrows, which dart above, then beneath her big white frame sunglasses. "I think I'm kind of genius."

"I know you are."

She swivels her head my way. "What's up?"

I peer over at her, heart tugging. I don't know what to say, when I know so much is about to change for her, when it's not my surprise to ruin, but I can't help worrying that she's not going to like it.

"What's your favorite thing about being six?" I ask her.

She turns her head back, facing the umbrella, brow furrowed. "All the words I know," she says. "Because the more words I know, the better stories I can write when I grow up."

"You want to write stories when you grow up?"

She nods. "Lots. Like Daddy does, but not about food. Stories like what Mommy teaches—people being brave and going on adventures and fighting monsters and learning something and coming home and being happy again."

I smile. "That's a good way to sum up a lot of great stories. I think you'll do an amazing job at it."

"Thanks," she says. "Maybe, first, I'll write stories like you read at StoryTime. For kids like me to use their 'maginations."

"You like using your imagination?"

"*Love* it," she says. "It's my favorite. Maybe *that's* my favorite thing about being six. My 'magination."

She turns my way again, this time propped up on her elbow, and shoves her glasses up on to her head. Every beat of that choreography is 100 percent Alex, and it makes my heart twinge with hope.

What happened last night is just a beginning. There's more I have to say to Alex, words and intentions we danced around last night. Tonight, I'm not going to play a single round of euchre; I'm going to lay down all *my* cards and tell him everything. I hope that means we'll figure out a relationship. I hope that means I'll get to watch Mia grow up, use her imagination, become a big girl, a tween, a teen, a woman I get to love.

"Thea?" she says.

I blink, pulled from my thoughts.

Mia's frowning.

"Sorry," I tell her. "You had to say my name a couple times, didn't you?"

"That's okay, I could tell you were dickstracted."

My mouth twitches as I fight a smile. I can't wait to tell Lauren this new Mia-ism. "I was distracted," I say to her, "but I'm listening now. What were you telling me?"

"I was telling you," she says, rolling onto her stomach, propped on both elbows, "that I guess you like 'maginating, too. Because you spend all day trying to get people to buy stories, and stories are all about 'magination."

"Yep," I tell her. "I've always liked imagining, and daydreaming, letting my mind wander to unexpected places. And I've always loved stories." My throat catches as emotion hits me, unexpectedly. I lean in and tell her, "I actually used to tell myself my own life story."

Mia tips her head. "Like what?"

I glance around, then back to her, like I'm sharing a secret I want no one else to hear. "Like, 'Once upon a time there was a girl named Thea. She had wild brown hair and eyes like the forest and sunshine kisses on her nose, and every day she woke up and wanted to climb trees.'"

Mia smiles. "You made your *life* a story."

"I did."

"Did you stop?" Mia asks. "When you growed up?"

"When I grew up," I tell her, weighing my words, "I still told my life story, but I started to get a little mixed up, which wasn't good. Like a lot of good things, when you use it the way you shouldn't, it can be not good anymore."

"Like eating candy for dinner instead of eating it for dessert."

I smile. "Kind of like that, yeah."

"So what happened?" she asks.

"Well . . . instead of listening to myself, telling my life's story as I went along, I started telling my life it had to *be* a certain story. I started trying to write chapters before they'd even happened. And then, I got all turned around."

Mia frowns. "You got lost," she wisely summarizes. Then she says, "That sounds scary."

"I did. And it was," I admit. "But the great thing is—just like you might eat jelly beans for dinner one day and *really* regret it, but then, the next day, you can go back to eating a yummy, helps-you-grow dinner and then have jelly beans for dessert—I realized I could find my way out of it. I could stop telling myself the story I thought my life should be, and start living it again, *then* telling myself the story afterward."

"Sort of like remembering!" Mia says. "But with your 'magination."

"Exactly."

"That's really cool." She flops onto her back, tucking her hands beneath her head. She's quiet for a moment, then says, "You know what word sounds like 'magination?"

"What word?"

"Magic," she says, smiling wide. "Wonder if 'maginations are magic."

I swallow the lump in my throat as I watch her dreaming, wondering, figuring out the world around her. "Yeah, Mia, I think they are."

She peers over at me. "Can I have a new word, Thea Thesaurus?"

"Sure," I tell her. "What word do you want? A synonym or antonym."

"Cinnamon," she says confidently, dipping her toes beyond the reach of the umbrella, wiggling them in the warm sun, then adds, "please. A cinnamon for . . . *sunbathing*."

"Ooh, that's a tricky one."

I glance out at the ocean, the waves rolling in, crashing on the shore, dragging back out to sea; Argos digging in the sand, filthy and euphoric, wagging his tail. I peer down the beach at the two specks that are Alex and Jen, gradually drawing closer, Alex's ball cap tugged low over his bedhead hair, Jen with her wide-brimmed straw hat.

I think of everything that brought us here, how I fought it, resented it, feared it, wrestled with it. How strange it is to look back on so much pain and realize, somehow, you're grateful for it, because it was necessary and true, the dark forest you *had* to stumble and claw your way through to finally emerge into the other side of your life.

"*Apricate*," I tell her.

"Ooh." Mia smiles. "I like that one. *Apricate*. Sounds like apricot."

"It does. *Apricate* is one of my favorite words."

"Why?" she asks.

"Because it comes from an old word that means *to open*. And it makes me think about flowers blooming, turning toward the light; that delicious shivery feeling you get when you stretch out beneath the warm sun.

"It makes me think about how, to soak up what's beautiful in life, you have to open yourself to it. You have to expose yourself. And that means not just to the beautiful stuff, but to the not-so-beautiful stuff. You can't pick and choose. You're either open or you're not. But the sun's worth that exposure. All beautiful things are."

"I love it." Mia stares up at me, a slow smile on her face. "I love *you*, Thea."

I blink, stunned, tears filling my eyes. I feel like I've been bathed in a bucket of sunshine. "I love you, too, Mia."

Mia turns back to the umbrella above her, wiggling her toes again. "Apricate," she says, like she's trying out the word, tasting it on her tongue. "Apricate."

Trying to keep myself together, I peer toward Alex as he walks toward us. My heartbeat thunders, pounding out its truthful rhythm.

I love him. I love him. I love him.

This time, I don't silence that voice or push it away or lock it up. I open myself up to it, my heart stretched out wide, exposed, reaching toward that beauty.

*

For as perfect as the day was, the evening is . . . not. We eat an early dinner, per Jen's request, which peeves Ethan, which peeves Alex, who suffers through cooking with him, even though Ethan is a shadow of the cook Alex is.

Mia has an after-dinner meltdown about not wanting to go to bed, which means she desperately needs to go to bed, and not even two requested verses of "I Am Here" help her settle. I step out of her and Jen's room, where Mia's cuddled up in her twin bed with Alex, who seems to maybe finally getting through to her, stroking her hair, doing something silly with her fingers that makes her laugh sleepily.

Just as I'm closing the door, I hear her say, "Apricate."

I smile as I close it with a click, and then my smile immediately dissolves. Down below, in Ethan's douche den, I catch voices. Yelling voices.

I hear the white noise machine in Mia's room go up in volume. Which means Alex heard them, too, and he's trying to cover them up.

I jog into our bedroom and unplug *my* white noise machine, then plug it into an outlet in the living room, right by Mia's door, twisting the lid until it's as loud as possible, its soothing roar so like the ocean, I haven't used it since I unpacked it, when I had the real thing right outside my window.

The yelling doesn't stop, but thankfully, it doesn't get louder.

I pass the time, nervous, by deep cleaning the kitchen. Not because I give a shit about making things nice for Ethan or his ancestral beach home. But because tomorrow Alex will cook here, tomorrow Mia will scrounge around for breakfast and snacks, twirling across the tiles. I can make it nice for *them*.

For half an hour, Alex doesn't come out of Mia's room. And neither Jen nor Ethan come up from Ethan's douche den. Finally, the yelling stops, dipping to murmured voices. I try not to hold my breath, to worry, to fill in the blanks. I keep on cleaning.

I've just finished scrubbing the floors, the last task I could think of, when I hear a car engine roar to life, the squeal of tires peeling out across gravel.

Then the slow, light tread of footsteps up the stairs. The door from the douche den swings open.

Jen stands at the top of the stairs, wide-eyed, looking a little shaken. Lauren was right. She really does look like Tinkerbell. Beautiful and pint-sized, a determined glint in those big blue eyes.

She looks at me on my hands and knees in the kitchen, the yellow rubber gloves I'm still wearing, and sighs. "No use doing that," she says, shutting the door behind her. "Ethan's gone."

I spring up, tugging off the gloves, chucking them in the bucket, then follow her out onto the deck.

Jen's staring out at the ocean, her back to me, still, silent. No sign of crying or emotion. I thought watching her break down in sobs outside The Bookshop was unnerving. This is much worse.

Slowly, I walk up to her. "Jen?"

"Hmm?" She dabs her nose with the back of her hand.

I come close enough so that we're nearly shoulder to shoulder. "What happened?"

"I told you, he left."

"Why?" I ask carefully.

She huffs an empty laugh. "Because I called him out on what he'd said to you, told him that I was tired of playing these games where it's me and him versus you and Alex, that I wanted to get past that and focus on Mia, and, because he's a manbaby, he told me he wasn't going to do that, that I had to choose. Him or her. My *daughter*."

She shakes her head, sneering at the deep-blue horizon. "That fucker actually thought I'd need a moment to decide.

"And when I told him 'Mia'—that it was always going to be

Mia—he didn't like that. So I told him he could leave." She peers over at me, eyes wide, triumphant. "I kicked him out of his own house."

"Badass, Jen," I say honestly.

"Was it?" she asks.

"You stood up to him more than I ever did."

"That's because you're nicer than me," she says. "And you were with him for pure reasons. I was not."

I feel a little unsteady, clutching the deck railing. "What?"

"It was a rebound fling. He was hot, I was angry and hurt. I could tell he was a selfish boy in a lot of ways. But he was also doting and spent time with me. We liked doing the same things, so, for a while, I enjoyed that. And then . . . you and Alex, you weren't a fling, either. And I was jealous. Not because I wanted Alex back, but because . . . I could tell, even when I'd blown up his life, he was still happier with you, more himself with you, than he'd ever been with me. And I wanted to punish you both for that.

"But then . . . I started to like you, started noticing the things Mia had learned when she was with you, the curiosity she brought home after being with you and Alex, the smart words she'd picked up, the books she was tearing through, the . . . joy she had. I started to see why Mia loves you, why Alex does. And I thought, maybe, we could make something better, the four of us, than we'd had before, a sort of odd, but good, adult blended family. I focused on what I liked about Ethan, told myself it could work, that there were enough things I liked about him that outweighed the things I couldn't stand. Until . . ."

"Until Alex told you," I say to her, "what Ethan said to me."

She sighs. "Yes. So now he's gone."

"For good?" I ask dazedly.

"From my life, yes. For the rest of our vacation, too," she says. "He's driving somewhere else now, I don't even care where, just that I told him he's made us all miserable enough to last a lifetime, and the least he could do was fuck off for three days and leave us in peace."

"Seriously, Jen. You are a warrior queen."

She laughs, before it catches at the end, thickening with tears.

I step closer and set my hand on her arm. "I'm sorry."

"You have literally nothing to be sorry for," she says. "Ethan is the one who should be sorry, but I don't even care if he is. It's done."

"I'm still sorry," I say again, quietly, "that he hurt you."

Jen nods. "He did, but only a little." Then she glances my way. "I never let him in much, never really opened up. Probably because I knew, all along, he was going to let me down."

A tear slips down her cheek, and I reach for her, the instinct to comfort her taking over, but she steps back, shaking her head. "I've cried in front of you enough, Thea."

"Jen—"

"Please." She takes another step back. "I swear, I'll be okay. I just need some time alone, with my own thoughts."

I nod, before retreating across the deck, then slipping inside, quiet as I drag the door shut.

CHAPTER 30

NOW

August 7, fifth day of "vacation"

I take a shower in our bedroom's en suite bathroom, hoping to scrub away the sadness clinging to me. It doesn't work. I knew it wouldn't.

Stretched out on the bed, I try to read a book, watching the clock creep into the early hours of the morning, my mind racing, too distracted to focus on the story as I think through what I was going to do tonight, questioning it, revising it. Everything's been turned upside down.

In a handful of hours, this morning, Mia's going to wake up and wonder where Ethan is, and even though she never struck me as particularly attached to him, I know it's going to impact her, that she's going to ask about the "special 'casion" and wearing her pretty white dress. I have no idea what Jen's going to tell her, how that's all going to play out. It makes my heart pinch with worry.

Outside my door, somewhere in the house, I catch the murmur of voices, Alex's deep pitch, Jen's soft and higher.

And then Alex walks in, carefully easing the door shut behind him.

I set the book aside and sit up, spinning on the bed to face him.

He looks at me, and he seems so tired, so weary. I open my arms.

Alex crosses the room, crawls across the bed, and falls onto me, pressing me down, smooshing me beneath him. I wrap him in a hard hug, rubbing his back, kissing his temple, comforting him, the way he's comforted me so many times.

"Cuddle talk?" he asks hoarsely.

I nod.

"Jen's going to tell Mia in the morning—well, later this morning—that she and Ethan aren't boyfriend-girlfriend anymore, and Ethan didn't say goodbye because he's hurting, not because he didn't want to say goodbye to her. I'm going to take point with Mia tomorrow, give Jen some to herself."

I sigh heavily. "That's a good way to put it. And a good plan. Jen's a good mom." I kiss his temple again. "You're a good dad."

He sighs, too. "Trying to be."

"You *are*."

Alex wedges his arms beneath me, squeezing me tight. "Before dinner, when we came in from the beach, you said you wanted to talk tonight?"

I swallow nervously. "I did. I still do. But we don't have to now. It's so late, and you have to be exhausted. I think . . . I think we've got a lot going on. It can wait."

Alex stiffens in my arms. Slowly, he pulls away, sits up, staring down at me. "What?"

I sit up, too, confused by his response. "What do you mean, *what*?"

"Why do you . . . Why did what happened tonight make you think we don't have to talk about what you wanted to talk about?" he asks. "Why does it have to wait?"

I search his eyes, trying to figure out what's upsetting him, where I went wrong. "Ethan blew everything up tonight, and now it feels weird and sad, and I just thought . . . maybe taking a beat, letting that settle, would be . . . helpful?"

"Helpful for whom?" Alex demands.

"All of us? Jen? Mia? Your ex-wife is hurting, and your daughter is going to be hurt when she wakes up, and she's going to pick up on her mom hurting, and that's a lot to handle. So I just thought it could wait—"

"Ted." He rakes both hands through his hair and tugs at the ends. "I don't want it to wait. I've waited a long time."

I stare at him, hearing what he's saying, understanding that he knew what this conversation was going to be. My heart tumbles in my chest, warmed that he wanted to talk about this as much as I did. And it falters when I realize how angry he is that I've tried to defer it.

"I'm sorry," I say quietly. "I wasn't trying to . . . make you wait longer."

"But you weren't interested in *not* making me wait any longer, either."

"That's not true." I reach for his hand, but he pulls away.

His eyes search mine. "Is this what it's going to be, Ted? You always waiting for the other shoe to drop, groping for any excuse, any theoretical obstacle to put between us, to avoid what you said—" His voice cracks. He stares down at the bed. "What you said you wanted."

"No, Alex, I just . . . I just didn't want to talk about all this when it's so precious and new and . . . well, when it's something

I've waited for, too, with Ethan's douchery and Jen's sadness and that impact on Mia hanging over us."

Alex stands from the bed and starts to pace the room. "That's nice. Good to know that's what you wanted." He rounds on me. "But what about what *I* want. Does that matter?"

"Of course it does." I feel unsteady, shaky, as I look up at him.

"You just told me you don't want to do this, though."

"Not now," I admit. "But I can, if you want—"

"It's not what *you* want, though," he mutters, scrubbing at his face. "You want to wait, until everything's just right, until it's storybook perfect."

"That's not fair—"

"You know what's not fair, Ted?" He steps closer, pain flashing in his eyes. "Waiting. And waiting. And waiting for the woman you love to think you're worth it. To choose you, even when it means sticking her neck out. To show you that she loves you even more than she fears what she'd be risking. And when, finally, you think it's going to happen, for her to decide, now isn't the time. Maybe tomorrow. Maybe next week. Who knows?"

"Alex, I'm sorry." Tears fill my eyes. "You *are* worth it to me—"

"Yeah, well." He grabs a pillow from the bed and storms toward the door. "You have one hell of a way of showing it. I'll be sleeping in the douche den. See if that fancy fucking pullout mattress is everything Ethan cracked it up to be."

When he pulls the door shut between us, he does so quietly, carefully. It still hits me like he slammed it, harsh and final.

I lie there for hours, warring with myself. Do I chase him down, follow him, push him to talk it out?

But then what? I tell Alex that I love him, that I want us to be more than friends, that I want every part of life with him, when he's angry, wounded, when we're both exhausted and spent and in a just few hours this morning, we'll be pressed in by even more very valid hurts, Jen's and Mia's.

Slowly, I sink lower in the bed, curled into a ball, listening to ocean roar. I tell myself that tomorrow, I can fix this. That tomorrow, it can be better.

I'll make sure of it.

*

When I wake up to the first stretch of sun on the horizon and wander out into the house, Alex is nowhere that I can see. Maybe he's still sleeping in the douche den. But it doesn't feel like he's here.

My stomach is an anxious knot as I set up the coffee, whisk batter for pancakes, and set out a pan to make eggs. I'm not a great cook, but I've learned enough to be a decent one. Decent is going to have to be good enough.

Jen and Mia come out of their room at the same time, Mia looking adorably sleepy, her hair sticking out every which way, her rainbow nightgown fluttering as she stumbles into me and gives me a drowsy hug.

"Morning, Mia."

She yawns. "Morning, Thea."

I glance up at Jen and smile encouragingly. "Morning, Jen."

"Morning, Thea," she says softly, sliding onto a stool at the breakfast bar.

"Coffee?" I ask.

Jen nods, looking exhausted, her hair in a messy high pony, her mascara smudged beneath her eyes. "With—"

"Cream," I tell her.

Jen smiles faintly. "Yes, thanks."

I serve Mia and myself blueberry pancakes and scrambled eggs. Jen sticks with coffee.

Mia's licking syrup from her plate when she stops, leaning to peer out the deck's sliding door. "Is that Daddy out there?"

Jen peers out, and I do, too.

"No," she and I both say.

"Is it Ethan?" she asks.

Jen tucks Mia's hair behind her ear. "No. Remember, I told you he's gone away, because that's how he handled being upset. And he's not going to come back, because of that."

"Sounds like he had a tantrum," Mia mutters, rolling her eyes.

Jen snorts into her coffee. I try to hide my laugh with a cough.

"I'm okay with it," Mia says. "He wasn't my favorite. I mean, he *did* buy me nice stuff, but I like heart stuff better." She smiles at us. "You give me nice heart stuff. So does Daddy."

Jen and I both stare at her, both of us blinking away tears.

"You give us nice heart stuff, too, sweetie," Jen tells her.

I smile, showing Mia I agree.

Mia smiles wider. "So. Where's Dad? Did he have a tantrum, too?"

Jen gives me a wary look, gauging what I'm going to say. I'm not sure how to handle this. I don't know where he is, what to tell her.

Jen leans in and tells Mia "Daddy texted me earlier, said he's going to a really nice grocery store outside of town, to buy the ingredients to make all our favorite foods tonight. He'll be back in a few hours."

She says that last part to me, and I feel like she knows. That even if he didn't tell her directly, Jen inferred. That he's angry, that he needs time.

There's a lump in my throat, and the anxious knot in my stomach has doubled in size, but I still manage a smile for Mia. "You know what that means?" I ask her.

"What?" she says, glancing back and forth between Jen and me.

"Girls' morning!" I tell her. "I can hang out with you, if Mommy needs some time to relax, or I can give you and Mommy some time together. Whatever anyone needs."

Mia tips her head. "I think I need to wear my pretty special-'casion white dress." She frowns. "When *is* the special 'casion?"

Jen suddenly looks as startled as I did a moment ago, when Mia asked where Alex was, when I had no idea what to say. She glances over to me, wide-eyed, panicked. *Help!* her expression says.

I'm still not quick on my feet, but a memory from a book I've read, a bittersweet moment, comes to mind. "Your special occasion," I tell Mia, "is today."

Mia squeals. "What is it?"

Jen looks just as curious.

"You and Mommy," I tell her, "are going to take showers, and do your hair, and make yourselves feel like your fanciest, happiest selves; then you're going to put on your pretty white dresses, come down to the beach, and I'm going to take lots of pictures of you."

Mia smiles. The girl loves having her photo taken. She loves dressing up. It's the home-run solution I'd desperately hoped it would be. "Yayyyy!!!"

Mia's sliding off the stool, sprinting to her room. "Mommy!" she yells. "Hurry up!"

Jen looks over at me and smiles tiredly, gratefully, I think. "That was . . . a really good save."

"Same to you," I tell her.

For a moment, she just looks at me, then, slowly, she stands and reaches for me, clasping my hand. "You and Alex . . . you'll figure it out."

I bite my lip as I fight tears. "I hope so."

"I know so," she says, squeezing, then letting go. "I'll get us ready, you'll take our photos, then Mia and I are going to spend the day all around Bethany, eating ice cream for lunch and buying crap we don't need, and hell, I think we'll get a manicure, while we're at it. So you two can have the place, okay?"

I smile faintly. "You don't need to do that. Who knows if we'll even need it."

Jen huffs a laugh. "Oh, Thea, you silly woman. You absolutely will. He's gone for you."

I watch her cross the living room, then stop just outside the door, turning around to face me. "When I told you, that night at The Bookshop, that I was glad you're in Mia's life?"

"Yes?" I say quietly.

"That wasn't entirely true. Or . . . it wasn't the whole truth." She smiles softly as she says, "I meant to tell you I'm not just glad you're in Mia's life. I'm glad you're in Alex's life, in my life. And . . . I hope you will be, for a very long time."

Jen slips past the door, shutting it quietly.

Leaving me alone in the kitchen, with a sink full of dishes I'm grateful to have to do. While I cry and feel and face it all—what I want, what I'm scared of, what I sense knitting back together inside me, healing what I never even knew was hurt.

CHAPTER 31

NOW

August 7, fifth day of "vacation"

Mia and Jen are off on their Bethany adventure, with a promise to come back manicured, stuffed with ice cream, and with new books in tow for Mia from the local bookstore.

While they've been gone, I've been making some important calls. First to my mother, then to Fern, and now to Lauren.

I'm on the phone with her, walking along the sand, beaming as Lauren yells, "Thea, YES!"

I grin. "You were right about calling her."

"As usual," she says smugly.

"You *and* Alex were right."

"Now, why'd you have to go and ruin it for me."

My smile widens. "It gets even better. Fern didn't accept my initial proposal to be co-owners." I bite my lip, shaking with the joy of it, still barely wrapping my head around the truth. "She told me she wants to sell me the store. For an abysmally low price that I'm not going to hold her to."

"THEA!" Lauren screams, so loud, I have to yank the phone away from my ear. "You! Boss! Ass! Bitch! I'm so proud of you. And I'm so happy for you!"

"Thanks, Lo." I smile as I stare out at the ocean. "I'm pretty proud of me, too."

We talk longer while I stroll down the beach, mostly Lauren peppering me with questions and me answering them. I tell Lauren what Fern told me—that she'd been waiting for me, holding out for me to show her I could be ambitious, push for what I believed the store needed, to demonstrate the leadership skills she knew I'd need to take over the way she wanted me to.

I tell Lauren that since I called Sue, that night after book club, and she encouraged me to tell my mom how I felt, that I was hurt, that I'd emailed my mom, and surprisingly, my mom had emailed back. She apologized for how she'd hurt me. Said she recognized something now that she hadn't recognized then—how deeply she'd been hurting, too. She told me she'd been recently diagnosed with depression and with ADHD, or what, when I was younger, was called ADD, mind racing, restlessness, struggle to focus, especially in overstimulating environments; how draining her job was for her because of that, and that she wished she'd known how long she'd been swimming upstream so she could have taken better care of herself and, in doing so, taken better care of me.

It doesn't magically fix everything. It doesn't change the past. But it gives me hope for the future. And it's given me food for thought, a hunch that maybe, I've got a brain like my mom's, that exploring that will help me in the future, too.

Finally, we get to Alex. I tell her everything that happened two nights ago, everything that happened last night. Everything I hope will happen today.

"Lady," she says, "you have been *busy*. Also, good fucking riddance to Ethan!"

"Right? Life is *a lot* right now."

"No shit. But so much juicy material for the memoir," she says.

I laugh. "Yes, I can see it now. Everyone will want to read *The Story of Thea Meyer: Behind the Scenes of the Titillating Life of a Weird, Goofy Bookworm.*"

"I'd read the hell out of that," Lauren says.

"That's because you love me."

"Yes, but also, because any book with *titillating* in the title has my money just for that."

I laugh again as I turn around, heading back up the shore toward the house. "Speaking of great words, guess what Mia said yesterday? *Dickstracted*."

Lauren cackles. "Oh. My. God. I love her. She's the best."

"She is," I tell her, eyes ahead as I gaze out toward the water, then the house. I freeze. Because I see him.

Alex, on the deck, standing there, watching me.

Waiting for me.

"Thea?" Lauren says.

I blink. "Sorry, Lo. I missed that."

A beat, before Lauren says. "Forget it, I was rambling. Get going—"

I'm speed walking up the sand, then jogging. "No, Lo, I can listen—"

"Thea," she says. "You're dickstracted, I can tell. And I'm so glad you are. Go. Get your man! Tell him you love him! Make wild, animalistic love to him! Then call me afterward and tell me all about it."

"Yeah, I'm not doing that last part."

She sighs. "Well, I had to try. Now go!"

She hangs up before I can, and it's the push I need, as bracing as the wind that rushes up behind me. I grip my phone tight in my hands, my eyes on Alex.

And I run.

CHAPTER 32

NOW

August 7, fifth day of "vacation"

I'm gasping for air as I stumble up the steps to the deck and launch myself at Alex. I throw myself at him, wrapping my arms around his neck.

"I'm sorry," I whisper. "I'm so sorry—"

"Ted, shhh," he murmurs, curling his arms around me, squeezing me to him. "I'm sorry. I was hurt and angry. I shouldn't have walked away—"

"You're allowed to be hurt, Alex. You're allowed to be angry. You're allowed to walk away." I pull back enough to meet his eyes. "I can wait, too, you know. I can be the patient one, the understanding one. Even when it scares me, even though it makes me anxious. You get to be just as much of a person, with just as many needs, as me. You're worth it. You're worth everything."

His eyes fill as he stares at me. "Thank you, Ted."

"Thank you for what? Protecting my heart over risking it for yours, like a pathetic scaredy-cat for two years? Torturing you with horny cuddles? Making you wait for me to find my guts and give you what you deserve?"

"For loving me," he says quietly. "All of me. For being brave for me. For thinking I'm worth it."

I shake my head and stare up at him, my heart so full. "I don't *think* you're worth it, Alex. I *know* it."

I press my hands up his chest, resting them both over his pounding heart. "I love you. Let me show you that?"

I cup his face, press up on tiptoe, so we're eye to eye, pounding hearts pressed against each other's chest. And then I kiss him, slow, savoring, pouring into every slide of my tongue, every slant of my mouth, every nip and lick and sweet touch, how much I love him. It's gentle at first, then it's urgent, hungry, teeth clacking, tongues tangled, gasped, fast breaths.

Alex pulls back, panting. His eyes are dark pools of midnight water. His hands clamp around my shirt to fists, yanking me against him. "You mean it?"

"More than I've ever meant anything," I whisper.

Alex's jaw works. His eyes shine with unshed tears. "Show me now?"

I nod. "Show me, too?"

He nods, sliding his hands around my back, down over my backside, before he yanks me up by the thighs, wrapping my legs around his waist. "We have the house to ourselves, right?"

"All day," I tell him.

He grins. "Thank fuck."

*

It isn't reverent or slow, this time. No careful, sultry undressing, no standing back and taking each other in. There'll be time for that, soon. But not now.

Now it's simply time to end the waiting, to finally give in.

I fumble with his shirt, tugging at the collar. He laughs, then yanks it over his head. I wriggle out of my tank top, then reach for my shorts. Alex tears them down my legs, then lifts and tosses me onto the bed.

I get a moment of stunning, glorious time to look at him as he steps out of his shorts, his boxer briefs, to see every golden inch of him, the white tops of his thighs at his tan line, the thick, hard length of him, before he's falling over me.

We gasp as our bodies touch, the mind-bending relief of every inch of us naked, finally touching. His skin is hot, the hairs on his chest coarse and springy, grating across my nipples, making them tighten to almost-pain, the pleasure is so intense.

He kisses me, hard and deep, as I reach between us and take him in hand, stroking, teasing, learning more to add to what I learned two nights ago. What makes him tremble, what makes his hip buck into me, what makes him beg.

Alex crawls down my body, grips me by the ass, and yanks me to the edge of the bed, kissing my thighs, my hips, then lower, softer, his tongue dipping, teasing, until finally he's there, and I arch up, sinking my hand into his hair as he learns me, drags his tongue up my center, swirls it lighter, then firmer when I beg him to.

My thighs shake, the promise of release building inside me, hot and crackling, a beautiful, desperate ache for relief.

"I need you," I gasp. "Please."

"Just a little more," he murmurs. He's edging me, letting off the moment I'm about to finally find release. And he's smiling while he does.

"Alex!" I tug at his hair. "I can't take it."

Alex pulls away, sighing, wiping at his mouth. His eyes are dazed and dark. He looks like he wants to do that forever. "Fuck, you taste good."

I blush spectacularly, slapping both hands over my face. Alex shoves me back up the mattress, climbing over me, and draws my hands away, then pins them over my head.

I arch up again, greedy for him, mindless with the need to feel him, heavy and strong and real, pressing me down. He takes my nipple in his mouth, sucking, swirling. I roll my hips into his. "Alex. Don't make me wait anymore."

"Coming from you," he teases.

I smile. "Fine," I whimper. "I can wait a few— Ah!"

Suddenly his finger is there, curled inside me, then another, curving, stroking. "With you," I whisper. "I want it with you."

He brings his fingers up, licking them as he looks at me.

I bite my lip, a shiver of pleasure wracking my body.

"I don't know how long this is going to last," he says roughly as he reaches for the nightstand and yanks open the drawer.

"Condoms, huh?"

He grins my way, breathing hard. "I had hopes."

"I'm on the pill," I tell him, just as breathless. "There's been no one. We don't have to, if you don't—"

"No one?" he growls. It sounds possessive and pleased. It makes me shiver again deliciously, curl myself against him.

"No one," I tell him.

"God, that makes me happy, and I know that's toxic as hell, but I don't care." He crawls back over me. "No one for me, either. Except my poor right hand. That guy has been working overtime."

I laugh, but then it becomes a gasp, as he eases in, just barely.

His eyes hold mine. "Ted," he whispers.

I set my hands on those glorious deep divots at his hips, the curve of his hard, beautiful backside, grip him steadily, and yank him toward me, drawing him in. I'm not making him wait a second longer.

Our mouths fall open, and Alex presses me down, seats himself deeper. It's full and overwhelming, so perfect, tears fill my eyes.

"Ted," he whispers. He wraps his arms around me.

"Alex,." My voice breaks as he drives into me. "Alex. I love you."

His hips lurch as I say it, like he's desperate to be even closer, for there to be not even the smallest space between us. "I love you," he gasps. "I love you."

It's fast and breathless, a sprint to the top that leaves us shaking as we near it, calling each other's name, crushing our bodies together, chasing closeness that has no bounds, no limit.

Alex shouts my name as he comes, burying his face in my neck, gasping for air He rocks into me still, kisses featherlight down my neck, drags his tongue along my collarbone, the swell of my breast, and reaches between us, rubs exactly where I need him to.

"Come on, Ted," he whispers. "Give it up for me."

And then it's there as I gasp for breath, sweet, lightning-sharp release flying through me. He pins me down, makes me feel every wave of pleasure, stretching it out with more kisses, tender, teasing touches traced along my body.

I hold him in my arms as it finally ebbs, his chest still heaving, his pounding heart thudding against me. And I smile, eyes shut.

"Ted," he croaks.

I press a kiss to his temple. "Yes, Alex."

"I think I died."

"No," I tell him. "You didn't. You are very much alive." I kiss him again, sweetly this time, his cheek, the corner of his mouth, his lips. "And so am I. We've got a whole life ahead of us to live."

"I'm not sure I'll have functional legs for it. They're gone."

A laugh jumps out of me. "Then I'll carry you until you find them. How's that sound?"

He presses a laughing kiss to my neck and sighs, sleepy, satisfied. "That sounds like an improbable but highly appealing plan.

CHAPTER 33

NOW

August 8, seventh day of "vacation"

I'm staring at the ocean, saying my goodbyes, doing everything I can to remember exactly what it looks like, to hold that memory close and dear, until I can see it again.

Alex walks up behind me and wraps me in his arms, drawing my back to his front. "Time to go, Ted. Argos is asleep, and we agreed we wanted to make sure we got as much time as possible on the road before his noxious nervous-car-ride farts made an appearance."

I sigh, still staring at the ocean. "Can't we stay here forever? Everything here feels . . . perfect."

He presses a tender kiss to my hair, swaying me gently side to side. "Nah. But we can come back."

I peer up at him and pout.

"Don't give me that sad-kitty face," he says.

Sad-kitty face.

I gasp as I turn inside his arms. "You remember that night at the bar?"

"Every moment. First time I told you I loved you. And you said you loved me, back. I could never not remember that."

I curl my arms around him, holding his eyes. "I do love you."

He smiles. "I know. I love you, too. And I love the life we've got back home, waiting for us. It's not perfect. It's not the beach. But it's ours. And . . . it's everything to me."

"It's everything to me, too." I set my hand on his chest, tracing over his heart the familiar shape with my finger. "Fine," I sigh playfully. "I guess we can go back home."

"Excellent." He hugs me to him, his eyes locked on mine. "I was thinking . . . maybe soon we'll find a house, a home that's good for both of us?"

That makes me smile so wide my cheeks ache.

"There she is," he murmurs. "Looking . . . almost happy-ish?"

I shake my head. "Even better than that.."

I rest my hand along his face, my thumb sweeping across his cheek. I know it won't always be this way, as close to perfect as it all feels right now, that we'll be sad and hurt and struggle. But I also know, through it all, we'll have what matters most, a love that lasts, two hands held, two hearts reaching for each other. An *us* that will tell a story that begins and ends with *we*.

Peering up at Alex, I do something I never have before. I open up my heart, as that little storyteller starts to weave her tale; I tell him exactly what she says.

Thea Meyer gazed at the man she loved, her best friend, the one who'd made her feel the most tenderly safe and the most wildly reckless. The one who'd changed her life for the braver, the more beautiful, always for the better.

She couldn't believe her luck, the chance to have found him, to love him for as long as he'd let her.

She couldn't wait for their story would bring. For whatever came next. Because finally, she had him.

Her happy ending.

EPILOGUE

It's my favorite time of day at the beach—sunset. The sky is a watercolor of glowing light, streaks of petal pink and violet, lush citrus orange, cool water blue. The waves roar steadily, and a warm sea breeze kisses my skin.

I set a plate down on the patio table, cup my hands around my mouth, and yell, "Come eat!"

My heart catches at the sight below me, on the shore. Lauren smiling wide, hand in hand with her partner, Zazie, who throws the ball for Argos to chase across the sand. Jen crouched over Mia's shell art as Mia explains the design to Jen and her boyfriend, Luke, a fellow teacher from another school whom she started seeing a little over a year ago. Luke is a soft-spoken, gentle giant whom I couldn't love more for Jen, though she's taking things very slowly with him—so slowly, I wish they'd hurry up, because he's perfect for her. Not that I'm one to talk. I know that, sometimes, you need time. That, as clichéd as the saying is, time *is* a healer and, maybe even more so, a teacher, if you let it take you where you need to go.

"Ted?"

The sliding door to our beach rental drifts shut, and I turn; my heart skips a beat. Alex smiles at me, two bottles of wine in one hand, a bottle of sparkling seltzer in the other.

"There you are," he says, leaning in for a slow, sweet kiss. "Anything you need, Chef, before you serve dinner?"

I glance from the spread of food I made entirely on my own, then smile up at him. "I did need something, but now it's here."

"Lemon seltzer?" he says. "For the nausea?"

I shake my head.

He sets the wine and seltzer down on the table, then steps closer. "Hmm. I'm all out of guesses, then."

I wrap my arms around his neck. "I needed *you*. But now I have you. Everything's perfect."

Alex smiles. "You always have me, Ted."

"I love you," I whisper, as he curls me gently inside his arms, my belly, which has finally started to show, bumping into his hard stomach.

"I love you, Ted."

I lean in and kiss him, tender, savoring. I press my body into his.

Alex groans in the back of his throat. "Ted, I'm gonna have a hard-on at dinner."

I snort as I pull away, affectionately patting his chest. "You'll be fine."

"Hey." He clasps my hands before they slip away and holds my eyes. "I'm sorry it took us this long to come back."

"Alex." I squeeze his hands in mine. "Two years is not a long time to wait for the beach, especially with everything we've had going on. The store, the restaurant, buying a house, moving in . . ."

He tips his head side to side. "I guess when you put it that way, it's not so bad. I just know I promised I'd bring you back; the beach makes you so happy—"

I tug him close again and kiss him one more time, before the deck is filled with the people we love. "Alex, I'm with you. And you love me."

He smiles softly. "I do."

I smile back, because I can't help it, because his joy never fails to spill into mine. "I could be anywhere in the world, so long as I was with you, and you know what I'd be. What I already am."

He smiles, then steals a swift, hot kiss, laced with promise, and whispers, "Happy."

ACKNOWLEDGMENTS

I held the concept for *Happy Ending* close to my heart for years, knowing I needed time before I wrote a story that touched on such a tender part of my life. When I finally felt ready to write it, it was because I felt safe to do so—I knew this story and I were in good hands, as I turned the page and reached for something new, and that is in thanks to my dear agent, Samantha Fabien, who walked so patiently alongside me as I worked up the courage to tell this story, heard my dreams for this next chapter, and fervently pursued them becoming a reality. I'm beyond grateful to have found such a welcoming home with Gallery/Simon & Schuster, with my phenomenal editor, Carrie Feron whose warmth, wisdom, and steady encouragement played an integral part in shaping *Happy Ending* into a story I'm so wildly proud of.

Happy Ending isn't only words from my heart put to page anymore but a book with a beautiful cover and interior design, an intentional marketing and publicity plan, and the efforts of a wonderful team supporting *Happy Ending*'s publication—Jennifer Bergstrom, Jennifer Long, Eliza Hanson, Ali Chesnick, Heather Waters, Lauren Carr, John Paul Jones, Caroline Pallotta, and Karla Schweer, thank you for everything you've done to make this book shine.

Thank you, Carolyn, for being so generous with your time and insight into bookselling and managing an indie bookstore. I couldn't have told Thea's story without you!

Thank you for Annie, my angel, Annie—thank you. As I wrote, you listened and made me laugh, and then you blazed through this story when it was finished with invaluable wit, joy, and keen insight. I have never finished a book so sure that I accomplished what I set out to, and I couldn't have done it without you. And I wouldn't have met you without Becca connecting us—thank you Becca, for the gift of Annie, for the gift of you, your true-hearted friendship, your tireless encouragement, and your beautiful writing that so deeply inspires me.

Thank you to my dear friends who've loved me through my long season of loss; who've met me in its wake, scarred yet stronger, and loved me in the midst of that complexity; who've celebrated my wins and cheered me on toward even higher hopes. You teach me, love me, challenge me, bring me joy. Life sparkles with you in it.

Thank you to my family whose presence and love colors my heart, every edge of my existence, with such a beautiful array of depth and dimension. I love you with all my soul.

And B, thank you—for promising to grow as we go, for showing up to do hard things even when they feel so damn hard, for believing in our happy ending, for dreaming and striving with me, for walking with me, hand in hand on this wild path called love.

evermore

Love, spice and sleepless nights.

The hottest new romance publisher at Penguin Random House UK.

Prepare for excessive swooning, devouring love stories and dangerously high standards for your own happily-ever-afters.

Proceed with caution... and an open heart.

FOLLOW US ON SOCIALS:

  @evermorebooksuk

On a station platform, with nothing to read,
and a four-hour train journey stretching ahead of him...

That's where the story began for Penguin founder Allen Lane.
With only 'shabby reprints of shoddy novels' on offer,
he resolved to make better books for readers everywhere.

By the time his train pulled into London, the idea was formed.
He would bring the best writing, in stylish and affordable
formats, to everyone. His books would be sold in bookstores,
stationers and tobacconists, for no more than the price
of a ten-pack of cigarettes.

And on every book would be a Penguin, a bird with a certain
'dignified flippancy', and a friendly invitation to anyone who
wished to spend their time reading.

In 1935, the first ten Penguin paperbacks were published.
Just a year later, three million Penguins had made their
way onto our shelves.

Reading was changed forever.

—

A lot has changed since 1935, including Penguin, but in the
most important ways we're still the same. We still believe that
books and reading are for everyone. And we still believe that
whether you're seeking an afternoon's escape, a vigorous debate
or a soothing bedtime story, all possibilities open with a book.

Whoever you are, whatever you're looking for,
you can find it with Penguin.